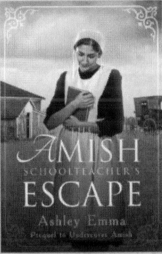

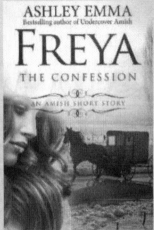

Other books by Ashley Emma on Amazon

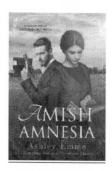

Coming soon:

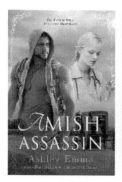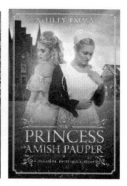

AMISH ALIAS

Ashley Emma

SPECIAL THANKS TO:

Fritzie

Julie

Abigail

Kit

Tandy

Robin

There were so many readers from my email list who gave me helpful feedback on this book, so I couldn't list you all here. Thank you so much!

Check out my author Facebook page to see rare photos from when I lived with the Amish in Unity, Maine.

Click here to join my free Facebook group The Amish Book Club where I share free Amish books weekly!

The characters and events in this book are the creation of the author, and any resemblance to actual persons or events are purely coincidental.

AMISH ALIAS

DEDICATION:

To Shirley C., the woman with the inspiring life story who never gave up.

Thank you for your encouragement and support all these years, and the beautiful dishes, of course, which I will treasure forever.

Table Of Contents

CHAPTER ONE

"**M**om, are we there yet?" nine-year-old Charlotte Cooper asked from the back seat of her parents' van. Her legs pumped up and down in anticipation. Mom had said they were going to a farm where her aunt lived, and she couldn't wait to see the animals. The ride was taking forever.

"Just a few more minutes, honey," Mom said from the driver's seat.

Charlotte put her coloring book down and patted the lollipop in her pocket Mommy had given her for the trip. She was tempted to eat it now but decided to save it for the ride home. She hoped it wouldn't melt in her pocket. The van was hot even though she was wearing shorts and her favorite pink princess T-shirt. Charlotte shoved her damp blonde curls out of her eyes.

The van passed a yellow diamond-shaped sign that had a black silhouette of a horse and carriage on it. "Mommy, what does that sign mean?"

"It's a warning to drive slowly because there are horses and buggies on the road here."

"*What?* Horses and bugs?"

"No." Mom smiled. "They're called buggies. They're like the carriages you've seen in your storybooks. Except they are not pumpkin-shaped. They are black and shaped more like a box."

Charlotte imagined a black box being pulled by a horse. If she were a princess, she would like a pumpkin carriage much better.

"Why are there buggies here?"

"The folks who live in this area don't drive cars."

They don't drive cars? Charlotte thought. "Then what do they drive?"

"They only drive buggies," Mom said.

How fast do buggies go? Charlotte wondered. *Not fast as a car, I bet.* "Why would anyone not drive a car? They're so much faster than buggies."

"I know, honey. Some people are just …different." Mom glanced at Charlotte in the rear-view mirror. "But being different isn't a bad thing."

Charlotte gazed out the window. Even though they had just passed a pizza place a few minutes ago, all she could see now were huge fields and plain-looking houses.

There was nothing around. This looked like a boring place to live. What did people do to have fun here besides play outside?

A horse and carriage rumbled past them on the unpaved road going in the other direction. A girl wearing a blue dress and a white bonnet sat on the top seat, guiding a dark brown horse. She looked just like a picture Charlotte had seen in her history book at school. "Look, Mom." Charlotte pointed at the big black box on wheels.

"It's not polite to point, Charlie."

Charlotte dropped her hand to her side. "Why is that girl dressed like a pilgrim, Mom? She's wearing a bonnet. Are we near Plymouth Plantation?"

Mom didn't answer. Maybe she was too distracted. She

seemed really focused on the mailbox up ahead.

"We're here," Mom said and turned onto a long driveway.

Charlotte gaped at the chocolate-colored horses in the fields and the clucking chickens congregating in the front yard. The van bounced over bumps on the gravel path leading to a huge tan house with bright blue curtains hanging in the windows. The dark red roof had a large metal pipe coming out of the top with smoke coming out of it, and behind the house stood a big red barn. Charlotte wondered how many animals were in there.

Mom parked the van and helped Charlotte out. "I'm going inside to talk to your Aunt Esther. I don't want to bring you inside because... Well... You should just wait here. I won't be long."

"Can I walk around?"

Before Mom could answer, a young boy about Charlotte's age walked out of the barn. He saw them and waved.

"Can I go play with him?" Charlotte asked.

"Hi!" The boy ran over. "I've never seen you around here before. Want to go see the animals in the barn?"

"Can I go in the barn with him?" Charlotte asked her mother.

"What's your name?" Mom asked the boy. "Is Esther your *Maam*?"

"I'm Elijah. No, she's not my mother. My *Maam* and *Daed* are out running errands, so I'm playing here until they get back. My parents are best friends with Esther and Irvin. I come here all the time. I know my way around the barn real well."

Mom crossed her arms and bit her lip, then looked at Charlotte. "I suppose you can go in. But stay away from the

3

horses."

"We will, ma'am," said Elijah.

Charlotte and Elijah took off running toward the barn. They ran into the dim interior and she breathed in. It smelled like hay and animals, just like the county fair she had gone to last fall with her mom and dad. To the left, she heard pigs squealing. To the right, she heard sheep bleating.

Which animals should we go see first? Charlotte wondered, tapping her toes on the hay-covered floor.

Elijah leaned over the edge of the sheep pen, patting a lamb's nose. He was dressed in plain black and white clothing and a straw hat. His brown hair reached the collar of his white shirt. He even wore suspenders. Charlotte glanced down at her princess T-shirt and wondered why he didn't dress like other kids at her school. Every kid she knew wore cool T-shirts. *Why are the people here dressed in such plain, old-fashioned clothes?*

Charlotte stepped forward. He turned around, looked at her, and grinned. "So what's your name, anyway?"

"I'm Charlotte. Well, you can call me Charlie."

"Charlie? That's a boy's name."

"It's my nickname. I like it."

"Suit yourself. Where you from?"

"Biddeford, Maine. Where are you from?"

"I live in Smyrna, Maine."

"Oh." Charlotte raised an eyebrow. Smyrna? Where was that?

Elijah smiled. "It's a bigger Amish community in northern Maine."

4

Charlotte shrugged. "Never heard of it."

Elijah shrugged. "Want to pet the sheep?"

"Yeah." They climbed up onto some boards stacked along the edge of the enclosure. Several of the animals sniffed their fingers and let out high-pitched noises. "They sound like people," Charlotte said. "The lambs sound like babies crying, and the big sheep sound like adults making sheep noises."

They laughed at that, and when the biggest sheep looked at them and cried *baaa* loudly, they laughed even harder.

Charlotte looked at the boy next to her, who was still watching the sheep. A small smear of dirt covered some of the freckles on his cheek, and his brown eyes sparkled when he laughed. The hands that gripped the wooden boards of the sheep pen looked strong. She wondered what it would be like if he held her hand. As she watched Elijah tenderly stroke the nose of a sheep, she smiled.

When one lamb made an especially loud, funny noise that sounded like a baby crying, Elijah threw his head back as he laughed, and his hat fell off. Charlotte snatched it up and turned it over in her hands. "Wow. I've never held a straw hat before. We don't have these where I live. I thought people only wore ones like these in the olden days."

Elijah shrugged. "What's wrong with that?"

"Nothing." Charlotte smiled shyly and offered it back to him. "Here you go."

Elijah held up his hand. "You can keep it if you want." He smiled at her with those dark eyes.

Charlotte got a funny feeling in her stomach. It was the same way she felt just before saying her lines on stage in the school play. She knew she should say, "Thank you," like Mom had taught her. But she couldn't speak the words. Instead, she took the lollipop out of her pocket and handed it to him.

"Thanks," Elijah said, eyes wide.

"You're welcome."

Elijah gestured to Charlie's ankle. "Hey, what happened to your ankle?"

Charlie looked down at the familiar sight of the zig-zagging surgical scars that marred her ankle. "I've had a lot of surgeries on my ankle. When I was born it wasn't formed right, but now it's all better and I can run and jump like other kids."

"Does it hurt?"

"No, not anymore. But it hurt when I had the surgeries. I had, like, six surgeries."

"Wow, really?"

"Charlotte!" Mom called. "We have to leave. Right now."

"Thanks for the hat, Elijah." Charlotte turned to leave. Then she stopped, turned around, and kissed him on the cheek.

Embarrassment flushed Elijah's cheeks.

Uh oh. Her own face heated, Charlotte sprinted toward her mother's voice.

"Get in the car," Mom said. "Your aunt refused to speak with us. She wants us to leave."

Charlotte had never heard her mother sound so upset. She climbed into the van, and Mom hastily buckled her in.

"Why didn't she want to talk to us, Mom?" Charlotte said.

Mom sniffed and shook her head. "It's hard to explain, baby."

"Why are you crying, Mom?"

"I just wanted to talk to my sister. And she wanted us to go away."

"That's not very nice," Charlotte said.

"I know, Charlie. Some people aren't nice. Remember that."

The van sped down the driveway as Charlotte clutched the straw hat.

"Why are you going so fast?" Charlotte said and craned her neck, hoping to see Elijah. She saw him standing outside the barn with one hand holding the lollipop and the other hand on his cheek where she'd kissed him. He was smiling crookedly.

Mom looked in the rearview mirror at Charlotte.

"Sorry," Mom said and slowed down.

Charlotte settled in her seat. She hoped she'd see Elijah again, and maybe he'd be her very own prince charming like in her fairytale books.

But Mom never took her to the farm again.

CHAPTER TWO

Fifteen years later

"Hi, Mom," twenty-four-year-old Charlie said, stepping into her mother's hospital room in the cancer ward. "I brought you Queen Anne's lace, your favorite." She set the vase of white flowers on her mom's bedside table.

"Oh, thank you, honey." Mom smiled, but her face looked thin and pale, a bright scarf covering her head. "Come sit with me." She patted the edge of the bed, and Charlie sat down, taking her mother's frail hand.

"You know why Queen Anne's lace are my favorite flowers?" Mom asked quietly.

Charlie shook her head.

"Growing up in the Amish community, we'd get tons of Queen Anne's lace in the fields every summer. My sister, Esther, and I would try to pick as much as we could before the grass was cut down for hay. At the end of every August, we'd also check all around for milkweed and look for monarch caterpillars before they were destroyed. We'd try to save as many of them as we could. We'd put them in jars and watch them make their chrysalises, then watch in amazement as they transformed into butterflies and escaped them. I used to promise myself that I'd get out into the world one day, just like the butterflies, and leave the Amish community behind. I knew it would be painful to leave everyone and everything I knew, but it would be worth it."

"And was it?" Charlie asked, leaning in close.

"Of course. It was both—painful and worth it. I don't regret leaving though. I never have. I miss my family, and I wish I could talk to them, but it was their choice to shun me. Not mine." Determination still shone in Mom's tired eyes. "I had already been baptized into the church when I left. That's why I was shunned. I still don't understand that rule. I still don't understand so many of their rules. I couldn't bear a life without music, and the Amish aren't allowed to play instruments. I wanted to go to college, but that's forbidden, too. Then there was your father, the Englisher, the outsider. It was too much for them, even for Esther. She swore she would never shun me. In the end, she turned her back on me, too."

Mom stared at the Queen Anne's lace, as if memories of her childhood were coming back to her. She wiped away a tear.

"And that's why she turned you away that day you took me to see her," Charlie concluded.

"Yes. Honestly, I've been so hurt, but I'm not angry with her. I don't want to hold a grudge. I can't decide if we should try to contact her or not to tell her I'm…" Mom's voice trailed off, and she blew out a lungful of air. She shook her head and looked down. "She wouldn't come to see me, anyway. There's no point."

"Really? Your own sister wouldn't come to see you, even under these circumstances?" Charlie gasped.

"I doubt it. She'd risk being shunned if she did." Mom patted Charlie's hand. "Don't get me wrong. I loved growing up Amish. There are so many wonderful things about it. They help each other in hard times, and they're the most tightly knit group of people I've ever met. Their faith is rock solid, most of the time. But most people only see their quaint, simple lifestyle and don't realize the Amish are human, too. They make mistakes just like the rest of us. Sometimes they gossip or say harsh things."

"Of course. Everyone does that," Charlie said.

Mom continued. "And they have such strict rules. Rules that were too confining for me. Once your father taught me how to play the piano at the old museum, I couldn't understand why they wouldn't allow such a beautiful instrument that can even be used to worship the Lord."

Mom shook her head. "I just had to leave. But I will always miss my family. I'll miss how God and family always came first, how it was their priority. Life was simpler, and people were close. We worked hard, but we had a lot of fun." Mom's face lit up. "We'd play so many games outside, and even all kinds of board games inside. Even work events were fun. And the food… Don't get me started on the delicious food. Pies, cakes, casseroles, homemade bread… I spent countless hours cooking and baking with my mother and sisters. There are many things I've missed. But I'm so glad I left because I married your father and had my two beautiful daughters. I wouldn't trade you two for anything. I wouldn't ever go back and do it differently."

Gratitude swelled in Charlie's chest, and she swallowed a lump in her throat. "But how could Aunt Esther do that to you? I just don't understand."

Mom shrugged her frail shoulders, and the hospital gown rustled with the movement. "She didn't want to end up like me—shunned. I don't blame her. It's not her fault, really. It's all their strict rules. I don't think God would want us to cut off friends and family when they do something wrong. And I didn't even do anything wrong by leaving. I'll never see it their way." Mom hiked her chin in defiance.

10

What had her mother been like at Charlie's age? Charlie smiled, imagining Mom as a determined, confident young woman. "Well, your community shouldn't have done that to you, Mom. Especially Aunt Esther, your own sister."

"I don't want that to paint you a negative picture of the Amish. They really are wonderful people, and it's beautiful there. You probably would have loved growing up there."

Charlie shook her head with so much emphasis that loose tendrils of hair fell from her ponytail. "No. I'm glad we live here. I wouldn't have liked those rules either. I'm glad you left, Mom. You made the right choice."

***

Elijah Hochstettler trudged into his small house after a long day of work in the community store with Irvin. He pulled off his boots, loosened his suspenders, and started washing his hands, getting ready to go to dinner at the Holts' house. He splashed water on his beardless face, the trademark of a single Amish man, thinking of his married friends who all had beards. Sometimes he felt like he was the last single man in the entire community.

He sat on his small bed with a sigh and looked around his tiny home. From this spot, he could see almost the entire structure. The community had built this house for him when he'd moved here when he was eighteen, just after his family had died. The Holts had been looking out for him ever since.

His dining room and living room were one room, and the bathroom was in the corner. It was a small cabin, but he was grateful that Irvin and the other men in the community had helped him build it. Someday he wanted to build a real house, if he ever found a woman to settle down with.

Another night alone. He wished he had a wife. He was only in his early twenties, but he had dreamed of getting married ever since he was a young teenager. He knew a wife was a gift from God, and he had watched how much in love his parents had been growing up. He could hardly wait to have such a special bond with one person.

If only his parents were still alive. Even if Elijah did have children one day, they would only have one set of grandparents. How Elijah's parents would have loved to have grandchildren. At least he had Esther and Irvin Holt. They were almost like parents to him. But even with the Holts right next door, he still felt lonely sometimes.

"At least I have You, Lord," Elijah said quietly.

He opened his Bible to see his familiar bookmark. His fingers brushed the waxy paper of the lollipop wrapper he had saved from his childhood. He had eaten the little orange sucker right away, since it was such a rare treat. But even after all these years, he could still not part with the simple wrapper.

Maybe it was silly. Over a decade had passed since that blonde *Englisher* girl had given it to him. How long had it been? Twelve years? Fifteen years? Her name was Charlie, short for Charlotte. He knew he'd never forget it because it was such an odd nickname for a girl. He remembered her laughing eyes. And the strange, exciting feeling she had given him.

Over the years, Elijah had been interested in a few girls. But he'd never pursued any of them because he didn't feel God calling him to. He never felt the kind of connection with them that he'd experienced with that girl in the barn when he was ten years old. He longed to feel that way about a woman. Maybe it had just been feelings one only had during childhood, but whatever it was, it had felt so genuine.

All this time, he'd kept the wrapper as a reminder to pray for that girl. For over fifteen years, he'd asked God to bring Charlie back into his life.

As he turned the wrapper over in his calloused hands, he prayed, "Lord, please keep her safe, help her love you more every day, and help me also love you more than anything. And if you do bring her back to me, please help me not mess it up."

He set down his Bible and walked to the Holts' house for supper.

The aroma of beef stew warmed his insides as he stepped into the familiar kitchen. Esther was slicing her homemade bread at the table.

"Hello, Elijah."

"Hi, Esther. I was wondering, do you remember that young girl named Charlie and her mother who came here about fifteen years ago? She was blonde, and she and her mother were *Englishers.* Who were they?"

"I don't know what you're talking about." Esther cut into the bread with more force than necessary.

"It's hard to forget. Her mom was so upset when they left. In fact, she said you refused to speak to them and made them leave. What was that all about?" He knew he was prying, but the words had just tumbled out. He couldn't stop them. "And I remember her name was Charlie because it's such an odd name for a girl."

"It was no one, Elijah. It does not concern you," she said stiffly.

"What happened? Something must have happened for you to not want to talk to her. Will they come back?" he pressed, knowing he should stop talking, but he couldn't. "It's not like you at all to turn someone away at

13

the door."

"It's a long story, one I don't care to revisit. I do not suspect they will ever come back. Now, do not ask me again," she said in such a firm voice that he jumped in surprise. Esther had always been a mild and sweet woman. What had made her so angry? Elijah had never seen her act like that before.

Elijah knew he was crossing the line by a mile, but he just had to know who the girl was. "Esther, please, I just want to know—"

Esther lifted her head slowly, looking him right in the eye, and set her knife down on the table with a thud.

"Elijah," she said in a pained, low voice. Her eyes narrowed, giving her an expression that was so unlike her usual smiling face. "The woman was my sister. I can't talk about what happened. I just can't. It's more complicated and terrible than you'll ever know. Don't ask me about her again."

***

The following night, Dad got a phone call from the hospital while they were having dinner at home. Since Dad was sitting close enough to her, Charlie overheard the voice on the phone.

"Come to the hospital now. I'm afraid this could possibly be Joanna's last night," the woman on the phone told them.

"What's going on?" Zoe, Charlie's eight-year-old sister asked, looking between Charlie and their father. "Dad? Charlie?"

Dad just hung his head.

Charlie's eyes stung with tears as she patted her younger sister's hand. "We have to leave right now, Zoe. We have to go see Mom."

As Dad sped them to the hospital, Charlie said, "Dad, if you're going

14

to drive like this, you really should wear your seat belt. I mean, you always should, but especially right now."

"You know I hate seat belts. There shouldn't even be a law that we have to wear them. It should be our own choice. And I hate how constricting they are. Besides, that's the last thing on my mind right now. Let's not have this argument again tonight."

Charlie sighed. How many times had they argued about seat belts over the years? Even Mom had tried to get Dad to wear one, but he wouldn't budge.

They arrived at the hospital and rushed to Mom's room.

It all felt unreal as they entered the white room containing her frail mother. Charlie halted at the door.

She couldn't do this.

She felt her throat constrict, and for a moment her stomach felt sick. "No, Dad, I can't," she whispered, her hand on her stomach. "I can't say goodbye."

"Charlie, this is your last chance. If you don't, you'll regret it forever. I know you can do it. You are made of the same stuff as your mother," he said and pulled her close, stroking her hair.

Compliments were rare from her father, but she was too heartbroken to truly appreciate it.

He let out a sob, and Charlie's heart wrenched. She hated it when her dad cried, which Charlie had only seen once or twice in her life. Zoe came over and wrapped her arms around them, then they walked over to the bed together.

They held her hand and whispered comforting words. They cried and laughed a little at fond memories. Her father said his goodbyes, Zoe said her goodbyes, and then it was Charlie's turn.

She did not bother trying to stop the flow of her tears. Sorrow crushed her spirit, and no matter how hard she tried she could not see how any silver lining could come from this. Was God punishing her for something? Why was He taking her beautiful, wonderful mother?

"Charlie, I love you," her mother whispered and clutched her hand with little strength.

"I love you too, Mom," Charlie choked out.

"Please promise me, Charlie. Chase your dreams and become a teacher."

"Okay, Mom. I will."

"I just want you to be happy."

"Mom, I will be. I promise."

"Take care of them."

"I will, Mom." She barely got the words out before another round of tears came.

"Thank you. I'll be watching."

Charlie nodded, unable to speak, biting her lip to keep from crying out.

"One more thing. There's something I need to tell you. Please tell your Aunt Esther that I forgive her. Promise me you will. And tell her I'm sorry. I am so sorry." Mom sobbed, and Charlie saw the same pain in her eyes she'd seen all those years ago after they left the Amish farm.

"Why, Mom? Sorry for what?"

"I lied to you yesterday, Charlie, when I said I wasn't angry with her. I didn't want you to think I was a bitter person. Honestly, I have been angry at her for years for shunning me. It was so hard to talk about. I'm

16

so sorry I didn't tell you the whole story."

"It's okay, Mom. I love you."

"I love you too. Tell Esther I love her and that I'm sorry. I forgive her. I hope she forgives me too…" Regret shone in Mom's eyes, then her eyes fluttered closed and the monitor next to her started beeping loudly.

"Forgive you for what? Why does she need to forgive you?" Charlie asked, panic rising in her voice as her eyes darted to the monitor. "What's wrong? What's happening?"

"Her heart rate is dropping," the nurse said and called the doctor into the room.

Charlie's heart wrenched at the sight of Zoe weeping, begging Mom not to die. Dad reached for Mom.

"Mom!" Zoe screamed.

"I'm sorry," the nurse said to Dad. "This could be it."

The doctor assessed her and slowly shook his head, frowning. "I'm so sorry. We tried everything we could. There's nothing more we can do. We will give you some privacy. Please call us if you need anything. We are right down the hall."

Charlie stood on shaky legs, feeling like they would give out at any moment. The doctor continued talking, but his words sounded like muffled gibberish in her ears. He turned and walked out of the room.

Charlie squeezed Mom's hand. "Mom? Mom? Please, tell me what you want Aunt Esther to forgive you for." It seemed so important to Mom, and Charlie wasn't sure if Dad would talk about it, so this could be her last chance to find out. If Mom's dying wish was to ask Aunt Esther's forgiveness for something, Charlie wanted to honor it.

Mom barely opened her eyes and mumbled something incoherent.

17

"Joanna, we are all here." Dad took Mom's other hand, and Zoe stood by Mom's bed.

Then Mom managed to whisper, "I…love…you…all." Her eyes opened for one fleeting moment, and she looked at each of them. She gave a small smile. "I'm going with Jesus." Her eyes closed.

The machine beside them made one long beeping sound.

She was gone.

Zoe cried out. They held each other as they wept.

Charlie's heart felt literally broken. She sucked in some air, feeling her chest ache, as if there was no air left to breathe.

When they finally left the hospital, she was in a haze as her feet moved on auto pilot. After they got to the apartment, hours passed before they finished drying their tears.

What would Mom say to make her feel better? That this was God's will? Charlie knew that was exactly what she'd say.

Why did God *want* this to happen?

Why didn't He take me instead? Mom was so…good, she thought glumly.

Her whole life she had been taught about the perfect love of Jesus and His wonderful plan for her life. Why was this part of His plan? This was not a wonderful plan.

She fell on her bed, put her head down on her pillow and sighed. "God…please just help me get through this. I don't know what to think right now. Please help me stop doubting you and just trust You."

Someone knocked on the apartment door. When neither her father nor Zoe got up to see who it was, Charlie dragged herself off her bed and went to the door, opening it.

"Alex!" she cried in surprise.

Her ex-fiancé stood in the doorway in his crisp police uniform. Dad and Zoe quickly came over to see what was going on.

"I need to talk to you, Charlie," he told her with determination. He glanced at Charlie's dad and sister. "Alone."

"Not going to happen, Alex," Dad said, stomping towards Alex. "In fact, you broke my daughter's heart. You cheated on her. If she doesn't want to talk to you, she doesn't have to."

"This is terrible timing, Alex. My mother just passed away," Charlie told him, tears constricting her voice. "You should go."

"I'm really sorry. But I've got to tell you something important, Charlie," Alex insisted, taking hold of Charlie's arm a little too roughly. "Come talk to me in the hallway for one minute."

"No." Charlie shoved him away.

"Charlie!" Alex yelled and pulled on her arm again, harder this time. "Come on. I wouldn't be here if it wasn't really important."

"Enough. Get out of here right now, Alex. And don't come back, you hear?" Dad's tall, daunting form seemed to take up the entire doorway. He loomed over Alex threateningly.

The police officer backed away with his hands up and stormed down the stairs.

Charlie let out a sigh of relief. He was gone. For now.

CHAPTER THREE

Charlie had mustered up enough courage to ask her dad about what Mom wanted Aunt Esther to forgive her for, but as she suspected, Dad wouldn't talk about it.

"It's too painful for me to talk about, especially now," he said. "And it is for Esther too, I'm sure. It's just something that should be left alone, Charlie. Please don't ask me again."

Defeated, she knew it was no use in prying. She'd asked her parents about her Amish aunt several times in the past and had never gotten any answers. After things settled down, maybe she'd give her aunt a call and let her know that Mom forgave her and was sorry. Right now, she had too many other things to worry about.

Over the next week, Alex called repeatedly, but Charlie ignored him.

Charlie checked her cell phone as her shift at the diner ended; she had seven missed calls and texts from him begging her to talk to him. Charlie rolled her eyes and ignored his communication attempts. He probably wanted her back, and she would never go back to him again.

As she was getting into her car after work, she heard someone shout, "Charlie!"

She whipped around and saw Alex waving at her.

So now he's coming to see me at work, waiting until my shift is over? I should call the police if he keeps this up. Oh wait… He is the police, she thought.

He jogged up to her. "I need to talk to you."

"I don't need to talk to you." Charlie got in her car and shut the door. *Please go away.*

He raised his hands, palms up, pleading with her. "Charlie, something has happened," came his muffled response.

She looked up at him. Worry furrowed his eyebrows, and his eyes held desperation, something she had never seen in him. *Something terrible could have happened. Maybe I should hear what he has to say...*

She rolled down the window.

"I need to talk to you about the ring. You still have it, right?"

"No, I don't." It was probably on the buyer's fiancée's left hand by now.

"What?" he shouted. He pressed his palms to his temples, his eyes widened. "What happened to it?"

Charlie stared at the steering wheel. Guilt gripped her for a moment, but she tamped it down. *It was* my *ring to sell.* "Look, my mom died, and my dad lost his job. I sold it."

"What?" He thrust his hands down on the hood of the car in anger.

"How do you think I got this car? From my meager college savings account? You think I could suddenly afford a car?"

"How could you do this?" He kicked the side of the car.

That was enough. He was acting like a child. She rolled up the window and started the engine. "Goodbye, Alex."

"Charlie, I need the ring back." He pounded on the window. "You don't understand."

She hit the gas and tore out of the parking lot. In the rearview mirror, she saw Alex running behind her car, shouting and shaking his fist.

"Sorry, Alex," she said as she sped around the corner and out of his sight.

When Charlie pulled into her driveway, she saw Alex's car parked in front of her apartment building.

Seriously? Is he stalking me?

Alex got out of his car and slammed the door shut. He marched up to her Honda and pounded on the window so hard it made Charlie jump in her seat. "I need that ring back."

Charlie got out of the vehicle and shut the door. "I don't care what you think you need, Alex. We're not together anymore, remember? That ring was mine to do with what I wanted."

His face turned red. He pushed Charlie up against the jagged bricks of the apartment building. His hands encircled her neck.

Shock and terror flashed through her. What had happened to him? Where was all this aggression coming from? He had always been so sweet to her...until he'd cheated on her and dumped her.

Now, as his hands gripped her neck, he wasn't trying to choke her but was trying to scare her. She knew if he really wanted to hurt her, he could. As fear coursed over her, she silently asked God to not let Alex hurt her or Zoe or Dad.

"If I don't have that ring soon, bad things will happen. To both of us."

"What are you talking about?" she choked out.

"Look, I need it, and that's all you need to know. But I'll be back. If you don't give me that ring, there will be serious consequences. For you. For Zoe. Even your Dad."

"Like what?"

"I'll put drugs in your apartment or your car. Then I'll tell my coworkers where to find it. After you're arrested, Child Protective Services will get involved."

Dad couldn't take care of Zoe alone. Especially since he no longer had a job.

"Even if the guy who bought it agreed to sell it back to me, I don't have the money to pay for it."

"I'll give you the money if I have to. I just need that ring back. Understand?"

Was he bluffing? She was too afraid to take the chance. "Okay, okay. I'll call the guy. I still have his number."

"Good." Alex released her.

She slumped against the wall of the building and rubbed her neck.

"I'll see you next week when I come back here around this time. And I expect you to have the ring for me." Alex stormed back to his car and drove away.

Charlie leaned against the wall, relieved he was gone but worried about what she would do.

She wanted so badly to tell her father about this. But Alex's threat echoed in her mind. She'd met several of Alex's coworkers from the police department when they were dating. Big, burly men in dark uniforms with guns and badges. And all close pals of Alex. She imagined them storming her apartment and finding drugs she had never seen in her life, then hauling her away in a police car.

She didn't dare risk crossing him.

Charlie ran up to her room and searched through the contacts on her cell phone. She called Brandon's number, and he told her he'd pawned the ring after his fiancée dumped him.

"What pawn shop was it?" she asked.

"Little Treasures Pawn Shop. Look it up. Now leave me alone, okay? If you call again, I'll call the police on you for harassment." He hung up.

Charlie searched for the pawn shop online, then called the number. The store owner remembered the ring when she described it, but the ring had been sold already to a buyer who had paid cash, so there was no way she could track him down.

She hung up, her stomach in knots.

Great. Now what, God? she wondered.

***

I hate cancer, Charlie thought the morning of her mother's funeral as a group of black-clad mourners surrounded the wooden coffin. Though it was still morning, the cemetery was gloomy with falling mist. The rain droplets fell on Charlie's cheeks, intermingling with her tears.

All her life Charlie had heard of people succumbing to cancer, but she never imagined her own mother would be one of its victims.

After the pastor finished speaking and the service ended, her Aunt Cheryl came up to her. "I'm so sorry about your mother's death, Charlotte. Joanna was a wonderful woman who will be missed by all of us."

Charlie wished everyone would just leave. She stared blankly beyond her aunt at the fading flowers on her mother's coffin that Dad had made to save money. He'd been doing odd jobs as a carpenter to earn some money while looking for a more permanent job. The grief had nearly killed him as he had crafted it, but they did not have the money to spend on a regular casket. They both knew Mom would not have wanted them to spend money they didn't have.

When Aunt Cheryl blocked her view of the simple coffin, Charlie gave up trying to keep her eyes on it. She nodded in acknowledgment, accepted Aunt Cheryl's hug, and thanked her for coming. It was the best she could do.

Dark storm clouds loomed overhead at the cemetery, casting eerie shadows on the gravestones. Charlie felt as though a piece of her heart was being buried along with her mother. It seemed as though Mom had died yesterday.

Their lives had changed when Mom had died, but they were managing. Zoe held Charlie's hand and stood by her. Zoe was mature for an eight-year-old and Charlie couldn't have endured the pain of losing Mom alone. As Charlie watched the box encasing her mother's cancer-ridden body being lowered into the ground, grief was a physical pain in Charlie's chest. It weighed her down, almost drowning her.

The guests lingered long enough to be polite, then disappeared. Charlie walked with her father and Zoe in silence to the old van parked along the curb.

Charlie and Zoe slid in the van and sat on the middle seat together. Rain poured as Charlie's father drove down a tree-lined back road. The windshield wipers cleared away the splattering raindrops. It was raining so heavily that it seemed as though God Himself was crying at her mother's death.

Mom loved God with all her heart, Charlie recalled, often waking up to see her mother reading her Bible at the kitchen table on most mornings in the past. *I know I will see her in heaven again one day*, Charlie thought. *I know I've made some huge mistakes in life, but who hasn't? Mom taught us that God forgives us when we ask Him to and if we repent and truly believe in Him, we will be saved.*

Dad turned on the radio to fill the silence. When the sound of a piano solo from the classical station floated through the van, Charlie wanted to switch the station. It reminded her so much of her mom playing pieces like that on the piano.

Her dad changed the channel before she could even reach for it.

The rain continued to fall, making puddles all over the road. Suddenly the van hydroplaned, sliding across the wet pavement, coming dangerously close to the side of the road. Charlie's stomach flipped, and for a moment she squeezed her eyes shut, her mind screaming, *No!*

She opened her eyes, commanding herself to stay calm. With one hand she reached out for Zoe.

"Dad!" Charlie grabbed the seat in front of her with her other hand.

Her father frantically turned the steering wheel, but the wheels did not respond.

They slid off the side of the road. The impact thrashed Charlie in her seat as the van rolled over and over.

Cover Zoe! she mentally ordered herself and moved closer to the screaming child.

The windows shattered, sending shards of glass into the van. The crashing made Zoe sob, and Charlie ducked her head and covered her sister with her arms.

"It's okay, Zoe," Charlie cried into Zoe's shoulder. Charlie felt Zoe clutching onto her so hard that her sister's small fingernails dug into her skin.

The van turned over a third time then stopped right side up. Charlie almost let out a sigh of relief, but she had to evaluate the situation first.

Charlie lowered her arms and looked over Zoe, checking to see if she had any cuts or injuries, but there were only a few scratches. "Are you okay?"

"I'm all right. Where's Daddy?"

Charlie looked at the driver's seat. Empty.

The windshield and the front windows were gone. *If Dad was thrown out of the car...could he survive that?* She felt sick just considering the possibility.

"Where's Daddy?" Zoe repeated, eyes wide and trembling. She began to look outside the van, but Charlie captured her attention.

"Don't worry. He probably jumped out so he wouldn't get hurt." Charlie smoothed back Zoe's hair. "Let's go find him."

Zoe unbuckled herself. Charlie reached for her own buckle and noticed the cuts on her arms from the broken glass. She looked out her window and realized they were near the edge of a cliff. The van was a mere few feet away from the edge.

Charlie didn't want Zoe to see that or risk her getting out of the van and falling. "Get out on your side of the van, Zoe," Charlie told her. Zoe didn't ask questions or complain. She just did as she was told.

As they were getting out, Charlie glanced back out her window. There was a wide, steadily flowing river below, the Saco River. What if her dad had fallen down there? The thought pushed Charlie into action. She followed Zoe out the other side of the van and walked ahead of her, crunching twigs and leaves. Charlie looked around desperately. She wanted to see him before Zoe. Just in case...

Charlie shook her head and focused. Where was he?

She whipped out her cell phone and dialed Dad's number.

Closer to the road, Charlie heard the faint ringing. She moved closer, then she saw the phone lighting up. Then she saw her dad. She saw his figure on the ground, unmoving.

27

Oh, no. Please, God, let him be alive. Don't take my dad, too.

Charlie whirled around and bent down to her sister's level. Zoe hadn't seen him yet. "Zoe, listen. I'm going to look over there." She pointed to an area near their dad. Then Charlie pointed to an area far enough from the street and cliff. "Go look over there, okay?"

"Okay," Zoe said, and she ambled away.

Charlie rushed over to Dad. His head was on a large rock. Charlie grabbed his wrist and felt for a pulse. Nothing. He wasn't breathing. She moved his arm aside then quickly looked away from the blood.

He was dead.

CHAPTER FOUR

Charlie slowly stood. Her head jerked up when she heard voices coming closer. Of course people who had driven by were coming to see if they were alive.

She desperately wanted to fall to the ground and weep, but she had no time. She had an idea and a choice to make.

Alex was looking for her. Charlie didn't know what he would do when he found her, and she certainly didn't want Zoe to get involved or hurt. She'd do anything to keep Zoe.

Charlie hurried to the edge of the cliff and looked down.

Her phone beeped.

It was a text from Alex: *You're running out of time, Charlie.* There was no hope in getting the ring back.

She felt where Alex had wrapped his hands around her neck. What would she do now without the protection of her caring father?

She had to protect Zoe. Charlie could not afford to hire a lawyer, and she would not risk Zoe being taken away from her. She knew she couldn't actually fake their deaths, but she could try to throw people off and give them some extra time to get away from Alex. A head start.

Charlie needed something that could fall off easily during a fall. After quickly checking on Zoe, she ran to the van. There wasn't much to choose from. She took one of Zoe's hats. Charlie threw the hat down into the river and dropped her cell phone onto the rocks. Hopefully it would make them think they had fallen off the cliff and been swept away by the river. It wasn't much, but it was all she could think of.

It was pouring so hard that their footprints would be covered up. As the voices neared, she scurried over to Zoe.

"We have to go home very quickly and quietly."

Zoe nodded her head and slipped her hand in Charlie's. "What about Dad?"

Charlie's throat tightened. "He'll meet us at home." She had to say something to keep Zoe quiet, just until they got home.

Charlie was overcome with guilt as she left her father's body behind, but it had to be done. She'd have to figure out what to do about his funeral arrangements once they were safe. She didn't know what would happen to her father's body, but right now Zoe's safety was her priority, and that's what her father would have wanted.

They crept away into the trees to their apartment.

They had almost been home when the van had crashed. When they finally reached their apartment, they were soaked through and Zoe was shivering. Charlie found the spare key and managed to calm her own shaking hand long enough to unlock the door.

Her plan was to let people believe they had not survived the car crash so they could leave quietly. After all, the van had crashed at the edge of a cliff with a river down below. Maybe, just maybe, Alex would believe they were dead and swept away by the river. Then he would stop harassing her.

She didn't know if it would even work. She didn't know what else to do.

"We have to leave, Zoe. We're going to go on a road trip," she said, trying to sound enthusiastic.

Zoe looked at Charlie with a serious expression. "What's going on, Charlie? Tell me."

30

Charlie sighed. She couldn't lie to her, and Zoe was old enough to be told. "Listen. Dad—"

"He's not coming to meet us here, is he?" Zoe asked quietly.

"No, Zoe, he's not."

God, why?

"He died in the crash, didn't he?" A tear fell from Zoe's eye.

Charlie held back her own tears and sat on the couch with her sister. "Yes... Dad is gone."

"Now Mom and Dad are both gone. What are we going to do? How are we going to pay the rent?" Zoe leaned forward and covered her face with her little hands. Charlie's heart broke when she saw the young girl cry. Charlie thought about how her parents would never see Zoe's graduation or wedding, and how Zoe would especially miss them at those times. Charlie promised herself she would always be there for Zoe in every way she could.

Charlie remembered the times she had heard about children losing their parents, and she had always thought that would never happen to them. But it had, and they would endure this grief together. Charlie wrapped her arms around Zoe as they wept in anguish.

Oh, God, I don't understand why this has happened. It makes me wonder sometimes if you really do care about us, and I am sorry. I know you care about us and love us more than I will ever understand. I really need your help right now. Help me take care of Zoe, she prayed.

Zoe was just a child. She was only supposed to be sad that her parents had both recently died, not worry about where they would live or how they would pay the bills.

Charlie knew if she stayed home, there was no way she could avoid

31

Alex. She had no choice but to leave. There was nothing here except an empty apartment that she couldn't afford.

Charlie wiped her tears away and silently vowed to herself that she would do everything she could to give Zoe a better life. She would put her sister's needs first. She would do whatever she had to do to protect her. Charlie wished she could shield Zoe from every hurt.

She willed the rest of her tears away. There was no time to grieve right now.

Charlie straightened and looked at Zoe's red face. "I know you're sad, but we have to pack what we need for our trip. We both got soaked from walking in the rain. Go grab some clothes, ok? We just need to pack what we absolutely need. Only a few things."

"Where are we going? Somewhere nicer than here, I hope," she said, the tiniest of smiles playing peekaboo on her face. She sniffed and wiped her nose on her sleeve.

"I don't know yet. Let me think. Go pack and make it quick. Really quick. We have to go," Charlie told her. Zoe walked into her room.

Charlie quickly grabbed some clothes and shoved them into a duffel bag. She only took a few things so Alex hopefully wouldn't notice them missing.

Who could we live with? Who has Alex never heard of? Charlie wondered as she packed. Dad's family lived in Canada, but Alex knew of them and that would probably be the first place he'd look.

Charlie went into her parents' room and dug the small safe out of the closet to get her mother's wedding ring. If she got really desperate, she could pawn it, even though it would break her heart. She also grabbed the little address book out of the safe.

32

Rummaging around, she accidentally knocked over a box on the top shelf. When it fell on the floor, Charlie stopped moving.

All that was in the box was a child's straw hat. Charlie bent and picked it up, feeling the roughness of it on her fingers. She remembered a barn full of bleating sheep. The smell of hay and farm soil. The wind in the grass and horses neighing. A young boy patting her hand and smiling at her so gently, laughing with her. She couldn't remember his name. Her memories pulled her by the hand to her childhood as she recalled coming home that day after they had driven all the way to the farm and back. Later that day, Mom had taken the hat away from Charlie, saying she didn't want to talk about it. Charlie had been so confused, and she never knew until now that Mom had kept it all these years.

She wondered if Mom's family still lived in the Amish community of Unity, Maine. She had never met them and never even seen any pictures of them. It would be a lot safer bet than going to Canada to stay with Dad's relatives. Aunt Esther's number was in that phone book, but Mom had always said never to call her unless it was an emergency. This was definitely an emergency.

Maybe an Amish community would be the last place Alex would look for her. As far as she knew, he had no idea she had Amish relatives, and they lived under the radar.

Charlie and Zoe needed to live with people Alex didn't know about. They would quietly disappear, even if Charlie didn't know where to go yet. Maybe if they went to live with her mother's family, Alex wouldn't be able to find them. Even if Alex used his police resources to search for Mom's relatives, he would probably have a hard time figuring out who they were. Charlie wondered if the Amish even got birth certificates or social security numbers.

Charlie opened the address book and found her aunt and uncle's phone number. Mom had told her they had a phone, but it was in their business, not their house. She couldn't call from here anyway in case the police pulled the apartment's phone records.

If her aunt and uncle didn't take them in… Well, Charlie would figure out what to do about that later. At least they would be away from Alex.

Zoe came out of her room, bag packed.

"You can only take a bag or two of clothes and shoes. We'll buy you a new toothbrush and things like that later. Are you all done packing?"

"Yes, almost," Zoe said. Then she asked hopefully, "Can I take Mr. Snuffles?"

Charlie smiled, picturing the stuffed elephant. "Sure, Mr. Snuffles can come. I'll check over your stuff."

Zoe finished up her packing. For a child, she was sensible. She had packed her rain boots, a few sweatshirts and her favorite purple jacket.

"What's going to happen to the rest of our stuff?" Zoe asked, gesturing to her clothes, furniture and collection of stuffed animals.

"We'll get it later," Charlie said, unsure of whether or not she was lying. Charlie hoped that if they left their things there, Alex would not think they had gone far. Maybe, if she got really lucky, the police would think that Charlie and Zoe had died in the accident, but it was a stretch.

Charlie left replaceable everyday items like her face wash and toothbrush. She took one photo album that had a lot of pictures of her mom and dad. She also packed clothes, shoes, and a few books. Regretfully, she left behind her keyboard. She couldn't lug that thing all the way to her aunt's farm. Besides, as soon as Alex saw it missing, he

34

would know that she had left and taken it with her.

There was still a bowl, spoon, and a box of cereal Dad had left out that morning. Mom had always hated that. She left everything the way it was when they had left that morning.

Then Charlie thought about her car. What if Alex realized it was gone? Charlie couldn't risk it. They'd have to take the bus, and maybe a cab once they got farther north.

"Ready?" she asked Zoe.

Zoe nodded, carrying her suitcase. Charlie ushered Zoe into the hallway. They didn't look back as they stepped past the crackled and paint-chipped door.

Charlie followed Zoe's lead and quickly locked the door behind her.

"Where are we going?" Zoe asked, struggling with the cumbersome suitcase.

Charlie reached out to help her. "We are going to Unity on a bus."

"Unity? Is Unity in Maine?" Zoe asked.

"Yes, it is."

After walking to the bus stop, Charlie stopped at a nearby pay phone while they waited for the bus. She picked up the phone and began to dial her aunt's number.

What if they turned her down? Butterflies whirled in her stomach. "Please, God... help me through this and show me what to do."

Charlie took a deep breath and told herself to calm down. She had to do this for Zoe. She shakily dialed the number and waited as it rang. It rang and then, went to voicemail. A man's voice, which Charlie assumed belonged to her uncle, said that she had reached the Unity Community Store. There had been a note in the address book about that, so Charlie knew it was the right number. There was a beep, signaling her to leave her message.

"Hi. This is Charlotte, Joanna and Greg's daughter. I'm Esther and Irvin's niece. Something awful has happened…" Charlie stopped as she willed her tears away. She knew this would happen when she spoke the words aloud. She couldn't stop the lump from forming in her throat and the hole that was forming in her heart.

She continued, "My mother, Joanna, has died of cancer. My father, Greg, died today in a car accident. My younger sister Zoe and I have nowhere to go right now. We don't have any other family near here. So, I was wondering if we could come and stay with you for a little while. This number I am calling from is a pay phone so don't call it back. I lost my cell phone." Charlie thanked them and hung up. Even though Charlie wasn't sure if they would take them in, she knew she had to try. If they didn't have a phone in their house, who knew how long it would take for Aunt Esther to get her message?

The bus pulled up to the stop, and Charlie led Zoe to it.

Hopefully, we will be welcomed there, she thought.

CHAPTER FIVE

Irvin Holt ambled to the phone to check his messages. He sat down on the stool behind his desk, glancing out the window at a patch of watermelons. Already tired even though it was only lunch time, he rubbed his eyes.

His store sold everything from tools and flour to souvenirs for tourists to take home. Business was booming lately, probably due to folks coming to see the fall foliage in a quaint Amish town. Irvin was thankful for all the new customers. *Thank you, Lord, for always providing for my family,* he prayed. He glanced up the driveway at his house that sheltered his family. He was a blessed man indeed. He had a thriving business, a wonderful wife, and six children. What more could a man want in life?

He pressed the button on the phone and listened to the messages.

"Hello, Mr. Holt. This is Mr. Laurence. I'd like to order several supplies in bulk from you..." Irvin listened to the rest and scribbled down the man's phone number.

"Hi. This message is for Esther. This is Sally just saying hi. Just have her call me when she can." Irvin scribbled down Sally's number and pressed the button again.

"Hello. This is DBGH Advertising. I see your community store doesn't have a website or online advertising, obviously because you're Amish. We would like to set you up with one for a monthly payment. Also—" Irvin didn't even listen to the rest of that one. He pressed the delete button.

Irvin laughed out loud at that one. "What nonsense. This business has never had a website and has thrived for over forty years, and I certainly

37

won't get one now," he muttered to himself. He pressed the button again to hear the next message. "God will continue to provide without it."

"This is Charlotte, Joanna and Greg's daughter."

Irvin nearly fell off the stool. How had she gotten this number?

"My mother, Joanna, has died of cancer. My father, Greg, died today in a car accident. My younger sister Zoe and I have nowhere to go right now…" He took in a sharp breath. Esther would be devastated, even though she hadn't spoken to her sister since—

"We don't have any other family near here. So, I was wondering if we could come and stay with you for a little while."

Of course, the Christian thing would be to take them in. But did Charlotte know the truth?

What should he do? He'd have to tell his wife about this. But how would she handle the news of Joanna's death? Not to mention the idea of her nieces showing up on their doorstep? After absentmindedly listening to the rest of the messages, Irvin trudged down the lane to his house.

"Esther?" he called as he opened the front door. "Something has happened."

Esther stopped sweeping the floor and her face paled. "What? What's wrong? Tell me."

Irvin had no idea how to break the news to her, so he walked to her, took the broom, and gently sat her down in a chair. "First of all… I'm sorry to tell you this. I don't know how else to say it—"

"Just say it."

"Your sister Joanna has passed away. It was cancer. And so has Greg. He was in a car accident."

"Joanna? No!" Esther cried, covering her face with her hands. "I never got to say goodbye. Why didn't she call? I had no idea she was sick."

"Well, you would have been shunned if you had gone to see her. And after everything that happened—"

"No," Esther said firmly. "Even after what happened, she still should have let me know she was dying."

"You would have gone to see her?" Irvin asked, surprised. "Even with the risk of being shunned?"

Esther nodded, wiping away tears. "It would have been hard after all these years, but I would have, even if I had to keep the visit a secret."

Irvin took a step back. His wife had refused to speak to her sister Joanna for over twenty years but would have dropped everything to secretly visit her if she had known Joanna was dying?

"We should treat every day as though it is our last. We should also treat others as though it could be their last day," Irvin said, barely above a whisper. He didn't want to upset her more than she already was, but he instantly regretted the words. He hadn't helped her feel better, that was for sure.

Esther sobbed, and he knelt down next to her, holding her as her body shook with sobs.

"If only I had known… Maybe I could have made things right between us before she died," Esther managed to say between sobs.

Irvin rubbed her back. "You didn't know, dear. And she could have tried to make things right with you but chose not to. She knew she was dying, but you didn't." He let her cry for several minutes, worried about how he would tell her the rest.

He stood up, pulled up a chair, and sat. "There is something else…" he began.

She sniffed and took a deep breath, her tears finally slowing for a moment. "What?"

"It was Charlotte who called. She asked to come stay here with her younger sister, Zoe."

"Zoe? I didn't even know about her." Esther sat up straight. "Of course, we should have them come. They are family. Right? What do you think? Isn't having them stay here the right thing to do?"

Irvin hesitated. "I'm not sure that's a good idea… What if—" His voice dropped to a whisper. "What if them coming here makes the truth come out? You know there have been rumors going around for years."

Esther held his hands. "No one will ever find out. It'll be fine. Charlotte and Zoe probably have no idea, so why would them coming here risk that?"

Irvin nodded slowly. "That's true, I suppose. But won't it be hard on you to have them here, especially after losing your sister?"

"Maybe. She'll probably remind me of Joanna. But I also want to see them."

"Are you sure?"

"Of course."

"And what if they start asking questions?"

"I'll figure that out. Besides, I don't have to answer anything. It's hard for me to talk about. But hopefully it won't come to that."

"Esther, are you sure about this?"

She sighed and patted his hands in her lap. "I've dreamed of meeting her for so long. Now that Joanna is gone, even though that is a horrific tragedy, that means I can meet Charlotte, and Zoe too. That's the one good thing that can happen as a result of losing my sister. Please, don't take this from me. Maybe God is giving me a second chance to make things right, even though Joanna is…gone."

Irvin's heart melted at the look Esther was giving him. Even after all these years, his heart still fluttered when he looked into his wife's lovely eyes.

"Fine. Maybe you're right. But we need to be careful. If the truth comes out—"

Esther touched his face. "You don't have to tell me the risks. I didn't make things right with Joanna, but the least I can do is take care of Charlotte and Zoe. We will trust the Lord. If the truth comes out, it'll destroy me. But I am willing to take that chance."

***

After almost an hour and a half of riding on the bus, Charlie heard her sister's stomach growl. Now that she thought of it, she was hungry herself. With the funeral and the car crash, they hadn't eaten lunch yet, and it was the middle of the afternoon. She wished she would have thought to pack a lunch, but she hadn't thought of it when she had left in such a rush. "Maybe we will stop soon and we can get a late lunch."

Zoe nodded. She hadn't asked any questions or made a single complaint since they got on the bus. She just stared out the window, cuddling her stuffed elephant.

Charlie also looked out her own window, her mind wandering back to the day Alex had asked her to marry him.

"Charlotte Cooper, will you marry me?" Alex had asked, down on one knee in an upscale seafood restaurant in Portland, Maine.

Charlie held back a squeal as she stared at the tiny velvet box with the sparkling diamond ring inside. She'd been waiting for this moment for what seemed like a century, even though she was only in her early twenties. Every detail had to be perfect, because she would remember it forever.

"Yes, Alex." She forced her voice to sound elegant and refined, keenly aware that everyone in the seaside Maine restaurant, guest and staff alike, was staring at this handsome young man, down on one knee before her. "I will." Unable to stifle her enthusiasm a second longer, she leapt out of her chair and vaulted into his arms, nearly knocking him over. Applause and cheers washed over her.

Alex laughed then gently helped her back into her seat. After taking the ring from its case, he slipped it onto her finger. She could barely breathe. Or sit still.

Charlie raised her hand and tilted it from side to side, basking in the brilliance of the diamond on her finger as it caught the chandelier light. Yes, this was the beginning of the fairy tale she'd always believed would come true for her.

They'd only known each other for eight months. But a girl just knows when a guy is "the one"—or so she had heard. Alex was gorgeous, intelligent, fun, witty, and he was a brave police officer. What else could a girl want in a—dare she say it?—*husband*?

"I can't wait to tell your parents."

Charlie gulped. Mom and Dad had liked Alex Henderson from the moment they first met him. But they wouldn't be thrilled about an engagement so soon. There was no doubt in her mind they'd say she should get to know Alex better before making a commitment to him.

But how could she say no to such a romantic proposal with so many eyes watching? And if she did, Alex would probably break up with her.

She might never find anyone so wonderful. So perfect.

"I was thinking the wedding could be in six months. What do you think? Why wait, right?" Alex said, eyes gleaming.

"Right. Why wait?" Charlie agreed, but she couldn't dismiss the niggling worry that this was happening too fast.

"Would you be all right with a large wedding? I'd like to invite my entire family and of course all my buddies at the police station."

"Sure. I always wanted a big wedding."

When they walked in the door of Charlie's apartment in Biddeford, her parents were sitting on the couch watching a movie with Zoe, who was snuggled in a blanket between them.

Zoe looked up. "Hi, Charlie. Did you have fun on your date?"

"I sure did. And we have something to tell you." Holding Alex's hand, she walked up to them and showed off her sparkling ring. "We're engaged."

"Oh, my," Mom said, her hand flying to her throat. "That's quite the ring."

Dad stood and shook Alex's hand. "Congratulations." Dad and Mom stood next to each other, smiling awkwardly.

That's it? That's all the enthusiasm they could muster? They were not very good at hiding their true emotions.

"It's beautiful." Zoe sighed. "I can't wait until I get a ring like that."

Charlie rested a hand on Mom's arm. "Will you help me plan the wedding? We were thinking it would be in less than a year."

Her mother bit her lip for only a second then smiled. "Of course, I will."

"Well, I better get home. I have an early morning tomorrow." Alex kissed Charlie on the cheek, and Charlie led him to the door. As Charlie watched Alex walk out their door, she dreaded the conversation she was about to have with her parents.

She turned around to face them, worry clearly written all over their faces. They were sitting on the couch, and she sat in a chair near them.

Dad leaned forward, elbows on his knees. "Are you sure you want to get married so soon? You've only known him for eight months."

"I'm absolutely sure. You two only knew each other a year before you got married. And you were eighteen. I just know Alex is the one for me. Why wait?"

Mom reached out to Charlie to touch her arm. Fatigue clouded her mother's eyes.

The fear of Mom's cancer returning weighed heavily on Charlie's mind. If Charlie married Alex within the year, then surely Mom would be able to be there, if the cancer didn't return.

No. She couldn't think that way. The cancer wouldn't return.

"It was different for us back then when we got engaged," Mom said. "I couldn't wait to leave the Amish community and marry your father. Not that I regret getting married that quickly." She smiled at Dad, and Dad squeezed her hand.

"We were lucky. We've been married over twenty years and are even more in love than when we got married. We're soulmates. Right, Joanna?" Dad said.

Mom kissed Dad's cheek. "Right. But things have changed nowadays. You haven't known Alex very long, Charlie. He may not be who you think he is. Sometimes it takes a while for someone's true personality to show," Mom insisted.

What do they think he is, a criminal or something? "But I do know him. Besides, he's a cop."

Mom glowered. "Charlie, no one is perfect. Who knows, he could have quite the temper, and you'd have no idea. At this stage in your relationship, he's on his best behavior when you're together. Don't be naïve, honey."

Charlie stood up. "I'm not, and you're wrong. He's a very decent man, and I love him. I want to marry him. And I will do it with or without your permission."

Mom and Dad looked at each other in silent communication that had been perfected by many years of marriage, as if to agree there would be no changing Charlie's mind.

Dad nodded. "Well, then, we will give you our blessing."

"The beach would be a lovely place for a wedding," Mom offered. "Just imagine it… A Maine wedding on the beach."

Charlie bounced up from her seat and clasped her hands together like an excited little girl. She was marrying the man of her dreams, and her mother would be there to see it.

Or so she'd thought.

A shiver snaked down her spine. Even if Charlie had gone through with the wedding, her mother wouldn't have lived long enough to attend.

Zoe yawned and stretched beside her, bringing Charlie out of her memories and back to the present.

A few minutes of driving down a shop-lined street led them to a small café. It reminded her of the diner where she used to work. She felt the sting of guilt at not even letting her boss know she would not be returning to work. She hoped Linda could quickly find a replacement.

45

The bus stopped near a diner.

"Come on. Let's get off and get something to eat, then we can take a taxi the rest of the way. The bus won't be going to the farm," Charlie said. "So take all your stuff with you."

"Okay. Mr. Snuffles can eat with us."

After going through so many traumatic events, the toy elephant was probably comforting to Zoe.

"As long as he doesn't eat all my food," Charlie said, hoping to lighten the mood a little.

Zoe stepped off the bus, the elephant dangling from her fist. With their luggage in tow, they entered the café.

Red checkered tablecloths and vases of sunflowers gave it a country look. There were only ten tables. Now that it was after the lunch rush, there were a handful of customers. Compared to the downtown trendiness of the diner where she'd worked in Biddeford, this one was quaint and rustic.

Linda and Tonya are going to be so worried about me when I don't show up for work at the diner for a few days… What will they think when they realize Zoe and I have disappeared? Will they call the police?

Charlie tried not to think about it as she looked around the café. A waiter took orders from an elderly couple, two middle-aged women chatted in hushed tones, and a man about Charlie's age sat alone, reading a thick book while waiting for his meal.

Charlie made herself stop thinking of back home and focused on the here and now. She had only brought a limited amount of cash with her and didn't want to spend much. She was afraid if she used her debit card or a check that somehow Alex would track her down. Even if she was a

46

little paranoid, she didn't want to take any chances. Now that she thought about it, she was glad she had ditched her cell phone. She had no idea if he would have been able to track her with it.

She didn't want to impose on her aunt and ask her for food when they arrived. Her stomach growled again, and she figured a hot meal would be worth dipping into their cash.

After seeing a sign that said to seat yourself, she considered the options and looked at all the tables.

The man sitting alone wore a blue shirt and brown pants with suspenders over his wide shoulders. His dark hair almost touched his collar. His clothes looked much plainer than what everyone else wore in the café. On closer inspection, Charlie noticed muddy boots and a straw hat hanging on the back of his chair. *He must be Amish,* Charlie thought.

She had to admit it. He was really cute, in a rugged sort of way.

"Can we sit down or what?" Zoe asked a little too loudly.

The man looked up. When his gaze met Charlie's, she could have sworn she'd seen those eyes before.

CHAPTER SIX

Elijah couldn't look away from the woman who had just entered the café. There was something oddly familiar about her, yet she and the girl who was with her had luggage like they were traveling. Maybe she'd come into the shop where he worked and that's where he knew her from, but it was unlikely.

Their unsettling eye contact ended when the young girl beside her led the woman to a table with four chairs right next to his. After they sat down, Elijah tried to return his attention to the Bible in front of him. The store where he worked had been busy today, so he was taking a later lunch than usual.

Elijah couldn't stop himself from occasionally glancing in the woman's direction.

Shoulder-length dark brown hair framed her lovely face. He guessed she was around his age, maybe in her early twenties. The little girl with her looked about seven or eight. Her sister perhaps?

When Jim came to take their order, Elijah took advantage of the distraction and stared, unable to take his eyes away. He ignored his mother's voice in his head, telling him that staring was impolite.

The woman was beautiful in her jeans and sweatshirt. Clearly, she was not Amish. Elijah knew he shouldn't be so interested in an *Englisher*, and usually he wasn't. But there was something very different about her.

"What is better," the woman asked Jim, "the spaghetti or the turkey dinner?"

"Turkey, definitely," Elijah said. When the waiter and both of the customers looked his way, he added sheepishly, "That's what I always get."

The woman nodded, then turned to Jim, "Guess I'll have the turkey dinner then." The little girl ordered a cheeseburger and fries.

After Jim left, the woman turned back to Elijah. "Thanks for the tip."

His stomach flip-flopped. He hadn't expected her to talk to him. "My pleasure."

She gestured toward his Bible. "What are you reading?"

Wasn't it obvious? Maybe she was just trying to make conversation. He smiled at the thought. "It's the Bible. I'm reading Psalms…again."

"Oh," she said, her own smile fading. "You read it a lot?"

"I read it every day. It helps me grow closer to God." It was a shame how many people missed out on reading God's love letter. "Have you read it?"

"I used to. When I was younger. Haven't lately. I did hear a pastor quote from it when…" Her voice trailed off and she got a sad look in her eyes. "Never mind."

Poor young woman, he thought. *What she really needs right now is to read it. Maybe it would help her understand whatever is troubling her… And give her some comfort.*

The little girl smiled at him. "Would you like to sit with us?"

The woman shot a glare at her.

She shrugged and whispered, "What? He seems nice. And maybe he's lonely, sitting all by himself."

The woman looked at him, her cheeks flushed. "Would you like to sit with us?"

What harm would sharing a table with this woman do? It was not against the *Ordnung* to share a meal with or befriend an *Englisher.* "Sure.

49

Thank you." Elijah moved his water glass, hat, and his Bible to the other table. "I'm Elijah Hochstettler." He extended his hand to her.

She took his hand and shook it. Her skin was soft, but her grip felt strong. "I'm Charlotte, but I go by Charlie."

Charlie? Could it be her, the little girl he'd met in Unity as a child, the girl who'd stolen his heart?

No way, Elijah thought, briefly shaking his head. He blinked and smiled, hoping he didn't look like too much of an idiot.

"I'm Zoe," said the girl.

"It's very nice to meet both of you," he said.

He hesitated. Charlie and Zoe sat across from each other. He wondered where to sit.

Zoe patted the chair beside her. "You can sit by me if you want."

"Thank you." Elijah set down his Bible and glass, then sat, grateful that the little girl had resolved his dilemma.

"Hose-settler is a funny last name." Zoe giggled.

"Zoe," her older sister chided.

Elijah laughed. "It's okay. I think it's rather amusing myself."

Charlie's cheeks turned a little red as she took a sip of water.

Jim walked by their table. "Oh, I see you have moved, Elijah. Want me to bring out your plate the same time as theirs?"

"That would be great. Thanks, Jim."

As Charlie and Zoe chatted quietly to themselves for a moment, a hint of doubt niggled at him. What would his community think if they saw him eating with an *Englisher* woman? He wasn't sure what they would think. It wasn't against his community's rules to eat with and talk to outsiders, so he was doing nothing wrong.

50

The truth was, at that moment, he didn't really care what the community thought. Besides, it was highly unlikely he would ever see this woman again.

Charlie didn't usually talk to strangers, but for some reason, this man made her feel comfortable and safe. In Biddeford, she would never have asked a strange man to sit with her in a café. There were plenty of odd characters in town, even though it was small, and her parents had always taught her to be careful.

"Where are you from?" Elijah asked, leaning back in his chair.

She knew he was just trying to make small talk. But if Alex showed up and started asking questions, the less that people knew about them, the better.

"We're visiting some relatives in Unity." She sent Zoe a glance, silently communicating that she shouldn't say anything else.

"Are they Amish too? I probably know them," he said.

Charlie looked him over again. He really was Amish, wasn't he? She didn't know if it would be rude to ask. "Yes, they are," she said. She wouldn't say more than that about it, and she hoped he wouldn't pry.

He looked like he wanted to ask more questions. "Everyone knows everyone around here," he added awkwardly.

Oh, great, Charlie thought as the waiter brought their food.

"Can we pray?" Elijah asked. Charlie felt a pang of grief. Her family had always prayed together before Mom had died.

Zoe took Charlie's hand and Elijah's hand and bowed her head. Charlie looked at Elijah. *This is so awkward,* she thought, but it would be more awkward if she didn't hold his hand. She held out her hand to him.

51

For a second, he only rested his hand on the table near hers hesitantly. Then he took it. They bowed their heads and closed their eyes.

Being so close to Elijah made her palms begin to sweat. She hoped the prayer would be short and he wouldn't notice.

"I will pray. Dear Lord," Zoe said, "thank You for this food. And thank You for us meeting Elijah today. Amen."

When Charlie opened her eyes, she saw Elijah smiling. She couldn't help but smile back.

"Let's eat." Elijah grabbed his fork and dug into his own turkey dinner.

While Zoe took a big bite of her burger, Charlie cut her turkey with her fork, inhaling the aroma.

"Who's your friend?" Elijah asked Zoe, referring to her toy elephant.

Zoe told Elijah all about Mr. Snuffles and how she had gotten him at a yard sale. He listened intently and laughed at her stories. Charlie wondered if the men in Unity were different from some of the jerks in Biddeford. Elijah seemed far more innocent and much kinder than Alex.

After they finished eating, Zoe rubbed her stomach. "That was really good."

When the waiter brought the bill, Elijah grabbed it before Charlie could. "I want to pay for this."

Though touched by his kind offer, Charlie said, "You don't have to do that."

"I don't get to treat people often. It would be my pleasure."

"Don't you have a girlfriend to buy meals for?" Zoe asked.

"Zoe." Charlie's face heated.

"No, I don't," Elijah said as he put money in the little black folder.

"Charlie's single too." Zoe looked at her for a reaction as she slurped the last of her drink through her straw.

Heat filled Charlie's face, and she could just imagine how red it had turned. "Thanks for the meal, Elijah."

He leaned back in his chair and gave her a warm smile. "You're very welcome."

Good grief, he is handsome, Charlie thought and mentally kicked herself. She couldn't afford to be distracted right now. "We need to go," Charlie announced, a little too suddenly.

All three of them stood up and collected their things. "Tomorrow's Sunday. If you're looking for a church to go to, the one in our Amish community welcomes visitors. We would love to see you there," Elijah offered. "If you want, I could show you around."

He was probably just being polite.

Not wanting to seem rude, she said, "We'll try to be at church." She put an arm around Zoe's shoulder, considering his offer. "Thanks again for lunch."

She didn't know much about the Amish, but she remembered learning from her mother that they didn't marry outsiders or even date them. But she wasn't here to find a boyfriend anyway.

As Elijah walked away, Charlie glanced out the window and saw Elijah getting into a horse-drawn buggy.

"He's cool." Zoe stared at the buggy outside in amazement. "I really like him."

"I do too. But we can't get to know anyone too well right now. We need to find Aunt Esther and ask if we can stay with her."

Zoe wrapped her arms around Mr. Snuffles and looked at Charlie sadly.

"I think it's time to call again." Charlie asked the waiter if there was a pay phone anywhere nearby. He pointed to one near the restrooms. Zoe stood near Charlie as she dialed. She called for a taxi first, then it was time to call Aunt Esther.

Charlie hoped her aunt would answer this time. *Will she be angry at me for bothering her? Does she even remember my mom?*

Charlie didn't really expect anyone to answer.

"Hello?" A woman's voice this time.

Oh, thank God. Charlie cleared her throat. "Um, this is Charlotte Cooper. I'm—"

"Charlotte. I was hoping it might be you. This is Aunt Esther."

Well, Charlie had not expected this. She felt tongue-tied, wondering what to say. Clearly her aunt had heard the message. Maybe Esther did have a phone in her home, after all.

"I'm so glad you called back. Are you all right, dear?"

"Yes, we are, considering the circumstances. I am guessing you heard my message?"

"Yes. When your uncle told me, I decided to stay right here by the phone in the shanty. Your message was a shock. I had no idea about Greg and Jo—" Esther's words were cut short by a mournful sob. Charlie winced. She hated that she had had to break the news to her aunt over an answering machine. Esther continued, "I haven't spoken to my sister in over twenty years."

She wanted to speak her mind, but instead, Charlie said, "Oh, I am sorry to keep you waiting there by the phone. And I'm so sorry I had to break such sad news over an answering machine."

"Don't worry about that, dear." Her aunt sniffed as if she had been crying. "Where are you now?"

"The Blue Moon Café."

"Do you need directions to get to our farm?"

So she was going to welcome them. Charlie felt some of her tension ease away. "Yes, thanks."

Esther gave her some simple directions. "I'm really looking forward to meeting you both. I never knew Joanna had a second child," Esther added quietly.

After what had happened between the two sisters, would her aunt be willing to take them into their home?

Should she tell Aunt Esther about Alex? What if she refused to let them stay with her? They were already so close to Unity.

Aunt Esther sighed over the phone, which made a muffled crackling sound, disrupting Charlie's thoughts. "Anyway, to answer your question, I do want you to come here. You are family, and you are always welcome in my home."

In relief, Charlie let out the breath she had been holding. They had already ridden the bus almost the entire way. She would tell her about Alex when she got there. "Thank you so much. I can't wait to meet you. You have no idea what this means to us. My father's family lives in Canada, but we couldn't afford to travel there." That wasn't entirely true. Charlie could have probably afforded the trip to Canada if she had withdrawn money from her bank account, but she was afraid of Alex looking into her bank records, so she was only using the rest of the cash from the sale of the ring she'd had at the apartment. She didn't know if police could access people's bank account information or not, but she

55

wanted to be on the safe side. But Esther didn't have to know about all that.

"I have wanted to meet you for a very long time, Charlotte. It will be wonderful to have you."

"I can pay room and board if you like…"

"No, no, that won't be necessary. You may stay as long as you like," her aunt said. "My dear, I do not know you very well, but let me cover some of the rules."

Visions of strict rules, white bonnets and long dresses filled Charlie's mind. Would she and Zoe have to dress and act just like them? Did they have outhouses instead of toilets? What would they think of her and Zoe?

Aunt Esther continued, "During your stay you must respect our lifestyle here. You don't have to dress like us, but you should dress modestly. There is no swearing, smoking or disrespect in my house. All I ask is that you obey the house rules, and help with the chores. Understood?"

"You don't have to worry about any of those things. We will do anything you ask." Charlie grimaced at the thought of doing laundry and dishes by hand, but then she reminded herself it was a small price to pay for what her aunt was offering, which was a safe haven.

"It is settled then," said her aunt. "We will see you soon."

Soon the taxi arrived, and she and Zoe got in with their bags.

CHAPTER SEVEN

Charlie and Zoe rode past quaint shops and over a small bridge. The number of farms passing by the cab's windows began to increase. Zoe pointed at some cows grazing. It was indeed beautiful here. It would be a great place to raise Zoe, if they stayed.

Charlie's thoughts drifted to Elijah and how he'd said he'd like to show them around. Could she trust him? All she knew about him was that he was extremely nice and that he was Amish. Were all Amish that nice?

Alex certainly hadn't been that nice. Well, he had played the part of a sweet gentleman when they'd dated and even for a while after they'd gotten engaged, but Charlie was thankful every day that she'd realized who he really was and hadn't married him.

Her mind went back to when they'd had dinner one night at their favorite seaside Portland restaurant where they had been engaged. She'd asked him, "Do you think after we get married, we could help my family get that big dent on the van fixed?"

Alex looked out the window at the white boats floating near the docks. The ocean sparkled in the sunset. "Maybe. We'll see how things go for us."

Charlie looked at him quizzically. What did he mean? While planning the wedding, he'd encouraged her to indulge in every fantasy that filled her head—no matter how silly or extravagant. Charlie was usually very careful with her money.

Surely, they'd be able to afford repairing her parents' van.

At the time, Mom's cancer had taken its toll on the entire family, even though it was in remission. Mom used to work full time as a music teacher, but she had reduced her hours because she still got tired easily. It had hit the family hard financially, and most of the time they went without whatever they could to save money. Like putting off getting the dent in the van fixed. Charlie just wanted to do this for her family, if Alex would be okay with it after the wedding.

The next morning Charlie awoke to the familiar sound of the family piano being played. It was not the staccato one-fingered playing of Zoe; it was the sound of intricately composed music that Mom loved to play. No one could play better than Mom.

Charlie opened her eyes to see the small, white-walled bedroom she shared with her younger sister. On Zoe's side of the room, a few pictures of elephants were taped to the walls.

Books on teaching school and sheet music filled Charlie's shelves along with pictures of her family. A picture of Alex was tucked into the frame of her mirror. He had acted strangely last night. What had been on his mind?

It was only seven o'clock. She pulled the blankets over her head and groaned. "Why does Mom have to play on Saturday mornings?"

Zoe finally woke up and rolled over, rubbing her eyes. "Because she teaches music lessons on other mornings or she's too tired on weekdays."

That had been a rhetorical question, but Zoe always seemed to have an answer for everything. "I know." Again, her mind wandered to Alex. Charlie told her mom everything. Mom would give her great advice, as usual. Charlie threw off her blankets, put on her bathrobe and slippers, and padded into the living room. She sat on the piano bench and waited for Mom to finish her song.

Charlie had been playing for years and still could not master reading music like Mom had. Mom could play any piece of music expertly, even if she had never seen it before. Charlie, on the other hand, could play by ear and memorize, but reading music was a bit difficult for her. Still, she loved playing the piano, especially with her mother, and wouldn't have given it up for anything in the world.

Mom finished the song with a flourish and smiled at Charlie.

"Perfect, as always," Charlie said.

"Thank you. Play a duet with me?" Mom's eyes twinkled.

"Oh, goodness. Only if I know it already. I can't just sight read flawlessly like you."

Mom flipped through a few books until she found a familiar piece that Charlie agreed to play. Charlie always felt so at home when she and Mom played together. It was something only they shared that no one could ever take away. A special bond, a unique communication known only to them.

After the music ended, Charlie sighed. "Alex is acting weird."

"How so?"

"Whenever I talk about life after the wedding, he becomes so quiet."

"Think it's cold feet? Second thoughts?"

"Maybe. What should I do?"

"If he's having cold feet, you'll know it. I mean, you two are moving very fast. Maybe he'll be fine in a few weeks, or maybe he really just isn't ready yet. If this isn't right, God will show you. Have you prayed about it?"

"I try. Maybe I should pray a lot more." Charlie had been so busy lately that she had been neglecting her prayer life. She knew busyness was no excuse not to pray. She had to get her priorities straight.

"Yes. Pray more. Ask God what He thinks and ask Him to give you a sign. Then just wait and see."

How could she have been so blind for so long?

The taxi hit a bump in the road, rudely jolting Charlie back to the present. It had turned onto a long dirt driveway, leaving the smooth, blacktopped road behind. The bumpy ride nudged Zoe awake after the smooth, paved road ended.

Charlie squinted against the sun and saw wide green fields through her eyelashes. The fields were outlined in jagged wooden fences and dotted with horses. Green and skeletal trees huddled together in the distance. Green was everywhere.

It was like they had entered another world. A world from two hundred years ago.

She suddenly hated it, even though it was beautiful. She wanted the silver and grays of downtown Biddeford back. She wanted the dirty sidewalks, the river, the brick buildings, and the noisy streets. She wanted her familiar apartment and her bedroom. She wanted to go home, and this was not home. Most of all, Charlie wanted her parents back for the hundredth time, and the regret of leaving her father's body behind struck her. She felt incredibly homesick. She wanted to ask the driver to turn the car around.

Instead, Charlie did what was best for her and her sister and let the driver take them down the long driveway to a huge tan house that had no shutters, but had bright blue curtains. It had three stories and a maroon roof with a large metal pipe coming out of the top. Behind the house was a red barn. Classic.

Charlie knew for sure this was the house that her mother had brought her to all those years ago. She recognized the house and the barn and the fields. This was the home of her Aunt Esther, the woman who had refused to speak to her own sister. Mom had been so hurt that day.

Why could Esther have turned her own sister away at the door? How could a person be so cold? Charlie pictured Aunt Esther in her mind as a mean, cruel woman.

Maybe she shouldn't have taken Zoe here to stay with these people. But they'd come this far. At least they could meet their relatives.

The taxi parked in front of the house and Charlie stared at it. In the movies, the Amish houses were usually white with black shutters. This house looked like any other house at first glance because the lack of power lines was not that noticeable at first. If she didn't know any better, she would have thought the house was not Amish.

Charlie looked around and sighed.

"It looks fake, like a story book," Zoe mumbled, still half asleep.

Zoe was right. It looked too perfect to be real. The strangeness of it all reminded Charlie that her parents were dead, and she had survived the car crash. How was she supposed to live with that? Charlie was usually more optimistic, but she was beginning to slip into a dark and numb frame of mind.

The image of her father's lifeless body flashed into her mind. How could she have left him there all alone?

Had she made a huge mistake by leaving him and coming here?

No one here could possibly understand.

She watched a family in Amish clothing walk down the lane in the other direction, probably towards their own home—a mother, a father, and two sisters. They reminded Charlie of happiness. Of her life before...

Before everything shattered to pieces like the windshield of her father's van.

She suddenly became very jealous of that family, and of all the families here. They seemed so sheltered from the pain of the world outside their community. Charlie thought in other circumstances she would have been happy to meet her biological relatives, but now it was a painful reminder of her wonderful past that she would never get back.

As Zoe stared at them through the car window, Charlie refocused. Her relatives came out of their house and approached them. She sluggishly picked up her pink bag, opened the car door, and they both stepped onto the dirt driveway embellished with horse manure. She paid the taxi driver and he drove away.

In her jeans, sweatshirt, and sneakers, she faced the family with Zoe beside her.

The fact that they all resembled her so much rattled her. She steadied herself and gave them the best smile she could manage. The woman and girls wore white bonnet-like head coverings that covered their hair, and the man wore suspenders and a vest. The woman, who had Charlie's eyes, smiled at Zoe and Charlie with as much love as her parents had.

Wait...what? They were happy to see her? Where was the hostility—where were the judgmental looks? They'd shunned her mother. Why were they being so nice to Charlie?

She had to keep reminding herself that this Amish family were her relatives. It was like they were from another century.

"Charlotte," the woman said, approaching Charlie with her arms open. "You have no idea how glad I am to see you." A tear slid down Esther's cheek and she hugged Charlotte. Charlie could barely hide her shock at seeing the woman's reaction. "I'm so glad you're home, Charlotte. I

62

mean—" The woman stammered, then hesitated. "I'm so glad you came."

They're actually glad to see us? Charlie thought, bewildered.

"We are your family now," said one of the girls.

The innocent comment caused an avalanche of grief to hit Charlie as Esther touched her arm. "I'm Esther...your aunt." Charlie jerked away from the woman's touch.

Even though she knew this fact, the statement still shocked her.

Charlie took a good look at Esther, who had kind eyes, graying hair under her prayer *kapp*, and a warm smile. How could this woman have treated Mom so terribly? Why were they being so nice now?

"I'm Irvin, your uncle," the man beside Esther said. His grin was so genuine, and his graying brown beard wagged when he talked. Charlie couldn't help smiling a sad smile, despite her pain. "You may call us Aunt Esther and Uncle Irvin. Or, if you prefer, calling us Esther and Irvin is fine."

Charlie had grown up not even knowing these people at all. She felt more comfortable calling them Esther and Irvin.

Besides, calling them her aunt and uncle would feel like a betrayal of her mother and remind her of her parents' deaths.

Irvin put his arms around his children. "These are your cousins," said Irvin. "Leah is the oldest," he began, gesturing to the young woman who looked about Charlie's age. "Second oldest is Ella Ruth, then Katie, then Lilly, then Debra and Seth. He is only two." Ella Ruth and Katie were teens, Lilly looked about twelve or thirteen, and Debra looked about six years old.

They just smiled at Charlie and Zoe politely, especially Ella Ruth. They seemed so mature for their ages.

63

Esther stood next to her husband. Even though Charlie had heard that the Amish did not allow their pictures to be taken, the family looked like they belonged on a postcard for the Amish country.

Would Charlie and Zoe ever know what it was like to have a family like theirs again? And how could Esther and Irvin have been so cruel to Mom, but act now like everything was just fine?

They were hypocrites.

That was when all Charlotte's sadness and grief reached out and tried to choke her. She couldn't stand to look at them one second longer. She dropped her pink bag and took off running as its contents spilled out over the ground.

Charlie didn't have a destination in mind, but she ended up landing in a sobbing heap right behind the red barn. She didn't care who saw or heard her. As she wept, her numbness temporarily broke and all she felt was pain.

"Why?" she asked God out loud. "Why did I have to lose what I loved most?"

Charlie covered her face in her hands. In the background, horses neighed.

"I asked God that same question a long time ago," said a soft voice. Charlie looked up to see Esther cautiously coming out from the other side of the barn.

"When?" Charlie asked incredulously. How could Esther understand what Charlie was going through? "Look, I know you think you can relate because you lost your sister, but you two haven't spoken in over twenty years. I lost my mother and best friend. I actually loved her. You shunned her."

64

The words had come out sharper than she intended, but she didn't apologize. Besides, weren't the Amish supposed to have unquestioning faith? She wiped her tears away. "I don't even understand why you're taking us in after how you treated my mom."

Esther looked at the grass. "Charlotte, I loved your mother. She was my sister. I've always loved her." Esther's voice was gentle, and guilt rose inside Charlie for what she'd said. Esther sighed. "I don't know what Joanna told you. But the entire community shunned her, even our parents. They passed away a few years ago. I didn't shun her. I even visited her in secret and paid dearly for it. I lost so much. My world fell apart when Joanna left. Things were never the same. After she left, we had an argument, and that's why we never spoke again."

A shadow crossed Esther's face. The older woman shuddered.

"But Mom said you shunned her just like everyone else. She told me that before she died," Charlie said.

"After Joanna left…" Esther paused as if searching for the right words. "Some things happened, and we had a big disagreement. We never spoke to each other again after that. But now I regret that so much… I'd give anything to go back and make it right."

"So, when I was little and Mom brought me here to visit, that's why you turned her away? Because of your argument?"

Esther nodded. "I hate that I did that. I know it's hard for you to understand, but what had happened between us was something devastating and life-changing. A few years later, I tried to apologize, but then she wouldn't speak to me. So, we were both in the wrong."

Charlie nodded slowly. Was that what Mom had been so sorry about before she died?

65

"I know this is hard," Esther continued. "And trust me, I do know how you feel. I also lost someone who meant everything to me a long time ago. Sometimes God takes things away from us and we don't understand why, but I promise you this: it's all part of God's miraculous plan for you. He's with you through it all. He has a reason for everything. Something good will come from this, even though it's hard to understand right now."

Charlie felt like she had been wrapped up in a warm blanket when Esther gathered her up in a hug.

"Charlotte, I know you miss your parents. But I think if you give this place a chance, you will grow to love it. Most importantly, I hope you will give us a chance to be your new family," Esther said. "I hope you stay for a long time. As long as you want."

What do I have left to lose? Charlie thought. She briefly considered telling Esther about her mother's apologies and forgiveness but dismissed the idea. She was already emotionally spent and could not handle anything else right now. Besides, she felt as though her mother's dying wish had a greater story behind it than she realized. She decided she would wait until the right time to tell Esther, maybe after they got to know each other better. Maybe then Esther would explain more of the story to Charlie.

Right now, she had something more pressing to tell Esther.

"There is something you should know," Charlie began.

CHAPTER EIGHT

"The other reason I came here is to hide from someone," Charlie said. It would be unfair to hide the truth from her relatives after they had offered their home to her.

Esther looked at her intently but didn't pry.

"My ex-fiancé gave me a valuable ring that I sold and can't get back. He keeps threatening me, so I thought I could hide out here. He's violent and angry at me. I'm sorry I didn't tell you on the phone earlier, but we were almost here anyway, and I wanted to meet you. I was afraid you wouldn't let us come."

"Nonsense. I'll discuss it with Irvin, but I'm sure he will still want you to stay. You're family, and that means we won't turn you away, ever. Besides, we will pray for God's protection over you, and He will hear us."

"Thank you so much," Charlie whispered, tears threatening once more, but this time they were tears of relief.

Esther helped Charlie up and gently piloted her to the door of the house which opened to a small mudroom. Rows of boots and black sneakers of all sizes lined the floor.

They went into the house and it was so ... uncluttered. The girls sat on a patterned couch draped with a white sheet. They all looked at her with concerned expressions. Zoe jumped up and ran to her sister.

"Are you ok?" Zoe asked with wide eyes, looking up at Charlie.

"I'm ok. I just…" Charlie couldn't find the words.

Zoe answered thoughtfully, "I know. You were thinking about Mom and Dad. It's ok. I cry sometimes, too."

New tears fell as Charlie hugged her little sister. Charlie looked

67

around. The house was open, and she could see most of it from where she stood. She was surprised that the room's walls had been painted with light blue, and the kitchen's walls were light yellow. To their left a huge unfinished quilt draped across a wooden contraption that resembled a table, the quilt as the tabletop. In the corner near the quilt sat a treadle sewing machine. A door led to what looked like a play room with stuffed animals on a bench. To the right of that stood a bookcase with encyclopedias and board games. The walls were bare save for a clock and a calendar. There were also a few pictures of animals, flowers, and scriptures.

To Charlie's right stood a long, plastic-topped kitchen table. There was also a sink with running water with cabinets below the counter. Graham crackers and cereals sat neatly organized on the shelves in clear plastic containers. The only thing that made their kitchen different than any other was the wood stove and no electronic appliances.

She heard chopping sounds and pots and pans clanging. Esther's daughters bustled around, already making dinner. From where Charlie stood, she could see the side of the stove, and she could feel its heat. Lilly took a lighter from Irvin and lit the gas lamp above the table which also gave off heat and surprisingly bright light.

Charlie realized that, even though there were so many children in the house, it was very quiet besides the sounds of the girls cooking. There was no TV or radio. Charlie's apartment, which had housed only four people, always had much more commotion than this full house. Charlie took in the comforting sounds around her.

"Come see your room," Leah said and ushered them deeper into the house. "Well, it's really Ella Ruth's and my room, but we are sharing with

Lilly and Katie while you're here to give you your own space."

"No, no, you don't need to do that," Charlie said, feeling guilty for imposing.

"You've been through a lot. We want you to feel comfortable here," Leah insisted. "Please, don't worry about it. Besides, Lilly and Katie's room is plenty large enough for the four of us. We want to do this for you."

Charlie smiled at Leah, grateful. "Thank you."

It wasn't long before Charlie and Zoe had finished bringing their few possessions into the room.

Everyone's rooms were upstairs except for Esther and Irvin's. Charlie and Zoe's room had blue walls, a small closet, a nightstand, and one full-sized bed for the two of them. It was simple and uncluttered. They put their suitcases down and went into the hall.

They got to take a look at the other girls' rooms as well. They were similar to Charlie and Zoe's room, except less cluttered, and there were no electronics, of course. They had mirrors, pictures, and lotion and perfume on their dressers, but there was no jewelry. Charlie was surprised to see the pictures because she had heard that the Amish were against taking pictures. But a closer look confirmed the pictures were postcards or pictures of people who were not Amish. There were no photographs of themselves or their family though. For example, there was a postcard of two young girls in jeans holding hands, walking down a road. They also had a calendar with photographs of people on it.

They ventured further down the hallway, and Charlie halted when she noticed the bathroom. An indoor bathroom. She had anticipated going outside in the middle of the night to an outhouse in the woods. She opened

69

the creaky door and grinned at the sight of a regular toilet and shower. She stepped in, turned on the faucet and felt the hot water run over her fingers. Well, the Amish were much more modern than she had expected. She was so grateful for the blessing. She chuckled at the thought of having to use an outhouse, then wrinkled her nose. She definitely preferred a modern bathroom over an outhouse any day. There were no signs of electricity anywhere, like light switches, but Charlie could live with that.

"Is this our home now?" Zoe asked Charlie as they walked back downstairs.

"Yes, it is."

"For how long?"

"I don't know, Zoe."

"Can we stay here forever?"

Charlie felt that sting of regret again. All she could think of was Alex and his hands around her neck, and the image of her father's limp body that she'd left behind. She hoped someone had taken care of him well.

Charlie's stomach twisted with guilt, and she grabbed a quilt and pulled it closer to her, hugging Zoe.

Zoe had comforted Charlie the night that Alex had dumped her and now giving Zoe a hug was the least Charlie could do.

As Charlie stroked Zoe's hair, she recalled the night Alex had dumped her.

He'd taken Charlie back to their favorite restaurant. At the time she had hoped a night out would help take her mind off her mother for a bit, who was in the hospital.

Charlie had hurried to the car when he'd pulled into her driveway. "Hi."

"You ready?" Alex replied, looking like he had just come from a funeral. Charlie wanted to ask him what was wrong, but she knew he would tell her when he was ready. Maybe he just felt bad about her mom.

The bleak expression on Alex's face that Charlie noticed when he picked her up remained throughout the evening. Charlie wondered what he was thinking about. Maybe something had happened at home or work…

"Charlotte." He reached for her hand across the linen tablecloth but did not look into her eyes. "I don't know how to tell you this."

Oh, no. What had happened to him? He looked so disheartened that she wondered if something terrible had happened to someone in his family.

"I'm really sorry to tell you this…" he began.

Sorry? He wouldn't be sorry if something bad had happened to him, would he? What was happening? Was he getting cold feet?

"Alex, if you are having second thoughts, I heard that's completely normal."

"I … I can't go through with this."

She needed to ask why, but her throat closed tight.

"I really thought I was ready to marry you. But …"

Maybe they just needed more time…

"Brooke called me. She said she wants us to get back together."

You're engaged to me *now,* Charlie's heart shouted, but her mouth still refused to utter a sound.

"I've been seeing her for two weeks now."

Charlie gripped her fork until it bit into her palm, glaring at him. "What?"

71

As he rambled on about how certain he felt about giving his relationship with *her* another try, heat coursed through Charlie's body from the top of her head right down to the tips of her maroon high-heeled shoes. What kind of lying, cheating jerk had she given her heart to? He had been off gallivanting with Brooke while Charlie was focused on her mother's health and taking care of her family. She had been too preoccupied to notice.

"She's perfect for me, Charlie. Smart, accomplished, high class."

"And I'm just a waitress in a diner?"

"Well… Yes."

With every word he spoke, the rage inside her grew hotter and hotter. "You've been cheating on me!" How had she not seen it?

"Charlie! Stop this. You're making a huge scene." Alex's face flamed as he looked around the room at all the people who were now watching them. "Maybe we should go."

"No. Let's do this right here."

"Fine. You want me to be honest? I just don't see you strong enough to get out of this rut you've been in and actually go to school."

"Excuse me? My mother is in the hospital with cancer. I have to work twice as hard at the diner just to help my dad provide for my family. School is on the back burner for now. And I am strong. My family has been through so much lately."

"You keep saying you want to go to school to become an elementary school teacher, but you haven't even applied yet."

"It takes a while to earn enough money for college. I don't have wealthy parents like you do," she retorted.

"My parents worked their way to the top, and they encourage me to do the same."

"Well, what about everything for the wedding that your parents have paid for? What do they think of this? Have you told them?"

"I only had them book a few things. They don't care, anyway, even if we lose some money. When I told them, they understood. Don't worry about all that; my parents and I will figure it out. I won't let that prevent me from ending this relationship."

How could he do this to her—especially here? Most of the wait staff had seen her joyfully accept Alex's proposal not long ago.

And how was she supposed to react to this? Cry and beg him to stay with her? Or throw the ring at him, like she'd seen in movies?

No. She wouldn't give Alex the satisfaction of watching her have an emotional melt-down. And she didn't want to give him the ring back. He'd given it to her as a gift. It was hers now.

"Face it, Charlie, your life is going nowhere." He smirked.

As she stood, rage roiling inside her. She wanted to scream at him, but she had a better idea.

Charlie picked up her glass and dumped her water all over him. Seeing him in his suit dripping wet made her feel just a little bit better.

His face turned almost the same color as the restaurant's pasta sauce as other dining patrons snickered, gasped, or laughed at him.

"At least I'm not a scumbag like you. This is over. Have a nice life." Charlie calmly grabbed her purse, and walked away, head held high.

Charlie pressed a hand to her aching chest as she left the restaurant and made her way down the street. "If only you were here, Mom." If it wasn't past visiting hours, she would have walked to the hospital. Since Alex had driven them to the restaurant, she had to walk all the way home.

She didn't mind the walk though—it gave her time to think.

In their apartment, she opened her bedroom door slowly, hoping it wouldn't creak, but it did anyway. She cringed, but Zoe was still sound asleep, and Dad continued to snore in his room.

She sat on her bed and rubbed her sore feet, quietly dropping one of her shoes on the floor.

"Shhh." Zoe moaned and rolled over, rubbing her eyes.

"Sorry." The word caused a sob to escape her lips.

Zoe peered at her in the dark. "What's wrong?"

"Nothing. Go back to sleep."

Zoe got up and embraced her sister. The warmth of Zoe's little arms around Charlie released a flood of tears.

"Charlie?" Her father's concerned voice came from the doorway. "What's wrong?"

"Alex broke up with me," Charlie managed to say between sobs. "He dumped me. He's been seeing someone else."

Zoe said nothing and continued to hold Charlie. Her father quietly sat down beside her and also wrapped his big arms around her. Silent sisterly and fatherly love was exactly what Charlie needed.

That seemed like so long ago.

Now, as Charlie hugged Zoe in the Holt's farmhouse, she felt Zoe slump against her, fatigue from the day's events taking its toll on her small body. Though Zoe was so young, she'd always been there for Charlie. She was steadfast.

Charlie thoughtfully eyed the Bible that was on a shelf. Maybe God had led them here. Maybe He had a purpose for them here.

Dear God, she prayed silently, *could you actually let us stay here and have a real home again? For Zoe?*

Charlie whispered to her sister in the dark among the sounds of the crickets outside, "I don't know about forever, Zoe, but if God wants us to, we can stay here for now."

CHAPTER NINE

Elijah always went to the Holts' house for supper. He was not hungry since he had stopped at his favorite café on the way home from picking up supplies, but he would visit with the family anyway and share dessert with them. The Amish here had dessert almost every day.

He lived in a small house behind the Holts' larger one. Elijah helped on the farm and helped run the store since Irvin's son Seth was so young.

He would love to see Charlie and her adorable younger sister more while they were visiting relatives here. At the café, he'd been dying to ask if her relatives were Esther and Irvin, but she seemed like she really didn't want to give him much information. It was such a small community, he figured he'd find out sooner or later.

Maybe he'd see them around. Since they were new to the area, he felt he was responsible to show them around...and protect them...and care for them.

Who was he kidding? He didn't feel this way just because Charlie was new to the area. He wanted to get to know her. She intrigued him. Not only that, if she really was the little girl who had given him the lollipop, he felt like he already knew her. She was mysterious and beautiful, and she unknowingly demanded his attention. He pictured her face framed by her shoulder-length dark hair, and he smiled. She was all he could think about since he had walked out of the café. But she was not Amish, which meant any future with her was out of the question unless she joined the Amish church.

A guy could dream, right?

Elijah didn't bother knocking. He'd been coming here every day for years to share meals and work for the Holts ever since he'd moved here, so he felt comfortable doing so. The Holts had assured him they were happy to have him over any time and to make himself at home. With his family gone, the Holts' house was like home to him now. His house was small and silent, and he liked it much better here.

He walked through the door. There stood Charlie, looking baffled. Zoe was behind her, setting the table.

His stomach flip-flopped, and he felt like a silly schoolboy with a crush. So, Charlie was visiting Esther and Irvin, of all people? That meant...

It was the girl he'd met as a child in Esther's barn. He'd been praying for her all these years, and here she was. He could hardly believe it.

And now he was standing before her, gaping like a fool. *Lord, please help me to not mess up this second chance,* he prayed. *Thank you for bringing her back here.*

"Are you following me?" she asked quietly but seriously. She looked behind him at the door, as if she was nervously expecting someone to jump out at her.

Elijah took a step backwards, surprised and confused himself. That reaction was definitely not what he was expecting. It made her even more interesting. Why was she so paranoid? "I work for the Holts," he stammered. "I usually come over for dinner."

"You're kidding, right?"

What if Esther and Irvin found out they'd eaten together? What would they say? His pulse quickened as the word *shunning* entered his mind. Then he felt foolish. The community would not shun him for simply eating with an English woman, because it wasn't against the rules to befriend Englishers. But they might if it led to something more.

Just then, Esther came into the room, holding a kitchen towel. "Hello, Elijah," she said with a smile. "Come on in and meet my nieces."

***

Charlie stepped aside and let him in. He walked up to Zoe, who was at the table.

"Hi, Elijah," Zoe said and stopped putting cups on the table to greet Elijah. "Why are you here, Mr. Hose-settler?"

Charlie watched the scene before her, so caught up in bewilderment that she didn't even correct Zoe's mispronunciation.

Elijah *worked* for them? He seemed like family to the Holts. The children chatted with him, and Leah offered him a drink. He messed up Seth's already unruly hair. Seth gave him a playful giggle as he batted the hand away. Ella Ruth, Esther, and Leah started setting the table. Lilly sliced a loaf of bread. Everything seemed to continue normally around her, but Charlie's brain was spinning.

"You've already met?" Esther asked.

Charlie snapped out of her daze.

"We met earlier today briefly," Charlie said.

"Oh really? Where?" Leah set a plastic cup on the table and filled it with water.

He seemed fidgety. Charlie wondered why he was so nervous. Elijah sat down and knocked over one of the full cups.

"I am so sorry. I'm so clumsy," Elijah said. He took a towel and started mopping it up.

"It's ok. It happens in a big family," Esther said, getting more towels. She then leaned in towards Charlie and whispered, "I talked to Irvin, and your circumstances do not change our decision in letting you stay here with us." She smiled and gave Charlie's arm a loving squeeze.

Charlie smiled back, gratitude filling her. "Thank you again, so much." Her relatives were so generous, she didn't know how she would ever show how thankful she was. She turned to the girls and asked, "What can I do to help with supper?"

"It's ok; we can do it," said Ella Ruth.

"There has to be something I can do," Charlie insisted, standing around awkwardly.

"You could peel these eggs for the egg salad for church tomorrow," Lilly offered.

She was relieved to have something to do. Once Charlie had them all peeled, rinsed, and mashed for the egg salad, she asked what else was left to do.

"We just have to mash the potatoes, but I can do it," Leah said.

"I really don't mind doing it."

"It's hard work, though…" Leah looked unsure.

"No, it's not," Charlie contradicted.

"How do you mash potatoes at home?" Ella Ruth asked.

"By hand, with a masher," Charlie said.

"Oh, ok," Ella Ruth said, sounding surprised as she gave Charlie the pot of potatoes.

Charlie did not count mashing potatoes as hard work. She did it the same way the Amish family did, except they added cream cheese to theirs, which made it really good. Soon dinner was ready. Charlie was surprised to see that they used plastic dishes. The tabletop was also plastic.

"Kinner, zeit fa essa," Leah said to Debra and Seth, who were playing

79

with puzzles on the floor. They stood, knowing it was time to eat. Irvin came inside.

Everyone sat down and everyone bowed their heads. Charlie and Zoe were raised in a Christian family, so prayer before a meal was normal to them and was done regularly. But when no one spoke a word of prayer after a few seconds, Charlie wondered why. She opened her eyes and looked at Zoe, who looked very confused.

"Does nobody want to say the prayer? I can do it," Zoe said.

Irvin picked up his head. "We say a silent prayer. I'm sorry I didn't tell you first; it is just habit."

Charlie was thankful they were not offended by Zoe's interruption.

"Oh, ok. I will say it in my heart, then," Zoe whispered. Everyone bowed their heads for a few more seconds and then the forks scraped against the plates as they started the meal.

They passed the potatoes, gravy, green bean casserole and corn that the girls had cooked. Esther hadn't needed to help with making dinner at all. Her daughters were great cooks.

***

Leah glanced at Elijah nonchalantly as she ate, then tried not to glare at Charlotte. Or Charlie, as she said people called her. What a weird name for a young woman.

Leah looked at her plate, trying to tamp down her anger and—she had to admit it—jealousy. She'd had to give up her bedroom for this stranger. Yes, they were related, but Charlie was a stranger in her flashy *Englisher* clothing. Leah caught Elijah smiling at Charlotte, and another pang of jealousy ripped through her.

Of course, even she could not deny Charlie was gorgeous, even though the Amish never complimented others on their outward appearances. Elijah must have found the young woman attractive. What man wouldn't?

Leah had been in love with Elijah for as long as she could remember. She'd imagined they'd get married ever since she was a little girl, and many women in the community had even told her they'd make a good match. Leah glanced at Elijah again, admiring his wide shoulders, the way his hair fell in his eyes, and his playful smile. He was always the first to offer help. Elijah was the kindest man she knew.

"Thanks again so much for letting us stay in your room, Leah and Ella Ruth."

Leah looked to Charlie when she heard her speak.

"We don't mind at all. We are happy to help you feel at home. This is your home now, after all," Ella Ruth said with a genuine smile.

Leah tried to make her own smile look as genuine as Ella Ruth's and hoped no one could tell it was fake. "Right. We really are happy to do it."

Leah gripped her fork with white knuckles, and her fingernails bit into her palm. Elijah smiled at her, and she felt her insides warm, then melt. Her fist loosened, then a real smile slowly spread across her face.

Then the moment ended as suddenly as it had begun as Ella Ruth passed around the pitcher of milk.

***

Charlie poured a glass of milk and gulped it down. Then a thought struck her. Where did this milk come from? The cows outside? What if she got sick from it? It was probably raw. She willed herself not to spit it out. She swallowed what was left in her mouth.

She tried to think of a way to ask the family without offending them.

"So…um…is this milk pasteurized?"

"No, it's not. But we have all been drinking it our whole lives, and we are fine," Irvin said with a grin.

Charlie figured it had to be safe enough to drink if none of them had ever gotten sick from it. Zoe looked into her glass of milk, shrugged, and gulped down half of it. As Charlie drank her milk, she was glad Zoe hadn't made any comments about it.

"This is all so good," Charlie said.

"Thank you," the girls replied quietly. Charlie felt like she hadn't helped much.

"This does look very tasty, but I had a late lunch," Elijah said, passing up a second scoop of casserole Leah offered to him. "I was famished earlier and stopped by the café. I came to visit with you anyway."

Zoe smiled at Elijah's comment. "We had a very good meal at the café today too before we came here. Didn't we, Elijah?" she asked.

This received many questioning glances.

"So, you met at the Blue Moon Café?" Leah asked, breaking the awkward moment.

"Yes," Elijah said with the slightest stammer. "I had lunch there today, and we met and started talking, since Charlotte and Zoe are new to town." Charlie noticed how he avoided everyone's eyes. He moved his small amount of casserole around his plate with his fork.

Was something wrong with them eating at the café together?

"He even paid for us," Zoe said, still smiling.

Charlie couldn't help but notice Irvin's raised eyebrows and Esther's questioning glance.

Yes, something was definitely wrong here. Charlie silently prayed

Elijah hadn't broken a rule that would get him in trouble. She wondered if the Amish had strict rules about associating with people who were not Amish.

She looked over at her sister, who was oblivious to the awkwardness she had just caused. Would Elijah get in trouble because he had eaten with them at the café?

***

After they were finished eating dessert, the Holt family and Elijah sang "God Our Father". Charlie and Zoe didn't know it, so they just listened, but the singing was beautiful. Even the little children sang every word. After dinner, Charlie and Zoe were beginning to help the other girls wash the dishes when Irvin motioned for Elijah to follow him onto the front porch.

Elijah got an anxious feeling in the pit of his stomach. He knew this wasn't about his schedule at the store.

"Elijah, what is going on? What happened at the café?" Irvin asked, scratching at his beard.

"Nothing. They're new in town and I just wanted to help them."

"They are English. *She* is an *Englisher*. You know that means you shouldn't buy her lunch, like you would on a date. Don't lead her on. What would people from the community think if they had seen you with her there? And the child? They could have thought many things. The Bible says to avoid even the appearance of evil. I know you did nothing wrong, but other people might have assumed that you were more involved with them, with Charlotte, if you know what I mean." Irvin's eyes communicated his concern for his employee and friend.

"I know. I'm sorry. It won't happen again." He had let his guard down

83

around Charlie too much already. He looked at the floor and dug his toe into a board of the expertly hand-crafted porch.

"Also, you don't want to give her the wrong idea. I care for you like a son, and I just want you to be cautious. Understand?"

"Thank you, Irvin. I will be careful." Elijah appreciated Irvin's concern, and he would have to be more careful. As they went back inside, he realized it would be hard to pretend like he wasn't already developing feelings for her. He felt a strange desire to be near her, unlike anything he had felt in a very long time. It was a feeling he did not think he would ever feel again, and now he had to tamp it down like it didn't exist.

***

After dinner, Elijah went home. Leah wondered what he and Irvin had gone outside to talk about. Elijah thanked everyone for the meal and walked back out the door. Before he did, he quickly glanced at Charlie. Leah couldn't decipher his expression, but she pretended that she hadn't noticed, even though her insides burned with frustration. Why didn't Elijah ever look at *her* like that?

Around eight o'clock, Irvin announced it was time to get ready for bed. He gave Charlie and Zoe a battery-operated stand-up light that resembled a lantern.

Zoe whispered, "I thought they would have the old-fashioned lanterns like in movies."

Charlie shrugged as they started to go to their rooms. "I guess not."

"Oh, we have those too," Leah said, coming up the stairs behind them. "I actually prefer the kerosene lanterns, but many Amish do use the battery-operated lights. They are safer and much less likely to cause fires."

"Has anyone here accidentally started a fire with a lantern, maybe by knocking it over or breaking it?" Charlie asked.

"Actually, yes. Elijah's entire family was killed in a house fire caused by a lantern. I think everyone in the community switched to battery-operated lanterns after that."

"I'm sorry... I had no idea," Charlie said sheepishly.

Of course Charlie didn't know. Leah was the one who had been friends with Elijah his entire life, especially after he'd moved here. She knew him and understood him better than Charlie ever would. Leah touched Charlie's arm, faking a smile. "Don't worry. You didn't know. He doesn't talk about it much."

***

At dinner, Esther had mentioned that Charlie and Zoe could go see the horses in the barn before going to bed if they wanted to. Zoe especially wanted to see them. Charlie grabbed her sweatshirt out of her bag.

They made their way downstairs with their lantern. Charlie pulled her sweatshirt tighter around her as she stepped out into the chilly evening with Zoe. They reached the barn and heard the whinnying before Charlie pulled open the red, rickety doors.

The horses all looked at the two sisters like they were intruders, but Charlie barely noticed because she was surprised by how huge they were. She passed every stall and read the names on the stall doors. She wanted to pat their soft-looking noses, but she was scared they'd bite her.

"Do you think they'd bite?" she asked Zoe.

"No." Zoe reached right out and scratched a mare's nose. "They are friendly."

"I've never touched a real horse before," Charlie said and cautiously reached out to the horse. She jumped a little when the horse nudged her hand and tried to lick her.

"It's okay, Charlie. Don't be afraid," Zoe said.

Charlie wished it was that simple. Though being afraid of a horse and being afraid of Alex were totally different, she still could not shake the fear of Alex finding them. She was also afraid she would not be accepted here. What if the other people here found out she was being hunted? Would they only let them stay for a short while? Would they make them leave? Charlie didn't know where else she and Zoe could go or how they would make it on their own. She didn't know how long she would have to stay here, but she didn't foresee them leaving any time soon.

Charlie looked out the barn window at the house where she saw the lanterns being shut off one by one, the darkness deleting the squares of light where the windows had been.

"Everyone is going to bed. Let's go," Charlie told Zoe. Zoe said goodnight to the horses, and they made their way back into the house.

Charlie realized this was going to be a rough night. She hoped she would be able to sleep with all she had on her mind. On top of that, Charlie was not used to going to bed so early. She came alive at night and usually got the most done during late hours.

Zoe yawned, changed into her pajamas and promptly fell asleep next to Charlie. Charlie tried to sleep too, but she was wide awake. The events of the day flooded her brain. The Amish had made a huge impression on her already. She envied their lifestyle and safe seclusion from the world. There was a great sense of home here. It was all around. Charlie hoped the impression would last on Zoe, too. Zoe needed a place to call home, even if it would only be temporary.

Charlie's thoughts drifted to Elijah. Okay, she'd admit it. He was cute. Extremely cute, in fact. Not that it mattered. He seemed to be really genuine. He also hadn't tried anything with her yet, but she wondered if he would have if he had not been Amish. He was one of the few young men who hadn't hit on her or asked for her number after having a conversation with her. She could tell he certainly was different...and someone worth getting to know. She hoped she would have the chance to do so.

Alex and Elijah couldn't have been more opposite. Was Elijah truly this genuine and sweet, or was he faking it like Alex had?

As Charlie pulled an expertly sewn quilt up over her and Zoe, her mind drifted back to the morning after Alex had dumped her in the restaurant.

That morning, Charlie had woken up to find Zoe cuddled up next to her like she was now. Charlie had stretched her arms above her head, then she'd seen the ring glistening in the morning sunlight. She'd been so overtaken by her emotions the night before that she hadn't even thought to remove it. She took it off and thrust it onto the nightstand like it was something poisonous.

As she stared at it, deep sorrow replaced her anger. No matter how angry she felt, she knew it wouldn't eclipse the heartbreak. That ring had meant too much to her. It represented their future together. All it represented was Alex's unfaithfulness. She pounded her pillow in frustration. "Oh, Lord, I can't believe I got in this situation," she muttered. "I never thought something like this would happen to me."

She continued to stare at the diamond, wondering how much Alex had paid for it.

I could sell it. We could really use the money…

"Hey," she whispered to herself. "That's not a bad idea."

Just to make sure it was legal, Charlie had checked what the law said. She learned that in Maine, engagement rings were conditional gifts. If the engagement was broken by the recipient, she must return the ring. However, if the engagement was broken by her fiancé or by mutual consent, the ring was hers to keep. Since Alex broke up with her, she could legally keep the ring.

She uploaded the photos she had already taken of the ring to an auction site, wrote a brief description, and considered an asking price. She decided to set the asking price a little lower than other ones like it to attract more prospective buyers.

Charlie clicked "publish listing". There. She had done it. She couldn't wait to see what it would sell for.

CHAPTER TEN

A door down the hall closed and the stocking-clad feet shuffled outside Charlie's door, waking her up.

The battery-operated clock read six o'clock. Charlie rolled over and groaned, then looked around at the simple wooden furniture, the picturesque farm fields outside, and the colorful quilt that covered her. It took her a moment to remember where she was—Aunt Esther's farm.

It was Sunday, and Esther had said the night before that they would be getting up early for church. She wished Esther hadn't meant *this* early.

Charlie propped herself up on her elbow and listened. She heard some feet shuffling but doubted anyone was in the bathroom yet. She jumped out of bed and scurried across the hall into the bathroom before anyone else. She wasn't going to wait until all the girls were done. She brushed her teeth, washed her face, and dashed back to her room. Zoe woke up, and they got dressed in their own clothes.

Charlie could hear pots and pans clattering and the smells of food cooking. The girls were already making breakfast. Charlie pulled her old Bible out of one of her bags, opened her door, and the two sisters went downstairs to the kitchen.

"*Guder mariye,*" several voices said. Charlie gave them a confused look.

"It means 'good morning'," Ella Ruth explained.

"Good morning," Charlie replied. "Need any help?"

Leah smiled. "We're all done. It's time to sit down."

The table was already set, and Charlie and Zoe sat down as the girls put the toast, eggs, and sausage on the table. They must have risen much earlier than she had. Feeling guilty, she wished she had been up in time to help them with breakfast. She promised herself she would be tomorrow.

This time before they ate, Irvin prayed out loud and they sang after they finished eating. The girls cleaned up while Irvin hitched up the buggy.

The morning was alive with birdsong and sunlight. Though it wasn't officially winter yet, it had snowed a little during the night. Zoe, Charlie and the Holt family bundled up and went outside. Charlie, Irvin, Esther, Debra, Seth, and Zoe rode in the buggy, and the rest of the girls walked to church.

Riding in the buggy was a terrifying but fun experience. All Irvin had to do was make a sound with his mouth and the horse sped up with a jolt. Most of the ride to church was uphill, and Charlie thought they were going to slide backwards down the hill or get stuck. Those buggy wheels were so narrow...sometimes she was sure the buggy was going to tip over. Zoe was nervous, too. She and Charlie held onto the seat with white knuckles, and Esther and the children laughed with them at their nervousness.

"That is my brother Andrew's house," Irvin said when they passed another Amish house. "He is soon going to host an applesauce party where we will make applesauce for several families."

"Sounds like fun," Zoe said.

They drove into the woods, down a dirt road, and finally they reached the church. Irvin drove the buggy in to the unpaved parking lot.

Charlie peered at the church from the buggy. The church building was surrounded by woods and looked like an unfinished ranch-style house. The walls were just boards and nails, though the only holes were the

90

uninstalled windows. The church was set on top of a hill, and down below Charlie could see several Amish homes including Esther's house in the distance. Inside, there was a large table where the women left their coats and bags, and downstairs there was a large room set up with chairs and long tables.

"I've always heard that Amish church services are held in people's homes, not in a building," Charlie said.

"I think most communities do that but not us. We decided to build a combination school and church building. We'll be finishing it very soon," Irvin commented as they walked in.

Most of the women at church wore light or dark blue dresses with buttons in the back. They wore a white prayer *kapp* with a black *kapp* over it for outside. They also wore black sneakers or black boots.

As Charlie and Zoe took their coats off, the Amish women and girls stood in small groups talking with each other and mingling. When they noticed Charlie and Zoe, they kept glancing at the two sisters, whispering in what sounded like German.

Charlie could hardly blame them for their reaction. She was an alien to them, and she felt like one. Charlie's embarrassment almost made her run out the door, but before she could, something interrupted her. An elderly woman entered the church and came right up to Charlie and Zoe.

"You must be Charlotte and Zoe. Irvin told me about you. I'm Irvin's mother, Abigail. Welcome. It is so nice to meet you," she said, smiling at them.

"It's nice to meet you too," Charlie said.

An elderly man with a long white beard also approached Charlie. "Hello, I'm Bishop Zook. You must be Charlotte. We are all glad to have you here. Welcome to Unity."

"Thank you."

The other women watched the introductions, then a line formed behind Abigail. One by one, each woman approached Charlie and Zoe.

"This is Charlotte," Esther told several women.

"But you can call me Charlie if you want," Charlie said. "It's always been my nickname."

This got a few strange looks, but she didn't care. They could call her whatever they wanted as long as they let her stay there.

She and Zoe met every female in the building. They did not meet any of the other men at church because they were standing in groups on the other side of the room. All Charlie and Zoe received from them were a few curious glances. Elijah stood among them, and he cast her a playful smile. She felt her insides warm instantly then ignored the feelings. Focusing on something else, she wondered if the other men were shy or just plain rude. Why wouldn't they speak to her?

Everyone went downstairs, and once again the women separated into groups where they stood and started talking again. The children grouped together and chattered in a language Charlie didn't understand. She tried to listen closer. The young girls noticed her and looked at her shyly. They were so adorable in their little prayer *kapps* and dresses that Charlie couldn't help but smile.

Charlie turned away with Zoe and they walked towards the chairs. After only a few people sat down, Charlie and Zoe took their own seats and waited for the service to start. After a moment, Charlie felt a tap on her arm. She looked up to see Abigail.

"Charlotte, the men sit on the right side and women sit on the left," the older woman whispered.

Feeling a sinking feeling in her stomach, Charlie's cheeks flamed in embarrassment. As she looked around, she realized she was indeed sitting among the men, who now glanced at her sheepishly. Except Elijah. He smiled at her forgivingly.

"Why do the men and women sit separately?" Zoe whispered back to Abigail.

"That's the Amish way, dear," Abigail said and steered them to the women's side. "The women sit in the back, and the girls sit in the front usually, but you may sit wherever you like." Charlie and Zoe decided to sit near her and Esther. Charlie took a deep breath, hoping the red in her face was disappearing. She felt like hiding under the bench.

Everyone opened their hymnals, and one of the men sang a long, loud note, then everyone else joined in. It took about ten minutes to sing just one song, they sang so slowly. Charlie stared at the words in the hymnal but understood none of it. Even if she had known the German language, the singing was so slow and drawn-out that she would have not been able to find her place in the song. So, afraid of singing the wrong words, Charlie and Zoe just listened to the a cappella worship for over an hour and tried not to fidget too much.

"What language is that?" Charlie whispered to Esther.

"Pennsylvania Dutch. It's a form of German."

Ah, so it was German. "Why no instruments?"

"We believe instruments are too prideful," Esther whispered back briefly. "It draws too much attention to the person playing."

Prideful? In our church we worshiped with many instruments. Even David in the Bible worshipped the Lord with an instrument... Charlie thought, completely baffled.

Even so, it was amazing how everyone kept time and sang together in the same key, even harmonizing. It sounded beautiful in that small church room. To Charlie, it seemed too bad that they were so far out in the woods and no other people could hear the singing.

After they sang, everyone stood and then kneeled facing their chair. Charlie and Zoe remained seated, wondering what they should do. No one seemed to notice or mind. After prayer, Irvin gave the message. The regular speaker was out of town, and Charlie hadn't realized until then that Irvin was a speaker. Then the entire first chapter of Corinthians was read aloud by the men in the congregation. Each man took a turn reading.

The service was from nine to eleven-thirty in the morning. When the women of the congregation began to mill downstairs, Charlie got up and gratefully stretched. Sitting on backless benches for two-and-a-half hours was less than comfortable. After the service, they went downstairs for lunch. The Amish women worked together so quickly and efficiently that Charlie and Zoe just stood out of the way, completely unsure of what to do.

***

Stop staring at her, Matthew Lapp silently told himself. He couldn't help but steal yet another glance at Leah. She was just so beautiful to him. He admired the way she carried herself, so humble yet also sure of herself. She placed the food she had most likely prepared herself on the long table covered in an array of homemade foods like casseroles, sandwiches, and pies. She looked around at the spread and smiled to herself, gently tucking a few escaped strands of hair back into her *kapp*. She smoothed out the front of her dress and smiled at all the other women and girls around her

94

who were setting up their own food to contribute to the potluck. He barely noticed all the chatter that filled the room.

Matthew watched as a subtle sadness clouded over Leah. She stared longingly at something or someone on the side of the room where the young men stood. Was she looking at a man? Who?

He tried to keep calm as he looked around nonchalantly. There were so many men around him that it was futile. He had no idea which one she was staring at.

She suddenly snapped out of it as Lilly asked her a question. Maybe she had just been daydreaming, not realizing where she was looking. *That had to be it.*

He imagined that look of longing he had just seen in her eyes. He would sure love to see her look at him like that. He would give his left pinkie just for her to notice him as something more than the boy down the road whom she had known her whole life. He would love to meet all her needs, to be what she wanted.

But he *was* just the boy down the lane from her house. He was just another Amish face in the crowd of young men at a church potluck. He was a family friend, just another worker in the fields.

Please God, one of these days, please give me the courage to offer her a ride home at a Singing...then maybe she will realize how I feel about her, he prayed for the hundredth time. He knew it would be inappropriate to speak to her at church since the men stayed separate from the women there, but at other places and times he had tried to approach her and talk to her. Every time he did, he forgot all he had planned to say and ended up talking about the weather, tripping over his meaningless words.

She is everything an Amish man could want in a wife. One day I will tell her that I have loved her for years, he promised himself. *I cannot wait for that day.*

CHAPTER ELEVEN

After lunch, Leah talked to Charlie about *Rumspringa,* a time in a young Amish person's life when they are allowed to leave the community to try living as *Englishers.*

"The Amish young adults in Unity do not go on *Rumspringa* anymore because they all choose to remain Amish without going into the world. For Amish young people who have, it was a shock for them once they saw the ways of the outside world. Sometimes they would become too involved with things like drugs and drinking."

"Anymore? You mean, they used to?"

"Actually, yes. *Rumspringa* used to be common here, but I heard that many years ago something bad happened to a young Amish woman in the city while on *Rumspringa* and she got hurt. I'm not even sure if that's true or just a rumor. No one has ever wanted to go on *Rumspringa* since then."

"Wow. That's terrible."

"No one knows who the person was or what really happened as far as I know. It's a topic people avoid, so I don't know much about it. But I wouldn't want to go on *Rumspringa* anyway. I'm happy here. Our parents don't make us remain Amish though. It is up to the child. And most of us choose to stay," Leah said. "Also, we do not try to recruit people to join. In fact, we discourage it. Regular people may be able to live like us for a while, but then they give up because it is too hard. To become and remain Amish, one usually has to be born Amish."

Leah grinned as Charlie tried to absorb all the information. Leah said, "I like your haircut. Do you like having short hair?"

"Yes. It's easier to take care of. How long is your hair?" Charlie asked, gesturing to Leah's white head covering.

Leah pointed to her leg, near her knee. "When it is down, it almost reaches my knee. You wouldn't know that since our hair is worn in a bun and covered. That is why your hair seems so short and different to me. I wonder what it would be like to have such short hair."

"Wow. Is your hair really that long?" Charlie asked, astounded. She could not imagine having such long hair. Wouldn't it get tangled or caught on things? Or shut in doors?

"Yes. We Amish girls and women do not cut our hair except for an occasional trim. In First Corinthians the Bible says a woman's hair is her glory, so we leave it long."

"That's incredible. How do you take care of it?" Charlie asked, still somewhat shocked.

Leah shrugged. "It has been like this my whole life. To me, it is not hard to take care of. Although sometimes it can get a little tangled."

They both laughed, and Charlie looked around and sighed. These people sure had some different customs. It might take her a while to get used to.

"I know it must be a lot for you, moving here and learning about how we do things, and losing your parents on top of that. I'm sure we are so different than what you are used to. I want to help you however I can, so just let me know if you ever need anything." Leah smiled, and Charlie thought for a fleeting moment that she saw something like contempt or jealousy in the young woman's eyes. Inwardly scolding herself, Charlie smiled back. Surely, whatever it was, she'd been imagining it. Leah had been nothing but kind and generous to Charlie.

Another young woman came over and smiled at Charlie. "Hi there, my name is Lydia. We are so happy to have you here."

"Hi, I'm Charlie."

"Please let us know if there is anything at all we can do for you, all right?" Lydia said. "I can't imagine what you're going through. I'm so sorry to hear about your parents."

"Thank you." Charlie was grateful for new friends.

***

After church, Esther and Irvin rode the buggy home with the younger children, but the others decided to walk home. Charlie and Elijah walked behind everyone else.

"I was so embarrassed when I sat on the men's side today," Charlie said, blushing.

"Don't worry. We do not expect you to know all of our customs. You will learn in time," Elijah reassured her.

Charlie wondered how long it would take.

"Can I ask if you know how long you will be staying here?" Elijah asked.

It was as if he had read her mind. "I don't really know," Charlie said, feeling uneasy. How long could she really stay there? Would Alex be able to track her and Zoe down?

"Well, we all like having you and Zoe here. I hope you know that."

Charlie smiled at him. He sure was sweet. She couldn't help but wonder if it was really his true personality. Her thoughts wandered to Alex, how she had thought he was so charming when in reality he was a complete jerk.

"I'm sorry about your parents," Elijah offered. "Irvin told me what happened."

"Thank you." She felt the fresh, deep pain of grief. She didn't know if her relatives had told Elijah about Alex, but she decided to leave that up to them. "And Leah told me about your family. I don't even know what to say."

He sighed. "I'm the only one left. I was eighteen when it happened."

"Oh…I am so sorry. How terrible that must have been for you." Charlie felt horrible for bringing up such a painful subject. Clearly, it still saddened Elijah to talk about it. "Does it ever get easier?"

"A little bit, with time. The Lord gives and takes away. They are in a better place now." He tilted his chin up and looked to the sky.

Charlie marveled at his steadfast faith. *We have a lot in common*, she realized.

She watched Zoe pick wildflowers as Leah, Ella Ruth, and the other girls pointed to different flowers, probably telling Zoe what they were called. Zoe sure looked like she was having fun. Leah looked up and looked at Elijah for a bit longer than necessary, then smiled at Charlie. Again, Charlie detected something like disdain hiding under Leah's grin. Charlie felt like something about Leah's smile seemed almost…fake. Or was she just imagining things?

"How did you survive?" Charlie asked Elijah softly. Immediately after, she hoped she hadn't pried too much.

"It happened in Smyrna, the Amish community I used to live in. I had a dog that was about to have puppies. I was so excited because I knew she would have them at any time. One night I had a feeling something was wrong, so I went and checked on her in the barn and she started having the puppies. While I was in the barn, the fire started in the house. I didn't realize it until it was too late. I tried to get inside the house, but I couldn't.

I ran to the nearest phone and called the fire department, but by the time I got to the phone shanty too much time had passed. I remember the flames... I even heard them scream. It still haunts me to this day."

She could not imagine such a horrific tragedy. Charlie saw a shadow cross his face as he spoke of the painful memory. He crossed his arms over his chest and looked at the ground as he walked.

"After that, I moved here, and Esther and Irvin hired me and have looked out for me ever since. The community all pitched in and built the little house I live in. We all take care of each other."

"That's so kind of them."

"They have good hearts. They're my family now." He swallowed. "You know, my father never had smoke alarms put in the house, saying he didn't need them. He said installing smoke alarms was putting faith in a manmade device rather than God. I wonder if that would have saved their lives."

Charlie was shocked. "The Amish don't use smoke alarms?"

"Some of them do, some don't. Depends on the community. All Amish communities are different. We never really found out what caused the fire, but the fire department suspected a kerosene lantern broke or tipped over. Amazingly, God called me out of there right before the fire started. I don't understand why I was the only one to survive, but God knows better than we do."

"God protected you," Charlie realized out loud.

"Yes, I think He did for a reason. Smyrna is much bigger than this community and several families volunteered to move here to help expand the community. When there was an opportunity for me to move right after I lost my family, I looked at it as an adventure and decided to come here

101

and work for the Holts, who have always been friends of the family. I had nothing to lose, anyway. For some reason, I felt God had something great He would reveal to me here someday."

"Has He?" Charlie pried.

"Yes. He has showed me many small things, but I am still waiting for greater things He has yet to show me." He cast a shy glance at her.

What was *that* supposed to mean?

She couldn't help it. Her heart fluttered. Her breathing quickened and she felt warmth and butterflies fill her belly. She quickly looked away. He couldn't possibly be talking about her, could he? She silently chided herself for being so self-centered. That statement probably had nothing to do with her. She wasn't even Amish.

She remembered the little boy she'd met in Esther's barn when they were children. Glancing at Elijah, she had to admit there was a strong resemblance. The boy had said he was here visiting and that he lived in Smyrna at the time.

Could that boy have been Elijah? Charlie wanted to ask, but when she noticed a sorrowful look lingering on Elijah's face, she couldn't bring herself to ask him.

The Holts' house was coming into view as the group walked over a hill. She tried to refocus as she looked over the field.

Zoe scampered over to them. "Look, Charlie! This flower is called clover, these are buttercups, and this white one is called Queen Anne's Lace. Look, it's made of lots of tiny little flowers. Isn't it pretty?"

Charlie's heart ached, but she tried to share Zoe's excitement. "Those are beautiful, Zoe. What a pretty bouquet."

"Leah said she'll put them in a vase on the table for me when we get home," Zoe said, bouncing on her heels.

Home. Did Zoe really feel at home here?

"Too bad it's too late in the season to find monarch caterpillars," Elijah said, interrupting her thoughts. "I would have liked to show you."

"What? What are those?" Zoe asked.

"You know monarch butterflies? The orange and black ones?"

"Oh, yes. I've seen those before," Zoe said.

"Well, this plant is called milkweed," he said, pointing to the dozens of dead plants that had several leaves. They were scattered all over the field. "The monarch caterpillars eat these plants until they grow large enough, then they encase themselves in a green chrysalis. They have these tiny golden dots on the outside of the chrysalis. It's really beautiful. Inside the chrysalis, the caterpillar changes into a butterfly, and it hatches and flies away. It is one of the most remarkable miracles God has designed. Have you ever seen it happen?"

"No, I haven't. I'd love to someday though," Charlie said.

"If you stay long enough, I'll show you next summer before they hatch," Elijah said with a smile.

"Okay! I hope we get to see those. That sounds so cool!" Zoe said before running ahead to tell the other girls.

Elijah's expression turned serious. "God changed me. I doubted Him for a long time after my family died. Then I asked God to prove that He was real to me, and He did...many times. Then I went through a metamorphosis."

"A what?" she asked with raised eyebrows.

"A metamorphosis. It's when a caterpillar changes into a butterfly. It goes through a huge transformation from an ugly little caterpillar, to

103

hiding away in a dark chrysalis, to becoming a beautiful flying creature. But it doesn't happen overnight."

Charlie nodded.

"Sometimes God puts you through hard times so you can become stronger and help other people who are going through similar things, or so He can get your attention. He loves you, and He wants you to love Him too. He has great plans for you."

Charlie thought about what she was going through. Maybe God was trying to get her attention. Maybe He had been for a long time and she had ignored Him.

She realized how the group had moved on without them and how silent it had become. Out of awkwardness, Charlie chose to be impulsive.

"Come on. I'll race you. Last one to the house has to do the dishes tonight," Charlie challenged and began sprinting towards the house.

"Hey, wait!" Elijah called behind her, and she heard him scrambling down the hill. Soon the other children began racing too, laughing all the way to the house. They all landed in a heap on the front lawn, and Elijah arrived last, all out of breath.

"You lost. You have to do the dishes tonight," Charlie said, laughing.

Elijah looked uncomfortable. "But men here don't do dishes."

Charlie laughed. Was he kidding? "Please. My dad even did the dishes sometimes. You probably just don't know how."

Leah looked serious. "He's right. Men here are not involved in kitchen chores. Cooking and cleaning are women's jobs."

Lilly, Ella Ruth, and Katie looked at one another awkwardly.

Elijah gave Charlie an apologetic shrug.

Charlie's cheeks flamed, partly from embarrassment, but mostly from annoyance. She hoped no one could see it since her face was flushed from the run, and she immediately stopped laughing. How could they live by such archaic rules? Were they really fine with them? Charlie wanted to state her opinions, but instead she just muttered, "Oh…I'm sorry. I didn't realize."

"It's all right," He flashed her a smile, and Charlie couldn't help but smile back. These were their silly rules, and she didn't have to follow them or like them.

Elijah took her hand and helped Charlie to her feet. His hand was gentle, but strong, just like the rest of him. She quickly let go.

"Well, I've got to get going," Elijah said. "I told the Yoders I'd visit them today."

Everyone said their goodbyes, and Elijah left. Charlie hoped she hadn't made him feel uncomfortable or embarrassed.

"Come on! We'll show you the barn," Lilly said, and they walked over to it.

Now that she was looking at it in the daylight, it was huge. When she and Zoe had looked at the horses in it on their first night in Unity, they had only looked at one section of the barn that held the horses. The Holts had cats, cows, horses and enormous pigs.

"This is huge!" Zoe marveled.

As Charlie looked around, she felt like she had been there before. The building, sounds and smells were so familiar.

She had been there. This was the barn where she had met the young boy. This was where he had smiled at her, and she had felt butterflies in her stomach.

Could it have really been Elijah? The more time she spent here, the more she suspected it. Soon she would bring herself to ask him. They'd been little kids. If it was him, he probably didn't even remember, and she didn't want to seem like she'd been pining for him all these years. She just had to wait for the right time.

They went into the greenhouse where the Holts stored peanuts and beans, and that was where they shelled beans for a while.

Charlie asked, "I've heard of Old Order Amish and New Order Amish. What are the differences?"

Katie answered, "Well, we are Old Order Amish, but we share many similarities with New Order Amish. We both wear plain clothing, we both travel by buggies, and we both speak Pennsylvania Dutch. Even though many people think New Order Amish is more modern, they do not allow electricity, and neither do we. However, some New Order Amish do accept some technology."

"Wow. I didn't think the Amish allowed technology at all," Charlie said.

"The Amish do not completely reject all things modern. We have indoor toilets and running water. We are allowed to ride in automobiles and will often hire car drivers for longer trips. We are just not allowed to own cars," Ella Ruth explained. "But all the communities are different. We ride bikes here, but in Lancaster they aren't allowed to, as far as I know. We don't use refrigerators, but they do. But we do use solar panels, and they do too."

"Wow," Charlie said, soaking it all in.

"Right. Every community has different rules and accepts different amounts of technology. If one of the church members thinks they need a certain modern device for their home or business that is not allowed, they

106

may ask the church elders and the bishop to allow the use of that item, but it may or may not be approved. However, they do allow electric devices for medical reasons," Leah said.

"As you have seen, we share phones in shanties between our houses. But some of the New Order Amish even allow telephones inside their homes. We do not allow that. But if a person owns a store, like Irvin does, that person may have a telephone for their business as long as it is outside the home."

"I had no idea there were so many differences between Amish communities and Old Order and New Order," Charlie said. How did they keep track of it all?

"New Order also do overseas evangelism and mission work, and they may fly in airplanes."

"You mean you are not allowed to fly in a plane? What if you have to visit relatives who live several states away?" Charlie asked incredulously.

"We usually travel by bus or train."

"That must take days."

"Sometimes it does, but it is the way we do things. Have you ever flown in a plane? Sometimes I watch them fly overhead and I think how scary it must be to be so high in the sky," Lilly said with wide eyes.

"Lilly!" Katie scolded, trying to stifle a giggle.

"What? Don't you ever wonder what it would be like?" Lilly asked.

"No." Katie folded her arms in all seriousness, then couldn't hide her smile any longer. "Okay. Maybe sometimes. Have you ever been on a plane, Charlie?"

"Yes, I have. I went on vacation to Florida with my parents when I was younger. It's a little scary the first time. But once the plane takes off, it is easy to forget you're thirty thousand feet above the ground because you can't feel the plane moving," Charlie explained.

"Wow. That's amazing," Lilly said wistfully. Then she countered seriously, "But I still would never do it."

"What is it like to be an *Englisher*?" Ella Ruth asked.

"Everyone is always in touch. We have the Internet, phones, and all kinds of ways to communicate, but sometimes it can hinder people from building actual relationships. Sometimes when people are together, they spend that time on their phones instead of talking to the people they are with.

"People always seem to be looking for the next big thing in technology, and really, people seem unhappy. They are hardly ever content with what they have, and they are always so busy that it seems like life just flies right by them. But I do miss my life there, my family and friends and my job.

"Also, so many people do not even believe in God, or they believe in other gods. Sometimes it is very sad to think of what their lives are like without the Lord," Charlie explained.

"*Ja*. I cannot imagine going through life with no hope of eternal salvation. I am so glad to know that I will go to heaven because I trust in Jesus as my Savior and love him. But why do you think people don't want to believe in God?" Leah asked.

"Well, I think they realize that if they believe in God, they will have to become accountable for the way they live. And people like to just have a good time and do what they want. They don't want to serve God, only themselves," Charlie said. "That's just a guess, anyway. Also, many people think that if they are good people, they will go to heaven."

"Really? That is not in the Bible. The Bible says God sends those who do not know Him to hell," Ella Ruth said.

"I know. But they don't read the Bible. Many people don't think it's true or accurate. A lot of people think it was changed over the years when it was translated so they don't bother reading it."

"Wow. It is too bad… I will pray for those who do not believe," Ella Ruth said somberly.

CHAPTER TWELVE

Later that day, Charlie and Zoe decided that Zoe would begin to attend school with the other girls after some much needed time off. However, Zoe was excited to start school and wondered what the Amish school would be like. First, she needed some time to grieve and adjust to her new environment.

About an hour after everyone went to bed, just as Charlie began to fall asleep, she saw a light and sat straight up. What was that? Had she been dreaming?

She rubbed her eyes and looked around the dark room. The beam of a flashlight darted across the room, reflecting off a mirror on a wall. It was coming in from the window that showed the backyard.

Who was doing that?

Charlie sprang out of bed and ran to the window where she knelt. She hoped she hadn't made a racket with her not so graceful movements. She didn't want to alarm anyone in case it was nothing as she peered over the windowsill, just enough to hide her face but to see what—or who—was outside.

There was no moon in sight, and the night was as black as an Amish buggy. The strange light continued to shine right into her room on her ceiling, but Charlie couldn't see the culprit. She scanned the yard once more then turned away from the window.

Alex wouldn't do something like this. If he was here, he would just come for her, not waste time pranking her. Or would he?

Maybe it was just being done unintentionally. Maybe it was nothing to worry about.

Or maybe someone in the Amish community didn't want her there.

***

The next morning in Unity, Charlie awoke to the girls and Esther singing downstairs as they worked. It seemed as though they all sang well, from what Charlie heard.

I guess that's all the music they have, since they don't have radios or other music, Charlie thought. Their voices were lovelier to listen to than the radio.

The memories of the night before filled her mind as she rubbed the sleep from her eyes. She shivered but was determined to not let it rattle her.

She hurried to find Esther and Irvin. She knocked on their bedroom door and they let her in.

"There's something I need to tell you," she began. "Someone was shining a flashlight in my window last night. I think it was Alex trying to scare me. If he's here, I understand if you want me to leave—"

"No, no. We want you to stay, no matter what. Right, Esther?" Irvin asked.

"Right. He doesn't scare us. It is all in the hands of the Lord. We trust that he will protect you," Esther said, resting a hand on Charlotte's arm.

"Aren't you worried about the safety of your family? Last time Alex saw me, he threatened me and had his hands around my throat. I don't know what he's capable of."

"It might not have been Alex last night, anyway. It could have been some rowdy *Englisher* teenagers from town trying to play tricks on us. Sometimes they do things like that. I'm not worried. As Esther said, it is all in the Lord's hands."

"As long as you are sure—"

"Don't worry, Charlotte. We are sure. Now, let's go have some breakfast, shall we?" Irvin led her out of the bedroom.

"Thank you again," Charlie said as they went into the kitchen. The couple gave her sincere smiles. They truly knew how to make a guest feel welcome in their home.

She would stay here and blend in as much as possible and hope that Alex would not attack her. Why would he with so many people around as witnesses? She was safer here than if she took Zoe and left, since they had nowhere else to go.

Charlie and Zoe helped make the meal, and after breakfast the other girls prepared to leave for school.

Charlie knew Leah was around her age, but Ella Ruth seemed around seventeen or eighteen years old and Katie looked about sixteen.

"Do you leave later for school?" Charlie asked the girls after she returned to the house and began doing the dishes.

Katie giggled. "We are all done with school. I finished eighth grade last year," she said, coming to stand by Charlie at the sink to rinse the dishes.

"Are you kidding?" Charlie asked in all seriousness. "What about high school?"

"The Amish finish school in eighth grade." Leah dried a clean dish that Katie gave her. "We don't go to high school."

No high school? "I wanted to go to college but never got the chance," Charlie said, trying to hide her shock.

"Really? Why waste so much time in school?" Katie asked, rinsing a dish.

Waste? Charlie had to turn away to hide her surprise. "Well, most people don't view it as a waste. Doctors go to college several years after high school so they can be qualified to save other's lives. It is a privilege to get that much education."

"The Amish see eight years of schooling as enough. Any more than that is considered prideful," Ella Ruth said, putting some cups away.

Charlie set a plastic cup down on the counter with a little too much force. *Prideful? Again? Instruments and now education?* Charlie thought, offended. She had worked so hard towards her college fund but never had enough time or money to begin college. Now she doubted she ever would with Zoe to take care of. She would love the chance to go to college, and these people thought that was prideful? And a waste?

Charlie crossed her arms, trying to hide the hurt that was now growing into frustration and resentment. Did they consider her prideful because she graduated from high school?

Isn't the idea that they have everything right and everyone else has it wrong prideful? Isn't shunning a family member because they didn't follow the rules prideful? Charlie wondered, resentment growing within her. *They would rather ignore a person than stand by someone like my mother during a painful time in her life.*

As if she read Charlie's thoughts, Ella Ruth piped in, "Not that we consider you or other *Englishers* prideful for going to high school or college. We do not judge the things *Englishers* do that are against the Amish church. Those rules do not apply to you."

Charlie didn't even try to fake a smile. She just turned away.

By saying the rules didn't apply to her as an *Englisher*, were they also saying she was an outsider in her own family? All because the community refused to accept her parents' relationship? Did they think that they had standards that she as an outsider couldn't possibly be expected to live up to?

Was that what they all really thought about her?

"Besides, we still learn everything we need to know after eighth grade. We get to stay home with our mother, and she teaches us everything she knows. Not being in school gives us the time to learn how to cook and clean, take care of a household and children," Leah said. "It won't be long until we get married and have houses of our own to manage."

"You mean, it won't be long for you the way Matthew fancies you," Katie said.

"Matthew does not like me, Katie. We are friends. How could you say such a thing?" Leah asked, her face reddening. Charlie turned away and busied herself with washing more dishes.

"Are you all really fine with those rules? Don't you want to go to school past eighth grade and have a career?" Charlie asked.

The girls looked at each other. Leah shrugged. "No. Not at all. It's my dream to become a wife and mother. That's all I want to do."

"Me too," Katie, Ella Ruth, and Lilly said.

"I don't understand. I don't see why the Amish see high school and college as prideful. I'm sorry, but I just don't agree with that at all. And men don't do dishes? That's just archaic." Charlie paused when she saw the girls' startled expressions. "Tell me honestly. Do you all see me as an outsider? That I can never belong here because my mother left the community?"

"No," Ella Ruth said, touching Charlie's arm. "Not at all."

"I don't think anyone thinks that," Lilly said.

"At least they shouldn't," Katie added.

"Charlie," Ella Ruth said. "We want you and Zoe here. We know our rules are very hard for people to understand. We see you and Zoe as family, not as outsiders. If you decide to stay forever, that would be wonderful, even if you don't decide to become Amish. And if you did, that would be wonderful too, even though it's really rare for an *Englisher* to become Amish. But we don't judge you, and I think I can speak for us girls when I say we don't judge your mother either. We've never even met her. We all love you and Zoe."

The girls nodded in agreement.

Charlie wiped away tears that stung her eyes. "We love you all, too."

Leah hugged her, but conflicting thoughts still swirled through Charlie's brain. Was that really true? And if she did stay, how could she ever come to accept their rules? She loved it here, and she wanted to feel at home, but Leah was right. Their rules were hard for her to understand.

CHAPTER THIRTEEN

"It's time to leave for school," Lilly said.

"You should come see the school," Zoe said to Charlie as she put on her coat. "Maybe you could help teach there."

Charlie doubted that she would be allowed to help teach, since she wasn't Amish, but she didn't see the harm of checking it out. "Okay, I'll come with you."

"Let's go," Lilly said, grabbing her backpack and heading out the door.

It was about a fifteen-minute walk to school. They walked past Andrew's house, went across the field, and up a hill through the woods which led to the road the school house was on.

"I usually walk to school alone, ever since Katie finished school last year. It's nice to have someone to walk with," Lilly said as they trudged up the hill. At least they did not have to walk along the road. This was much safer, away from the eyes of anyone not trustworthy.

They reached the school, and Charlie and Zoe both asked, "Isn't that the church?"

Lilly laughed. "The church is also the school. It is all in the same building."

"Oh," Charlie and Zoe said in unison.

"I guess it was so busy with you meeting everyone we forgot to show you the school section of the building. The church is made up of three rooms. The first floor is a hall where the after church luncheons are served. The floor is cement and there is a wood stove and propane burner. Upstairs is divided into two parts, the church and the school. There is a room divider we take down for special occasions, like weddings, to make it all one big room."

They walked in the door that they had walked through on Sunday, then went through another door that opened to the classroom.

It was a one-room school with all grades in one class from what Charlie could tell. Children of various ages sat at desks or put away their backpacks and hung up coats.

Charlie looked around the room at all the wonderful artwork that adorned the walls, drawings of cats and horses and Amish homes and families. Various grammar charts were hung up, along with a border that listed numbers and the alphabet. Bookshelves held text books and dictionaries, and there were cubbies for the students' belongings. There were several simple wooden desks and chairs that looked handmade. She looked to the front of the room to the teacher's desk.

"Hi!" Lydia called. She was the teacher? Why hadn't she mentioned that yesterday? Charlie realized it was probably because Lydia was so modest, and it was not the Amish way to talk about themselves.

"I didn't know you were the teacher," Charlie said, walking over to her.

"This is only temporary. I teach part of the week and another woman teaches on the days when I bake with my family. There was another teacher before us, but she got married a few months ago and moved away, so I've been filling in with the other woman. But I can't for much longer because my family needs my help with the bakery, and the other woman has to quit soon, too. We are looking for a full-time teacher to replace me. Yes, we only do school until eighth grade. We do extra schoolwork each year, and the curriculum is advanced."

Charlie's ears practically perked up and she asked, "Does the teacher have to be Amish?"

Lydia nodded. "Yes, the elders and Bishop Zook would want an Amish teacher. Why; you know someone?"

Zoe piped in, "Charlie wants to be a teacher."

Charlie shrugged and smiled. "It's always been my dream. But I couldn't. I'm not Amish."

"The Lord will provide just the right person," Lydia said, smiling.

Charlie wished she could be the one to teach these children, but she understood if they wanted someone of the same religion. She looked around the room at the quiet students and told Lydia, "They are all so well behaved, but not all classes are so respectful. Right, Zoe?"

Zoe said, "Yes. At my old school some kids were really rude in class, especially to the teacher, and some kids bully other kids. I went to public school, but I'm glad I'm not anymore. I didn't like it that much."

"Well, I am so glad you'll be at this school now," Charlie said. "Ready to go back to the house?"

"Can I stay here? Please? If it's okay with Miss Lydia?" Zoe pleaded.

"I don't mind at all. We'd love to have her," Lydia said. "You can watch and see how we do things to prepare you for when you start attending full time. You can shadow one of the other girls if you'd like, just for the day, then start attending whenever you're ready. What do you think?" Lydia looked at Zoe and Charlie.

"She can sit with me," Lilly offered.

"I think that's a great idea, if you want to, Zoe," Charlie said, patting her shoulder.

"Yes! I want to stay." Zoe scampered over and one of the other children showed her an extra desk, then they moved it near Lilly.

"Thank you," Charlie said. "This actually might be really good for her." Maybe school would actually be a needed distraction after their parents' death, since Zoe loved learning so much.

Lydia nodded. "I agree."

"I'll let you start your day. Thank you. Bye, Lydia." Zoe was already settled and chatting with the other students.

"You're welcome. It's our pleasure. See you later," Lydia said and returned to her desk.

When Charlie returned to the house, Ella Ruth, Katie, and Leah were leaving. Then it was just Charlie and Esther who remained.

"Do the children speak Pennsylvania Dutch?" Charlie asked as they cleaned the house.

Esther explained, "Yes. Amish children speak it half or most of the time, especially at home."

"Even when people here are speaking Pennsylvania Dutch, so many English words are thrown in that I still can usually understand," Charlie said.

Esther nodded. "We try to speak English when there are *Englishers* around. But the younger children only know Pennsylvania Dutch until they go to school, where they learn English. The form of the language varies with different communities. We probably speak it differently than the Amish of Pennsylvania, actually."

"Well, the children speak Pennsylvania Dutch to me, but I can somewhat understand what they are saying. I have learned the words *spiele* which means 'play,' *esse* which means 'eat' and simple words like that which are said often. But I am learning."

119

One of the things Charlie had also noticed about Amish children was that they all highly respected their elders and their parents. That was not as common where Charlie came from.

"It is so peaceful here compared to the city," Charlie told Esther.

"Though it is peaceful here, there are still dangers. We were in a buggy once and Debra wanted a drink, but the motion of the buggy kept sloshing the drink on her. So, we stopped while she drank as another buggy and a car passed each other on the road ahead. I am sure that if we wouldn't have stopped, there wouldn't have been enough room on the road for the two buggies and car. I believe God saved us from all passing each other at once. There most likely would have been an accident."

"Wow. God did protect you." She paused and asked, "So, you're not allowed to own cars?"

"We may ride in cars, but we cannot own a car. It is against our beliefs. It says in the Bible to be content with what you have, and we are content with our buggies."

Charlie asked Esther about what the Amish thought of photos. Esther told Charlie that all communities are different, but in Unity they would not pose for pictures.

"I don't mind if I'm driving my buggy or walking down the road and someone takes a picture of me, but I will look away from the camera," she said.

While lunch was cooking, Charlie picked two big boxes of grapes off their stems, cleaned them, and put them into jars for canning. Esther used them for juice and jam. While they worked, Esther told Charlie about how she met Irvin.

"We courted for a year or so until we were married. I had a few other proposals, but I had said no. I knew when it wasn't right. But when Irvin proposed, I knew he was the one."

Charlie smiled and asked her, "What is the average age of people who get married here?"

Esther told her, "It's usually between 20 and 25, sometimes older. Most people think the Amish marry very young, but the marrying age is generally the same age as non-Amish people. Dating in the Amish community is strictly hands-off—as in no physical contact of any kind until marriage, which includes holding hands. Usually a courtship starts with 'dating', where the couple may have one date every month until they are engaged. When they are engaged, they can have one date a week until they are married. Usually a couple does not date without serious intentions of marrying. Amish marriages last. There is no such thing as Amish divorce."

Charlie was stunned. Almost everywhere else divorce was common, and she knew several people who were divorced.

After they finished cleaning the grapes and eating lunch, Charlie washed the dishes and Esther pressure cooked the grapes.

"So, Lydia told me that people here don't go on *Rumspringa* anymore because something bad happened to a young woman," Charlie said.

"Yes. It was a terrible thing."

Charlie turned to her. "Do you know what happened? Lydia said she didn't know."

"No. No one knows." Esther looked away, and sorrow clouded her face.

"Was it you?" Charlie blurted, then covered her mouth. Why had she said that? Guilt swept over Charlie for bringing it up. "I'm so sorry."

Esther looked at Charlie again, her eyes filling with tears, which she quickly swiped away.

"It was you, wasn't it?" Charlie asked,

Esther put a hand to her forehead. "Something happened to me when I was visiting Joanna."

"Oh… I'm really sorry. I shouldn't have asked."

"No, no. It's not your fault. I don't like to tell people, so please don't tell anyone. I don't want anyone to feel bad for me."

"What happened?" Charlie blurted, then instantly regretted the words.

"It's what started everything that led up to the fight between Joanna and me." Esther slowly shook her head and swatted at a tear on her cheek. "I should have never gone to Portland alone that day. But then I wouldn't have… Never mind. Sorry, but I don't want to talk about it."

"I'm so sorry," Charlie apologized again. What had Esther meant by saying she wouldn't have something—or someone? Or maybe she wouldn't have done something in particular?

Charlie desperately wanted to know but knew it would be rude to ask, especially when Esther quickly changed the subject.

***

"Irvin?" Esther whispered as she turned down the quilt on their bed. A horse neighed in the barn, but other than that, the farm was quiet.

"What's wrong?" her husband asked, setting the battery-operated lamp on the bedside table and getting into bed.

"Charlie started asking questions about…the incident. I told her something happened while I visiting Joanna." Esther climbed into bed beside him.

"Did you say anything else?" He wrapped his arm around her.

She shook her head. "Of course not. But what if she keeps asking questions? What if she figures out what happened?"

Irvin rubbed her arm consolingly. "Just don't tell her anything you don't want to tell her. It'll be all right."

"But what if people find out? What will people think?" Fear rose inside her at the very thought, and she trembled.

"No one will find out."

"But what if they do?"

Irvin reached over and turned off the battery-operated light. "Then we must pray for strength."

CHAPTER FOURTEEN

A week passed as Charlie and Zoe continued to adapt to the Amish lifestyle. Zoe started attending school and was absolutely loving it. Every day after school she would tell Charlie all about her day and what she learned.

They felt more comfortable in the Holt household, and they became more helpful as they learned how to do things. Charlie was glad to help out around the house as much as she could and no longer felt like she was in the way all the time.

"So the church is going to be finished tomorrow," Esther said that night as they washed dishes.

"Are they really going to finish building the church all in one day?" Charlie asked, astounded.

"Oh yes. They've been working on it for a a while now, so it just needs to be finished up and the toilets need to be installed. We have so many people help that the work gets done quickly and efficiently," Esther explained.

"Well, I can't wait to help. I'm not very good at building, but I helped my dad fix things around the house sometimes," Charlie said, sweeping the floor.

Esther laughed. "Oh, Charlotte. I forgot to mention that the women don't help with the building; only the men do the construction work. We go to bring food and serve the men and to clean up afterwards."

Charlie felt a strange feeling of disappointment followed by confusion. Why weren't the women allowed to do things the men did?

And why weren't men allowed to do dishes or other kitchen work?

She wanted to ask more about why they had such odd rules. But she held back her words. Charlie loved these people, and the last thing she wanted to do was offend them as they offered their home to her and Zoe.

"Now, let's make some potato salad for tomorrow," Esther said and began washing potatoes.

An hour or so later, Ella Ruth and Katie came home after going to a friend's house. For a snack, they made popcorn in an old kettle on the gas stove top.

Charlie asked Ella Ruth if she had ever had popcorn with nutritional yeast in it. She said no and thought that was funny.

"It does sound weird, but it tastes very good," Charlie told her. "My dad used to like it like that." Mentioning her father filled her with sadness again, bringing back memories of her parents. Tears came to her eyes as she worked, but she turned so no one could see them, and quickly wiped them away.

Later that day at a store, Charlie found some nutritional yeast and bought a container of it for Ella Ruth's popcorn. When Charlie got back, Esther helped her make mozzarella cheese from scratch. They mixed some ingredients with milk in a big pot. When it started to solidify, Esther showed Charlie how to cut it with a long knife while it was still in the pot, stir it and strain it.

Katie asked Charlie, "Did you have TV where you lived?"

Charlie told her, "Yes, but we didn't have time to watch it much. We were so busy all the time."

The younger girls came home from school that afternoon, and Leah came home from running some errands.

125

Elijah came over and he and Charlie played jump rope for about an hour with the children. Then they played limbo and the high jump. Charlie tied the ends of the rope together to make one big circle. They held it and ran around. Little Seth laughed so hard and ran as fast as his short legs would go and Charlie laughed until her sides hurt. She couldn't remember the last time she had had so much fun.

Charlie adjusted more and more to the Amish way of life. In the middle of the night, when Charlie would look for the bathroom, she had finally stopped habitually feeling the walls in the dark for light switches. She was beginning to get used to the lack of electricity. She really didn't miss it. It was so peaceful in Unity without the distractions of blaring radios, TV's or computers.

She wondered how long the peace would last.

***

"Rise and shine!" Irvin called through the house the next morning. Charlie pulled her pillow over her head and groaned.

"I'm so tired. I miss sleeping in." She quickly wished she could take back her words. They hardly ever got to sleep in at home because Mom used to play piano in the mornings. Charlie recalled complaining about it, and now she regretted it. Right now, she would give anything to hear Mom play again, even if it was 5:45 in the morning.

"Let's go. We have a church to finish!" he yelled again, this time at the bottom of the stairs.

Zoe continued to sleep soundly. Charlie nudged her. "Wake up. Time to go to the church with everyone."

Zoe snorted a little and rolled over. Charlie laughed. "Come on. Everyone will leave without you."

126

"Okay, okay," Zoe mumbled, sat up and rubbed her eyes. They dressed quickly in jeans and sweatshirts. It would be cold out today. Charlie pulled her hair up in a short ponytail. A few pieces of her brown hair fell in wisps around her face, but she left it, tucking some behind her ears. This was as good as it was going to get.

She walked downstairs and shared a quick breakfast of oatmeal and fruit with the family. Everyone was excited about the work day, since it doubled as a social day. They gathered up their potato salad and some pies the other girls had made the night before and loaded up the buggy.

Charlie and the other girls decided to walk while Esther and Irvin rode with Debra and Seth in the buggy with the food. The children were too young to walk all the way to the church unless they were on the shoulders of a parent.

When the girls arrived, several people were already at the church gathered around outside talking. Zoe ran off to join some new friends she'd made. Charlie saw Lydia and approached her.

"Hi," Charlie said. "Beautiful morning, isn't it?"

"Oh yes. I'm not sure if you've met my boyfriend, Luke. Luke, this is Charlie, or Charlotte," Lydia said.

"Nice to finally meet you, Charlotte. I've heard a lot about you," Luke said, tossing his blond hair out of his eyes.

"You have?" Charlie asked. Who had talked about her?

"Oh, I mean, you know. It's a small community," he said. "Word gets around."

I wonder if Elijah told him about me. Charlie thought, then ignored the notion. They were friends, but that didn't mean she could jump to conclusions.

"Well, I have heard a lot about you, too," Charlie said, glancing at Lydia, who blushed.

"Good morning, Charlotte." Charlie heard the deep, wonderful voice from behind her. She turned to face Elijah, looking great in his wide-brimmed hat and coat. His hair had been cut a little. She wondered if he did it himself. It actually looked really good, the hair in the front peeking out from under the hat and just brushing his eyebrows. She wished she could reach up and gently push it back...

"When did you get here?" she asked.

"About an hour ago. I helped set some things up. Did you make any food yesterday?"

"Yes. I helped Esther make potato salad. It was my first time, but it turned out pretty good, thanks to Esther."

"I'm sure it will be great." He smiled at her for a bit longer than necessary. Butterflies erupted in her stomach.

More families arrived, and Bishop Zook began giving instructions.

"I'll see you around," he said, walking away with Luke.

Soon everyone else arrived, and already Charlie wished she could go sit by the wood stove in the church. She pulled her coat around her tighter and bounced on her heels, trying to stay warm as snow began to fall lightly. It was sunny, however, and still a good day to finish building a church.

"Want to help me make drinks for the men?" Lydia asked.

"Yes. Will it be warmer inside?" Zoe asked excitedly.

"Oh yes, definitely." Lydia laughed, and Charlie and Zoe followed her to the first floor of the church. They heated up the stove top and began boiling water for the cocoa. The women and girls opened the cocoa mix,

128

pouring it into mugs along with hot water and mixing it together. Each one of them took two mugs outside to give to the men. Charlie wondered if she should give some hot chocolate to Elijah. She didn't want to make her feelings towards him obvious. As she carried out two mugs and looked around the churchyard bustling with people, she realized that probably no one would think twice about it or even notice.

She gave one mug to Andrew, who was hammering something, then turned and walked around the other side of the building towards Elijah. She had seen him go around the other side and start working there.

"So, would you ever consider marrying an *Englisher*?"

When she heard the male voice, Charlie halted so abruptly that some of the hot cocoa sloshed over the edge of the mug onto her mittens. She bit her tongue to hold back a yelp.

Had that been Matthew's voice?

"Of course not. I will always be Amish, and that means I could never marry an *Englisher*. You know that," Charlie heard Elijah say. She felt her heart sink down to her boots. What had she been thinking? Had she really thought a man like Elijah would ever love her? She was about to turn and hurry away, but stopped when she heard him continue.

"Unless, of course, she decided to become Amish. Then I would marry her if we loved each other," Elijah added.

Become Amish? Charlie almost laughed out loud. Her? Amish? No way. She could never give up the piano, dress like a pilgrim all the time, and follow their many strict rules.

Besides, this community shunned her mother for leaving to marry her father. Even if she did ever join the Amish—not that she was considering it—wouldn't that be a betrayal to her parents? Wouldn't joining the

129

community that shunned Mom be like turning her back on her mother?

What would Mom think if she were here? Charlie wondered.

"You know that *Englishers* hardly ever join the Amish and last more than a year. They can't handle it and usually go back to the *Englisher* life," Matthew countered. "It's really rare that they stay. Actually, to be honest, some of us don't really think she belongs here. She could corrupt the youth if we aren't careful."

"Nonsense. Come on, Matthew. This isn't like you. Charlie came here in her time of need, and God calls us to take care of those in need. Besides, she's Esther and Irvin's family. And if she really wanted to for the right reasons, I think someone could become Amish for life and not go back to their old ways. Just like when one becomes a follower of Christ. You have to really mean it and really want it. You never go back to the way you used to live."

"Well, I'm just saying. A few of the men have been talking, and there is some uneasiness about her being here. An outsider staying in an Amish community? It just isn't normal. We separate ourselves from the world for a reason," Matthew persisted.

Had Matthew been the one who had shone the light in her room? Was he trying to scare her out of Unity?

"I can't believe this. Our church should be welcoming her and Zoe, not talking about her behind her back. Who said those things?"

"Andrew, Luke, and their fathers. Look, I don't think anyone is going to make her leave, but people talk."

Charlie turned away, a sick feeling filling her insides. Was it true? Did people not want her here?

Who was she kidding? Maybe Matthew was right. Maybe she didn't belong here after all.

Charlie did love the Amish way of life, but there were rules she didn't agree with, like not being allowed to play instruments or go to college. She watched the commotion all around her, the perfect picture of a community helping each other. She was uncomfortable with the different roles of males and females, and how women could not read in church and had to always keep their hair covered. But she was beginning to see that the ways of the Amish worked. The roles balanced out their way of life.

She watched the women begin to set up the lunch tables and realized that if the men tried to prepare lunch and the women and children hammered away, it would be confusing. She could only imagine the chaos. But the way the women worked with the food with the kids hiding and playing around their skirts while the men built their church, using their refined skills, everything just flowed harmoniously. Everyone had their own jobs and worked at them diligently.

Maybe it wasn't that one job or one sex was supposedly more important than the other—they were just different.

"This hot chocolate is good," Matthew said.

Hot chocolate. Right. Charlie still stood there like a fool with the now lukewarm drink in her hands. She still had to give it to Elijah. She walked around the side of the building and offered it up to him. Matthew made himself scarce.

"Thank you," he said. "Having fun so far?"

"Oh, *ja*. You? Are you freezing?"

"Not too bad. Moving around and working keeps us warm."

"Good. Well, keep up the good work." She smiled awkwardly and walked away, feeling his eyes on her. She went back inside to help Lydia and Leah make more hot chocolate.

"What else can I do to help?" Charlie asked Leah, who was bustling around.

"I will go bring these mugs outside. Can you heat up more water?" Leah asked.

"Sure."

Leah and Lydia grabbed four mugs and took them outside to the workers.

Charlie set to work, filling up the kettle with water, turning up the heat and waiting for the kettle to whistle. When it did, Elijah walked in, probably on the way to the bathroom which was near the kitchen.

He smiled at her as she went to pick up the kettle. She felt her insides heat up like the kettle had at the sight of his charming grin. Distracted, her hand slipped a little from the handle and touched the hot outside of the kettle. She cried out in pain.

"Charlotte! Are you okay?" he exclaimed and ran over to her.

Charlie bit her lip and clenched her other hand over her burn. She did not want to look it at it. Even though it hurt terribly, she knew it wasn't that bad. She fell onto the nearest chair.

"Let me see it," Elijah coaxed.

She clenched her grip harder over her hurt hand.

"It's ok. I won't touch it. I just want to see how bad it is." He gently eased her clenched fingers away from her injured hand. He pried them away and held her burned hand in his own as if he was holding something expensive and fragile. She let him move her fingers away, almost completely forgetting about the pain as she relished the welcome warmth of his fingers on her own. She would have let him hold her hand if he

132

wanted to. He did for a moment, only to inspect the burn.

"It's not too bad. Some of the ointment they keep in the first aid kit should do it," he said, and he briskly stood and retrieved it from a closet. He lifted her hand again in his own and rubbed some of the ointment onto her burn. Then he opened a bandage and applied it to her hand.

No one else in the world could have bandaged a hand more tenderly.

"There you go. Good as new," he said.

He looked up. When his eyes met hers, she knew she should look away. She knew she should control the butterflies in her stomach and the desire to kiss him, which was so much stronger than she had ever felt for Alex. This was completely different, and she knew this was wrong. She knew it would never work out, that it was forbidden for an Amish man to love a woman like her. She didn't want to risk getting him in trouble.

Yet, that made her want to pursue him so much more. It was all so deliciously intriguing. Then she told herself that must be it. That was what attracted her to him, the game of pursuing him even though she knew he would never date or marry her.

This was so wrong…

This man was deeper than the Atlantic, and she wanted to leave him unharmed. He was too beautiful, too simple and honest to hurt.

Even though she really wanted to lean closer to him, she sat further back in her chair, trying to distance herself before she did somehow kiss him. He held her gaze and gently squeezed her hand.

Dishes crashed noisily, and Charlie looked up to see Leah setting down a tray of mugs.

Elijah gathered up gauze and tubes of ointment and put them back in the first aid box. "Charlotte burned her hand," he said. "But it's not bad."

133

"Oh, no. I shouldn't have left you to do that alone," Leah said.

"It's not your fault. I may not be the best cook in the world, but I can usually manage to boil water without hurting myself," Charlie said, forcing an awkward chuckle.

"I'll let you ladies get back to work. I was on my way to the bathroom, so I better go and get back outside," Elijah said, giving her one last look of concern.

"Yes, right. Of course. Thanks for your help," Charlie said.

He smiled at her again, and she wished he would stay there with her and talk, but he walked to the bathroom.

Leah cleared her throat, then set to work washing the empty mugs she'd just brought in. The awkwardness was unbearable. Charlie busied herself with making more hot cocoa, pretending as though none of that had just happened. She waited for Leah to say something. Had she seen Elijah holding Charlie's hand? How long had she been in the room? Had anyone else seen them?

She should have been more careful. The last thing she wanted was to get him into trouble with his community.

But Charlie couldn't help but smile as she thought of the way Elijah had tenderly held her hand in his or how her heart had sped up at his touch.

Was it just her or had Elijah felt the same way she had?

134

CHAPTER FIFTEEN

O he church had indeed been finished that day. When it was over, as the sun set behind the hills, everyone went home exhausted. Charlie tried not to think about the strange encounter she had shared with Elijah and whether other people had witnessed it. Maybe if she made herself forget about it, it would be as though it had never happened.

Well, that's what she wished. But the burn on her hand would not let her forget.

Her mind was still mulling over what Matthew had said about people not wanting her there, and she wondered if one of the men he had mentioned had been the one shining the light in her room. Did they really want her to leave bad enough to try to scare her, or had it just been unintentional or a coincidence?

When dinner was almost ready, Irvin and Elijah came in and sat at the table, and they all ate rice with beef, vegetables, bread, cantaloupe, and watermelon.

Afterwards, the girls cleaned up. Esther said, "There are so many dishes with such a large family." There had been a lot of dishes even at Charlie's house with half the amount of people.

Esther asked Charlie, "Is it very different than what you expected here?"

"At first it was. I didn't know if you would have electricity or even bathrooms. I really didn't know what to expect."

Irvin led the evening devotions. They read Matthew 6, and each person took turns reading a verse. In the home, the girls and women read, but not in church. Afterwards, Irvin went around asking what they thought

135

of the passage.

Charlie said, "Sometimes the good things you do in secret make more difference than the things done in the open."

"Well said," Elijah added. Irvin agreed.

After devotions, Charlie, Esther, Zoe, and all the girls decided to make apple dumplings. They almost always had homemade dessert with lunch and supper, sometimes even with breakfast. They put their dessert in their bowls and poured milk over it. Charlie thought it would taste weird at first, but it was delicious.

As Charlie swept the apple peelings off the floor and washed dishes, Esther asked, "Did you have a dishwasher back at home?"

Charlie said, "Yes, but sometimes it didn't work well. I'm used to doing dishes by hand."

Esther said, "It is refreshing to see a person who is not Amish and willing to do work."

Charlie shrugged sheepishly. "I just like to help." She ended up accidentally spraying herself with the sink hose, and the other girls laughed with her, and Elijah chuckled too.

"Stop it," Charlie said.

"Sorry," Elijah said. "We aren't making fun of you. It was just funny."

Charlie smiled and let herself forget about her problems. At least for a little while.

As they cleaned up the dishes from dessert, a rubber band fight started. They ducked and ran and fired bands at each other, running around, laughing hysterically the whole time.

Elijah asked Charlie, "Did it ever get this crazy at your house?"

Charlie said, "Sometimes. But we didn't have quite as many people in my family."

"Sometimes when I had friends over it got this loud," Zoe added.

Lilly said, "We have so many people living here we don't need friends over to have fun."

Even Esther and Irvin laughed at the game. Elijah picked up Seth and ran around with him. Seth was too little to know how to shoot them like the girls did, so he just threw them. Whenever one of the girls shot a rubber band at him, he shrieked with laughter. Elijah laughed so hard he could barely breathe, and Charlie watched him play with the children.

She could not deny it. She knew he would make an excellent father. She couldn't help but picture him like that in her future, playing with their own children.

She shook her head to clear her thoughts. Elijah was Amish, and she was an *Englisher*. There was no hope of them ever being together. He had said he would never even date an *Englisher*. She knew it was out of the question. They were from two completely different worlds. She grabbed several rubber bands off the floor and flung them at the children, forcing all romantic thoughts out of her brain. Zoe took a handful and threw them back at her.

Once the fight died down, they drew pictures and painted at the table. It was great to see them all having so much fun and learning, and she smiled as she watched Zoe laugh. As they painted, Leah made more popcorn for everyone with the yeast Charlie had bought for them.

Charlie drew the profiles of everyone and they marveled at how some of the pictures really resembled them. Elijah smiled at her.

"You're really talented," he told her. "That's incredible."

She blushed, said a quiet thank you, and looked away. She noticed

Lilly, Katie and Leah looking at her and Elijah. When they met Charlie's eyes, they quickly looked away, obviously not wanting to stare.

She had to be more careful. If they told someone that they suspected Charlie was developing feelings for Elijah, he could get in trouble with the Amish church. One could never know how one small action could spark a fire.

CHAPTER SIXTEEN

A week later, after Zoe and the other children had gone to school, Esther started making lunch for everyone else on the farm at nine in the morning. It was early to begin cooking lunch, but it took so much longer to make without electricity and modern appliances.

Charlie sighed heavily, frustrated. She felt like they were constantly cooking or cleaning up after cooking. Sometimes, she felt it was unfair that the men had no involvement in the kitchen whatsoever. However, there were things Charlie was glad that she didn't have to do that the men did have to do, like milk cows at four-thirty in the morning or work in the fields.

She glanced at the bandage on her hand. The burn was healing.

After helping Esther, Charlie went outside so she could walk to Lydia's house for lunch. As she approached the family's buggy, she gasped. Someone had written the words *she should leave* in large, red letters with paint on the black siding of the buggy. Charlie clapped a hand over her mouth to keep from crying out.

She shuddered. Who would do this?

Had one of the men who didn't want her here done this? Why didn't they just ask her to leave directly and say it to her face?

Charlie went to the barn and looked around for a while until she found a few cans of paint. She grabbed some black paint and a brush, then painted over the words.

Again, she doubted Alex had done this. It wasn't his style at all. And if he had, he would have written something a lot more vulgar. No, if Alex were here, she would know it.

I could just tell Elijah... Even though the thought of it made her sick. If she told him about Alex, he might make her leave, unlike her relatives, in order to protect the community. But she knew she would have to do it, and she had to do it soon. Then she would be able to decide what to do about Alex, and maybe Elijah would help her, maybe even protect her and Zoe. Alex had not hurt her or threatened Zoe so far...but she didn't want to take any chances.

For now, she had to go to Lydia's for lunch. She didn't want to let her down. It wasn't like Charlie could call Lydia on her cell phone and cancel.

When Charlie arrived, Lydia and her big dog came out to greet Charlie. Lydia's sister, Tabitha, and her mother were inside. They owned a bakery where they baked from five in the morning to noon every Thursday and Friday, and they sold their goods at a market on Saturdays. Their home bakery was open all week, though, located in a building right next to their house. They made whole wheat breads, pies, rolls, turnovers, and more. They had an oven with several doors and compartments where they baked several different things at once. Thursdays and Fridays were Lydia's days off from teaching school so she could bake with her family.

When Charlie got there, she helped them make blueberry turnovers. It was a time-consuming process. There were lots of dirty dishes to wash, and then they ate lunch. Lydia's father and brother came in, and everyone sat down and had the silent prayer. Lydia's father asked Charlie about herself, and somehow the dinner conversation turned to Noah's Ark.

Charlie told them about a church sign she saw once that said, "Where did Noah put the woodpeckers?" They thought that was pretty funny as Charlie had when she had first seen it.

After a lunch made from scratch, Charlie asked, "Do you think you'll get married to Luke?"

"Yes, I do. We have been dating for almost a year now." Lydia smiled at the mention of his name.

Luke had been one of the men who wanted her gone, but Charlie didn't want to say anything to upset her new friend.

"All Amish dating is done with the intention of marriage. And yes, I do believe we will get married. I know I want to marry him. In fact, I expect a proposal any day now," she said excitedly. "Secretly, that is the biggest reason why I have to quit teaching school. Yes, my family does need my help throughout the week, but once I get married, I want to stay home and have lots of children. I'll be too busy to teach school."

"Wow, that's great news. I'm really happy for you," Charlie said.

"You know, there is a young man named Matthew who likes Leah."

"Oh, yes. I've met him." Charlie tried not to frown at the mention of another man who wanted her to leave. "Does Leah know?"

"They have known each other their whole lives, so I think Leah is rather oblivious to it. But Matthew told Luke, since they are friends, that he is planning on asking Irvin if he can court her," Lydia told her, smiling. "He is such a nice young man. I'm sure Irvin will approve."

Luke and Matthew didn't seem so nice to her, but Charlie smiled and scrubbed a pot vigorously.

Lydia watched her for a second. "So…"

Charlie knew what was coming. She scrubbed even harder.

"What is going on with you and Elijah?" Lydia asked.

Charlie didn't even deny it. She let out the breath she had been holding, somewhat grateful to finally confide in someone. "Something is going on, but I am not sure what."

"It is obvious that he has an interest in you."

"What? Of course not. I'm not Amish."

"I know Elijah well. He wants to marry an Amish woman," Lydia told her gently.

"Exactly."

"Would you join the church to marry him? I mean, everyone knows your mother was Amish. Wouldn't you consider joining?"

Charlie shook her head. "No, I don't think so. He hasn't even told me he loves me or anything like that. I think it is a little soon to think about joining the church and marriage."

"I don't think it's too soon. I think it is something you really need to consider."

Charlie scrubbed the pot with even more intensity than before. Lydia rested a hand on Charlie's arm, and Charlie stopped.

"For what it's worth, I think you two would make a great couple," she said quietly, her big blue eyes twinkling.

"You do?" Charlie was so happy to hear someone say something encouraging about her and Elijah.

"Yes. If you become Amish."

"And just how would I join the church?"

"In one way it is just as simple as coming before our community and saying, 'Here I am. I want to be a part of your community. I am here to learn and help.' But on the other hand, if I would try to define all the adjustments a person goes through in the process of 'pulling out of society' and blending into a plain community, it could sound pretty complicated. Of course, the biggest requirement in actually becoming part of our group is sharing the same faith and values. Faith in God and Jesus and a dedication to taking the Bible very seriously and being willing to let it order your life is a must. Basically, I am not sure, since we have never had an outsider join our church here before, but I think you would stand before the church and ask to be accepted as an Amish church member. And you'd probably have to be baptized into the church.

"As I said, I do think you and Elijah would make a fine couple, but only if you joined the church, and if you joined it for the right reasons."

That was just the thing. If Charlie did join the church, would she do it with the right motives?

"You have faith in God, yes? And you trust Him with your life?" Lydia asked.

"Yes, I do. Always have, but I understand it fully now."

"And you would be willing to commit your life to serving Him and giving up worldly things?"

"Yes." It would be so much better, so much more peaceful than the life she would go back to if she left here and went home. "The thing is, this community shunned my mother. I feel like I would be betraying her by joining the Amish."

"Don't you think she'd want you to be happy?"

Charlie hesitated. "Yes...I think so. But there are still some things that need to be resolved."

Did she forgive these people for shunning her mother?

When Charlie didn't elaborate, Lydia said, "Well, that's between you and God. I think you would make a fine Amish woman, Charlotte."

Charlie smiled. "Well, I haven't been here very long, so I don't even know if I could do it yet."

"And, hey, if you get married and join the church, then you could be the next teacher," Lydia said excitedly, smiling.

"Really?"

"*Ja.* Of course."

"That would be a dream come true…" Charlie sighed. What a perfect life that would be if she was married to Elijah and lived out her dream of being a teacher. An Amish teacher. She envisioned a quaint and tidy Amish home filled with their children, warmed by the wood stove and the love of their family. And her own classroom full of eager students, thriving in their schoolwork. In a perfect world, maybe it would have been possible. But she didn't even know if Alex was looking for her, and she had no idea how long she'd be staying here.

Either way, could she really live with the people who shunned her mother just for leaving to marry her father? Charlie wasn't even sure if she had really forgiven them yet. She wanted to, but had she truly? Charlie also could tell there was more to the story between Esther and Mom, but would she ever get Esther to tell her everything?

Even if she could stay and forgive the community for shunning Mom, and even if there was no Alex, could she really make a good enough Amish woman…and wife? Could she live the rest of her life like this, with all these rules, strict dress code and no musical instruments? If she was able to stay here forever and make this place her home, would she ever really fit in? She just wished Alex would leave her alone so she could fully consider the possibilities.

CHAPTER SEVENTEEN

After lunch at Lydia's, Charlie went back to the Holts' house. It was time to tell Esther what had happened to the buggy.

She walked into the house and saw Esther cleaning the kitchen.

"How was visiting Lydia? Is her family well?" Esther asked.

"It was great. Yes, they are all doing well. Actually, there's something I need to tell you. When I walked outside earlier, I saw the buggy was vandalized. Someone had painted *she should leave* in red letters."

Esther gasped. "What? Who would do such a thing?"

"I think…" Charlie hesitated. "I think it's someone here in the community who wants me to leave."

Esther paused to look at her. "Who?"

"I'm not sure who exactly."

"We are peaceful people. This is not something an Amish person would typically do." Esther sighed. "But everyone sins. Maybe it is possible."

"I painted over it with black paint. I hope that's okay. I just didn't want anyone to see it. I didn't want it to start any drama."

"That was the right choice. Thank you."

"I'm really sorry me being here is causing so much trouble. I would understand if it got to be too much and you asked me to leave."

"No. I want you and Zoe here. Our whole family does. Don't think you're a burden for a moment. You're our family now, and we should stick together no matter what."

Charlie grinned; her insides warmed with gratitude. "Thank you, Esther. I really appreciate that."

145

Esther hugged her. "Come on. It's time to do the laundry."

Washing clothes took her so much longer without an electric washer and dryer, and it was physically taxing. The Holts used a Maytag washer run by gas that swished the clothes back and forth, and then they put the clothes through a ringer that squeezed most of the water out. Then they rinsed them in a large container and sent them through the ringer again before hanging them out on the clothesline. Charlie was afraid her fingers would get caught in the ringer, which could happen if she was not careful. She had heard a few stories of people who got their arms caught in the ringers. There was a button to push that opened the contraption if that did happen, but Charlie didn't want to find out what that would be like.

Charlie put her and Zoe's clothes in the wash with the Amish dresses and pants. The jeans and t-shirts looked so out of place among the old-fashioned clothes.

After all the laundry was washed, rinsed, and wrung out, Charlie offered to hang the clothes on the line. That was one chore her family and this family had in common, and she knew how to do it well.

When all the laundry was hung, she moved on to washing dishes. She was surprised after she had finished washing and drying every dish. She didn't really remember doing it. Her hands had seemed to move on their own as she stared out the window before her at the fields and the stretching, gravelly lane that bent around the trees. She was becoming accustomed to doing so many dishes three times a day, although it often felt like more.

However, that wasn't the case today. In her mind, she was so deep in conversation with Elijah that she was not thinking about the dishes at all. How would she find the right words to tell him about Alex? What would he say? Would he reject her? She pictured his dark eyes and warm smile, always so forgiving, so genuine.

When she started to put the dishes away, she absentmindedly put a fork in the cabinet and tried to put a mug in the silverware drawer. It clanked against the edge of the counter when she shut the drawer on it.

"What are you doing?" Esther asked Charlie, looking at her strangely. Charlie hadn't even noticed the older woman had also started working in the kitchen.

"Nothing," Charlie said automatically, about to put another fork in the bowl cabinet. She looked at her hand and realized what she was doing. "Sorry. My mind is somewhere else today."

"Sure seems that way." Esther slowly shook her head, smiling a little as she swept the floor.

Charlie was thinking about what to say when she would tell Elijah about Alex. Charlie caught onto that little knowing smile of Esther's.

"What?" Charlie asked, waving her dish towel. "Why are you smiling?"

"I know who you are thinking about. It's obvious to everyone that you two care about each other." Esther's smile faded, and she stopped sweeping to look at Charlie. "But if that is going to go on, you really need to think about some choices you have to make. You know what I mean." Esther's broom continued on its course, bristling against the floor like Charlie's unmade decisions chafing against her heart.

Of course, Charlie knew what Esther was talking about. The problem was that Charlie had no idea what to do. She placed her hands on the edge of the sink and looked out the window. She watched Amish workers mending fences in the fields, and she heard the squeaking of the

147

clothesline as the wind blew. There was so much work all the time. Back at her apartment in the city, some of the work could be done twice as fast, like cooking and laundry and dishes. Charlie missed her microwave that enabled her to have a meal ready in minutes. All this work took up time they could use to do other things.

Then she saw Elijah working on a fence outside, and he looked towards the house. Charlie wasn't sure if he could see her, but for a moment it seemed like he was looking right into her eyes.

Charlie's cheeks burned, and she looked away. Maybe there really were some kind, selfless men in this world, contrary to what she'd believed ever since Alex had bruised her heart and her neck.

The memory of driving to work in her old car flashed in her mind.

Charlie had walked into the diner after she'd bought the car. She'd put on her apron and hung up her keys.

"Whose car is that?" her boss, Linda, had asked.

"Mine. I bought it yesterday," Charlie said.

"You were just saying how you were really low on money the other day," Tonya commented, wiping down tables.

"I used some of my savings to buy it."

Linda and Tonya gave her questioning looks, clearly wondering how she could afford a car.

"Look, don't tell anyone, ok?" Charlie said.

"Okay," they both said in unison, leaning forward in anticipation.

"I sold the ring online. That's how I paid for the car."

Linda and Tonya looked at each other, then back at Charlie, eyebrows raised.

Charlie put her palms up. "You must think how awful that is, but with my mom gone and my dad losing his job, I was desperate for money—"

"No. After what that man did to you, he deserved it," Linda cut in.

"Any man who treats women disrespectfully deserves it!" Tonya cried.

"When you said all men are deceitful, I should have listened to you. I shouldn't have been so naïve." Charlie sighed, leaning against the counter. "I fell for his stupid flattery."

"They *are* deceitful. That's why none of us are married and I'm divorced," Linda said and began sweeping the floor vigorously.

Charlie continued to believe all young men were deceitful and that they put on a mask of kindness until their true personalities showed. She stopped trusting all of them because of her past experiences. And when boys would want to date Zoe in the future, Charlie would do whatever it would take to protect Zoe from them.

"I know you're still way too young to date, but even when you are older don't trust any boys," Charlie had told Zoe. "Even when they tell you that you're pretty and special and that they love you. Anyone can say those things, and they will. Alex said those things to me, and then he broke my heart. Don't ever fall for it, okay?"

Zoe looked up at her older sister and replied seriously, "Okay. I won't."

Now, as Charlie swept the floor in her aunt's farmhouse, she sneaked another glance out the window at the kindest, most gentle man she'd ever met besides her own father. Elijah truly was like no one she'd ever met.

Of course, all the extra work here was worth it. But the Amish lifestyle wasn't really what was making her decision difficult.

The thing that was holding her back the most was feeling like she was betraying her mother by considering joining the Amish. What would her mother say if she was here now and saw Charlie cleaning the kitchen with Esther, who had shunned Mom?

Also, she had no idea how she would give up playing the piano, the one thing that still connected her to her mother. She missed it already. It had only been a few weeks, but she was used to playing every day. She wondered if there was some place nearby where she could play. Besides, she wasn't Amish yet, so she could.

As for going to college, she knew she would have had to give up that dream anyway. She couldn't afford college now that she was solely responsible for Zoe.

"Are there any places nearby that have musical instruments?" she asked Esther. It was a long shot, but she could try. Just as she did, Elijah came inside, followed by Katie, Ella Ruth, Leah, Zoe, and Lilly.

"No, not really," Esther said, and everyone said hello to each other.

"Actually, there is a small museum a few miles down the road that has dozens of player pianos," Elijah said. "Joe, the owner, calls it a museum, but it's really more like an antique store. He loves when people go in and play the pianos. It's laid back. They have old stoves, toys, antique cars, and all sorts of things. Zoe would love it. We should go over after dinner tonight. Anyone else want to come?" He looked to all the girls. "Do you all want to come with us?"

The girls nodded their heads.

"Yes! We'd love to," Katie said.

"That sounds like fun!" Charlie said, the anticipation of playing piano again running through her.

"That might not be such a good idea," Esther said, frowning.

150

"Why not?" Charlie asked.

Esther's brows knit together, a worried look on her face. "It's just…
The Amish don't play musical instruments, so I can't see the good in you
all going."

"But Charlie isn't Amish, and the rest of us won't be playing the
pianos. We don't know how anyway," Elijah said. The girls went upstairs.

What was Esther so worried about?

"Well, let me know later," Elijah said to Charlie after an awkward
quiet moment, then he went back outside.

"What's going on? Why don't you want us to go to that museum?"
Charlie asked Esther once they were alone.

Esther sighed. "It's the museum where Joanna met Greg. He worked
there, and he taught her to play piano there in secret. It's what started the
series of events that led to her leaving, and it's where they fell in love. It
just holds bad memories for me. As I said before, I was devastated when
Joanna left."

"That's the museum where they met?" Now she had to go. Maybe
she'd feel a little closer to her parents if she went there. "I'd really like to
go. I hope you don't mind too much."

"Of course I'm not going to stop you. You're an adult—you can do
what you choose. It's just a painful reminder of everything that happened
between us."

Charlie did feel sorry for Esther, but now she just felt frustrated.
"That's the problem. I don't know what really happened between you
two. I know she left, and I know it upset you and there was an argument,
but what's the real reason why you didn't talk for over twenty years?
What happened to you when you visited my mother? I just wish you

151

would tell me what happened."

Esther set the broom down against the wall, sat down at the table, and rested her hands in her lap. She took a deep breath and looked Charlie in the eye, then Charlie sat across from her.

"You're right. You don't know the whole story. It's really painful for me to talk about it, so I don't. And I'm sorry. She was my sister, but she was your mother too. I need to remember that," Esther said. "I'll tell you what happened."

Charlie folded her hands on the table, listening intently.

Ester took in a shaky breath and continued. "After Joanna left, I was attacked when I visited her in Portland. I was traveling alone, which was a terrible idea, because I lied to everyone about where I was going. I was going in secret, so I didn't ask anyone to go with me. I was pulled into an alley and raped at knifepoint by two men. People even walked by... No one stopped them. I guess they thought someone else would, but no one wanted to get involved. I never even reported it. I was so ashamed and embarrassed. No one knows except Irvin."

Charlie gasped and rested her face in her hands. "Oh, Aunt Esther... I'm so sorry. No wonder you don't want to talk about it."

"Even after all this time, it's still hard. But it was a long time ago, and God has healed me. The incident caused so many problems... Even problems in our marriage. And it led to Joanna and me not speaking. But it all started with that museum," Esther said. "We didn't speak for so long, and I didn't even get to see her before she died. If Joanna and Greg hadn't met there, then none of those bad things would have happened. She'd still be here, at home in this community with us."

"But then I would have never been born," Charlie realized out loud.

"Oh, of course. You are a good thing that came out of it. God uses bad things for good, see?" Esther patted her hand. Longing filled her eyes, and sorrow. Charlie still felt like there was so much more her aunt was keeping secret, but when tears filled Esther's eyes, Charlie couldn't bring herself to pry anymore. This woman had been through enough as it was.

Esther leaned back in her chair. "So, I hope you understand when I said I didn't think it was a good idea. But I know you must miss playing the piano. So, if you want to go, that's fine. I won't stop you."

"I do miss the piano. Mom and I played so much together. She was amazing at playing. It was something special we did together. I hope that going there might help me feel a little closer to my parents."

Esther nodded slowly. "Of course. You should go then, in their memory."

Later on, during dinner, Elijah asked, "So are we going to go to the museum, Charlie?"

Charlie glanced at Esther, who just stared at her plate. "Yes, if you're all still up for it."

"I'd love to. I used to go when my family would visit here, back when I lived in Smyrna. I haven't been in so long. Zoe, you'll love it. They have all kinds of old things, even a room full of old dolls and puppets that dance when you press a button."

"That sounds so fun!" Zoe said and finished eating quickly. "You're all still coming, right?"

"Oh yes, I'd still like to go," Ella Ruth said.

"Me too," Katie and Lilly added.

"I should probably stay here and help *Maam* with cleaning up," Leah said.

"It's all right, Leah," Esther said. She smiled at Charlie. "If you all want to go, you should go. I don't mind cleaning up alone tonight."

"I want to go, too," Debra said.

"Me too," Seth chimed in.

"You two need to go to bed," Irvin told them. They frowned in disappointment but continued eating.

"Thank you, Aunt Esther." Charlie really meant it, and Esther gave that knowing smile again.

Charlie couldn't wait to get to the museum. It had been clear to her that the Amish did not allow music besides what was in their little German hymn book. She couldn't imagine not being allowed to listen to regular music. She listened to mostly Christian music, and it was such a big part of her life. She listened to a lot of classical too, or just instrumental piano. She had memorized many of the dozens of songs she and her mother used to play together. It was one piece of her mother she could take with her anywhere, even if it was just in her heart.

How could she ever give up music, her last connection to her mother?

CHAPTER EIGHTEEN

The group walked to the museum parking lot. A sign read Joe's Museum and advertised old stoves and player pianos, but since everything was for sale, it truly was more like an antique store. Zoe marveled at all of the rusty old stoves lined up in the yard.

"What are all those for?" she asked. "Do people cook with those?"

Elijah chuckled. "No, they're too old. People like to look at them and buy them sometimes."

Zoe was flabbergasted. "Why? What are they for?"

"Some people just like old things. They like antiques," Leah told her.

They walked into the museum. It didn't look like a regular museum. When they first walked through the door, it looked like the inside of a house. There were newspaper articles on the walls about the museum and its owner, who apparently lived here.

They went into a large room with more stoves, and Zoe wondered what was so great about this museum. There wasn't anything very interesting, except the huge collection of goofy salt and pepper shakers.

Zoe saw a sign with an arrow.

"Come on! Let's go," she said, grabbing Lilly and Katie's hands and hurrying with them down the hall. Ella Ruth followed right behind them.

They followed the arrow into a huge room with a high ceiling that was filled to the ceiling with a myriad of toys. Zoe noticed a switch on the wall that said "activate toys". She flipped it, and to her delight, many of the toys came to life. Music that sounded like a marching band blared as everything moved, twirled, or danced.

"Isn't it wonderful?" Ella Ruth yelled above the noise.

"Yes!" Zoe clapped with excitement.

There were dolls, puppets, trains, cars, marionettes, and wooden planes hanging from the ceiling with whirling propellers. Zoe and the girls walked around the entire room, fascinated at the colorful and complex arrangements.

She laughed at the silly ostrich marionettes marching around in a circle that were almost as tall as her. She leaned over the side of a fenced-in area containing mini cars that zoomed around a racetrack and wondered who had made this amazing room.

***

Down the hall, Charlie sat down at a piano and laid her hands on the old keys. Elijah came and stood beside the piano bench.

"You sure it's okay if I play this piano?" she asked.

"Of course. Joe doesn't mind at all. Go ahead."

She turned to the keys and played one of her favorite songs. Her hands ran up and down the octaves, almost floating. Elijah watched her expression of concentration and her love for music. He knew what was happening before him was amazing.

Once Charlie finished with the classical piece, she played a different song and started singing a song she'd heard on the country radio station by a local band called Forgiven.

I'm just one in a million,
Just one in a billion, I see
I'm one in a trillion
So there must be someone else that feels like me...

Stunned, Elijah watched as Charlie's fingers danced across the keys. Her sweet voice surrounded him like a warm blanket, and he couldn't stop his eyes from closing just so he could focus on the sound more intently.

When he opened his eyes, he stared at her. She sang as though no one else was around, as though nothing else mattered except the lyrics to her song and the notes of the piano. Locks of hair fell into her eyes, but she didn't seem to notice, not like he did. He stepped closer, close enough to see every strand, but Charlie was so engrossed in the music that she didn't see him. And he didn't want to interrupt her.

He had never been in love before, and he didn't know what it felt like, except for that day when he'd first met Charlie in Irvin's barn when they were children. That day he had felt something a little like love. He'd thought over time he would forget her name or find an Amish woman who would stir the same feelings in him, but that had never happened. God had brought her back to him, but she was just out of reach. What was he supposed to do now?

Now, as he watched Charlie play the piano, Elijah knew he was falling in love with Charlotte. He felt those same feelings he had experienced in the barn that day.

And she was completely off-limits to him.

Would she ever give up music to be with him? And all of her *Englisher* ways? He would sure be asking a lot of her if he ever told her the way he felt about her.

He knew this woman was different, even though she wasn't Amish. That wasn't what made her different. He wasn't sure what it was, but he suddenly knew he wanted to spend the rest of his life figuring it out, and he would do whatever it would take to make that happen.

***

Leah wandered the different rooms in the museum. Charlie and Elijah had headed off to the piano room, and the other girls were in the toy room. She was the odd one out. Why had she even agreed to come? She should have just stayed home and helped *Maam* with the dishes.

The sound of the girls' laughter floated down the hall from the toy room, then Leah heard the sound of a piano being played beautifully. She followed it to the piano room.

Charlie was seated at one of the old pianos, playing and singing a hauntingly lovely song. But the music faded into the background when Leah saw Elijah standing there, staring at Charlie in amazement. He took a step closer to her as she played.

Though Leah had looked at Elijah like that many times, she'd never seen him look at her that way.

Pain crushed her heart when she realized Elijah was obviously smitten with Charlie. And why wouldn't he be? Charlie was beautiful, interesting, and could play piano and sing like an angel.

I'm just the plain girl next door. Nothing special, Leah thought, jealousy tearing through her. *He'll never love me like he clearly loves her.*

Tears filled her eyes, and no one saw her run from the room.

***

Zoe turned away from the puppets she was playing with, giggling. She stopped at the sound she heard. Charlie was playing one of the pianos. She hadn't played since Mom had died, and Zoe had missed it.

Zoe crept out of the toy room and into the piano room. She peeked around the corner and listened to Charlie play the rest of the song. Charlie stopped playing and looked up shyly at Elijah, who had been intently watching her play. They stayed like that for a few more seconds, just staring at each other.

What were they doing? Zoe had never seen any two people look at each other like that in her entire life except for her mom and dad.

Charlie and Elijah were acting weird, but Zoe was happy for them.

**

Charlie finished the song and looked up at Elijah, who was grinning.

"I don't call that playing the piano a little," he said with a laugh. "That was amazing."

Applause came from the back of the room.

"Well, someone can play," someone piped from the other side of the room.

They turned to see an elderly man in a wheelchair approaching them. "I'm Joe, the owner. It's nice to hear someone who actually knows how to play this old thing."

"Thanks. I'm Charlotte Cooper. This is Elijah, and the girl in the corner is my sister Zoe. Yes, I see you over there."

Zoe came forward and smiled shyly at Joe.

"Charlotte Cooper? As in Joanna and Greg's daughter?" Joe asked.

"Yes. I heard they used to come here a lot, and that this is where they met. You knew them?"

"Oh, yes. I watched them fall in love here. Your father taught your mother how to play piano right here. In fact, that was their favorite piano." Joe pointed to the one Charlie had just played.

Charlie swallowed a lump in her throat and swiped away a tear. Afraid of bursting into tears, she didn't say anything.

"How are your parents?" Joe asked.

Now she really couldn't speak. She glanced to Elijah, hoping he'd answer for her.

"Her parents passed away recently. Joanna died from cancer and Greg was killed in a car accident," Elijah told the museum owner.

"No!" Joe cried. "I haven't seen them or talked to them in years… We just fell out of touch. I had no idea. I'm so sorry."

Charlie nodded and managed a thank you.

"Would you like me to tell you more about their time here?" Joe offered.

"I'd love that. Thanks," Charlie said.

"Well, let me show you around while I tell you," the owner said. Zoe and Charlie went with him and Elijah excused himself to go find the girls.

They walked down an aisle of pianos and Joe stopped his wheelchair at one. "This piano was Joanna's favorite. She started coming here secretly as a teenager to come play the pianos. She used to tell me all about how she was going to be a concert pianist one day. In fact, I was surprised when she was baptized into the church after talking about leaving for so long. Maybe she didn't want to disappoint her parents, or maybe she thought she was going to stay Amish. Then she met Greg.

"She and Greg were almost like a son and daughter to me back then because they spent so much time here together after I hired him. They'd meet up here often to play the piano, but they also would talk a lot too. I was glad to have them here. They kept me company, and it was a safe place for them. Your mother was uneasy about leaving the Amish, but she was a determined woman. I wasn't surprised when they told me they were leaving to get married and move to Portland," Joe told Charlie and Zoe.

"They confided in me. I think Joanna saw me as a father figure after she left home. They visited me after their wedding and told me that the Amish community was shunning Joanna. Is that really true? That even her family wouldn't talk to her?"

Charlie nodded. "Yes. Hard to believe, but it's true."

"Well, after what Joanna did to her sister after her pregnancy, I can see why Esther shut her out, but it's a shame the whole community shunned her."

"Zoe, go find the other girls," Charlie told her. Zoe gave her a look then walked down the hall. "What pregnancy? Whose pregnancy?" Charlie persisted once Zoe was out of ear shot, heart pounding. Was this the secret Esther and her mother had been keeping from her for so long? "What did my mom do to Esther? Does this have to do with the disagreement between them?"

Joe scratched his head and looked away and stammered, "Never mind. I'm sorry. I shouldn't have said that."

"No, please tell me. My mother died without telling me what really happened. You know the whole story, don't you?"

Joe glanced at Charlie, worry lining his face. "Well, as I said, your parents were like a son and daughter to me. So, yes, they told me what really happened. I'm sorry, Charlotte. I think I've said too much. It's really not my place. Maybe your aunt should tell you."

Charlie looked Joe in the eye, who was still looking at the floor. "Did she get pregnant? Who was the baby? Is that what their fight was about?"

"Look, Charlotte, just forget I said anything. You need to talk to Esther about this, not me. You just need to ask her directly, okay? She'll tell you when she's ready. It was hard on both of them, believe me. Your mother felt terrible after what happened. I'm sorry, but I just can't say anything more."

Questions stormed through her mind. What had happened to the baby? Who was it? What horrible thing had Mom done that had caused the sisters to not speak to each other ever again?

CHAPTER NINETEEN

Leah sniffed and wiped her tears on her sleeve when she heard someone coming closer. She stood up from where she'd been sitting on the floor and let out a breath of relief when she saw it was only Ella Ruth.

"Leah, what's wrong?" Ella Ruth asked.

Leah swallowed the growing lump in her throat. "You should have seen the way Elijah looked at her."

"Who?"

"Charlie. Who else? He's obviously in love with her."

"You think so? But he could be shunned if he decides to leave with her."

"I know." Leah sniffed again. "Someone should remind him of that."

"Why are you so upset?" Ella Ruth asked. Realization lit up her face. "Wait... Are you in love with him?"

Leah only nodded, and a new round of tears came.

"Oh... Leah. I had no idea," Ella Ruth murmured, wrapping her arms around her sister. "Why didn't you tell me?"

"I guess I was worried that maybe you liked him. I didn't want it to drive us apart."

"No, of course not! He's like a brother to me."

"I've thought for a long time that we'd get married. And then Charlie came here, and he's obviously fallen for her. She's beautiful and interesting... And I'm just a friend to him. Maybe not even that. I'm just the girl next door, the daughter of the man he works for. He doesn't even notice me."

163

"Leah, you are beautiful and interesting. And he's a fool if he doesn't see you that way." Ella Ruth rubbed Leah's back comfortingly.

"That's kind of you to say," Leah said with a sigh. "I just wish he'd notice me."

"So, let's get him to notice you," Ella Ruth said.

"How?"

Ella Ruth held Leah at arm's length and smiled at her. "You need to tell him how you feel."

Leah nodded, determination setting in. "You're right. I'll do it tonight."

As the group walked home, the sun was setting. The other girls chatted amongst themselves, but Charlie was oddly quiet. Leah also remained silent, completely focused on what she was going to say to Elijah.

Her heart hammered harder and harder as they neared the farm. Once they arrived, everyone else headed toward the house, and Elijah said goodnight, about to head home.

Leah waited until the other girls were inside, especially Charlie. Then she forced herself to speak, knowing that if she waited any longer, she'd be too afraid to say anything. "Wait. Elijah, can I talk to you for a minute? It'll be quick."

"Sure."

They stood near the porch steps. Leah knew it would be more proper for them to be on the porch, but she didn't want to risk anyone overhearing them.

"There's something I've been wanting to tell you for a long time now. And I don't know if it's proper or how to say it eloquently, so I'm just going to say it," she began.

164

Elijah smiled warmly at her, and her insides turned to pudding. "Leah, we've been friends forever. You can tell me anything."

Friends? Her heart sank. Was he on to her and trying to send her a message?

She had to say it now or else it wouldn't happen, and she'd regret it always. "Elijah, I love you. I think I always have. There, I said it." A weight lifted off her chest, but once she saw the look on his face, the full realization of the situation fell on her like a hundred bales of hay from the barn loft.

He really was in love with Charlie. He didn't even have to say it. He never saw her as anything more than a good friend.

Elijah sighed. "Leah, I'm flattered, I really am. Any man would be beyond blessed to have you as his girlfriend or wife. You're beautiful, an amazing cook, and so kind. But—"

"But you love Charlie," she finished for him.

He nodded slowly.

"I just need to know. Did you ever have feelings for me? Ever?"

He shook his head. "Honestly, you're like a sister to me. All the girls in your family are. You're all lovely. But no, Leah. I've never been in love with anyone else before Charlie."

Leah's eyes overflowed with tears. A sob escaped her lips, and she covered her mouth.

Elijah gently touched her arm, and even though she loved the sensation, she jerked away.

"I'm sorry. I hope I didn't ruin our friendship," she said.

"Of course not. I'm glad you were honest. You'll find a wonderful man one day, one who will be madly in love with you. God has someone else for you," he said. "But it's not me. In fact, it might be someone you know here. You just have to open your eyes."

She didn't want anyone else but him. The thought of marrying someone else made her sick.

Leah turned and ran off into the field, tears spilling down her cheeks and onto the grass.

***

Charlie took a deep breath and approached Esther, who was reading in her favorite chair in the living room by lamplight, a colorful and intricate quilt spread over her lap.

"Can I talk to you?" Charlie asked as everyone else headed to bed.

Esther looked up and eyed her tentatively. "Sure," she said slowly.

"At the museum, I was talking to the owner, Joe. He knows you and he knew my parents."

Esther closed her book and looked down at the quilt.

"Is that why you didn't want me to go to the museum? You didn't want me to talk to him and find out things?" Charlie asked.

Esther hesitated. "Well, yes. That was part of it," she admitted. "Actually, if I'm being honest, that was most of it. What did he tell you?"

"He mentioned a pregnancy. And that my mom did something horrible to you. What happened? Who got pregnant, and who is the baby? Or did it even survive?" Charlie asked, trying not to be too demanding. This was obviously painful for Esther, but Charlie's need for answers made her keep persisting. "Please, tell me something."

"No. I can't believe Joe told you that much." Esther's eyes reddened with tears. "That was not his place."

"He regretted telling me that much right after he said it, but I'm glad he did, because you're keeping so much from me, just like my mother. Why wouldn't she tell me anything? Why are you keeping secrets?"

"Some secrets should never be told. Did that ever occur to you, Charlie?" Esther stared at her right in the eye, and her voice dropped to a whisper. "You are not entitled to know everything, as much as you might think so. You can't force me to tell you things that I don't want to tell." Esther covered her mouth and turned away, then her tears began to flow. "I'm sorry. I didn't mean to be harsh. It's just too painful." Then she set her book down on the side table, stood, and threw the quilt on the chair.

Guilt filled Charlie as she realized how thoughtless she'd been. "I know it's hard for you… I'm sorry I was so demanding." She just wanted to know what her mother had kept from her.

Leah burst through the front door, sobbing uncontrollably, and ran upstairs.

"What happened to her?" Charlie asked.

Esther ran after her.

CHAPTER TWENTY

"Leah?" Esther asked cautiously as she followed the sound of weeping to her daughter's room. Katie, Lilly, and Ella Ruth were all sitting around her on Leah's bed, trying to console her.

"Girls, go get ready for bed. I will talk to Leah," Esther said to her daughters, and they quietly left, shutting the door.

Esther climbed up on the bed and put her arm around her eldest child. "Darling, what happened? What's wrong?"

Several moments passed as Leah continued to sob so hard, she couldn't speak. Once she finally calmed down enough to talk, she took a few deep breaths. "I... I told Elijah I'm in love with him."

"What? I had no idea you were interested in him. You certainly hid it well," Esther said, trying to remember even one time when Leah had done anything to express her interest for the man. "Oh, dear, why didn't you ever tell me? Did your sisters know?"

"No. I never told anyone. And I guess I hid it too well. I was worried maybe Ella Ruth liked him, but she just sees him as a brother. I didn't want it to come between us, you know? So I never told anyone." Leah sniffed and wiped her nose on her sleeve.

"Yes, I understand," Esther said solemnly. She understood all too well how situations could drive even the closest of sisters apart. "So, what did he say?" She guessed it hadn't gone well at all, obviously.

"He's in love with... Charlie," Leah spat, then buried her face in her pillow and sobbed some more.

"Oh. Oh, dear. Did he really say 'love'?"

By the way her daughter cried even harder, Esther took that as a yes.

She rubbed Leah's back, her mind reeling. She figured Elijah was interested in or even maybe infatuated with Charlie, but she hadn't realized how far it had gone. He was really in love with her?

"I'm so sorry, honey," Esther murmured. "Sometimes things just don't go the way we planned. God has a wonderful man for you. What about Matthew? He's obviously interested in you."

Leah shook her head. "I only want Elijah. I can't even imagine marrying anyone else. I always thought I'd marry him, but then Charlie came along and now he's in love with her."

"Did he love you before she arrived?"

"Well, no. He said he's always seen me as a sister. But maybe if she'd never come here, he would have fallen in love with me instead." Leah swatted away a tear and sat up, crossing her arms. "I wish she never would have come here."

"Leah," Esther said firmly. "That's a terrible thing to say. Even if she never had come here, Elijah even said he's always seen you as a sister. You grew up together."

"Right. But maybe I could have made him see me as someone other than the daughter of the man he works for. But now my chances have been ruined... All because of *her*."

Esther shook her head. What could she say to make Leah feel better? "God created a wonderful man to be your husband, and maybe Elijah is not that man. Maybe God has a much better match for you. I know it's hard to imagine now, but in the future, you will look back on this day and thank God He had a different plan for you."

Leah just cried harder.

Esther pulled her daughter close to her and hugged her, her heart

169

breaking at the sight of her daughter's tears. "You're a wonderful young woman, Leah. I'm so happy you're my daughter. You're kind, caring, smart, and good at so many things. You'll make your future husband a wonderful wife. You just have to trust God to lead you to the right man. And you have to be patient. Over time your heart will heal, trust me. It will get easier."

"Promise?" Leah said into her shoulder, her voice muffled.

"I promise."

***

The next morning before breakfast, Esther opened the wood stove's door and pulled out the bread Charlie had made. Well, Charlie had done the mixing. Esther had measured the ingredients and guided her through the entire process. Throughout it all, Charlie had felt so awkward, contemplating how to bring up what had happened last night so she could apologize. She wanted to say she was sorry, but also hated to bring up such a painful subject again.

"Well done, Charlotte. This looks *wonderful gut*," Esther said.

"Yes, it does look good, thanks to your help." Charlie hesitated, then added, "I'm really sorry for how insensitive I was last night. I shouldn't have pried so much. It's obviously hard for you to talk about. I'm really sorry."

Esther patted Charlie's arm. "I understand why you want answers so badly, Charlie. I forgive you."

Charlie also hoped she'd get those answers soon, but she said nothing. She'd caused the woman enough pain already.

"That bread smells so good," said Zoe, who was setting the table.

"Next time I'll let you do it on your own, *ja*?" said Esther with a grin.

170

She placed the cinnamon raisin bread on the breakfast table next to fruit, cereal and a big plate of eggs.

They could hear the sound of Irvin stomping his boots in the entryway. He swung open the kitchen door so hard it thudded against the wall. He looked at her, concern written on his face.

"Charlie, someone shredded all of Zoe's and your clothes that you left on the clothesline last night but left our clothing alone," he said, looking surprised and confused. "I don't know who would do such a thing."

Charlie knew who would do this. But she had to see it for herself. "I forgot to bring the clothes in."

She and Zoe ran out the door, wearing their last set of *Englisher* clothes. On the ground were shreds of her and Zoe's jeans, t-shirts, and sweatshirts. They looked like someone had taken a pair of scissors and mercilessly cut them up.

"Who ruined all our clothes?" Zoe cried out, voicing Charlie's thoughts. She looked like she was about to burst into tears.

Those clothes were some of the last things she had here that connected Charlie to her former life. Though she clung to the porch railing, she sank to her knees, just staring at her vandalized garments on the ground. Tears stung her eyes. Without those clothes, she had no things of her own here. Later on, she would probably think it was silly, but she felt a piece of her fade away.

Who would do this? "It's just clothing," she said, mostly to herself.

"What's done is done. There is no sense seeking revenge, seeking answers or being sad. We accept what has happened and move on." Esther touched her shoulder.

"We have dresses that will fit you. Perhaps Zoe can wear one of

Lilly's old dresses and you can wear one of Leah's," Ella Ruth offered.

Leah smiled at Charlie and Zoe. "What a good idea."

Ella Ruth put her hand on Charlie's shoulder, and she took Zoe's hand. "Come on. Let's go try some on you."

Charlie and Zoe let the two girls lead them upstairs. While Lilly and Zoe looked for a dress for Zoe to wear, Ella Ruth and Leah rummaged through Leah's closet and pulled out a few dresses. One was brown, one was dark blue, and one was pale blue. All three of them fit Charlie very well. Apparently, she and Leah were the same size.

Before she let them in to see her, Charlie looked in the mirror. She took a white prayer *kapp* off Leah's bureau and tried it on. She hoped Leah wouldn't mind, but Charlie just wanted to see and feel what it would be like on her.

Charlie stared at her reflection. She could certainly pass as a young Amish woman in these clothes. Even without the prayer *kapp,* she blended in well with the family. She hoped Alex wouldn't be able to recognize her and Zoe now if he came to look for her here.

She pulled the *kapp* off and thrust it back onto the bureau. That was wishful thinking. She was almost certain he already knew she was here. He was probably just playing mind games with her, making her wonder when he would really strike, making her fear him like the manipulative man he was.

She could play dress up all she wanted, but it was only a matter of time before he would make his final move.

Unless someone inside the community was doing these things, someone who really wanted her gone.

She pushed those thoughts away and opened the bedroom door. Leah and Ella Ruth grinned at her.

"You look very Amish. It is a very nice dress on you," said Ella Ruth.

"Thank you, Ella Ruth. And Leah, thank you so much for letting me borrow these dresses."

"You're welcome. I am glad to help," said Leah. "Let's go see Zoe's dress."

Zoe came out of Lilly's room into the hallway wearing a brown dress. She looked cute in it, Charlie had to admit. Zoe twirled like she was wearing a fine ball gown.

"I like this better than my clothes," she said, grinning. They all went downstairs and finished preparing breakfast.

CHAPTER TWENTY-ONE

Elijah took off his boots and went into the kitchen. The aroma of cinnamon greeted him. He looked around for Charlie in her usual jeans and sweatshirt, but he couldn't find her. Maybe she was still sleeping. Then he heard Zoe's laugh and he saw her in an Amish dress. Why was she wearing that?

Then he saw Charlie, the only other female in the room not wearing a prayer *kapp*. She was wearing a blue Amish dress and slicing a loaf of bread, looking beautiful. The hem of the dress brushed against her ankles gently.

Blue was often the color of Amish wedding dresses. He couldn't help but wonder what it would be like to come in after his chores every morning to her making breakfast in his house as his wife. But one thing separated them, and it was as clear as her lack of a head covering. She wore no prayer *kapp* because she was not Amish.

He wondered if she would ever join the church. Maybe she had had a nice house or apartment in the city somewhere before she came here. Why would she want to give that all up? Would she really trade it all for a life of simplicity and plainness? What about her love for the piano?

Would she ever give up all she had known for him?

"What are you doing, Mr. Hose-settler?"

Elijah looked down to see Zoe standing right in front of him. He hadn't even noticed her.

Talk about letting his guard down.

"I was just thinking. Don't mind me," he told her, shaking his head as he sat down at the table. He glanced at Charlie, who was still slicing bread.

174

She looked so focused on not chopping her fingers off that he was sure she hadn't seen him gaping at her.

Everyone sat down at the table, and Irvin gave Elijah a questioning glance. Elijah had to be more careful, no matter how he felt. He was risking his reputation, the Holts' reputation…and worst of all, he could even be shunned.

But then he realized Charlie would be completely worth it. Maybe he was acting *ferhuddled,* but he would have to be dragged away by stampeding horses before he would leave her side.

***

"You know what would be really good for dessert tonight?" Esther asked Charlie and Zoe one evening a few days later.

Esther and Charlie had spent the past two days cleaning the house with the older girls while Zoe and the younger girls were in school. Instead of vacuuming, it took Charlie hours to sweep all the floors. They'd also washed the windows and the floors, cleaned the bathrooms, and washed all the bedding by hand. But she was so grateful for the safe haven the Amish family was providing that she did it as joyfully as she could.

"What would be good for dessert?" Zoe said eagerly.

"A fruit pizza," Esther said.

Zoe made a face with her nose scrunched up. "Ew. That doesn't sound very yummy. What is that?"

Esther laughed at Zoe's reaction. "It's not like a regular pizza with cheese and tomato sauce. It has a shortbread crust with fruit and a sweet glaze on top. I have plenty of fruit, but I don't have any flour left."

Zoe reconsidered the fruit pizza, tilting her head to one side and smiling. "That actually sounds good."

"I can go down to the store and get some flour," Charlie offered.

"That would be great," Esther said. "I'll start chopping the fruit. Want to help, Zoe?"

"Sure," Zoe said and helped Esther get out the cutting board.

Charlie grabbed her coat and put on her boots and went out the door. Elijah was walking towards the house.

"I'm going to the store. Want to come?" Charlie asked.

"Sure. I'm on my break," he said and began walking next to her. She thought about how maybe this wasn't such a good idea, them being seen alone together.

But honestly, she just didn't care. She couldn't lie to herself any longer or to anyone else about how she felt about Elijah.

***

As they walked down the lane to the store, Charlie felt something happening. She felt it even more intensely than she saw the fiery shades of the leaves and felt the chilling breeze. She even saw a few snowflakes drift through the air. There was something happening between the two of them, and it had been happening for the past few weeks she'd been here, ever since the day they'd met. But at that moment she knew that whatever this was, it was at a turning point and something was about to change.

The air was completely silent other than the swaying of tree branches, their footsteps crunching in the gravel and the noise of distant passing cars. She knew he was about to tell her something important, and that's why he was taking so long to find the words.

"Charlotte, I need to tell you something."

And so it began. The apex, turning point. She knew this was where things would change. It was up to her which way the relationship would go now. She glanced at him in his suspenders, black boots, and simple clothing. His dark hair flapped in the breeze and he stared intently at his shuffling boots. He looked absolutely beautiful to her. Just plain beautiful.

She didn't want to hurt him. The burden she carried wasn't fair to him. All she had to offer was a damaged heart, unpleasant past and a younger sister to take care of.

It just wasn't fair to him. He deserved so much more. He was so genuine and unmarred…so innocent.

She realized she had not yet replied. "What do you need to tell me?"

"I know we have known each other for a short time, but I think that you, along with several others in the community, have noticed how much I…care about you," he began.

"Yes, I have. And I care about you, too." She wanted to say she loved him, but she couldn't. She knew she loved him for sure. She thought she had loved Alex, but now she could see she was only entertaining a fantasy. He never loved her. He was only using her, and she had fallen for it.

Elijah stopped walking, turned to her, and smiled. He looked relieved. She wondered if he knew from her eyes that she wanted to tell him she loved him.

He said, "I'm so glad to hear that. I also have some other things to tell you." He hesitated again.

"Look, I already basically know what you're going to say. And I can tell you right now I want the same thing. So, don't be afraid. You can just tell me. I just wanted to be straightforward with you, and I want you to be straightforward with me."

He raised his eyebrows and hooked his suspenders with his thumbs. He let out a long breath. "Well. All right, then. Well, as you know, I really

177

do care about you, more than anyone I've ever known, in fact. Honestly, I want to spend a lot more time with you, if you know what I mean." He looked at her, his eyes flickering with desire. "Really, I want to start a life with you."

And she thought he was just going to ask her out. Or to court her. Was he…proposing? Is this how the Amish proposed? A million butterflies launched in her stomach. She had been proposed to before, but this…

"Charlotte," he said, putting his hand on her arm. "I love you. I know it is an awful lot to ask, but would you consider starting a relationship with me?"

She looked at him. Her head was saying one thing and her heart argued another, but nothing came out of her mouth. Would he be willing to take care of Zoe too? They were a package deal.

"I want to court you with the intention of marriage," he explained. "And I know what that means, that you would have to join the Amish church. I was just wondering if you had considered it. You belong here, Charlotte. It is so clear. We could build a life together here. You, me and Zoe."

"You want Zoe too?" she blurted.

"Of course. I love that precious girl and you with all my heart. I want to take care of you and her for the rest of my life. I'd give anything to do that."

She could not believe what she was hearing. How could she possibly have such a great man basically asking for her hand in marriage?

"Look, I know three weeks is not a long time at all, and some people might think this is crazy, but I've never been surer of anything in my life. I love you, Charlotte, and I don't need more time to think about it, but I understand if you do," he said.

I've never met anyone kinder or more generous than him. I don't even know how to respond to respect from men. I've been mistreated so long...and he wants to take care of not only me but also Zoe? Charlie thought in disbelief.

She was waiting for him to say something else, something negative, but he didn't. That was not like him.

Where has he been my whole life? I do love him... I love him and I wish it was that simple.

"Elijah, there is something you should know about me. Certain people in my past haunt me. I wish I could forget the memories. Not to mention there are secrets my mother kept from me that are troubling me..."

"Don't let it keep us apart," he said. "I am praying for you." He brushed a strand of hair back from her face. "Do you believe God can heal you? That He can protect you?"

"I think so. I want to," was her quiet answer.

"And do you want to join the Amish church?" he asked.

"I do. But I want to make sure I do for the right reasons. Maybe I should pray about it."

"Yes, you should. I will wait for you. No matter how long it takes. I love you."

At that moment Charlie knew without a doubt this was the man she wanted to marry, and he wanted the same thing. She was so ecstatic that tears welled up in her eyes. She let them fall. She didn't care who saw her.

Elijah knew it was not proper to hug before marriage, but he forgot about that for the moment. He wrapped his big arms around her, and she let him hold her in his safe embrace. She felt so warm despite the cold weather, and she wished they could stand there together in the lane all day, holding one another. Amid the quiet of the green fields and the far-off laughter of children, she said softly to him, "Elijah, I love you too. I love you more than I even understand."

CHAPTER TWENTY-TWO

Welcome to Unity.

The sign flew by as he drove past, and Alex snickered smugly when he saw a yellow sign with a buggy on it.

He finally had arrived at the quaint little Amish town.

He had searched online for the Amish community in Unity and found the Unity Community Store address, which he'd found with his GPS. After arriving, he pulled in to the parking lot of the store to stop and get some snacks and to use the bathroom. He went in and realized immediately that it was quiet. Very quiet. With the lack of music, it was almost eerie.

After using the bathroom and collecting an armful of purchases, he was about to ask the store clerk at the register if he knew a Charlie Cooper, but then Alex saw her.

He did a double take. There she was. Finally, after three long weeks, he'd found her.

What was she wearing? She had on a long dress and her hair was completely different, but it was definitely her. He ducked behind a shelf, almost dropping his snacks. Now that he was here, this would be much easier than he thought it would be.

A man in suspenders came around the corner and walked up to her, talking to her. Alex saw the way Charlie looked at the man.

Anger boiled in his stomach.

Charlie had never looked at Alex like that. He didn't like the guy already. He didn't like the idea of him with her at all. Not one bit.

Did she already have a boyfriend? If so, that man was going to find out just how conniving and deceptive Charlotte Cooper was.

Of course, she had a boyfriend already. A woman who looked like that wouldn't stay single for long. Plenty of his police buddies had asked him to set her up with them after they had heard about the breakup, but Alex had said no. She was still his ex-fiancé and was off limits to his friends.

Alex quickly paid for his purchases while they weren't looking and rushed to his car to wait for them to leave. He watched them exit the store, the man carrying a sack of flour. They walked back up the lane. Alex followed them at a safe distance until they reached a house. They went in together, but Alex knew the man would leave before nightfall.

An Amish man would not sleep under the roof of an unwed woman his age. That was one thing Alex knew about the Amish, besides the fact that they dressed weird and refused electricity. Had she joined the Amish? Is that why she was dressed like them?

Either way, the boyfriend would leave sooner or later, but it didn't matter. Alex could see several people moving around in the house. He wouldn't be able to get her alone tonight. He would have to wait until there was no one else around.

Alex opened a bag of pretzels and grinned, his teeth glinting in the moonlight. In the meantime, Alex could think of some ways to keep himself occupied. He knew another fact about the Amish: they were very nonviolent, and they usually didn't lock their doors. He also knew that when they were robbed, they did not seek justice.

"Vengeance is mine, says the Lord..." he muttered.

That could come in handy for a guy like him.

***

"You were right, Esther. That fruit pizza was good!" Zoe exclaimed later that evening, rubbing her full belly.

"When it comes to food, I am almost always right," Esther said with a smile.

"And you're always right when it comes to advice," Ella Ruth added.

Esther chuckled and began clearing the plates. "Hey, what took you two so long at the store, anyway? Did they run out of flour and have to order more?" she asked jokingly.

"No, we were just talking and lost track of time," Charlie explained, glancing at Elijah, who sat at the table with them. He gave her a heart-stopping, crooked grin.

Esther stopped gathering the plates for a moment to give Charlie a knowing look. She said nothing.

"Well," Elijah said, breaking the awkward silence. "I should turn in. It's an early day tomorrow, as usual. Goodnight, everyone."

"I will walk you to the door," Charlie said quietly and followed him. Ella Ruth and Esther exchanged questioning glances, wondering what was really going on between the two of them.

"Remember what I told you, Charlie," Elijah said gently when they reached the seclusion of the mud room. "Think about it."

"I will." She smiled up at him. "Thank you for being so honest with me. I have a lot to think over."

"I anxiously await your answer."

Warmth flooded through her from the look he gave her, especially when he gently touched her cheek.

They wished each other goodnight, and he went home. For a moment she watched him walk down the driveway then went back into the kitchen.

"*Maam*, why don't you let us clean up tonight? Go rest or read. We can take care of this," Leah said.

Esther rubbed her lower back. "That would be very nice. Thank you, girls. Goodnight," she said, and she went to her room.

Leah looked at Zoe, Lilly, Katie, and Ella Ruth, who were about to wash the dishes. "You girls go on up to bed. Charlie and I can clean up by ourselves, right, Charlie?"

Charlie looked up. "Sure."

The girls said thank you and went upstairs, all except Leah.

"And then there were two," Charlie muttered, knowing something was going on.

"I wanted some time to talk to you alone," Leah said.

"I was wondering what all that was about," Charlie said, knowing exactly what Leah would talk to her about.

"I know Elijah likes you. Maybe even loves you. He's always been so serious about the store, so he never dated. I'm just worried because you're not Amish and he would not be able to marry you unless you join the Amish church."

"I know. And it certainly has been weighing on my mind, and tonight we talked about it. I wonder if this is the life I am meant to choose. There are some things I am afraid of."

"If it is God's will, you will have the strength to live this way. But you also have to think about the faith part of the Amish ways. Can you love the Lord and live to serve Him?"

"Yes. I mean…I don't know," Charlie stammered. "I just want to do it for the right reasons. This is such a big decision and commitment. It's for life."

184

"I love you, Charlie; we all do. But I am just watching out for you. If you don't think you can join the Amish church, I would encourage you to end the romance between you and Elijah. You would do it if you truly cared about Elijah, or else he could be shunned."

Charlie stared at the floor, feeling ashamed. She could never live with herself if she caused such an honorable man to be shunned. How many people thought the same thing as Leah?

"Have you already heard this speech before from someone else?" Leah asked.

"Oh, yes, I have. And I am sure many want to give it to me, but they remain silent. I appreciate your concern, though. And I really will think about it. It is a hard decision to make. And it also tremendously affects Zoe, too. Although I think she would like to live the Amish life."

Leah smiled. "I think so, too."

After they finished cleaning up, Charlie said, "Well, I am going to bed. Goodnight and thank you so much for talking with me."

"Any time. Goodnight," Leah replied, and they both went upstairs.

Charlie meandered up to her bedroom where Zoe was already sound asleep. Charlie read the Bible for a while then sat by the window. She looked up at the plethora of stars, wondering how God made all of them. There were thousands and thousands, way beyond what her tiny mind could comprehend. She stared, amazed. Surely, such a powerful God could heal her heart and protect her and Zoe.

"Dear Lord, I know it has been a while since I have really talked to you. You know I love Elijah, and to be with him I would have to join the Amish church. I want to join, but I want to do it for the right reasons, and I want the best for Zoe. I think you have shown us that this is where you

185

want us. We could belong here and build a life here.

"Elijah truly does love me. I want to say yes to him, but there is one thing that is holding me back. I am afraid Alex will come for me, and it is so hard for me to trust Elijah, even though he is such a good man, because Alex made me afraid to ever trust again. God, please show me if Elijah is as genuine as he seems. Please let me let go of my past and stop remembering how Alex treated me. Please show me what to do about being with Elijah, joining the church and taking care of Zoe. And most of all, please protect us from Alex. I know he may already be here, but please, if it is possible, let Zoe and me blend in enough so that he won't recognize us. And if he does, please, even if everything else falls apart, please let Zoe and me stay together."

CHAPTER TWENTY-THREE

On Saturday afternoon, the Holt household went to the Singing. Usually Singings were on Sunday afternoons but this one was scheduled on Saturday due to a possible snowstorm coming on Sunday.

Everyone was asked to read a story or poem at the Singing, and Charlie looked through her Bible for something. Zoe, Charlie and all the Holt girls took a pony wagon to the house where the Singing was to be held. Everyone else took a buggy. Their pony wagon was like a buggy except it was open, with no roof. Cars flew by them, and mostly every one of their drivers waved politely. The girls talked with each other as Charlie leaned back on the pony wagon seat, thinking how content she was.

They rode by a huge hole the size of a pond. Ella Ruth told Charlie it was an old manure pit they wanted to make into a pond for cutting ice to keep their food cold. While Charlie was wondering if that was sanitary, Ella Ruth said they also planned to skate on it and to go sledding down the huge hills when the snow came.

They arrived, and the horse walked right up to his post. The rest of the Holt household, including Elijah, got there soon after, and they all went inside.

Everyone got a song book that had mostly English songs, which Charlie was happy about. First, they each read a poem or story, but when it was Charlie's turn, she explained that all she had with her was her Bible, and she read Psalm 96. Ella Ruth read a funny story about a princess who couldn't cry. As each person took turns, many poems were read. When everyone was done reading, they began singing.

This was how it worked: one of them would choose a song and say the song number out loud. Everyone would find the page, and the person who picked the song had to start singing it alone, then everyone would join in, like in church. This happened at the beginning of every verse. That is how they all started and ended in the same key without instruments. When it was Charlie's turn, she led all the others in song. She chose "Take My Life and Let It Be" because it was the only one she knew. The group sang it beautifully.

She glanced at Elijah, and she felt a physical pain in her chest, guilty for not telling him about Alex. He had the right to know everything, but she couldn't bring herself to tell him.

But she had to do it. It had to be done. It was time, before their relationship progressed any further. Especially if Alex was in the area, Elijah had to know.

She stopped singing.

Ella Ruth noticed and leaned close to Charlie as everyone else continued singing. "Are you all right?"

"No...I think I'm coming down with something. I think I'll walk back to the house. It's not far," Charlie whispered.

"All right. Would you like me to come with you?"

"No, thank you. I'll be fine. I'll see you all later." Charlie quietly stood and walked out, leaving Zoe with the others. Zoe could return to the house with them later.

Charlie walked back to Esther's house and ran up to her room. She sat on her bed and wondered why she was hurting so much. The only other pain she had known like this was when her parents died.

All she wanted at that moment was for them to hold her and tell her everything would be okay. She wanted to drive home and be able to find them there.

But she knew no one was home at the apartment. Guilt swept over her again for leaving her father's body at the scene of the car accident. Had there been a funeral for him already? She wished she hadn't just left him there like that, but she'd done what she thought was best for Zoe at the time by leaving so quickly.

Charlie prayed for God to comfort her, and she prayed for the right words to tell Elijah. Would he reject her when he found out that she was being hunted by an angry, violent man?

Her past could cost her the one man she had ever truly loved.

***

It's now or never, Matthew told himself as the singing ended. As always, Leah looked lovely in her blue dress. As people gathered up hymnals and stood, stretching out their legs, Matthew made his way towards Leah.

"Hello, Leah," he got out. He twisted his hat in his hands. Could he finally do it today?

"How are you, Matthew?" Leah asked, her eyes twinkling. Did she have any idea how lovely she was? The way her hair peeked out from under her *kapp* simply intrigued him.

"Very well. I came over here to ask you..."

Why couldn't he just say it? He desperately wanted to but somehow couldn't force any air out of his lungs. He felt as though his tongue was dysfunctional.

Leah looked around, brows furrowed. "Where's Charlotte?"

"She went home. I think she's sick," Ella Ruth said softly.

"Oh, no. I hope she feels better. We should go make sure she's okay." Leah turned to Matthew. "What did you need to ask me?"

His stomach felt like it was sinking. He couldn't do it. "I had noticed she had left, and I was just wondering if Charlotte was all right." It was not a lie; he had seen her go and had been concerned.

"Thank you, Matthew. I'm sure she's all right. If you will excuse me, I have to go. Have a nice day." She smiled at him, gathered her things and left with her family.

Another opportunity wasted. I must look like a fool.

***

Charlie woke up when she heard the downstairs door open to the sound of stomping boots and chattering voices. She looked around, realizing she had fallen asleep while she was praying.

She became fully alert when she heard Elijah's voice and felt a surge of anxiety.

Charlie would tell him everything tonight after dinner. She went into the bathroom and splashed cold water on her face, trying to make the redness from crying fade.

"What's done is done," she told herself. "It's time to move on with my life. Just like the Amish do."

She went downstairs, and the others greeted her.

"Are you feeling better? Ella Ruth said you felt like you were getting sick," Esther said.

"Yes, I feel a little better. I slept for a while and that helped." It was the truth. She had felt terrible…with guilt and anxiety.

"That is *wonderful gut.* Let's start supper then," she said.

***

After dinner, Elijah announced that he was heading home.

Charlie wanted to run away and hide, but she followed him to the door. "May I talk to you in private for a minute?"

"Sure. Let's go outside," he said. They put on their shoes and coats and walked out to the barn.

"So. What is it that you wanted to talk to me about?" Elijah asked.

Charlie took a deep breath, trying to calm her racing heart. She glanced up at him and he gave her a smile.

It would help if he wasn't so good looking, Charlie thought to herself.

She forced herself to begin. "I have to tell you something about my past."

When she hesitated, he said, "It's all right. Just tell me."

She prayed for strength. "All right. Before I met you, I met a man named Alex, and now he is after me. I am afraid if he finds me, he might hurt me or Zoe. And I believe he knows where I am."

"Why is that?"

"Someone cut up my clothes. Someone painted the words *she should leave* on Irvin's buggy, and someone flashed a light into my window when I first came here. Either someone in this community is trying to scare me, or it could be Alex, even though it's not his style. I think he would have attacked me by now if it was him. Even if it's not him, he could be looking for me."

"Why didn't you tell me before?"

"I couldn't. If I told you that I thought Alex found out where I have been hiding, I was afraid you or someone else here would send me away."

Elijah looked her in the eyes with concern. "No, we'd never send you away, especially when you need us most. Why is he after you, Charlie?"

191

"I sold the engagement ring he gave to me. I don't know why it is so important to him, but he will stop at nothing until he gets it back. I can't get it back from the man I sold it to. I tried, but he broke up with his fiancée and sold it to a pawn shop. It's long gone. I don't know what to do." She covered her face with her hands. Voicing her problem aloud made it seem even more real. "He's a cop, but he's not a good person. He could hurt me or Zoe. He's already hurt me before. I need your help." She reached out to him.

"He's hurt you before? What did he do to you?" Fire flickered in Elijah's eyes.

Charlie's hand instinctively went to her neck. "He tried to choke me once, but I think it was just to scare me."

Elijah's hands turned to angry fists. "How dare he. How could anyone ever hurt you?" He reached up and gently touched her face.

She leaned into his touch. "But if it's not him doing these strange attacks, someone in this community is trying to scare me into leaving. I think it's one of the men here, maybe Matthew or Andrew or Luke," Charlie said.

"My friends are good men. They'd never do that."

"I heard Matthew talking about me on the building day at the church. He said some of the men were talking about how they didn't want me here."

"That's true, but they'd never do that."

"Then who did?"

"I don't know. Look, you must be scared and confused. I'll do everything I can to protect you from this guy."

"Elijah, I hate to accuse your friends, but I really had to tell you what

I thought. I'm sorry I didn't tell you about my past sooner."

He slowly nodded. "I have to admit, they have not been acting like themselves lately, but I still don't think they'd ever do anything like this. You don't know them, but I've known them for years. We'll figure out who's doing this. And in the meantime, I will do everything I can to protect you."

CHAPTER TWENTY-FOUR

Sunday morning in Unity was bright and sunny, but also chilly. The Amish milled into church as was the norm on Sunday mornings, greeting each other with holy kisses, which no longer fazed Zoe or Charlie. To everyone's relief, there was only a light dusting of snow instead of the possible storm that could have hit Unity. Traveling anywhere in a buggy in a snowstorm was not ideal.

They sat on their backless benches, and the service began. After singing hymns in German from the *Ausbund,* the speaker began.

"This morning's message is about forgiveness," Irvin began, looking at all of them.

Charlie saw Alex's face in her mind. She wished she could forgive him and forget all about him and what he had put her through. She wished she'd never met him or let him hurt her. She regretted her relationship with him and how it prevented her from trusting Elijah. She heard his threats in her mind, felt his hands around her neck.

She looked over at Elijah, who gave her a small smile in return, which surprised her. She felt her mood lift when she saw that smile. She hoped it was a sign that in time he would fully accept and forgive what she had done. She knew it was the Amish way, and she hoped it wouldn't hinder his love for her.

She wondered how long it would take for her to completely heal. She had thought Alex loved her, but in the end, he had only hurt her physically and verbally.

She loved Elijah even though she hadn't let go of the pain from Alex's abuse.

Then there was her mother's shunning. If Charlie was completely honest with herself, she still couldn't fully forgive the community—especially Esther—for shunning her mother, not to mention being frustrated with her for withholding secrets that Charlie felt she had the right to know.

There was no way she could move on until she learned the truth from Esther—then, Charlie hoped she could forgive her.

And now she'd hurt Elijah by accusing his friends and by not telling him about her past until yesterday. She should have trusted him with her secret. How long would it take for him to forgive her?

Charlie felt her eyes sting from unshed tears. She would not allow herself to cry in front of everyone. She looked for the quickest, quietest way out. Charlie stood and hurried past people. Many people looked at her with concern. Embarrassment heated her cheeks and made her want to cover her face, but she pushed on towards the back door of the church. She ran down the stairs and stepped out into the cool of the morning.

Elijah flung open the church door and walked up to Charlie. "What's wrong?"

"I'm fine. I just have a lot on my mind. Things I have to deal with. I'm going back to the house, ok? I'll see you all later. Watch Zoe for me," she said and turned away before he saw her tears.

As Charlie began to run, the sun effortlessly tossed light on the country fields behind her. She heard Elijah say something, but she did not turn back. She ran all the way to the house. She ran into the barn and leaned against the wall. She wished more than anything that she had her parents to lean on. She missed them so much it hurt. If her mom had been here, she would have given Charlie advice that would make everything seem clear. They would have sat at the piano together, and she would have cried on Mom's shoulder, and Mom would have rubbed her back. Then, when Charlie's tears slowed, they would have played a song to cheer her up.

Instead, she was alone. Charlie's knees gave out, and her back slid down the coarse barn wall until she plopped down onto a pile of hay.

She was burdened with memories, grieving her parents' death, feeling guilty for abandoning her father's body, wondering how to provide for Zoe, and confused about Elijah, and terrified Alex would track her down. Her hand flew to her throat, and for a moment she felt like she couldn't breathe.

She let herself stay in that one spot as she cried in anger and frustration. She picked up handfuls of hay and let it fall through her fingers repeatedly.

No matter what, she silently promised herself, *even if other people leave me or let me down, I will not lose Zoe. I will always take care of her, no matter the cost.*

She heard something. A crash coming from inside the house. What was that?

On complete alert, she choked back her tears, and peeked over the cobweb-draped windowsill. She stared intently at the house windows, watching for any slight movement...There. A dark figure crept past one of the bedroom windows. No one was supposed to be home. They were all at church.

She gripped the windowsill, her fingernails digging into the wood of the barn window. Fear clenched her heart, which felt like it had fallen into her stomach. Was it Alex? Or some thief?

Suddenly, the back door opened and the hooded figure, dressed in all black, skirted around the house and started coming towards the barn. She had to hide, but where? Her eyes frantically searched the barn. Then she realized what she was sitting on: a large pile of hay. She burrowed herself into the pile as deep as she could. She covered herself with the hay and stayed as still as possible. She squeezed her eyes shut and waited.

She heard feet stepping into the barn and walking down the aisle between the stalls filled with cows, pigs, and horses. The footfalls sounded ominous among the innocent noises of the barn animals. They echoed through the barn like thunder.

Please don't let him find me, Charlie silently pleaded, her heart racing. She squeezed a handful of hay even though it felt like it was piercing her palm. She could barely breathe with the straw blocking her face. Her lungs burned from lack of oxygen.

She heard the figure searching the barn, knocking things over. She wondered if the Amish ever kept cash in their barns, and if that was what the intruder was looking for.

She felt a tickle in her nose, and instantly she knew she was about to sneeze. She remembered that someone had once told her if you say or think the word "pineapple" when you feel like you are going to sneeze, it will stop you from sneezing. She had always thought that sounded ridiculous, but she tried it. She thought the word "pineapple" over and over, and miraculously, the tickle in her nose faded, and she didn't sneeze. She prayed a silent thank you. That could have ended horribly.

She realized the intruder had moved from one end of the barn to the other and now was walking towards the shelf next to her. She heard the shuffling of things being moved around on the shelf next to her, and she

197

held her breath.

She heard the sound of metal scraping metal, and another box being opened. She heard a quiet chuckle, and the box was slammed shut. The intruder began to walk out of the barn, and there was silence. A few painstakingly long moments later, she heard the distant sound of an engine, which faded as the vehicle drove away.

Charlie jumped up and pushed all the hay off her, terrified and baffled. What had just happened? If that man was Alex, why wasn't he looking for her? He had told her he needed the ring back as soon as possible. Would he really waste time stealing from the Amish before he came for her? If he knew she was here, it was a small town and he could easily figure out where she was staying. And he could easily attack her and take her.

By the sound of the chuckle she had heard when the intruder opened the box, he had clearly found what he was looking for, but she couldn't tell by the sound of it if it had been Alex's voice or not. But if the man was Alex, it wouldn't be long until he came for her.

Tonight, since the Amish rarely locked their doors, she would be sure to lock them after everyone fell asleep. She sank back down onto the hay, hugging her knees to her chest, wondering how things had become so complicated. She wondered if and how she should tell Irvin and Esther about the robbery.

Time slipped by. She wasn't sure how long she stayed in the barn, but when she heard the staccato of the horse's hooves on the lane and the creaking of the buggy, she willed herself to stand.

She pushed herself to her feet and walked out into the yard, towards the buggy, determined to confront Esther about the secrets she was

198

keeping, once and for all. And this time, she would demand an answer. Then she'd tell her and Irvin about the robbery.

"Esther? Esther!"

CHAPTER TWENTY-FIVE

Esther had heard her name called like that before. That was how Irvin had sounded right after Charlie had called them for the first time, saying her parents had died. She heard the distress in Charlie's voice now, and Esther knew something was wrong.

"Aunt Esther, I need you to tell me the truth. The whole truth. This time, I'm demanding answers," Charlie said, marching toward her.

"What's going on?" the children inside the buggy asked.

"Nothing that concerns you. Now go on inside the house." Esther took a breath and steadied herself. She stepped on the grass. She had always known this day would come. No matter how much she had tried to avoid the secret from coming out, she always knew she couldn't hide it forever.

Now she only prayed no one else would find out. She didn't want anyone overhearing besides Irvin, who already knew.

"Let's take a walk," she said, thankful the children were going inside.

They started walking along the path that led to the woods behind the house.

"I will tell you my side of the story, Charlie. The whole story," Esther told her.

"Thank you," Charlie said.

"There's no easy way to break this to you, so I'm just going to say it. After Joanna left to marry Greg, you know she was shunned, so I had to visit her in secret in Portland. That's when I was attacked and raped. I became pregnant"—Esther paused—"with you and your sister... Leah."

Charlie stopped walking and pivoted towards Esther. "Pregnant with me? And my sister?"

"Leah is your twin, and I am your biological mother."

Esther could see that Charlie didn't know how to handle this news. Esther had expected this. Charlie had grown up thinking Joanna and Greg were her biological parents, and now she was slammed with the truth. Everything she had thought she knew had been a lie.

"That can't be true. My parents would never lie to me for my whole life. My mom and I were best friends. I don't believe you," Charlie said and started to walk away.

"Remember when you first got here, and I found you crying behind the barn? Remember I told you I had also asked God why I had to lose what I loved most? You didn't believe me then either," Esther said in a quiet but strong voice.

Charlie stopped walking.

"I was talking about when I lost you," Esther said.

Charlie whirled around. "But why didn't my parents ever tell me? Why and how did you lose me? Why didn't you keep both of us? Wait a second… Leah and I don't even look alike," Charlie argued, throwing her hands in the air.

"You are fraternal twins. You are both very different from the other."

"So…why was I adopted by my parents but not Leah?" Charlie demanded.

"I'm getting to that part. I had to stay with Joanna until you and Leah were born so no one would know I had been raped. I wasn't married to Irvin yet, and I was so ashamed and embarrassed. I was a pregnant, unmarried Amish woman. I didn't want people to get the wrong idea. I had told everyone here that I was visiting relatives for a while. I was afraid that if people knew, they would pity me and treat me differently. I was afraid Irvin wouldn't want me, but that was never true. All I wanted was to get married and start a family, and I was afraid that the truth of my past would have ruined that.

"Joanna offered to take care of you and Leah temporarily until after I was married, then I was going to take you both back and tell everyone I adopted you. They were unable to conceive a child of their own at the time. That's why I was surprised when I found out about Zoe. I didn't even know she'd been pregnant. She must have been a miracle baby. Anyway, when you were born the doctor told us you'd need several surgeries to heal your malformed ankle, possibly until you would be about seven or eight years old. We don't have medical insurance and they have the best specialists in Maine at the Portland hospital, so we decided it would be best for you to stay with Greg and Joanna so you could get the best medical care for your ankle.

"Before my wedding, I couldn't keep the truth from Irvin any longer, and I told him what had happened, but he still loved me and married me anyway. We got married just a few weeks after you were born. After the wedding, I took Leah back, but you stayed with Joanna and Greg."

"You split us up?" Charlie asked.

"We all agreed it would be best for you. Joanna and Greg adopted you. We took Leah home, and we let everyone believe that she was adopted, that her mother gave Leah to us to take care of because she couldn't. We never told anyone the truth. And because Joanna was shunned, no one was allowed to speak of her, so no one asked any questions. Many people assumed your mother had given her to us to raise. I think even the elders suspected it, and that I had been communicating with Joanna about the baby even though she was shunned. No one ever seemed to mind, though, considering the circumstances. They looked the other way. I mean, they thought I was taking in her child, and we are called to care for those in need. So, I never was shunned for speaking to my sister, even though I could have been.

"When you had your final surgery at eight years old, I desperately wanted you back, but Joanna and Greg refused, of course. They'd adopted you, after all. You were all so close, and they didn't want to uproot you and turn your world upside down by sending you here. I don't blame them. However, I was bitter. I felt like I had the right to have you back, and that they should give you back to me, but they felt as though they should have you. It caused a huge argument between us, and after that, we never spoke again."

"I'm sorry. I had no idea," Charlie said, shaking her head in disbelief. "So that's why you never spoke to each other again. It all makes sense now."

Esther nodded. "Also, Joanna had hated giving Leah back to me so much that she couldn't bring herself to speak to me or write to me for years. Then, one day, she came to my door trying to apologize. By then you and Leah were around nine years old, and she was home with me that day. It must have been about a year after your last surgery. I did not want Leah to meet Joanna and start asking questions, and I definitely didn't want her to see you. I was afraid of losing Leah again. So, I had to do the hardest thing I have ever done. I had to turn my own sister away at my front door." Esther remembered the piercing pain she had felt in her heart as she had watched Joanna walk away in anguish.

Charlie's face paled. "I remember. I was in the barn looking at sheep while she went to talk to you. She came back after a few minutes saying you had refused to speak to her, and we left."

Esther anticipated Charlie would start yelling in anger, but the younger woman did not. Instead, Charlie looked at Esther, clearly shocked. She held a hand to her heart. "I can't believe this. My whole life I have been lied to," she said, her eyes wandering to the forest. "Why didn't they tell me?"

"Because of the shunning," Esther said. "You would never have been able to meet me. People would have found out the truth about what had happened to me, and my lies, and I didn't want anyone to know. That's why your family never told you about me. She was protecting me and you. And I'm sure your mom was hurt too deeply to ever tell you the truth."

Charlie briefly closed her eyes, then looked at Esther. "Why...?" Charlie began to ask, then broke down. Esther pulled her daughter into her arms and held Charlie as they wept. After several minutes, Charlie pulled away and wiped her nose on her sleeve. "How did you ever overcome it?"

Esther gave her a sad smile. "I was broken for a long time, but the Lord has healed me and made me stronger. I prayed constantly and grew closer to Him by reading the Word."

Charlie nodded. "Maybe He'll do that for me, too."

"He will if you ask Him to, but it is a process."

"I think He already has begun."

"Me too. I can see already how much you have changed for the better since you arrived. You are healing too. I am so deeply sorry for hurting your mother, Charlie," Esther said.

"I forgive you. You were in a difficult situation," Charlie said sincerely. "And I'm so sorry for how I treated you... I thought you had been the only one in the wrong. I had no idea what my mother did to you. I should have never been so insensitive. I'm so sorry."

"I forgive you, my dear. You didn't know the whole story."

Charlie nodded and wiped away a tear.

"Charlie, there is one more thing. No one can know about this. Joe at the museum knows though, of course. He was like a second father to Irvin and me, and my parents wouldn't have understood. I trusted him with my secret, and it wasn't his place to tell you what he did."

"I think he assumed I knew," Charlie said.

"What's done is done. I'm not angry with him." Esther sighed. "It's for the best."

"What about Leah? Does she know?"

"Well, she knows now. When you arrived, she realized that both of you were about the same age. She confronted me, and I told her everything. I think most people always assumed she was Joanna's baby, and I was worried someone would accidentally let it slip and she'd hear about it. We told her when she was young that Joanna was her biological mother and we'd taken her in when her mother couldn't take care of her. We hadn't told her any more than that until after you got here, when she'd figured out you were twins. All these years, I wanted to tell her she's my biological daughter, but I couldn't. It killed me, year after year. But to tell her that meant I'd have to tell her about the rape. I thought it would be too painful to tell her. Irvin is her true father anyway. He's the one who's always been there for her. Now I'm actually so glad I've told her the whole truth. I felt such a burden lifted from my heart, and it wasn't nearly as painful as I thought it was going to be. She was angry and upset at first, but now I think she's accepted it. But you must promise not to tell anyone." Esther said. "I don't want anyone else to know."

"I promise. Also, there is something I have to tell you. On her deathbed, my mother made me promise to tell you that she was sorry about what happened and that she forgave you. I had no idea what she was talking about at the time, but now I understand. I'm sorry I never told you before now. I guess it's because I was holding a grudge against you for shunning her. I'm sorry."

Esther cried tears of joy. "All is forgiven. Oh, I'm so glad to hear that. All this time I wondered if she hated me when she died or if she missed me at all. You have no idea how much that means to me to hear you say that."

Charlie nodded. "I know she loved you."

"I loved her too."

"I need time to think about all this," Charlie said. "Alone. Thank you for telling me the whole story. I'm going to take a walk."

Charlie walked away towards the woods. Esther turned around and walked inside the house. She needed to tell Irvin that Charlie knew the truth.

CHAPTER TWENTY-SIX

Storm clouds loomed overhead as Charlie walked. Now that she thought about it, she had always suspected something had been off in her family, especially as a teen. Then again, maybe many teenagers felt that way.

It wasn't that she didn't look like her parents or Zoe. They had looked enough alike, since they had still been related. Charlie had just always had the feeling that there was a lot more to her story than she knew, and it had started when Mom had first brought her here.

And now she knew. She had been deceived her whole life, even if it had been in her best interest. Dad hadn't been her biological father, but he'd been a wonderful father to her. Her biological father was a terrible person, someone she'd never meet, nor did she want to.

How could her parents have kept all this from her?

What if she had been raised Amish? How different would she be now?

Would she have been married to Elijah by now if she had grown up here?

Charlie shook her head. This was not about him. This was about her. Her and Leah.

Why had Leah been raised Amish and not Charlie? What if it had been the other way around, and Charlie had been raised Amish? Charlie wondered what Leah would be like if she had been raised in an *Englisher* home.

Charlie was not very close to Leah. In fact, she'd felt as though something separated them, preventing them from connecting. This must have been it. Until soon after Charlie had arrived, Leah had thought she was Joanna's daughter, given up by a mother who couldn't cope. Leah must have started wondering why Joanna had chosen to keep Charlie instead of herself when they were babies. How must she have felt when she'd found out from Esther that they were twins? She must have felt so confused and hurt that she'd been lied to. It must have been a lot to take in. Leah probably felt like Charlie was trying to push her way into the family—or worse—take Leah's place as Esther's eldest daughter. No wonder she had been cold towards Charlie.

They were not close, but could they be? It would be better than letting it weigh down her heart.

Now Charlie finally realized that her mother hadn't been the only victim in all this. Leah was a victim too. Yes, Esther had hurt Mom, but Mom had also deeply hurt Esther. Charlie shook her head. She should have never been so insensitive to Esther, resenting her for thinking she'd been so cruel to Mom, when in reality Mom had betrayed Esther. Esther had endured so much pain… Charlie admired how her faith remained strong even after everything that had happened to her. She hoped to have faith that strong one day.

But there was a more urgent matter at hand. She needed to tell Esther and Irvin that they had been robbed.

***

Esther walked to the barn, figuring she'd find her husband there, taking care of the animals. She walked in to see Irvin tenderly brushing his horse, Penny. How she loved that man. He was so kind and gentle, even to his animals. Even after all these years, seeing him stroking his horse made her heart flutter like she was a teenager again, and she smiled.

Then her smile faded as she remembered why she was here and what she had to tell him.

"Irvin…"

He looked up. "What's wrong?"

"I told Charlotte the truth."

"All of it?"

"All of it. Now she and Leah both know."

Irvin lowered the brush and faced her. "We knew this day would come. We couldn't keep it from her forever.

"I asked Charlotte not to say anything to anyone else. I don't think she will. She just kept asking so many questions… I knew I couldn't keep it from her much longer. I just hope no one else finds out."

Irvin closed the gap between them with quick strides and wrapped his arms around her. Amish couples usually didn't show physical affection outside of their home, but no one was around.

"I've thought about Charlotte every day for over twenty-four years. I've wanted to hold and comfort her like this so many times as I have with Leah. I've been wanting to tell Charlotte I'm her mother for so long, but it didn't go the way I'd imagined it at all." Knowing she'd been responsible for Charlie's tears prevented her from treasuring the moment in the way she had imagined. "I thought it would be a happier occasion. And now that she knows—"

"It'll be all right," Irvin whispered into her ear as if reading her thoughts. "Even if others find out."

"I pray it never comes to that."

"There's something else. Leah apparently has been in love with Elijah for some time, and she told him, but he is in love with Charlotte. That's what he told her."

"I had no idea she felt that way about him." Irvin pulled away and held her at arm's length. "Esther, do you think maybe it was a bad idea to let Charlie come here? Elijah could be shunned if he lets it go too far."

"The Lord calls us to help those in need, and she was in need. She just lost her parents. How could we have turned her away? Besides, you know how badly I wanted to meet her."

"I know. But her being here is causing so many problems. Some of the men feel uneasy about an *Englisher* staying in our home, in our community. And she's been pestering you about what happened with you and Joanna, and I know that was hard for you. And now Elijah's fallen for her. What next?" Irvin walked toward the barn doors to head back inside the house, and Esther fell in step beside him.

"All I know is that I believe God wants her here," Esther said. "We just have to trust in His plan. People will come around. She's a wonderful young woman. They just need to see that."

***

Charlie trudged back into the house. She heard the shuffling of feet as the girls scurried around, removing the black *kapps* they wore over their white ones to church. Some of the children sat down on the floor with puzzles, and some began to read in the living room.

Irvin followed suit, taking a book off the shelf and sitting by the window. Esther came in from putting some leftovers out in the cold on the porch. She made eye contact and gave a sad smile to Charlie.

"There's something I need to tell you. I need to talk to you and Irvin. Privately."

"Let's go in our room, Irvin," Esther said, and the three of them went inside the couple's bedroom.

Irvin sighed. "We are sorry we had to keep this from you. We both knew we would have to tell you and Leah one day. But you won't tell anyone else, will you?"

"No, of course not. I am so grateful for you taking me and Zoe in," Charlie said.

"Thank you. No one else must ever know," Esther said. "I lied by telling everyone Leah was Joanna's daughter. Even so, I don't want people to know how you and Leah were conceived. I would be embarrassed, and I don't want anyone to see me differently or pity me." Her eyes welled up with tears. "I just don't want anyone else to know what happened to me all those years ago."

Charlie rested her hand on Esther's arm. "It's not your fault that you were raped," she whispered.

Esther nodded, letting a few tears fall. "I know that now. But I still don't want anyone to know." Irvin wrapped his arm around her shoulders.

"I have something to tell you. When I came here today and was sitting in the barn, someone was in the house. They came into the barn after and I am pretty sure they robbed you. I was hiding, but I heard them open a metal box," Charlie said.

Esther gasped. "No."

Irvin said, "That was where I kept my cash for emergencies. But it doesn't matter. It was really God's money, not mine. The Lord gives and the Lord takes away."

Charlie marveled at his calm reaction. Who knew how much money had been taken from him? "I think I know who robbed you," Charlie said. "The same person who destroyed my clothes. I think it was Alex."

"It doesn't matter. We don't need to seek answers or press charges.

211

What's done is done," Esther said gently.

"Don't you want to know who broke into your home?" Charlie said with disbelief.

"No. What good would that do?" Irvin said.

"It might help catch the guy and prevent someone else from getting robbed or hurt," Charlie exclaimed. "Why don't we call the police?" If Alex was robbing houses, that meant he could be arrested, and then Charlie and Zoe would be safe.

"We will not go to the police. The Lord calls us to forgive and forget," Irvin said. "It is the Amish way."

"It could have been some thief, or it could have been Alex. He may have decided to break into Amish homes before coming after me. And I am afraid he will take revenge on me by either hurting us or trying to get the state to take Zoe away from me. I told him I can't get the ring back, but he may just want revenge anyway. What will we do if he comes here?"

"The Amish are non-violent. We will not protect ourselves against someone intruding in our home. We just let them take our money and leave. As we said, we believe whatever happens is God's will and we should turn the other cheek instead of engaging in self-defense," Irvin said.

Charlie could not believe her ears.

"We have guns, but we only use them for hunting. We believe that to use guns for any purpose other than hunting game is a sin," he replied. "Taking a human life, even in self-defense, is out of the question."

"So, if Alex barges into this house in the middle of the night and takes me and Zoe, you wouldn't defend us?" Charlie cried.

"It would be against our beliefs. God will protect you and all of us if

212

it is His will. We still haven't told the children about this. We don't want to frighten them."

"He is only after me. I don't think he'd hurt any of you. Hopefully, he's not that cruel," Charlie said quietly. Charlie took a step back, distraught. She would have to protect herself. But how?

"I am truly sorry about your predicament, Charlie. We will pray earnestly for your safety, and you are still welcome here. But your future is up to the Lord, and there is nothing we can do but pray. We must have faith," Irvin said.

"You will stay, won't you?" Esther asked.

"Yes." As tears blurred her vision, she looked downwards. She noticed Esther's and Irvin's hands. They wore no wedding rings. She realized none of the Amish wore rings. She had noticed their bare, work-worn hands before but had never really thought about it until now.

"Why don't you wear wedding rings?" Charlie asked.

"The Amish do not wear any sort of jewelry, especially wedding rings, because it brings too much attention to the body, and it may cause the wearer to be prideful. Besides, we do not need rings to symbolize our love and commitment. Amish marriages last. As you know, there is no such thing as Amish divorce," Irvin told her.

Charlie looked at her own hand. Her entire life she had looked forward to receiving a wedding ring.

She wondered if she would ever wear one, and if that would be a good thing.

When she went to her room the snow came, and Charlie stared out her window and prayed for safety.

CHAPTER TWENTY-SEVEN

The next morning, Elijah carried a box of canned goods into Irvin's store. The snow had hardly been anything at all, certainly not anything worth worrying about. It was often hard to know what to expect with snowstorms and other types of weather. That was one disadvantage that came with not being able to check the weather on a television, cell phone, or radio, but they made do and trusted in God. They'd been doing it for generations.

Elijah put down his box. Irvin bought canned goods and jams from a woman down the road, Mrs. Brown, who made the best canned tomatoes in town. With a sigh, Elijah took the box and set it down on the floor next to where Irvin stood, who had almost finished stocking a box of jams.

"How are you doing, my friend? I mean, how are you really doing?" Irvin asked Elijah, turning to him with jars in his raised hands.

Elijah raked a hand through his dark hair with a heavy sigh and ripped his box open.

"What has happened? Is it Charlie?" Irvin prodded, seeing Elijah's obvious frustration.

"Yes." Elijah started taking out the jars and stocking the shelves. "She told me the truth."

"What, about her ex-fiancé?"

"Yes."

"Look, this man is after her. There is no telling what he might do, so we need to be praying for Charlie and Zoe's safety. The Lord calls us to forgive and forget, Elijah. She was just too afraid to tell us sooner," Irvin said.

"Not only that, she accused people in this community of doing those cruel things to her to try to scare her away. You know some of the men have said they don't think she should be here, but they aren't capable of doing those things."

"She's just scared, Elijah. Maybe telling herself someone inside the community did those things helps her feel safer. She's dealing with a lot right now, first with the death of her parents, all these cruel pranks, and her ex. It's understandable that she might make false assumptions."

Elijah knew the older, wiser man was right. To change the subject, he said, "Do you know why she ran out of church yesterday?"

"I figured she was not feeling well," Irvin replied.

"That's what she said, but I think it is more than that."

"I'll talk to her," Irvin said, putting the last jars of jam up on the shelf. He turned again to look at his employee and friend. "Do you love her?" he asked abruptly.

Elijah was taken aback, but he could not deny it. "Yes, I love her. More than anything."

"You're sure you love her?"

"Positive."

"And does she love you?"

"Yes. She told me she does."

"You better be careful, Elijah. Remember what I told you about risking getting shunned? If you love each other, she needs to join the church. Do you think she would?"

"I don't know. I guess she would if she truly loves me."

"That woman and little girl are precious." He looked around and said in a quiet voice, "If she would join the church, I think you three would make a fine family. And you would have my blessing."

"Thank you, Irvin."

"You are like a son to me, Elijah."

"And you and Esther are like second parents to me."

Irvin smiled at him, picked up the boxes and walked away, leaving Elijah with his thoughts.

***

As Charlie helped Esther prepare lunch, Elijah and Irvin came into the kitchen from the store for their midday meal.

Irvin stepped up to her and smiled. "I think you and Elijah would make a good couple once you join the church. And with Zoe, you'd make a great family. You have our blessing."

She nodded, truly grateful. "Thank you, Irvin."

"Now, let's go eat some of that food you've made. It smells delicious. You have already learned so much from Esther, I see."

Elijah met Charlie's eyes. Irvin walked over to Esther and started talking quietly to her. Elijah walked towards Charlie, gently took her hand and led her back onto the porch.

She nodded, blushing. "Irvin knows you love me," Charlie said softly.

"Yes, he does. He's known for a while. He also told me if you join the church, we would have his blessing. He thinks we'd make a fine family someday. You, me and Zoe."

The way he smiled at her almost made her look away in shyness. But she held his gaze.

"I am going to consider joining the church, but joining the church won't protect me from Alex."

"God will protect you if it is His will, Charlie."

"What if it's not His will?" she countered.

"Then we will have to accept that."

She didn't want to accept it. She wished again she could call the police on Alex, but out of fear she could not. She certainly did not want Alex to put drugs in the Holts' house or to hurt them in revenge. She didn't want to risk losing Zoe.

"Come on. Let's go eat. We have the applesauce party soon."

***

Later that day after school, Charlie, Zoe, Esther, and the Holt girls drove to Esther's neighbor Andrew's house to make applesauce. Andrew's family had grown and picked the apples themselves.

Charlie and Zoe helped them gather apples outside into a huge container. They washed them, cut them up and boiled the apples. Charlie helped a girl named Sharon put all the boiled apples into a device secured to a table. Hot juice splashed them occasionally as it dropped into a bucket, and Charlie guided it in with a spatula. The apples were strained by the device, and the peelings came out one side while the liquid emptied into a bowl. While the liquid was still hot, they canned it. They made one hundred quarts of applesauce for several families to share.

The younger children busied themselves by looking at books and playing with homemade play dough. Charlie took a break to read them a few books. Even though they didn't know English, they seemed to understand for the most part. They giggled when Charlie did funny voices.

As Sharon, Zoe and Charlie strained the apples, Sharon told Charlie about all her siblings.

"Charlotte and Zoe, would you go get another bucket full of apples in

217

the front yard?" Sharon's mother, Mrs. Duncan, asked Charlie a few minutes later.

"Sure," they answered.

Charlie grabbed a bucket and headed outside to get more apples with Zoe trailing behind.

Andrew's white turkeys jumped up on the buckets of apples and started pecking. Charlie started toward them to scare them away, but a few charged at her. She had heard a farmer say once that turkeys could bite, and she panicked.

"Zoe. Run back inside!" she shouted.

Frightened, they quickly ran back inside and shut the door. They leaned against the door of the mud room, trying to catch their breath.

After a moment, Charlie and Zoe looked at each other and laughed.

"Being chased by a turkey certainly wasn't on my bucket list," Charlie said.

"I had no idea they could be so mean!" Zoe said. "That was kind of scary but also funny."

They began to walk back to the kitchen to tell the women about the turkeys.

"The cash we kept in our house is gone."

Charlie's heart felt like it had dropped into her stomach.

"And ours is as well."

"What are they talking about?" Zoe whispered, seeing Charlie's shocked expression.

Charlie quieted her sister. "Shhh. Listen."

"It was there on Saturday before we went shopping for supplies. It must have gone missing during church yesterday."

"Who do you think did it?"

"Many of us agree... We think it was Charlie," one of the women said.

CHAPTER TWENTY-EIGHT

"Hey, Elijah," Andrew said. "What's the situation with that girl, Charlotte? Or Charlie, as she says people call her."

"She needs a place for her and her sister to stay for a while. Their parents just died." Elijah plucked several apples from Andrew's tree and placed them in his bucket with a little more force than was necessary. Matthew added a few more.

"*Ja.* That is a hard thing. She must be lonely." Andrew gave him a sideways glance.

"What?" Elijah asked.

"He likes her," Matthew said.

Elijah threw a bunch of apples in the bucket. He clenched his teeth. He did love her, but he didn't want everyone to know it yet.

"Aha. It is true," Andrew said. "Finally, you have an interest in a woman. Too bad she's an *Englisher*. And I dare say…she is a pretty one. But this is a really bad idea, my friend."

"Don't make such a racket. You know I could get in huge trouble."

"Relax. No one is around," Andrew told him.

"You could get in huge trouble, Elijah. It's called being shunned. Ever heard of it?" Matthew crossed his arms. "It's going to happen to you if you keep getting involved. That girl needs to leave before she causes any more problems."

"What problems?"

"Have you heard about the thefts in the community over the weekend? Some people think Charlie is the thief. She did leave the Singing early, and yesterday she left church early. She doesn't have an alibi."

"What has gotten into you, Matthew?" Elijah shot back. "I've never seen you like this."

"Shhh. They're coming," Matthew warned. Irvin and Luke came to join them after bringing buckets of apples to the women.

"What are you three talking about?" Irvin asked, smiling.

"Charlie," Andrew said, looking right at Elijah, eyes narrowed.

Elijah tried not to rebuke Andrew out loud. Would Andrew get Elijah in trouble with his quick tongue?

"Say, some cash was stolen during the Singing. Do you know anything about that, Elijah?" Luke asked.

"No. Why would I?"

"Well, Charlie left church early yesterday…" Luke's voice trailed off.

"And?" Elijah pressed. What was that supposed to mean?

"Well, she just arrived, and the money went missing during the same time she left the Singing and church early. That seems suspicious. I know this is hard for you to hear. But her parents just died, and she had to come live here. Grief can make people do things," Matthew said.

"Enough. Come on. Charlie would never do that," Elijah told them. "Why don't you all ask her and see for yourself?"

"Charlie has a kind heart," Irvin said. "It's not possible."

"What do you know about her? Do you know her that well?" countered Luke.

"Even though she's your niece, you really don't know her well at all," Matthew added.

"Yes, we only just met her, but I can tell that she is too kind-hearted to do anything like that," Irvin told them.

"I've spent some time with her because I work for Esther and Irvin. I also know she wouldn't do that," Elijah said.

"Elijah and Irvin, I think you both need to be cautious. It is very easy to be deceived," said Matthew.

"Indeed," Elijah replied solemnly and walked away towards the house. What had gotten into his closest friends?

***

"Calm down, ladies," Charlie heard Esther say to the group of women inside the house. "The Bible says not to judge. So, before you point any fingers, I suggest you think before you speak."

Charlie silently thanked her.

"Esther, did your cash go missing over the weekend, too?"

"Well...yes. But that doesn't mean she—"

"Come on, Esther. Who else could it be? That outsider comes here, and people's money starts going missing. She left the Singing early on Saturday and church early yesterday. What are we supposed to think?" Charlie could tell that was Mrs. Duncan making most of the accusations.

"Yes, what should we do?" said another.

"The Bible says to turn the other cheek," another said meekly.

"Ladies. Please. The Bible also says to not be so quick to judge," Esther challenged firmly. "Besides, when I got home yesterday, Charlie was in the barn and told me she saw someone go into our house, then someone had come into the barn and stolen from our cash box. It wasn't her. I know it."

"She could have easily made that up."

Charlie covered her mouth with one hand to keep from crying out, dropping her bucket. She ran outside, despite the turkeys that now seemed so small. She just stood there in shock. They thought she was a thief.

222

There was no way she could live among people who thought she was a thief.

It was clear she didn't belong here.

Zoe ran outside after her. "Charlie." Zoe hugged her sister around the waist, aware of her pain.

Hot tears stung Charlie's eyes, and she choked back a sob when she noticed Elijah walking toward her. Great. He was the last person she wanted to see her like this.

Before he could see her obvious distress, she started towards Esther's house, hurrying Zoe along.

It was time for her and Zoe to leave. It would be better that way for everyone. "Come on, Zoe." Charlie started running down the lane towards Esther's house, with Zoe following.

"Why are we running? Where are we going?" Zoe called.

"Back to Esther's house."

"Why?"

"Because I forgot something we really need there," Charlie lied. If Charlie told Zoe the truth, Zoe would never cooperate.

They ran down the lane, along the road, and down Esther's driveway. Charlie burst into the house, knowing no one was home.

"Okay, Charlie, what is really going on?" Zoe asked, placing her hands on her hips and staring at her older sister defiantly.

Charlie had forgotten how intuitive Zoe was. Sometimes she acted like an adult in a child's body.

Elijah crashed through the mudroom and landed in the kitchen. "Charlie, What is wrong?" he demanded.

Zoe gave Charlie a questioning glance.

Charlie saw the two of them staring at her and realized they would not budge until they got an answer.

"Zoe and I are leaving."

"No!" Zoe protested, crying. It was not a cry of a child frustrated because she was not getting her way. It was the cry of a child who was truly devastated.

Charlie was taking away the one stable thing Zoe had in her life since their parents had died.

But what choice did Charlie have? She didn't want to be accused of something she hadn't done.

Defeated, Zoe turned away and ran upstairs.

"Everyone here thinks you stole money from houses when you left the Singing early and when you left church early," Elijah told her. "Do you know anything about that?"

"What? You think I did it?" Charlie took a step back, feeling like her heart had been twisted. That was not what she wanted to hear right now. "No. I took nothing from anyone here. I love everyone here, and I would never betray them."

"Well..." Elijah said slowly, "it is suspicious that the robberies happened during the time you were absent from church and the Singing."

"I left because I was upset. You don't believe me? I swear, I didn't do it. The Holts have done so much for me. I would never do this to them. And I won't live among people who think that of me. Families are supposed to trust each other, not accuse each other. I don't want Zoe growing up in that kind of environment. And besides. I thought that wasn't the way of the Amish to go around accusing innocent people."

"Charlie, don't you see why everyone thinks you did it?"

"Yes, I can see why they think I did it. Yes, I left the Singing early and I left church early. Everyone knows about my parents and what I've been through. It looks obvious that I did it. I get it. It would be hard to convince them otherwise. I guess you are just like them… And you don't believe me."

"Charlie…" He started to reach for her hand, but then he stopped.

Charlie heard Zoe cry upstairs. "You should go, Elijah. I'm sorry this didn't work out," she said solemnly. She turned away and started towards the stairs.

The one man she loved saw her as a thief.

Elijah backed away, and she watched him walk out the door. She let out a sob, unable to control her sudden tears and the same ache in her chest that she had felt when her parents died.

Except this was worse. Unlike her parents' deaths, this was her doing. She should have been more cautious.

CHAPTER TWENTY-NINE

Elijah walked away from Esther's house, wondering why his heart hurt so much. He loved Charlie, that was for sure.

He had not felt pain so terrible since he lost his family in the fire.

He didn't want her to leave. He wanted her here forever as his wife. But not if she was a thief. Had she really stolen from people in his community? How could she have lied to all of them after they took her in? How dark could her heart truly be?

Should he side with her or with his community?

Elijah trudged across the yard to his tiny house, feeling destroyed and torn. He turned to take one last look at the house.

He knew he would never love another woman like he loved her.

***

It was time for Alex to make his move.

He'd been waiting for the right time to go after Charlie. Taking his time, he'd robbed several homes in the process over the weekend. He'd had his first robbery rampage when everyone in the community had left to go to some singing event on Saturday, and of course he knew they'd all be at church on Sunday morning. Each occasion had been over two hours long each, so he'd had enough time to search and steal from several homes. The homes were so uncluttered and organized that he hadn't had to make a mess while searching around for cash. In fact, he was careful not to make a mess while searching so that it would prolong the families from noticing that they'd been robbed, which would give him more time to keep stealing before they raised the alarm and did something about it. Or maybe they did know, but still weren't doing anything about it. He'd heard the Amish don't report crimes, but wasn't sure if it was actually true.

Alex chuckled to himself. These people were so naïve that they didn't even lock their doors, which made it even easier. It was too easy. Just too easy.

Leaving his car on a road in the woods behind the house, he walked up the lane to the house so Charlie wouldn't hear the motor. A sound like that would stand out to her after living among horses and buggies for a while. He marched up to the door and knocked.

After a moment, a small voice on the other side of the door asked, "Elijah?"

That was Zoe.

Elijah must have been the boyfriend. "Yes, it's me, Zoe. I have to talk to Charlie."

"Okay." Zoe opened the door. Before she could let out a peep, Alex grabbed her and covered her mouth.

"You stay here and don't make a sound. No matter what happens. Got it?" Alex ordered through gritted teeth. The young girl nodded with wide eyes. Alex shoved her down to the floor, and he heard a thud when her head hit the mudroom wall.

Good. That would keep her quiet.

Alex raced up the stairs to find Charlie.

***

"Owww," Zoe moaned. She slowly opened her eyes and reached up and rubbed her head where it had hit the wall. She heard him yelling questions at Charlie upstairs, and then she heard a lot of noise that sounded like Charlie was fighting against Alex.

227

"Where is the ring?"

"I don't have it. I don't have it!"

Alex could hurt Charlie, Zoe thought. *I have to find Elijah.*

She remembered Alex's order to stay there and not make a sound, but Zoe didn't care. She bolted out the door and sprinted down the lane to Elijah's house.

***

Elijah opened his Bible to Psalms and began to pray. "Dear God, please don't let Charlie and Zoe leave. I love them both too much. I want to make them my family. If that is meant to be, if it is Your will, please don't let them leave."

He was interrupted by a fierce pounding on his door.

"Elijah. Help!"

Zoe.

He jumped up, knocking his chair over, and quickly crossed the tiny room. He pulled open the door to see Zoe's tear-streaked face.

"Alex found us. He found Charlie, and I'm scared he might hurt her. You have to do something." she pleaded.

The Amish were usually nonviolent. But what was Elijah going to do? Go in there waving his Bible around? Adrenaline surged through him, and he momentarily forgot the ways of his people.

He wouldn't be able to live with himself if he let something happen to Charlie. He couldn't let that happen.

His eyes scanned the cabin for a weapon. Even if he only used a weapon to scare off the guy. His eyes landed on his hunting rifle.

The sixth commandment rang through his mind. *Thou shall not kill…*

Elijah would never kill a person. But, he sure could scare someone off. He grabbed the rifle and started running to Esther's house.

"Go call the police in the phone shanty!" Elijah called to Zoe over his shoulder. The Amish were usually against asking for help from the police, but at that moment Elijah was only concerned about Charlie's safety. He saw Zoe run in the direction of the phone shanty, and he sprinted even faster towards the house.

CHAPTER THIRTY

Charlie heard a commotion downstairs. Zoe cried out and… Was that Alex's voice?

No.

Charlie froze. Should she try to run, leaving Zoe here alone? Before she could sort her thoughts, she heard pounding footsteps on the stairs. Then he stood in her doorway, pistol drawn, aiming for her heart.

"Where is the ring?" Alex demanded in a gravelly voice, intense hatred burning in his eyes.

"I told you, Alex. I don't have it." Panic infused Charlie's veins. "How…?"

"How did I find you? It took a while. I had to do a lot of digging and had to make several phone calls. A lot of it led to dead ends. I had no idea you had Amish relatives and they live so under the radar that when I searched for your mother's relatives, I couldn't find anything at first. It was a ton of work. Why did you have to make this so hard, Charlie?" He pushed her back against the wall. He rammed the gun into her ribs. "With every passing second, I'm more likely to get in huge trouble. And searching for you was a huge waste of time. Now, enough stalling. Where is the ring? What did you do with it?"

Charlie winced from the shooting pain that snaked down her spine, feeling the cold metal of the gun through the fabric of her dress. "I told you already, I sold it to someone. It's gone."

"Do you have any idea how badly I need that ring back?" Alex's face turned red in anger, but there was also fear in his eyes, something Charlie had never seen before in him. "I stole it from evidence at a police department. It was a cold case, so I thought no one would notice, but it just got reopened and they noticed it's missing. Now the case is on the news. I'm panicking here. And if I don't put it back soon, they might figure out it was me. I'd lose my job, my entire career that I've worked so hard for. I'd lose everything and go to prison. So I have to get it back."

"Why can't you just get one that looks like it?" Charlie offered, knowing that was not a good suggestion. But she was running out of options. "Or why don't you just confess?"

"Because. It's an antique and very unique. Extremely valuable. I looked everywhere and can't find a look alike. So you see why I need it back? And now it's gone, and I could go to prison. There's only a few people who had access to that evidence, and they'll figure out it was me eventually. But not if I put it back first. So where is it?"

Charlie swept the room with her eyes for a way out, even though he was still pinning her against the wall.

Before she could react, he hit her. The side of her face throbbed and she covered it with her hand. She stared at him angrily, tears blurring her vision. How could he do this to her? It wasn't even her fault.

"Answer me!" he shouted.

"I have no idea where it is! You shouldn't have stolen it in the first place," she retorted. What had he been thinking? She had never thought stealing was among Alex's many faults.

"I didn't think they'd notice it. It's the only thing I took. But now they're starting to figure it out. It's all your fault." He grabbed her shoulders tightly. She tried to wriggle free, but she was trapped like a butterfly in a net.

"You'll pay for this, Charlie!" he shouted at her. "And you're going

231

to get me that ring back. Listen. Zoe is downstairs. If you don't come with me and do what I say, she'll get hurt. Your boyfriend will, too. Understand?" He pressed the barrel of the gun even harder into her side.

Charlie saw the fire in his glare, and she did not doubt his words for a second. She nodded.

But there was no way she could get that ring back. What would he do to them when he finally realized that?

"Now, go change into your normal clothes."

"I can't. You destroyed them all, remember?" she retorted.

He laughed crazily. "Why would I do that? I don't want to take you wearing that. You'll stand right out. You look like a pilgrim."

"You didn't tear them up?" she asked.

"No. I don't even know what you're talking about. Just go get your old clothes."

If Alex hadn't shredded them, who had?

"I told you I don't have any more regular clothes. If you don't believe me, go look in my closet."

"Forget it. I'll get you some on the way." He forced her to get her wallet, then he propelled her through the house and out the back door, jamming the gun into her back. She didn't even get to see Zoe and tell her she was leaving. But it was better than risking Alex hurting Zoe. Zoe would eventually be all right when the Holts came home. Charlie knew they would take care of her.

I hope she's okay and getting help, Charlie thought.

"Oh well. Let's get out of here." Alex led Charlie down the lane and behind the woods to where his car was parked. She saw the license plate number and said it in her head over and over so she would memorize it.

He opened the driver's side door for her. "You drive," he said, pointing the gun at her.

She slid onto the seat, and he got in on the other side, keeping the gun pointed at her the entire time.

"So who did you sell the ring to?"

"A guy named Brandon Francis who got it for his fiancée. But—" She was about to explain that Brandon had sold it to a pawn shop and that it was gone, but Alex cut her off.

"You have to convince him to get it back," he reminded her.

Charlie hesitated. She knew she couldn't get the ring back, and she knew Alex would hurt Zoe if it was not recovered. She had one choice: let Alex think Brandon still had the ring, buy herself some time, and plan an escape. She had to make him believe she could still get the ring back until she figured something out. "I guess I could convince him to give it back...but how?" she lied.

Remembering how Brandon had threatened to call the police if she contacted him again, she hoped he'd keep his word. If he did call the police when she arrived, then maybe she could use that to her advantage and blindside Alex.

Brandon was her only hope.

"We'll convince him," she said.

"We'll need to offer him more money than what he paid you. And if that doesn't work, I can think of some other ways to convince him to give it back." He looked her in the eyes intently. "And if you escape, you can be sure I will turn right around and go after Zoe and your boyfriend. Got it? Now let's go."

She drove out from behind the woods and down the lane. She prayed

Elijah and Zoe realized what had just happened and that they would call the police. Charlie didn't know what Alex would really do when he found out that he wasn't getting the ring back. She had to find a way to let the police know where they were going. She needed a plan for when they got to Rhode Island. But for now, she just needed to stay alive.

CHAPTER THIRTY-ONE

Elijah fell to his knees, physically incapable of holding himself up. He threw the rifle on the ground, feeling like a boulder was crushing his chest. He shouldn't have left her alone at the house. He should have stayed and protected her. His eyes fell on the rifle. How far would he have gone to protect her and Zoe?

He shook his head and focused on praying. "God, please bring Charlie back to me. Please don't let that man hurt her. Please show me how to bring her back safely."

"Elijah!" Several voices cried.

He turned his head to see the Holt family returning from the applesauce party.

"*Was ist letz?* What is wrong?" Esther asked.

"Charlie has been kidnapped," he told them, standing. "A man took her in the car that just drove away."

Everyone began speaking at once, all of them in shock.

"Where's Zoe?" Leah asked.

"She is calling the police," he told them, anticipating an argument.

"Charlie's fate is in the Lord's hands. All we can do is pray," Irvin said.

Elijah wanted to scream in anger, but that would do no good. Zoe was an *Englisher*, so she could call the police if she wanted to. "I know that is how we were taught. But I think God would want us to seek help in this situation. If we don't and something happens to her, I don't know what I'd do… I love her so much."

The Holt family stared at him quietly for a second. They had all been able to see for some time now that Elijah cared deeply for Charlie, but his words had confirmed it, finally making it real.

Leah broke the silence. "Let's go check on Zoe in the phone shanty. I'm sure she's really scared," she said, and they ran to the phone shanty.

Even before they reached the shanty, they heard Zoe's cries. Elijah ran in and held her close. She was still on the phone with the police.

"Are you all right?" Esther asked.

"Yes." Zoe sniffed. "I'm fine. Just worried." She paused to listen to the speaker on the phone, then she held it to Elijah. "The police want to talk to you. You are the only other person who saw what happened."

"Elijah—" Irvin began to argue.

"Irvin, I have to tell them what I know," Elijah insisted.

"It is against our ways!" Esther cried. "It is up to God now. We must accept whatever happens as the Lord's will."

"I know God would want me to get help for the woman I love. I must do this. I'll accept the consequences later," he told them and took the phone from Zoe.

He gave the police all the information he could about what he had seen and about what Charlie had told him, but when they asked him the make and model of the car, he could not answer.

"All I know was that it was black or dark gray. I'm Amish. I know nothing about cars. I'm sorry. I wish I could tell you more. I saw the car only for a few seconds."

They also asked if he had seen the license plate number, but he had not. The car had been too far away when he had seen it. How would they find Charlie if they didn't know what vehicle to look for?

Then he heard a tiny voice in his heart say, *Have faith.*

236

CHAPTER THIRTY-TWO

"So, what's this guy's address?" Alex demanded as she drove. "And don't even try lying to me about the address, Charlie. I need his real address if you don't want me to turn this car around and go after your boyfriend and little sister."

She gripped the steering wheel so hard her knuckles turned white. "It's 110 Lincolndale Street, Providence, Rhode Island." She remembered writing it on the package when she had mailed him the ring.

"Pull over here, behind the building," Alex said, and Charlie drove in to a lot with an abandoned gas station. The car was hidden by some trees and the building.

"Get in the trunk," Alex ordered, pointing his gun at her.

"What? Are you serious?"

"I'm going inside a store to get you some clothes. I'm not going to let you in the store dressed like that. You'll stand right out. People will wonder why an Amish woman is with a regular guy. And if you go in the bathroom dressed like that, and then come out wearing regular clothes, it will cause even more attention."

"Alex, come on. Just let me stay up front. I won't try to escape, I promise." Just the thought of being locked in the trunk made her mouth go dry and her heart hammer.

"I can't risk it. I'm sorry. But you have to get in. Go."

He looked almost as if he felt bad for making her do this, but Charlie wondered if he had a sympathetic bone in his body.

"And if you try anything, remember what will happen to your sister and that guy. Is that clear?" he added.

Charlie nodded, got out of the car, and willed her feet to move toward the back. Alex came around the other side, looked around, opened the trunk and motioned for her to get inside. She eyed a roll of duct tape and some rope.

"Really, Alex, you don't need to—" she began.

"Stop. Yes, I do. I'm sorry."

He glared at her, and she got in the trunk, then he put duct tape over her mouth and tied her hands together.

"I'll be quick. Then I'll get you out before you know it," he said apologetically before closing the trunk.

Darkness enveloped Charlie, and her hands became clammy as the engine started. Her breathing and heart rate sped up along with the car.

She hoped he'd be really quick, because she was becoming more claustrophobic by the minute.

The car came to a stop, and the door opened and shut as Alex went inside the store.

Before she could think up any possible escape plan that actually made sense, Alex returned. The car started and drove a minute, then stopped again. She heard the driver side door open again, and he opened the trunk. She winced when he ripped off the duct tape. At least he'd been quick as he promised.

He handed her a bag containing a shirt and pants. "Put these on."

"Here?"

"Yes."

"Seriously?"

"There's no one around."

She grabbed the bag and crawled into the back of the vehicle. She pulled out the clothing and a slip of paper fell out of the bag. A receipt. A piece of paper. A sliver of hope. She looked around madly for a pen and found one on the floor under the seat.

Thank you, Jesus.

She changed her clothes and shoved the receipt into the side of her pants.

"What's taking so long back there?" Alex pressed.

"These Amish clothes are held together by pins. They are not so easy to get off." She tucked the receipt into her pocket.

"Well, let's go already."

She crawled over the seats to the front of the car. "I have to go to the bathroom. Really bad."

"Can't you wait until we get to the bank?" Alex asked, exasperated.

"No. I really have to go now," she said with determination. "It's a feminine problem, if you know what I mean."

He rolled his eyes. "Fine. But I'm going in the store, too," he said. She had expected that.

She was disappointed to find no one else in the bathroom. She pulled the receipt out of her pocket and wrote on it: *HELP. Charlotte Cooper, Kidnapped. Call police. Taken to 110 Lincolndale Street, Providence, Rhode Island.* She then quickly described the color and model of his car and the license plate number.

Then she had an idea. She could also leave a message on the bathroom mirror and write it with soap, like she'd seen on a movie once.

"Charlie?" she heard Alex call. "That's enough. Let's go."

She had to hurry before he got suspicious. She quickly repeated the same message on the mirror but in a more abbreviated format, then came

239

out of the bathroom.

"Women always take forever." Alex rolled his eyes. "Let's grab some snacks for the road," he added and picked out a few items.

They went to the cash register. The cashier was a middle-aged blonde woman who looked Charlie up and down. The woman's name tag said "Diane." Charlie wondered why Diane looked at her like that, but she didn't think about it for long. As Alex paid for the food, a plan formed in Charlie's mind. She took one of the filled grocery bags from the cashier and purposefully dropped it on the floor. Cans of nuts fell out and rolled a short distance away.

Alex gave an annoyed sigh and bent down to pick up the contents. In the brief second, he was turned away, Charlie put the receipt right in front of the cashier, but since the cashier was also distracted, she did not see it either.

Charlie then quickly reached down to pick up the remaining items on the floor. "Sorry. I'm so clumsy."

Alex grunted in response, shoved the rest of the items in the bag, and paid. "Let's go."

As Alex stormed out of the store, Charlie risked one look over her shoulder. Charlie had just enough time to see the cashier reading the receipt with a concerned look on her face. The cashier looked up and made eye contact with Charlie.

Charlie gave her a pleading look, clasped her hands together in a praying position, and followed Alex to the car.

Lord, please, compel her to call the police.

***

Elijah didn't know how much time had passed, but it seemed like hours. He had left Zoe with the Holts and had taken his buggy to the nearby police station. He had been waiting there, answering questions from the police and staring at the pages of his Bible. The police were somehow trying to track Charlie down.

A police officer finally came in to talk to him.

"We got a call from a cashier at a local store. She got a note from Charlotte asking for help and saying she was kidnapped. She also left a message on the bathroom mirror with soap. Charlotte wrote the make and model of the car and an address the kidnapper is taking her to in Rhode Island. We called the resident at the address and asked him some questions."

"It's Alex Henderson, her ex fiancé. She told me he was intent on getting the ring back. She was convinced he followed her here and has been trying to scare her into giving it to him."

The police officer nodded.

Elijah said, "I can give you more information."

CHAPTER THIRTY-THREE

"**I**'m tired, and I don't want to drive all the way to Rhode Island tonight. Tracking you down has been exhausting," Alex whined.

Charlie looked at him, thoroughly disgusted with his entire being. What had she possibly ever seen in him?

"Let's stop at a hotel and go to Providence in the morning," Alex said, yawning.

"You could nap while I drive," Charlie offered.

"No way. I don't trust you."

"I don't trust you either," she spat.

They pulled in to the nearest hotel and went to their room.

"If you leave this room, I'll hurt you, your sister, and your boyfriend. Understand?" Alex said, gripping her arm roughly. He made her sit on one of the beds, then pulled some rope out of his bag and tied up her hands and feet. He walked over to the other twin bed. "I'm going to sleep now, and I am a very light sleeper."

Alex fell asleep right away. Charlie was relieved. She had been prepared to fight him if he had tried anything with her. She had no idea how, but she would have tried.

She thought of ways she could escape, but she knew Alex truly was a light sleeper and she wouldn't even be able to open the door without waking him up. She'd go out a window, but they were on the fourth floor. She could call someone on the phone, but he would hear. And if he woke up, she knew he would hurt her or Zoe or Elijah.

Thinking of ways to escape was useless. She didn't want to put anyone else in danger.

She tried to sleep, but it was impossible. She worried about Elijah and Zoe and the rest of her family. She knew they must be worried sick. Especially Elijah.

She really loved him. Now that he was apart from her, she missed the warmth of his touch and longed for the feeling of his lips on hers. She remembered him falling to his knees. He must have felt so helpless as he watched her being taken away with nothing he could do to stop it.

To ease her mind, she imagined their future. Would she marry him? Though the thought of a marriage commitment frightened her, she still fantasized about it. She wondered what their life would be like together if they were married.

In the deepest part of herself, she knew it would be a wonderful life, the best she could possibly hope for. It would be if she could let go of her fear, forsake her past full of sorrow, and run towards a new life full of redemption and simple happiness.

In the morning, Alex cut off the ropes, and she rubbed her wrists where they had turned her skin red. It could have been worse.

They got back in the car and kept driving. Eventually, the GPS announced they were approaching their destination.

As they reached Brandon's house at 110 Lincolndale Street, Charlie's pulse raced. She prayed with all her heart that the cashier had called the police.

"Get out," Alex said when she hesitated after the car stopped in the driveway. While Alex waited in the car, she made her way to the front door and shakily rang the doorbell.

Then the door opened and Brandon stood in the doorway.

"Hi. My name is Charlotte Cooper—"

243

"Charlotte? What are you doing here?" he asked, looking angry. "I told you to leave me alone."

"I need the ring back. I know you already gave it to your fiancée, but I'm willing to pay double for it this time," she blurted before he could stop her, hoping he wouldn't contradict her.

She knew Alex had rolled the window down and could hear every word. Brandon's eyes strayed to the car and the dark figure waiting inside.

"Come inside, okay?" he said, motioning her in. She followed him inside and he closed the door. She figured Alex would think they were going inside to talk.

"Are you okay, Charlotte?" a female voice asked.

Charlie turned to see a female police officer in the kitchen, away from the windows. She nodded, speechless with relief.

"We've got her. Go," the police officer said into her radio, and Charlie heard sirens wail and tires squeal as vehicles pulled in to the driveway. Blue and red lights flashed along the walls of Brandon's kitchen.

From what Charlie could see out the window, Alex started to back out of the driveway, but not before the police cars barreled onto Brandon's street and around his driveway, blocking Alex's escape. The police got out, and Charlie watched as they handcuffed Alex and hauled him away to the police car. As they did, Alex looked over his shoulder at Brandon's house. For the first time since she had met him, Charlie realized he looked afraid.

"It's over, Charlotte." The police officer placed a gentle hand on her shoulder. "I just need you to come with me to give a statement, and then we'll get you back home."

***

When he'd been questioned by the police, Alex had admitted to the robberies and the kidnapping. But he continued to insist he had nothing to do with cutting Charlie's clothes, writing on the buggy, or shining a light in her window. The Rhode Island police called Charlie's hometown police and let them know Charlie and Zoe were safe. They explained why they had fled town without telling anyone where they were going.

The police explained that after Diane, the woman from the department store, had called and told them Brandon's address, the police had gone to Brandon's house to wait for Charlie and Alex to arrive. Brandon had even apologized for how he'd treated her and wished her the best. He'd been glad to help the police.

As for the ring, the police continued to search for it.

But Charlie was still baffled. In the police car on her way back to Unity, she wondered who had done the strange attacks on the Holt farm.

Who was trying to scare her out of Unity?

Her mind wandered to the cashier, Diane. Once things settled down, Charlie decided she would thank the woman for her kindness. Charlie shivered at the thought of what could have happened if Diane had not called the police. She wondered if Alex would have killed her.

The police car turned in to the Holts' driveway and the entire household flowed out onto the front yard. Charlie quickly climbed out of the car and ran to them.

Elijah sprinted wildly towards Charlie, then wrapped his arms around her so tight she thought she'd crack a rib.

"I was so scared," he said. "I told them everything I knew."

"Thank you." She closed her eyes and relished the warmth and security of being in his arms.

Then she was smothered in hugs and reassuring words. She found Zoe in the chaos and hugged her tightly.

"I was afraid Alex was going to hurt you!" Zoe cried.

"God protected me," Charlie told her. "Everything is okay now." Even after she said the words, the worry about who had been trying to scare her off the farm lingered in the back of her mind. "I love you."

"I love you, too."

The police officer who had given them a ride exited the car, and Esther invited her into the house. As everyone else went inside to talk to her, Elijah wrapped his arms around Charlie. She could feel and hear his heart pounding, and she treasured the sound.

Elijah pulled away from her but held onto her hands.

"Charlie, I love you. God can give you a new life here. Please don't leave."

His eyes held honesty and gentleness. The statement was so simple, like his people, in a good way.

Before she could answer she heard footsteps and commotion coming out of the house.

"Charlotte? Charlotte!" Voices called her name. Zoe and the older Holt girls ran out onto the porch. "The policewoman says you didn't steal the money. Wait until we tell everyone else." They excitedly ran back into the house.

Elijah chuckled. "You know they'll tell the entire community. Everyone will know you are innocent, Charlie. What is holding you back?"

She thought for a moment.

He held her close and whispered into her ear, "Will you stay here with me, Charlie, and consider marrying me one day? I mean, this isn't my official proposal, and I know so much is happening right now. I just want you to know my intentions."

Charlie's eyes filled with joyful tears. She desperately wanted to stay with him, but there was still something holding her back. She had trusted Alex in the beginning, and he had hurt her and kidnapped her, and he had hurt Zoe. Could she ever trust a man again?

"Elijah..." She didn't know what to tell him.

"It's all right. I just want you to think about it." He released her and took her hand. "Let's go inside and celebrate your return."

CHAPTER THIRTY-FOUR

Over the next few days, Charlie focused on arranging a memorial service for her father. Because Charlie and Zoe had missed it, she still wanted to have a service for Dad that they could attend. Now that she was safe and able to, Charlie called Dad's relatives in Canada and invited them, even though they'd already had a funeral for him, and they agreed to come. She and Zoe took a bus to Biddeford and held the small service at a chapel there.

Now that she had properly laid her father to rest, Charlie let go of the guilt she'd been holding on to for leaving his body behind after the crash. She was thankful Dad's relatives had seen to his burial in such a timely manner when she wasn't able to. The pain of losing her parents was far from being healed, but at least she had closure now.

During the funeral, Charlie and Zoe held hands, both with tears of sorrow coursing down their cheeks as they stood before both of their parents' graves, which were side by side. Charlie took comfort in knowing that not only were her parents laid to rest next to each other, but that they were together in heaven.

As for her family's belongings, Charlie called the landlord and found out he'd put everything in a storage unit so he could continue renting out the apartment, and Charlie reimbursed him. She decided to keep the things there until she decided what to do with it all.

As Charlie and Zoe returned to Unity, she couldn't stop thinking about Elijah's unofficial proposal. She loved him and wanted to marry him more than anything; that was certain. But she could not make up her mind. She argued with herself in her head, going back and forth. She knew there was no such thing as Amish divorce. Once they were married, it would be forever, and forever was a long time. The thought thrilled her and frightened her at the same time. She prayed earnestly about it day and night. She prayed for God to give her a sign. Was this the life she was meant to choose?

She sighed and looked down at her Amish dress that Leah had given her to wear. Even though Charlie had the set of clothes she had bought at the store with Alex, she preferred to continue wearing Amish clothing. Regular clothes reminded her of her old life.

A few days later, to clear her head, she drove the Holt's buggy to the museum to play one of the pianos. She sat down at the keys and played song after song. Joe had wheeled by in his wheelchair, once again commenting on how lovely it was to have someone play.

As Charlie played, it brought back memories of her mother. Before Charlie's mom died, she was Charlie's best friend. A lot of daughters say that, but Mom really had been. Charlie had some friends in high school, but she had lost touch with them after they left for college.

Music was Charlie and Mom's language. Charlie recalled all the times they had sat at the keys for hours, showing each other the pieces they had been practicing. And Mom had always encouraged Charlie to write her own music, even if it was just for fun.

Charlie's mom supported her dreams of being a teacher. When Charlie was a child, she would bring her written music masterpieces to Mom, and she would always edit and write little notes to Charlie on them. It was a fun game they had, writing to each other while they lived in the same house.

Mom had always wanted to be a concert pianist, but life had gotten in the way and she'd never had the time. Charlie knew what she really meant when Mom had told her that: she was too busy raising Zoe and Charlie.

As Mom's cancer became worse, Charlie remembered that she had begun to fear that Mom would never see her go to college. But to Mom, other things were more important than college. She had always told Charlie to love God and love people and do what she loved. That's what Mom told Charlie that last time they talked.

"I know you'll be a wonderful teacher one day, and keep writing music," she said. "Write to me when I'm in heaven."

The melodies were therapy for Charlie's storming mind and heart. Her tears fell onto the keys as the memories of her parents' deaths came back to her for the thousandth time.

She played until she heard a throat clear behind her. Startled, she jumped and turned on the bench.

Bishop Zook stood in the doorway, holding a black hat in his hand. "Charlotte, how are you today?"

"Oh, hi, Bishop Zook. I've been better, actually. I just returned from my father's funeral."

"I'm very sorry to hear that. I was just stopping by to visit Joe. I'm surprised to see you here. I hear that you are considering joining the Amish church and marrying Elijah. Is this true?" he asked. He sure cut to the chase.

"Yes, it is."

"Do you not know that playing instruments, including the piano, is forbidden in the Amish faith?"

"I am aware of that."

"Well, Charlotte. It looks like you have some choosing to do. Once

250

one truly joins the Amish faith, there is no turning back. Do you believe you could give this up?" His hand gestured to the piano.

"Yes." For Elijah, she'd do anything.

"Also, check your heart. Make sure you are considering joining the faith for the right reasons. One should not join for the sole purpose of marriage. It is a commitment to wholeheartedly serve God above all else. To deny yourself of luxuries the world has to offer. And the chaos and distractions that come with it. It is not worth gaining the world to only end up losing your soul."

She didn't see how playing the piano could lead to her losing her soul, but she nodded. If she was going to join the church, she had to respect their ways, even if she didn't understand.

He gave one last look at the instrument, his eyes moving over the keys. Charlie wondered if he had ever even touched a piano. She couldn't imagine being denied such joy. But she supposed he had never known it, so he would never miss it.

But she had known it her whole life, and if she gave it up, she would miss it incredibly. It was one of the last links she had left to her mother. The piano was something special that they'd shared together.

Wait...it's not the last link, Charlie realized. Besides Zoe and her relatives and this place, the Amish faith was also a strong link to her mother. By becoming Amish, Charlie would be embracing her mother's former faith, even though her mother had let it go. She'd be living where her mother had grown up.

"I hope you consider this decision very carefully. It is life-changing," the bishop told her, touching his dangling white beard.

"Believe me, I think about it all the time. I pray that God will show me what to do," Charlie said.

"In due time, He will show you. Just be patient." The bishop gave her a rare, wise smile and left her alone with her tumultuous thoughts. She stared at the keys until her vision blurred with tears, then pulled the cover down over the keys and drove the buggy back to the farm.

CHAPTER THIRTY-FIVE

Elijah carried the last box of canned tomatoes from Mrs. Brown's house to his buggy. Mr. Brown had brought Elijah into the barn to show him his new horse, and they had chatted longer than Elijah had planned. It would be long past sunset when he got home. He did not like driving his buggy in the dark, but he didn't want to disappoint Mr. Brown.

"I know it's none of my business but..." Mr. Brown began.

Elijah should have anticipated that he would ask about Charlie.

"We hear you're planning on marrying Charlotte Cooper," Mrs. Brown said behind her husband as Elijah secured the box in the back of the buggy. Just the mention of Charlie's name made his heart leap.

"Yes. I have asked her to marry me."

"And I hear she has not yet accepted," Mrs. Brown said.

"No, she has not. She is taking some time to think about it. The past year has been hard on her. Have people been talking about it?"

Mrs. Brown absentmindedly fiddled with the white ribbon on her *kapp*. "Well, *ja,* it's a small town. Everyone knows everyone. We would certainly welcome her into our community. I have known you for some time now and have gotten to know you quite well. You are an honorable person, and I think Charlotte is too. I look forward to when I attend your wedding, Elijah, if it is God's will."

"And I do too," Mr. Brown added.

Here were two more people who believed Elijah should marry Charlotte. Elijah wondered if God was speaking through the Browns and also Irvin. It only confirmed in his heart that he and Charlie were meant to be together.

253

If only Charlie would accept his proposal.

"Thank you, Mr. and Mrs. Brown. I appreciate your encouraging words. I hope one day she will feel at home here and be accepted by everyone as you accept her."

"Well, we have never had someone who was not born Amish join this church before, but God calls us to love everyone," Mrs. Brown said.

"Yes, He does." Elijah looked to the horizon, where the sun splattered orange and pink streaks across the sky like it had been painted with finger-paints. He marveled at how each sunset was one of God's unique masterpieces and proof that He loved mankind.

"Well, it is time for me to go. I want to get home before it gets too dark," Elijah said, shaking Mr. Brown's hand.

They said their goodbyes. Elijah got in his buggy and started driving back to the store to drop off the canned tomatoes. Twenty minutes into his drive, Elijah saw a bright pair of headlights speeding up behind him, approaching him rapidly. Usually at that point the car would start to slow down and go around the buggy, but the car was still driving straight, right towards Elijah's buggy.

There was not enough time to move the buggy out of the way. There was nothing that Elijah could do besides close his eyes and pray that the car would miss him. The car veered at the last moment but still hit the buggy from the side. Elijah heard a deafening crash and the cries of the panicking horse as the buggy toppled over. Elijah saw Charlie's face in his mind right before the world went black.

***

Charlie walked up the lane to the Holts' house. As soon as she stepped foot onto the front yard, the children ran outside of the house.

"Charlie! Charlie!" Lilly cried. "Elijah was in an accident."

Charlie halted. A thousand questions erupted in her brain. Before she could choose which one to ask first, all the children were speaking at once. Charlie couldn't decipher any of it.

Is he hurt? Is he...dead? She could barely breathe at the thought. She felt as though her heart would stop if she heard them say he was gone. How would she go on without him?

Visions of their wedding day and future came into her mind. She imagined their first child, their home, their life together with Zoe. Could that all still happen?

And that's when she knew what to do. If Elijah was still alive, she realized she wanted to marry him more than anything.

She knew Elijah was a gift from God, and not accepting that gift would be complete foolishness. It was so clear that they were meant for each other.

The children were still all speaking at once. She put her hands to her head and said, "One at a time. What happened?"

Ella Ruth spoke first. "We found out soon after you left. He was picking up canned goods for the store. He stayed a little longer than he planned. On the way home it was getting dark, and a drunk driver hit him from the side. The buggy tipped over. He's at the hospital now but we haven't heard any word since then."

"I'm going to the hospital," Charlie said. "Where are Esther and Irvin?"

"They already went there," Lilly said.

"Are you going to be okay here?" Charlie asked them.

"Yes. Leah, Lilly, Zoe, Debra, Seth and I are staying home," said Ella

Ruth.

"Can I come?" Zoe asked.

Charlie didn't know what kind of condition Elijah would be in or what he would look like. "I think it's best if you stay here and help take care of the little ones with Leah and Ella Ruth. Besides, I could be there a while."

"All right," Zoe said, looking as though she had an important job to do.

Now that she was alone, the full impact of the news crushed her. She broke down in tears. If only she hadn't been at the museum... She could have been there for him. What if he had a brain injury? What if he had fatal injuries? She couldn't bear the thought. And she couldn't waste one more second. She went to the phone shanty and called for a taxi, so thankful that the Amish were not against accepting hospital care when it was needed.

She had to get there as fast as she could to be with him. And as soon as she could, she would tell him she had made her decision. She didn't want to live the rest of her life without him. She wouldn't.

When Charlie finally reached the hospital, she hesitated before walking into Elijah's room. She willed herself to step into the room, but fear held her still. Would he be okay? She prayed for strength. *Please, God, heal him.* Then, somehow, she gathered the courage to step inside.

First, she saw Esther and Irvin, who looked so out of place in the modern hospital with their plain clothing. The dark clothes against the white walls were like black horses in a snowy field.

Charlie's eyes found Elijah. His eyes were closed. He was on the hospital bed with one foot in a cast and a bandage around his head. Was he in a coma? Her heart pounded harder, her hands shook, and she almost

256

panicked.

"Charlotte." Esther stood and enveloped Charlie in a hug. Charlie let Esther hold her, grateful for the small comfort.

"How is he?" Charlie asked.

Esther pulled away. "The horse didn't make it, but God protected Elijah. He has some broken bones, but he'll be all right. A broken foot and some cracked ribs, and a minor concussion. He will probably wake up soon."

Charlie breathed a sigh of relief. "I thought it was worse."

"No. Thank God it isn't any worse," Irvin said. "How are the children?"

"They're all right. Just scared."

"We should go home to be with them," Esther said. Irvin stood. "Call the phone shanty if anything changes. We'll check for messages every now and then."

After the couple left, Charlie pulled a chair up next to Elijah. She took his hand without the IV in it and held it in hers. She looked at his face, speckled with cuts and scrapes and those few freckles she loved so much.

"I love you," she whispered.

He slept for a few more minutes, then he slowly opened his eyes. He looked at her then stared at the cast on his leg in confusion.

A shadow crossed over his face. "I remember it. I remember the accident."

"It was a drunk driver."

"We will not seek justice or revenge… It is in the Lord's hands," he said softly.

She was still holding onto his hand. She didn't know what to say. Of

257

course, they would not even try to find out the name of the driver. They accepted it as God's will and moved on. Part of her was angry with the driver, and the rest of her was in awe of the Amish faith.

All she could think of saying was, "You're going to be okay."

***

When Charlie got back to the Holts' house late that night, everyone was asleep. She let herself in through the unlocked door, crept up the stairs and quietly went into the room she shared with Zoe. Charlie put on her pajamas and slipped into bed. Zoe stirred and turned over in bed to face her.

"Is Elijah really going to be okay?" Zoe asked.

"Elijah is hurt very badly, but he will be okay," Charlie said.

"Good. I love Elijah," Zoe said in her small voice.

Charlie smiled in the darkness. The moon offered just enough light for Charlie to see the edges of Zoe's face.

"I love Elijah too. Which reminds me of something I need to talk to you about," Charlie said.

"I already know. Everyone is talking about how he wants to marry you. Do you want to marry him?" Zoe asked her. Charlie should have known that Zoe already knew.

"I do want to marry Elijah, but it's not that simple. Did you know there is no such thing as Amish divorce?"

"Yes. So that means you and Elijah and I will be together forever?" Zoe asked with hope in her voice.

"Well, yes, but I was going to ask you first—"

"Charlie, can't you see I love it here? I want to stay here forever. I want to be an Amish girl, too, just like Ella Ruth and Leah and the other girls. We have a real family here. And I'm not afraid when I am here. When I am here, I know I'm home, and I never want to leave."

Tears stung Charlie's eyes. "I feel the same way. I'm glad you want to stay." Moved by Zoe's words, she almost burst with happiness, even though she had already known Zoe wanted to stay in Unity.

"If you marry Elijah, would he be my new daddy?" Zoe asked.

"Well… no. He would be your brother-in-law, technically."

"My brother? I always wanted a big brother. Me, you, and Elijah…we'd make a good family, wouldn't we? And then if you and Elijah have kids would they be my brother or sister?"

"My child would be your niece or nephew. You would be an aunt," Charlie told her. "Wouldn't that be great?"

Charlie heard Zoe suck in a breath. "Oh, yes."

"So, you would be okay with Elijah marrying me?"

"Yes. I really want you two to get married. I can't wait for us to be a family. Will he give you a ring, Charlie? Will you keep this one?" Zoe asked.

Charlie laughed a little. "No, the Amish don't wear rings or any jewelry at all."

"I guess you won't ever get a ring after all," Zoe said, laughing.

Zoe giggled as Charlie pulled the blanket over her little sister, kissed her on the head, and watched Zoe fall asleep.

CHAPTER THIRTY-SIX

The next day, Charlie put on her dress and prayer *kapp* while getting ready to visit Elijah. Today, she was going to do it. She was going to ask Elijah if he was the boy who had given the hat to her all those years ago. Part of her hesitated because she wanted it to be him so badly. Of course, she suspected it was him, but what were the odds? Maybe it was silly, but she truly hoped it was him. But if not, so be it. She stuffed the hat into her bag and got into the car of the driver she'd hired.

After arriving at the hospital, she quietly approached Elijah's room, not wanting to disturb him if he was sleeping. He was sitting up in bed, reading his Bible. Her heart warmed at the sight of seeing the man she loved reading God's Word, and she thanked God again for Elijah. A lock of his dark hair fell over a bandage on his forehead, almost touching his eyebrow. Before coming to Unity, she had no idea men like him even existed.

He looked up. "Charlie. Hey."

Charlie smiled at the sound of Elijah's tired voice. "Hey yourself." She walked toward him, and her smile fell when she saw what was on the pages of his Bible.

It was an orange lollipop wrapper, crinkled, faded, and folded over a thousand times with age.

It couldn't be, could it?

"Where did you get that?" she asked incredulously.

"This? My bookmark?" He grinned mischievously like the little boy he once was and picked it up, handing it to her. "A special little girl gave it to me once in a barn. She kissed me on the cheek that day, and I've been

in love with her ever since, and I've been waiting for her all this time."
His eyes were filled with love and devotion, and she reached for his hand.

"You kept a lollipop wrapper for more than fifteen years?" Charlie
asked in disbelief.

"Of course. It's no ordinary lollipop wrapper." Elijah gently touched
the side of Charlie's face. "It's one of my most precious possessions,
really, besides this Bible."

"So it *was* you," she murmured. "I suspected it, but I wasn't sure. It
was so long ago, I didn't think you'd remember. And if you did, I didn't
think it had affected you like it had affected me. I thought maybe I was
kind of silly for hanging onto the memory so long."

"Same here. But I remember it well. I figured you were that little girl
as soon as I met you in the diner and you told me your name was Charlie.
That's a hard name to forget for a girl. But when I found out you were
Esther's niece, I knew for sure."

"Why didn't you say anything?" Charlie laughed, playfully batting
him on the arm.

"I was waiting for the right moment. I didn't want to seem too eager,"
he said with a grin. "Or I thought you'd think it was silly of me."

"I guess we each felt the same way." She pulled the straw hat out of
her bag and showed it to him. "Does this look familiar?"

He reached out an unsteady hand and touched the hat, his brow
crinkled. "Wait a second..." Elijah said, flipping the hat over.

Something caught Charlie's eye on the inside rim of the hat. "Look.
What's that?"

Faint but visible, two words were written on the inside of the hat that
she had not noticed before: *Elijah Hochstettler.*

"You kept it all this time?" he asked.

"Well, my mom did. She took it from me after we left here because she was so upset. She didn't want the reminder of her argument with Esther, I guess. She kept it in the closet, and I only found it just before I came here. I thought she'd thrown it out years ago. She'll never know how much it means to me that she kept it." Charlie's eyes welled up with tears. "She didn't know it, but this was her final gift to me."

Elijah patted her hand. "Maybe she had a feeling we'd meet again. I always hoped we would. I knew I loved you from the moment we met in that barn, when you kissed me on the cheek. And all these years later, God brought you back to me."

Charlotte's thoughts ran so fast, they jumbled together. It was him. He was the boy—the boy was Elijah. The fact that the little boy who had given her butterflies and a straw hat had grown up and proposed to her astounded her. If this wasn't a completely obvious sign from God, she didn't know what else to expect, like letters in the sky saying, "Marry Elijah."

Memories of her time in Unity with him and when she had found out about Elijah's accident sent Charlie's brain somersaulting with emotions and questions. Like her parents' deaths, it reminded her life was short, and now was the time to treasure what was most important, and to not put things off. It excited her and scared her.

Thank you, God, for making this all so clear, Charlie prayed.

She didn't feel the hesitation like she had with Alex. She'd never been more positive of anything in her life.

"I've made my decision," she said quietly.

"You mean…" He looked at her expectantly.

She smiled, barely able to contain her joy and excitement.

When she said nothing, he said, "So, I need to officially ask... Will you marry me, Charlie?"

Elation rushed through her, making even her toes tingle. She wanted to fly, to shout from the sky, "Yes!"

Elijah grinned. "If I wasn't in this hospital bed, I would get down on one knee, pick you up, and twirl you around. I'm the happiest man in the world, Charlie." Tears streamed down his face and he laughed.

Just by seeing the smile on his face, she knew he was right.

"God has truly brought us together, Charlie. I have been praying for you all these years, hoping you'd come back to me. That's why I kept the lollipop wrapper as a bookmark in my Bible, as a reminder to pray for you. I loved you even back then, Charlie, even though we were kids. I never felt the same way about anyone since. I have been waiting for you my whole life." He took her hand, kissed it, and pressed it against the side of his face.

Tears of joy ran down Charlie's cheeks. "I love you too. I did then, and I do now. And I always will." She gently rested her forehead on his arm and closed her eyes.

***

As soon as she had said "yes" to Elijah's proposal, Charlie knew what she had to do. She must sever every other tie to the English world. She took a bus to the storage unit, gave away or sold almost everything in it, and packed what little would be allowed by the Amish in a bag to take back to the farm. But before she left, she stopped by the diner.

She walked in and heard the familiar sound of the bell tinkle above the door. Linda looked up and saw Charlie, who just stared at her for a moment.

"Charlie? Is that you?" Linda asked.

"Yes, it's me."

"Oh, my goodness! Wow, you look different! It's so good to see you!" she cried and ran to hug her former employee. "Tonya! Come here."

Tonya came out from the back of the diner and hurried over. "Whoa! What's with the pilgrim outfit?" she asked, looking over Charlie's dress and prayer *kapp*.

"I'm joining the Amish," Charlie explained. "This is how we dress."

"What? You have to tell us everything. We need details. We heard what happened, about the car crash. We thought you were dead. The police came here to ask us questions after you and Zoe disappeared at the scene of the accident. They thought maybe we'd know where you were. We had no idea what had happened to you!"

They explained how so many people in town were wondering what had happened to Charlie and Zoe when they'd escaped to Unity, wondering if they had died or disappeared. They were glad to spread the word in town that the sisters were safe now.

"Alex threatened to get the state to take Zoe away if I didn't give his ring back. But he's in jail now, and we are safe. We've been living with my Amish relatives this whole time."

"Seriously?" Linda laughed. "And that's why you're dressed like that?"

"Actually, I met a man there, and I'm marrying him. I absolutely love it there, and I love their way of life. That's why I'm joining the Amish," Charlie said and waited for their reaction.

They looked at each other. "Wow. That's amazing," Tonya said.

"Tell me about him. Does he wear a straw hat?" Linda asked.

"Yes, actually, he does." Charlie laughed.

"Is he hot? Does he have a farmer's tan?"

"Do you have to wear a bonnet?"

They bombarded her with questions, just as she had expected. She gladly answered every single one. It was a slow time of day, so they sat in a booth and chatted for a while.

"So... I don't see a ring on your hand," Tonya commented.

"The Amish don't wear rings, so ironically, I'm ending up with no ring at all," Charlie said.

Linda and Tonya laughed. She looked around, wondering if she would ever come here again. It was time to put her past behind her, even though she would keep in touch with these two women.

"So, do you want to come to my wedding?"

CHAPTER THIRTY-SEVEN

Charlie was ready to move ahead with her new life and never look back at her old one. Besides the love of her parents and Zoe, her old life had only been filled with emptiness compared to her new one. Serving God and belonging to this wonderful Amish community mattered so much more to her now than any material objects. And of course, Elijah was completely worth it.

But there was one thing that was by far the hardest to give up.

Charlie took the bus back to Unity, to the old museum to play the piano one last time.

"Good morning, Charlotte." Joe greeted her with a ready smile. "Have you come to play the old piano? You know I love to hear you play, just like I used to love listening to your mother play."

Mom used to say the same thing. She had loved to hear Charlie play.

"Yes, I have. But I'm sorry to say it will be the last time. I have decided to join the Amish church," Charlie told him. "The Amish do not allow the playing of any instruments. Once I join, I must give up the piano."

"Why don't the Amish allow instruments? What is the harm in playing piano? I could never understand that. That seems ridiculous to me, especially since it can be used for worship," Joe said in exasperation, throwing his hands up. "Absurd."

"I know... It's hard to understand. They don't allow instruments because they believe it calls unnecessary attention to the individual playing. I believe playing piano is a way to worship the Lord, but if I am going to join the church, I must abide by their rules and beliefs," Charlie explained.

"Why are you doing all this?" Joe asked her, gripping the wheel on his wheelchair.

"I have fallen in love with this place, the Amish community, and Elijah Hochstettler. Zoe and I have chosen to live here, and I am going to marry Elijah," she said with excitement.

"Congratulations. Well, I guess you have made up your mind. Now let's quit yammering and hear you play."

Charlie felt a rush of anxiety from the thought of playing the beloved instrument one last time, the last tangible connection to her parents that she had left. She rested her fingers gently on the keys. She had already picked out what song she would play. It was the best piece her mother had written.

Charlie played the song perfectly. She poured everything she had into it. A few tears fell onto the keys, but she continued playing until the song was finished.

Joe remained silent as Charlie stood. Sorrow gripped Charlie's heart as she lowered the cover over the keys, feeling like she was closing the coffin that contained her past.

As hard as it was to give up the piano, she knew Elijah and her new life were completely worth it. She loved Elijah and Zoe so much more than any instrument. She would give up all music just to be with them forever.

She forced herself to turn away from the instrument and faced a baffled-looking Joe.

"You know, you're invited to the wedding," she stated with a small smile, wiping a tear off her cheek.

"Wouldn't miss it for the world," he told her. "That was the most beautiful thing I've ever heard anyone play."

"Thank you. My mother wrote that."

He gawked in amazement. "She is an amazing composer."

She was *an amazing composer*. Charlie didn't have the heart to correct him on his present tense. She couldn't handle any more pain at that moment. She said goodbye to him, saying she would see him at the wedding, and made herself walk away.

CHAPTER THIRTY-EIGHT

Elijah was sent home with strict orders of resting his foot and ribs. Charlie began planning the wedding and sewing her wedding dress. Sharon and Lydia came over frequently to help her sew it, and Leah and Ella Ruth helped, since Charlie had not sewn much before. But she learned quickly. They also worked on other clothes that had to be made or mended.

Charlie's dress was blue cotton with a simple apron and *kapp*. All her life she had dreamed of a flowing white gown that sparkled in candlelight, but now this blue dress seemed more beautiful than the type of elaborate dress she had always wanted.

Now that she and Zoe were wearing full traditional Amish clothing, the plain dresses were normal to her. As Charlie sewed, she smiled as she thought of the way Elijah would look at her. She wasn't sure if it was because she had joined the church, or that she wore Amish clothes, or that they were getting married. It could have been all three. But Charlie loved the way Elijah grinned whenever he saw her. She could not wait to be his wife.

While the women were busy with preparations for the wedding, the men set to work on building Elijah and Charlie's new barn. They decided that they would enlarge Elijah's tiny house later on, and Zoe would stay with the Holt's until then, once she had a room of her own built. They needed a barn first because they would get animals before they would have children. Elijah bought the piece of land from Irvin that his little house was on with money his father and grandfather had left him. The land was set far back from the road, surrounded by fields and hidden by clusters of trees. Best of all, it was close to the Holt family.

The word spread that Elijah needed a new barn, and soon a barn raising was organized. Everyone called it a "frolic", a day of work which is also a time for food and socialization. Elijah explained to Charlie how work frolics brought the community together so they could all work together to accomplish something while also having fun.

"The Amish work together to help a friend in need. Sometimes, natural disasters destroy barns or rowdy teenagers will set a barn on fire, and we come together to build a new one," Elijah told her.

"Has that happened here?" Charlie asked, shocked. "That's awful."

Elijah shrugged. "Not much here. Where I grew up in Smyrna, I saw it happen, other than when my own home burned down. These things happen sometimes. Some people simply do not like the Amish, or they just target us because they know we will not report them. We like to help each other out. Where would we be without friends?"

"You're right. It is a very good system, always taking care of each other. No one here is ever alone." Charlie's mind wandered back to the barn raising. "How will so many people know what to do in order to build a barn correctly?"

"Irvin and I will be in charge. We drew up the plans together and we already bought the supplies, and many community members are donating lumber. Irvin has experience in building barns, so he will be in charge of telling everyone what to do. Don't worry, it always goes smoothly."

***

Before the barn raising, the foundation of the barn was built. The women spent the day preparing food which they would bring to the barn raising for everyone to share. Leah, Ella Ruth, Charlie, Lydia, Sharon and

270

some of the other girls and women came together to make an enormous amount of food. They made the classic shoofly pie, breads, stews, and salads. They peeled dozens of potatoes for mashing and gathered dozens of jars of applesauce from the applesauce party.

At the end of the day, Charlie was exhausted. She sank into one of the chairs near a large window in the Holts' living room.

She heard the door open and the familiar sound of stomping of boots in the mudroom. Instantly, she knew it was Elijah. Once his boots were removed, he flew into the living room.

"Charlie. Great news. The community came together and has donated animals for our barn, including a horse to replace my horse that was killed in the accident. Isn't that wonderful?" he said, grinning.

Charlie sat up in her chair. "Really? But they don't even know me well. That is so nice of them. How can I repay them?"

Elijah crossed the room and knelt before her, taking her hands in his. He smiled up at her. Elijah continued, "They do not ask for us to pay them back. This is the way of the Amish. We help each other, my dear. And remember, if some other person in the community loses their barn to a fire or needs to build their first one, we will help them rebuild one with the community. So maybe we will pay it forward someday."

She smiled and nodded. They said goodnight, and Elijah went to his cabin so they could both get some rest.

***

In the morning, the men arrived at Elijah's place early when the sun was barely peeking over the pine trees. Some women arrived with them and began setting out the food.

Elijah and Irvin separated the men into teams to accomplish different

271

jobs. As they set to work and the skeleton of the barn began to take shape, Elijah thought about *Englishers* he had met who thought that the barn was built in one day at an Amish barn raising. He chuckled at the thought. He supposed that maybe if the barn was small enough it could be done, but usually in Unity they spanned the building work over a few days.

"What do you think so far?" Elijah asked Irvin as they looked around at the volunteers.

"It's going so well. The barn frame should be finished by the end of the day, but the entire barn will probably take about a week."

"I think they will do better once they eat breakfast," Elijah said.

"The women should be here soon. It is still early, but it will take them a while to set out the meal. Ah, I see them coming now."

Elijah turned and smiled when he saw the large group of women in their black, gray, blue, and brown dresses coming towards them over the hill, as determined as a faithful marching army in the morning sun. Almost every one of them carried a dish or basket. Even little girls walked with them and helped carry the food, all ready to serve as one. They set the food out on several large rectangular tables. Though the women did not help in the actual building of the barn, they kept the men fed and hydrated. Throughout the day, they served the men, and then cleaned up after everyone was finished.

As those women greeted the women who had arrived earlier to set the table, Elijah figured the entire community had attended. He quickly counted and estimated that over seventy-five of their Amish friends had shown up.

Some *Englishers* driving by caught sight of the commotion and came to watch for a bit. This was not unusual. Elijah remembered seeing

Englishers watch a barn raising from a distance when he was a child growing up in Smyrna. He had attended one with his own family and helped the other boys his age move supplies and help the men.

Elijah smiled as he saw a group of boys helping out their fathers and older brothers. One of them said something, and they all laughed. Elijah remembered having fun with his own siblings and wished they could be there to see his barn being built.

Elijah felt a tap on his arm and turned to see Charlie's beautiful face smiling up at him. Her already big eyes, framed by her white *kapp*, were wide as she took in the scene.

"This is amazing," she said in wonder, "that they are doing all of this to help us."

"I told you. We take care of each other here." For a brief moment, he rested his hand on her long-sleeved arm. "How did the food preparation go this morning?"

"It went well. It was a little chaotic, but Esther took charge and managed everything. It took us a while to gather together all the food and bring it out, but we did it." She looked around. "I am so grateful for everyone's help."

"They know you are. Speaking of help, that is what I need to do. It's our barn after all." He smiled, kissed her on the cheek, and hurried off to join the other workers. Charlie smiled in surprise. She knew that they were not supposed to kiss on the lips until marriage, so she had not anticipated a sweet kiss on the cheek that no one seemed to have noticed.

Charlie returned to the tables with the other women and helped them set everything out. Before lunch, Elijah said the prayer, and also thanked everyone for coming. He also told everyone how grateful Charlie was for their help.

After lunch, the women gathered up the food and put it away. They filled large plastic containers with soapy water and washed the dishes in an assembly line. Charlie was surprised at how quickly their work was done. Or so she thought. That was when the women took out clothes that needed to be mended, sewing supplies, and quilts to work on. Charlie shook her head and smiled. Of course, their work was not done. It was never done.

As she sat down with the other Amish women, Zoe, and her other female family members who were now all her dear friends, she looked around at the familiar smiling faces framed by their white *kapps*. Charlie knew she wouldn't have it any other way. And now that she also had Elijah, she felt like the most blessed woman in the whole world.

***

That night, Elijah woke up to get a drink of water. He walked sleepily to his small kitchen. He opened the cabinet near a window, grabbed a cup and glanced outside. Instantly, he was fully awake. He shook his head to make sure he wasn't dreaming.

A dark figure was walking near the barn holding a kerosene lantern. Who on earth was snooping around his barn in the middle of the night? He dropped the cup, letting it clatter to the floor, and dashed out the door.

He heard a crash as he ran around the side of his house. When the barn came back into view, he realized the trespasser had started a fire with the lantern, and now flames leapt up the frame of the barn. He searched the field frantically for the dark figure, but whoever it was had run off.

"Fire!" he screamed at the top of his lungs several times, hoping the Holts would hear. "Fire!"

Memories of his house burning down jarred his mind as he ran back into his cabin. Visions of his childhood home burning with his family inside flashed through his head. He had promised himself that he would never let anything like that happen again.

Fire extinguishers were frowned upon on in the community here, but no one knew that Elijah secretly kept one in his house. He quickly retrieved it, hurried back to the barn, and put out the fire as quickly as he could.

Elijah stared at the damage. A section of the framework was charred and smoking from the blaze. Elijah wondered if the fire would have spread to his house. Probably not, because there was quite a distance between the two structures, but Elijah shivered at the thought.

Elijah heard a shout as Irvin ran towards him, followed by Esther, Charlie, Ella Ruth, and Leah.

"What happened?"

"Are you all right?"

They all started asking questions at once. Elijah told them, "Someone set the barn on fire. I saw someone holding a kerosene lamp. They set the barn on fire with it and ran off before I could see who it was."

"Are you sure you saw someone? Maybe your eyes were playing tricks on you," Irvin suggested.

"As sure as I am standing here, I saw someone holding a lantern near the barn," he said, his voice rising. How could someone do this to him? He had never hurt anyone here.

"Well, thank God you are safe. And it doesn't matter who did it. God will punish the person if it is His will," Irvin told him, resting a hand on Elijah's shoulder.

Elijah looked at Charlie, who was looking confused and worried. "At least you're all right. Leah saw the fire and woke us all up."

Leah said, "I was on my way back from the bathroom, and I saw the fire. I'm so sorry about your barn."

"It's all right. We'll repair it tomorrow. At least the whole thing didn't burn down," Elijah said.

"You put out the fire?" Irvin asked, his gaze falling on the fire extinguisher that was on the ground. "You have a fire extinguisher? That's putting your faith in a man-made device instead of God. What God wants to happen will happen. We trust in God to protect us, not smoke alarms or fire extinguishers."

"Well, after what happened to my family…" Elijah looked away.

Esther touched Irvin's arm, sensing that Elijah didn't want to argue about the fire extinguisher at that moment. "It's late. Let's all go back to sleep. All is well now," she said softly. She led her family back into the house.

Charlie looked over her shoulder and gave Elijah a sad smile. He smiled back, but once she turned back around, he scanned the field and woods once more for the dark figure. He looked around for a few minutes, and when he saw nothing, he warily went back to bed. The arsonist was probably just some rebellious teenager wanting to start some trouble for a simple Amish man.

***

Charlie settled back into bed, wondering if someone was still trying to scare her out of Unity. Was the same person now attacking Elijah, too? Did someone not want her to marry Elijah?

In her mind, Charlie made a list of people who might have something against her besides Alex. This started before she was suspected of robbing the Amish homes, so she knew it was most likely not because of that. It all started not long after she arrived. Why had someone shredded her clothes and painted *she should leave* on the Holt's buggy? Who wanted her gone? And when would they give up?

Charlie was not going anywhere.

She considered suspects. Other than Alex, she could not think of any. And Alex was behind bars.

Then Charlie had an idea. Did the barn arson have a connection to whoever had hit Elijah's buggy with their car?

Did the attacker have something against Elijah too? Who could possibly hold a grudge against him? Elijah would never hurt anyone.

Had someone started out just trying to scare Charlie away and was now trying to hurt or even kill Elijah for some reason?

Charlie thoughts churned like clothing in a Maytag washer. She knew it was against the Amish rules to seek a culprit and justice, but Charlie could not suppress her desire to do just that. She wanted to find the culprit before someone got hurt...or worse.

***

After dinner the next evening, when Elijah and Charlie usually spent quality time together, Charlie decided to voice her suspicions.

They sat in handmade wooden chairs, the kind that was a classic representation of Amish furniture. Charlie looked over at Elijah, who was gazing at the fields surrounding them. She wondered what he was thinking about.

"I have something to tell you," she said.

"What is it, my dear?" he said to her with concern.

"I think someone is trying to hurt you."

"Why?"

"I think the car that hit your buggy and the barn burning down are attacks that are connected somehow. We also never discovered who cut up my clothes, or who vandalized the buggy, or who shone a light in my window shortly after I got here. I think someone started out by just trying to scare me away, but now they are going after you, too, since we are engaged."

Elijah pondered her words. "Are you planning on solving this mystery?"

"I want to try, but—"

"The Bible says to turn the other cheek."

"The Bible also says your body is a temple of the Holy Spirit and to take care of it. That means to protect it," Charlie countered. It was the best comeback she could think of.

Elijah smiled. "You are correct in that. But we must give this over to God. We must not worry. It is all in His hands. Okay, darling?"

"What if... What if the attacks don't go away? What if they get worse? What if someone gets killed because of our wedding, Elijah? Is this a sign we shouldn't get married?" Charlie asked.

"No. I know with all my heart it is the Lord's will for us to be married. Now we must obey Him and trust God, and whatever will happen is His will. We will not let fear control our lives, Charlie."

Charlie desperately wanted to find the culprit so she could stop worrying about their safety. She realized there was something else that would be hard to give up now that she was Amish: the freedom to seek justice. She had to trust that God would do that for her.

278

CHAPTER THIRTY-NINE

When all of the Amish men and women showed up at the site of the barn the next morning, everyone began asking questions. Elijah stood before them and told them what had happened.

"What if someone burns down the barn right after we complete it?" someone in the crowd asked. "If it's a bunch of rowdy *Englishers,* they might do just that."

"Then we build another one for Elijah," someone countered.

Elijah told them, "I would appreciate that, but I understand that this barn may not survive long before being destroyed. As some of you may know, there have been some attacks on my fiancée, Charlotte, ever since she arrived. Someone has destroyed her clothing, vandalized the Holts' buggy, and now has trespassed onto our property last night. Someone also hit my buggy with their car, even though that could have been just a coincidental accident. Last night someone tried to burn down this barn, but they failed because, I must confess, I put the fire out. I did not want your hard work to go to waste. I'm sorry. I used a fire extinguisher."

The bishop and several church elders conversed quietly among themselves then told Elijah they forgave him, considering the circumstances and how his family died in a fire.

Elijah thanked them and looked at all the workers. "If you think it is a waste of time to build something that very well might be destroyed in less than a day or two and you don't want to help build this barn, I understand. I will not hold it against you."

Elijah waited and there was a minute of silence. Eyes glanced around warily, questioning who would turn away. But even after several moments, no one left.

"We stand with you, Elijah. No work, if done in the Lord's name, is ever done in vain," Andrew said.

"Then let's repair the frame and continue building this barn. I thank every single one of you," Elijah said.

A week later, the barn was complete. Elijah and Charlie stood side by side, admiring the structure that symbolized their new life together.

"Do you think it will last?" Charlie asked.

"I honestly don't know, Charlie. But we can't worry about it," Elijah told her.

Charlie sighed. She wouldn't admit it, but whenever she woke up in the middle of the night, she would look out the window to watch for any trespassers. She never saw anyone. She prayed for God to reveal the trespasser or make the person stop their attacks so they could live in peace and begin their new life.

***

The following Sunday, the bishop approached Charlie after church as she was leaving.

"Charlotte, I'd like to speak with you for a moment," he said. His long beard bobbed up and down as he spoke. "As you know, we have been looking for a new teacher here at the schoolhouse. Lydia and our other temporary replacement can't continue teaching much longer. I was talking to Lydia recently, and she said that you want to be a teacher."

Excitement welled up inside Charlie, but she told herself not to get her hopes up yet. "Yes, to become a teacher has always been my lifelong dream."

"Do you have any experience?" he asked.

"I apprenticed with teachers when I was in high school, I took a few classes on teaching, and I have taught Sunday School at church. However, I do not have a college degree."

"A degree does not matter to us. Our teachers only have an eighth-grade education. What matters is a person who truly cares about her students and will work hard to teach them everything she can. Someone dedicated and committed. Are you willing to be such a person?"

"Oh, yes, I would try my best!"

He stroked his gray beard. "I believe it. You have completed high school and have some experience. After you officially join the church, I think you'd be just the right person for the job."

"Really?"

He smiled, the wrinkles around his brown eyes crinkling. "Absolutely. You have come a very long way since you first arrived here, learning about our ways. Everyone here loves you as our own. Talk to Elijah about it and let me know. All right?"

She willed herself to not jump up and down. "Yes. Thank you." If Elijah was fine with her teaching soon after the wedding, and she was sure he would be, she would want to start a few weeks after the wedding. She would need some time to adjust to married life before launching herself into teaching.

"Good. Thank you, Charlotte. If the answer is yes, meet with Lydia soon so she can show you what the students have been learning so you will know what they need to learn. Have a great day," he said, tipping his hat and walking away.

Charlie smiled to herself. She looked heavenward and whispered, "Thank you."

Elijah came up behind her. "What did he talk to you about?"

"He asked me to be the next teacher after I join the church!" she cried. She wanted to leap into his arms, but that would be wildly inappropriate, especially in front of the church. Instead, Elijah touched her arm for a brief moment.

"I'm so happy for you," he said, his eyes twinkling. "This has always been your dream. Did you tell him yes?"

"Well, I was going to talk to you about it first. It would be a few weeks after the wedding."

"Of course, you should do it! Whatever makes you happy."

"I can't wait to start. I'm going to tell him our answer is yes before he leaves," she said, hurrying towards Bishop Zook as he was getting into his buggy. After she gave him her answer, she stopped to talk to Lydia, who was standing outside after talking to some other woman.

"Thank you so much for telling the bishop about me," Charlie said. "I'll be starting soon after the wedding."

"You're welcome. I can't think of anyone better for the job than you, Charlotte. You will be a great teacher for those students. They will learn so much from you."

"I am excited beyond belief to start. All my life I dreamed of being a teacher, and now I finally can be. And I don't even have a degree."

"What's important is the attitude of the heart," Lydia said, stroking the mane of her horse. "And your heart is in the right place."

"Thank you. Really, I can't thank you enough for this."

"This is God's plan for you. He's the one who brought you here. We are all your family now. We all take care of each other."

Charlie looked around, feeling more blessed than she had in her entire life. Tears of joy stung her eyes, and she blinked them back. "God has brought me so far and given me more than I ever dreamed of. I can't believe how much He has given me. I don't deserve this."

"It is all by the grace of God." Lydia smiled and reached for Charlie's hand. "Isn't God so good?"

"Yes. I knew that my whole life, because my parents always taught me that, but I never fully realized it until now."

CHAPTER FORTY

That night, Charlie went out to the new barn and walked through it alone. Elijah already had their new animals in their pens, and Charlie breathed in the scent of hay, imagining what other animals would fill the stalls. A horse, a pig, some sheep and goats slept in their barn. She imagined their children and Zoe taking care of the animals and running around the property. What would their life be like? What things would they overcome together? Charlie knew life could be hard, but now that she had Elijah and her stronger faith, nothing could be that bad.

She heard a noise. She heard footsteps behind her. She knew Elijah and everyone else was asleep. Who else would have followed her out here?

The trespasser.

Heart racing, she ran into one of the stalls and crouched in the corner. She tried to quiet her breathing and her heart. She waited as she heard the footsteps come closer. Then Charlie panicked.

What if the person set the barn on fire and Charlie couldn't escape?

Charlie didn't know what to do. She had no way of knowing if the intruder had a weapon. She might have a greater chance of being killed if she ran rather than waiting and trying to escape the possible fire.

Charlie began to tremble, fearing the worst. She tried to think straight, but fear clouded her brain. Before she could make a decision on what to do, she heard a soft voice.

"Charlotte? I know you're in here. I followed you."

Leah?

Charlie slowly stood and looked out from the stall. Leah stood in the middle of the barn, looking around for her.

"I'm here. I'm sorry. I thought you were someone else." She felt foolish for hiding from Leah.

"I came here to talk to you." Leah timidly stepped forward, holding a can of red paint.

The same color that had said *she should leave* on Irvin's buggy.

"Where did you find that?" Charlie asked, hoping Leah had found the culprit. "Did you see who did that to your family's buggy? Whose paint is that?"

"Mine."

Charlie stared at her, astonished. What was Leah saying?

"I'm the one, Charlie. I tried to scare you with the flashlight that night when I shone it in your window. I cut up your clothes and I vandalized our buggy with this," Leah held out the paint, and a tear fell from her eye.

"Why?" Charlie asked incredulously.

"Because, don't you see? Everything in my life was great until you came along. I always thought I was in love with Elijah. I was the oldest child. He worked on *my* farm, and I always thought *we* would get married. Of course, I never told him that, because I didn't want to seem improper. Besides that, I was way too shy. Then you came along, and I thought you were going to take my place and Elijah would love you instead of me. And he does. He truly does love you, not me." Leah thrust the paint towards Charlie like it would burn her hand if she held it any longer. "Not only that, but I think I've been lied to my whole life. It didn't take long for me to figure out that we're twins. Now I finally know the truth."

Charlie felt sympathy for Leah for a moment, but it was quickly replaced with anger. She'd talk with her about the fact that they were

285

twins later. "What about the barn? Was that you?"

"It was me. Honestly, I didn't mean for that to happen. I was taking a walk because I couldn't sleep and walked by the barn. I was so angry that Elijah rejected me and chose you instead that I threw the kerosene lantern on the ground. Clearly, I wasn't thinking logically. When the fire started, I panicked. Once I realized it was getting out of control, I ran back into the house before Elijah could see me. That was when I woke everyone up, even though I knew Elijah had already put it out anyway with the fire extinguisher. I was afraid someone would see the fire and wonder why I wasn't in bed.

"Then I thought maybe Elijah would give up and it would stop the wedding. But you and he and everyone persevered, and that was when I realized I cannot stop the two of you from getting married. Clearly, it is God's will, and I am so terribly sorry I was so horrible. And about your clothes, that was only meant to scare you away. I thought that if I destroyed everything you'd brought with you, you'd have to leave. I didn't think you'd want to wear Amish clothing. Instead, you ended up borrowing *my* dress. The plan backfired. I am so sorry." She hung her head in shame. "Guilt has been plaguing me so badly that it is consuming me, and I knew I had to tell you tonight."

"What about Elijah's buggy accident?" Charlie demanded. "Did you have anything to do with that?"

"No, I swear, I did not. That was just a random drunk driver, like the police assumed. I had no connection to that accident. But I am so sorry for all the trouble I caused…" Leah said, and she began to cry. Quiet tears turned into sobs that wracked Leah's body. She covered her face with her hands.

For a few moments, Charlie stared at Leah and let her anger control her. How could her own twin sister treat her and Elijah like this? What would ever possess someone to do such things?

"You could have gotten someone killed by setting that barn on fire, Leah. Elijah's own family died in a fire. Do you know what burning that barn did to him?" Charlie shouted in anger. "It brought back all those horrific memories."

"I know, I know. I didn't mean for it to go so far. And I have never regretted anything more in my entire life," Leah said between sobs and short breaths.

"How could you do this to us?" Charlie cried and threw the can of paint as hard as she could. It hit the ground with a *thwack* that echoed through the barn. "You terrified me, letting me think Alex was stalking me. I thought he was going to attack me. You cut up my clothes, burned our barn that everyone worked so hard to build... What kind of person can be that heartless?"

Leah crumpled to the ground, overtaken by sobs.

Charlie felt a stab of guilt. She knew she had to forgive Leah, but she didn't know how. *Lord, give me the strength to do the right thing,* she prayed.

Suddenly, despite all her anger, the verse about forgiving seventy times seven times popped into her head. Who was Charlie to judge and be angry with Leah? Clearly, Leah had been so blinded by anger and jealousy that she hadn't been thinking rationally.

Recalling when she had sold the ring from Alex after she had caught him with another woman, Charlie remembered feeling the same way. She had been so angry she had acted impulsively and recklessly, though she never would have gone as far as Leah had.

But she had learned her lesson, and now Leah would learn from her own mistakes as well.

"I'm sorry. I'm sorry for being so harsh." Charlie took a deep breath and knelt beside Leah, taking her hand. "There's something else we should talk about. Esther told me everything. She told me how you figured out that we're twins soon after I got here."

"I figured we had to be close in age. I thought at first that Joanna had chosen you over me when we were babies, and that she'd discarded me like trash but kept you to raise. I was so confused, hurt, and jealous. But then I confronted *Maam,* and she told me everything."

"I know this must be a shock. It was for me. At least you now know that Mom—Joanna—didn't choose me over you. In fact, it's the other way around. Our biological mother raised you and not me, even though she wanted both of us."

"I know. She's been through so much. But they lied to me my whole life," Leah swatted away a tear, anger crossing her face for a moment. "They lied to both of us."

"They were just trying to protect you. Besides, Irvin is your true father who raised you, not some stranger, a heartless criminal. Sometimes DNA doesn't matter."

Leah nodded slowly. "You're right."

"We are sisters. Sisters always forgive each other, no matter what," Charlie told Leah, holding onto her twin tightly. "I'd be a fool to push away my own sister. I forgive you, Leah. All those things that you did, they don't matter anymore. I'm sorry how I reacted. I love you."

Leah sniffed. "I love you too. I am happy for you and Elijah. I pray for the best for you. When you wed Elijah, you can count on me being your biggest supporter, helper, and best friend."

"Best friend?" Charlie asked. "Honestly, I have never had a best friend before, so I might not be that great at it."

"I've had many friends here in the community, but I don't think I've ever had a true best friend in a long time. We can learn together."

CHAPTER FORTY-ONE

Now that she knew who had been behind the campaign against her, the following Sunday, Charlie joined the Amish church. She had previously asked Bishop Zook and the elders if she could stand before the church and be baptized, and they had readily approved.

She would stand alone because Zoe was too young to join. She would make that decision on her own during or after her teen years. Once a year all the young adults who chose to remain Amish were baptized sometime in the fall together, but that had already gone by, so she stood alone.

"Good morning," she said to the audience of faces. "I am standing here before you today to ask you to accept me into your church and community. I have given up everything I had that was worldly. I want to become Amish and devote my life to serving the Lord and live here with my younger sister." Fear rose in her stomach. What if someone objected?

She searched the faces before her. Silently, several of them began to slowly nod. She waited a few more moments, but all she received were smiles and expressions of approval.

"Do you commit your life to serving God and serving others as is the Amish way of life?" the bishop asked her.

"Yes."

"And you accept Christ Jesus as your savior, loving Him with all your heart?"

"Yes," she said.

"Then I baptize you in the name of the Father, Son and Holy Spirit." He cupped his hands into a basin of water and poured it over her head three times, baptizing her into the church.

"Welcome to the Amish church, Charlotte Cooper," Bishop Zook said to her.

Overflowing with joy, Charlie expressed her gratitude and took her seat. By then everyone had heard of the robberies committed by Alex and how Charlie was innocent. After church, several people apologized to her. From the ones who did not speak their regret out loud, she received apologetic looks and smiles.

Among the people who told her they were sorry was the group that had been at the applesauce party. One by one they expressed the regrets they had about talking about her that day. Charlie graciously forgave every one of them. She could see how they could have made the assumption that she was guilty of stealing their money after all that had happened.

"Charlie?"

Charlie turned to see Matthew, Luke, and Andrew approaching her.

"We are so happy that you've joined the church, and for you and Elijah," Matthew began, awkwardly shuffling his feet. Luke and Andrew smiled but could barely maintain eye contact.

"Thank you." She tilted her head.

"We have to apologize," Andrew said.

"We jumped to conclusions about you, and we were wrong. So terribly wrong," Luke added.

"We feel awful about it. Could you forgive us?" Matthew asked.

"Of course." Charlie grinned, filled with encouragement that she was now on good terms with Elijah's dear friends. "It means so much to me to hear you say that. And I also have to apologize to you all too. I thought you were behind those mean pranks because I had heard you didn't want me here. I was also wrong and jumped to conclusions."

Matthew waved his hand. "All is forgiven. We are human and make mistakes."

"I probably would have thought the same thing in your shoes." Luke smiled at her, and it was genuine.

"Elijah is one of my closest friends. I can see now he chose a wonderful woman to be his wife," Andrew said.

"Thank you all so much."

"We had to speak with you, but we don't want to keep you. People are lining up to talk to you," Luke said.

"I pray you have a happy life together." Andrew nodded.

"And welcome to our community," Matthew added before they walked away. "We are happy you are here."

Mrs. Duncan was the last to apologize to Charlie. She stepped up to her and rested a hand on Charlie's shoulder.

"I am sorry I suspected you at the applesauce party and tried to make everyone think you stole the money. I watched and listened to you talking to Sharon about planes and asking her questions while you were making applesauce, and I assumed the worst, especially after you left church early the day before. I thought you were a bad influence. It seemed like it made sense at the time, but now I see how blind I was. I am so sorry, Charlotte. My daughter, Sharon, loves you. I'd love to see the two of you become good friends," Mrs. Duncan told her with kindness in her eyes. "I am very happy you have joined the church, and I welcome you to our community."

Charlie's eyes misted. "Thank you," she whispered and gave her a hug. "That means a lot to me."

Sharon came up behind her mother and touched her arm. They

exchanged smiles, and Sharon took Charlie's hands. "I am so happy for you, Charlotte. I'd love to have you come to my house sometime so we can talk about it."

Even though Sharon was a few years younger than Charlie, she was grateful for another friend. "I'd love that."

As she looked around at all the genuine smiles that were directed her way, Charlie felt truly accepted into the community.

As Elijah gazed at her and smiled in joy and approval, she finally felt at home. And, especially after she and Elijah were married, she knew she would never leave. She had everything she needed here. She thanked God for His abundant blessings.

CHAPTER FORTY-TWO

On the day of her wedding, Charlie put on her simple blue dress. As she sat down among her friends and family, all smiling at her, she knew this was all she wanted. Elijah's aunts, cousins and uncles were there, along with the Holts, and Lydia, even Joe the museum owner, and all of the people she loved.

Charlie wished her parents could be here. She looked heavenward, hoping they were watching. Then she looked at the front row, where two seats were saved by two candles. One for her mother and one for her father. She teared up at the sight but felt a peace in her heart. She knew they were watching, and she knew they would be so happy with her decision to marry Elijah. But she was thankful for all the people who were able to attend.

Elijah's friends had moved the school room divider aside, so it was all open and connected to the room where church services were held. The chairs were set up in a circular shape, so they all faced a pulpit in the middle of the large room where the rooms met. That was where the speakers would stand. And at the end of the service, that was where Charlie and Elijah would stand as they were married.

The classroom section usually looked like a classroom with educational decorations like posters and students' artwork on the walls. Where the walls and ceiling met, a border of numbers and letters remained. Bookshelves still stood, holding encyclopedias and textbooks. The chalkboard and dry erase board remained on the walls, but everything else that was school-related had been temporarily moved out. Charlie loved all of it.

There were no decorations or finery. Charlie and Elijah wore clothes that looked just like clothes they usually wore, and they did not at all stand out from the guests.

As each guest got a pamphlet with chosen songs from the *Ausbund,* Charlie greeted Linda and Tonya.

"We are so happy for you!" they squealed and began to chatter excitedly. Charlie sure would miss these two women, even if they could talk your ear off.

When they received their pamphlets, Charlie saw Tonya whisper to Linda, "This is all in German."

"The English part is written right below the German words," Charlie pointed out.

A Mennonite girl beside them offered, "I can sing the English part with you if you want. Do you know German?"

"No," they replied.

"It's okay. A translator will be sitting near you so that you will not have to listen to three hours of German and have no idea what is going on," Charlie told them.

"Oh good."

Charlie continued to look around the room. Even Diane was at the wedding, the lady who worked at the store and had called the police when Charlie had left the note saying that she'd been kidnapped.

When Diane arrived, Charlie approached her.

"I would like to officially introduce myself." Charlie took Diane's hand. "I'm Charlotte Cooper, and I want to thank you for calling the police for me that day. I do not know where my younger sister and I would be without you. We, along with Elijah, sincerely thank you."

"It is so nice to meet you, Charlotte. As soon as you handed me that slip of paper, I knew what I had to do. I called the police right away. Then someone reported the message in the bathroom, so I reported that too. I hoped you would find me. I know the Amish don't have phones, and so I had no clue how I would ever be able to track you down. I am so happy you put in the effort to call the store, ask for me, and invite me to your wedding. Thank you." Her eyes sparkled as she smiled warmly at Charlie.

The bishop signaled to Charlie that the wedding was about to start, so Charlie thanked Diane for coming and hugged her. As Charlie walked towards the front of the church, she saw that Matthew, the young man who would court Leah soon, was there. Charlie could tell just by the way he looked across the room at Leah that he was in love with her. Charlie wondered how long it would be until her twin was also married.

Keeping her word, Leah had risen hours before everyone else, making preparations. It seemed she had done more work than all the women combined. Now, as Charlie approached the front of the church, Leah squeezed Charlie's hand. They smiled at each other, silently communicating their happiness and redeemed relationship. Charlie took her place next to Elijah in their seats at the front of the church, near the bishop.

The wedding started a few minutes before nine o'clock. There was no grand entrance with Charlie's walk down the aisle. There were no romantic, self-written vows. There was no white gown or veil, and there were no flowers or instruments. There were only the people she loved in their plain clothes sitting in their plain, rugged church.

Everyone stopped talking as the wedding started. They sang the German hymns for the first hour. Some of the *Englishers* started getting fidgety after a while. It was a long time to sing songs you didn't understand, and the songs were very slow. And since they did not understand the words, it probably seemed a lot longer than an hour to them. However, her friends were completely patient throughout the entire service, although Linda and Tonya seemed to get a little antsy and anxious for it to be over so they could move around. Charlie was feeling fidgety too. She just wanted it to be over so she could be married. Charlie grinned at Elijah briefly, and he smiled back. She had never seen him look so happy.

An Amish man, one of Elijah's friends, gave a message in German. Right before the man started to speak, another man came into the room and sat among those who were not Amish. The Amish speaker began his message in German.

The man who had just arrived also began speaking in a loud voice, saying, "Brothers and sisters, we are gathered here today to celebrate the marriage of this young man and woman…"

Charlie thought at first, *Why is he talking like that? What is he trying to do, disrupt the wedding?* She was not the only one who thought that because he received several strange looks. She then realized this was the translator some of the men had been talking about. Charlie had never experienced listening to a translator before, except for when Esther had once translated the church service for Charlie. But she had been very quiet, and this man was speaking loudly so the other half of the room could hear him. It was strange to hear both the translator and the speaker speaking at once, especially since Charlie now knew bits of what the man was saying in German.

Every now and then the translator would pause and say, "I didn't get

297

that…. Anyway…" and continue on. The man speaking in German was across the room so sometimes the translator didn't hear him. After the man speaking in German was done, the translator slipped out as quickly as he had slipped in. Charlie wondered why he did not stay. Perhaps he had done his job and saw no reason to stay if he did not personally know the bride or groom.

Irvin spoke next. He spoke in English, and Charlie was grateful to fully understand him. He talked about when Elijah was little and also about the responsibility of the man being the leader of the household. He said a good marriage takes two good forgivers. Charlie liked that point. He spoke of when Elijah's family died, and Elijah let a few tears fall. Charlie desperately wanted to squeeze his hand in comfort, but knew that would be inappropriate.

Next to speak was Bishop Zook. As the speaking carried into the third hour, Charlie felt very fortunate to have a chair with a backing. Many people sat on not so comfortable benches for the three hours. The group of boys who sat on benches across the aisle put their elbows on their knees and their chins on their knuckles, looking like they would much rather be doing something else. But everyone was patient throughout the long service. Charlie supposed they must be used to it because their regular church services were about two-and-a-half hours long.

The actual vows and marriage ceremony took about five minutes out of the entire service. The bishop called her and Elijah forward and asked them vows similar to the ones Charlie had heard at other weddings, but they were worded a little differently. Instead of saying "I do" in response to the vows, Elijah simply said, "Yes." At the end, Bishop Zook joined Charlie's and Elijah's hands together.

When Elijah smiled at Charlie and took her hand, her heart felt like it would burst because it was so full of joy. Her groom did not place a ring on her finger. Instead, he just held her hand, promising to love her for the rest of her days. In that moment she knew nothing that life would throw at them would be that bad because she would have him with her.

Bishop Zook said, "A three-cord strand is not easily broken. The three-cord strand represents the husband, the wife, and God."

When the bishop pronounced that they were married, Elijah and Charlie grinned at each other like the first time they had met when they were children. Charlie wanted to skip around the church, jump for joy and run out the door giggling with Elijah, but she told herself to wait and contain her happiness. There was no kissing the bride, only simple words promising their lives to one another.

As people approached them one after another, so many kind words were spoken, they muddled together in Charlie's brain. She was thankful for each and every word.

***

After the last few guests trickled out of the church and everything was cleaned up, Zoe went home with the Holts, and the newlyweds rode to Elijah's little house.

The buggy jostled along the rocky lane, and the sun reclined on a bed of hills and distant mountains. Elijah leaned in and kissed her for the first time, now that they were alone, and her head spun in delight. Finally, she had found peace and happiness. She was so content, more content than she ever thought she would be in life.

"If I had given you a ring, would you have kept it?" Elijah asked Charlie jokingly.

She leaned her head on her husband's shoulder and smiled. "I don't even want a ring. Your love is all I need."

"Well, I do have one small gift for you to express my love for you." He reached for something at his feet and handed her a cloth bag. She opened it and pulled out a Bible with her new name, *Charlotte Hostettler,* on the front.

"Oh, Elijah, I love it. This is wonderful."

He gave a crooked smile. "Open it."

She opened the book and it fell open to a few famous verses about love in 1 Corinthians, where a crinkly orange wrapper marked the pages. "The lollipop wrapper." She laughed and squeezed her husband's arm. "Thank you, Elijah."

And she treasured that orange lollipop wrapper more than any diamond ring.

EPILOGUE

One Year Later

Matthew glanced at the clock. The three-hour church service was almost over. He was glad not only because he was stiff and famished, but because he was anxious to talk to Leah.

Another speaker began closing the ceremony, which signaled that the church service was over, and some of the girls and women left the room to prepare lunch.

Today was the day, Matthew was sure of it. Love permeated the church, flowing through all the worshipers and bursting through the windows. It was especially filling his heart as he gazed at Leah. He promised himself that today he would tell Leah how he felt. He had already asked Irvin, who had readily approved of their courtship. Now all he had to do was ask Leah.

He approached her, and today she seemed to glow brighter than he had ever seen her before. Her smile was dazzling, and her skin was luminous. She talked with the other women much more sociably than he had seen her in a long time. Before he could think twice, he walked right up to her.

"Hello, Leah."

She turned to him and grinned. "Well, hello, Matthew. A lovely day, isn't it?"

"Yes, it is. Did you help with the food?" he asked. She was an amazing cook.

"Oh, yes. I made shoofly pie and sandwiches."

"You are so thoughtful and kind, Leah."

Well, that was a start. She blushed and toyed with one of the ribbons on her *kapp.*

"I just like to help," she said softly.

He took a deep breath and willed the words to come. He was on a roll. He couldn't stop now.

"Leah, I'm just going to say it. I was wondering if you would do me the honor of letting me court you. Or at least if you would consider it..."

Her hand fell from her ribbons and she stared at him. Her smile faded, and she looked right into his eyes, her own widening. Then her grin quickly returned.

"Yes. I would love that." She covered her mouth in surprise. "We've known each other so long. I have been wondering lately if our relationship would turn into anything beyond a friendship."

"I've wanted to ask you for a long time. I'm sorry I never had the courage to tell you until now," he said, his eyes shying away from hers.

"No. Don't be sorry. Honestly, I wouldn't have been ready. It wouldn't have been the right time. In fact, I thought I was in love with someone else until a year ago. Recently I came to some realizations about myself. But I am feeling pretty guilty about some things I did a while back to Charlie when she first came here. I can tell you more later, but I was unkind to her. I was awful to her. I'm having a hard time forgiving myself, even after all this time."

"It couldn't have been that bad, Leah. Why, you wouldn't hurt a fly." Matthew could not picture Leah intentionally harming anyone.

She laughed out loud and gave him a sidelong glance. "You'd be surprised."

"Well, I don't need an answer on the courtship today. You should

302

think about it. But maybe we could spend some time together and you can tell me more about it," he said, hoping she'd agree. He'd be so happy if she would just go out with him once.

Concern lined her face, and she took a step back, crossing her arms over her chest. "Matthew, I do care for you very much, but I don't know if I could tell you what I did…"

He took a step towards her and quickly whispered in her ear when no one was paying attention, "There is nothing you could do that would make me love you any less." He quickly took a step back and waited, heart pounding. He looked around inconspicuously, hoping no one had noticed.

She only stared at him for a moment, and he was afraid he had offended her and crossed the line. Then the smile came, starting in her eyes and slowly spreading across her lovely mouth.

"I'm free tomorrow. Where do you want to go?" she asked.

***

As Charlie, Zoe, Elijah, Leah and Matthew walked home from church, their world unfolded before them in the rolling hills. Spring and summer had ended, and the trees would soon become ablaze with color again, but for now thousands of yellow flowers and green plants covered the fields. Charlie loved summer, and sometimes she wished it would never end. She took a deep breath, taking in the smells of the country.

She let her mind wander back to a few weeks ago when she had been subpoenaed to testify in court against Alex.

She had worn her best Amish dress, and she had to have a driver bring her to court in his car. He was one of the drivers many of the local Amish had recommended when they needed to take trips that were too long for a horse and buggy.

She had not expected the news channel to be at the courthouse with all their cameras. She should have figured as much; local crimes associated with the Amish were rare. As soon as she stepped out of the driver's car, they encircled her.

"Charlotte, did you really join the Amish after Alex Henderson threatened you?"

"Are you going to remain Amish forever?"

"What about your younger sister?"

She felt claustrophobic, as though they were closing in on her. She hid her face with her hands and walked away from them as quickly as possible. She certainly did not want to be seen on the news. She was already nervous to testify, and she did not need this added stress.

The D.A., Cindy Whiting, rushed to Charlotte's side. "The Amish do not like people to take pictures of them or record them. It is against their religious beliefs. Now, please, leave Mrs. Hochstettler alone and stop harassing her." She shooed them away sternly with one hand, and rested her other hand on Charlie's elbow, guiding her into the court house.

The door shut and the quietness settled around them. Charlie realized she had been holding her breath, and she sighed deeply. Video cameras had always made her nervous.

"The public and the media are fascinated with Amish stories. I wish they would just leave you alone. It's none of their business," the D.A. said, emptying her pockets into a round black container which she placed on a conveyor belt.

Charlie nodded in agreement, feeling like her privacy had been invaded. "A big reason why I joined the Amish was to get some peace."

"No doubt. Here, empty your things into this container. They have to put it through this machine for security." Cindy tossed back her blonde hair.

Charlie placed her wallet into the container then they stepped through a body scanner. The security guard gave them back their things and they went upstairs to an office near the courtroom. Charlie sat down and tried to calm herself.

Cindy had prepared Charlie well for testifying, practicing with her and asking her possible questions she would be asked. Charlie knew exactly what the truth was. Yet she knew Alex's lawyer would try to sandbag her, so she fought the butterflies in her stomach. She clasped her hands together in her lap to stop them from trembling.

"Are you ready?" Cindy asked.

"Yes." Charlie nodded firmly. "Just nervous."

"It's good to be nervous. It means it is important to you that you do well, and you will. We practiced this a hundred times."

"Right." Charlie took a deep breath, trying to lower her heart rate.

"Time to go," Cindy said, leading her to the courtroom.

Her stomach jumped at the words, and they entered the courtroom. Charlie had been here before, when the D.A. had met with her other times to prepare her for the case. She looked up at the portraits on the walls of former judges and the words above the windows which said words like Justice, Honor, and Integrity.

Charlie and Cindy took a seat on the middle left side of the room on wooden pews that looked like they belonged in a church. Alex entered, escorted by someone who looked like either a marshal or security guard; she wasn't sure. Alex was in a suit. She had expected him to be in orange and in chains, but that wouldn't be until the sentencing.

305

"He has an ankle monitor on, but you can't see it," Cindy explained.

Charlie's eyes widened.

"Don't worry. He would never get far."

"All rise for the jury," one of the marshals announced.

The jury filed in, each taking a spot on the front right side of the room. The judge entered, then everyone was seated. The prosecutor made an opening statement, then the defense made an opening statement. Charlie started to tune them out as she went over the questions and answers in her head.

"The court calls Charlotte Hochstettler to the witness stand."

Oh, God, help me do well.

Charlie stood and walked in front of where the people who came to watch were seated. She walked right past them and past the jury to where the witness stand was. She ignored them, focused on what she had to do.

A woman with a Bible approached her, telling her to raise her hand. "Do you swear to tell the truth, the whole truth and nothing but the truth, so help you God?"

"Yes."

The woman motioned for her to sit. A marshal poured her a cup of water and slid it behind her on her right side.

And so it began.

Cindy stood at a stand before her. Beyond her sat Alex, staring at Charlie blankly. She quickly looked away before he distracted her.

"Charlotte Hochstettler, do you know Alex Henderson?" Cindy asked her.

"Yes, I do. That's him." Charlie motioned to Alex. "We were engaged before I married my husband."

"What happened when you broke up with Alex?"

"I sold the ring he gave me online."

"Which was legal in this case, just so the jury knows. In Maine, engagement rings are conditional gifts. Since the giver of the ring broke off the engagement, the recipient could legally keep the ring," Cindy commented, turning towards the jury. "What happened after you sold the ring? How did Alex react?"

"He threatened me, but the man to whom I sold it had sold it to a pawn shop. It was bought by an unidentified customer with cash, and I couldn't get it back. Alex told me if I did not get his ring back that something bad would happen to me, my sister, or my dad. He also said he would put drugs in my house or car so the state would take my younger sister Zoe away from me. He also tried to choke me outside my house."

After she was questioned, the rest of the day passed in a blur, but Charlie knew she had done the best she could. Diane was called to testify.

Alex had been charged with assault, embezzlement, and kidnapping. After deliberating, the jury found him guilty on all three counts and the judge scheduled Alex's sentencing.

As Charlie watched Alex being led away, she realized she could finally start to live her life in peace.

***

Elijah gently took Charlie's hand as they watched Zoe run and jump through the grass. She also grinned at the sight of Matthew and Leah, who were walking to the Holts' together, much closer than usual. It was easy to see that Leah was happy. Had Matthew finally asked her to be his girlfriend? They walked down the hill and disappeared from view.

Charlie sighed contentedly, so thankful that she had made the choice

307

to join the church, marry Elijah, and raise Zoe here. Zoe deserved such a happy childhood.

In the time they had spent in Unity, Charlie had seen Zoe grow in confidence and in her walk with God. Elijah also told Charlie how she had grown in the same ways. The sisters were finally free to prosper.

Shortly after the wedding, Charlie began teaching in the schoolhouse. Her dream to be a teacher had finally come true after all, and she absolutely loved her students and her job more than she could have ever imagined. The Amish did not really care about diplomas that were just pieces of paper, but instead they valued kind hearts, a strong work ethic, and a willingness to learn.

On the horizon, Charlie could see their home, which had been completed. It was a large house with many windows and bright curtains. It was beautiful, and Elijah and Charlie planned on filling it with several precious children. Charlie could not have dreamed of a better house. It was not as she had imagined growing up, but now she was so thankful to call it home, wood stove and all.

"I can't wait to see our own children run around with Zoe," Elijah said with a smile. "Along with children Leah and Matthew will have someday."

"Speaking of children," Charlie said and turned to Elijah. "I have something to tell you."

Elijah stared at her in anticipation.

"We're going to have a baby."

Charlie barely got the words out before Elijah picked her up and spun her around. He kissed her, tears filling his eyes. "I'm so happy," he said softly into her ear.

Zoe ran over to them and asked what all the commotion was about, and they told her the good news.

Zoe shrieked, "I get a little niece or nephew?"

"Yes, but the baby will probably seem like more of a brother or sister to you."

"I wish we could find out if it is a boy or a girl before you have the baby," Zoe said, then gasped. She put her small hands on her face, her eyes wide with wonder. "Maybe you'll have twins! Oh, I really hope we get twins."

Charlie and Elijah laughed.

"That would be amazing. We will have to wait and see what God gives us. It will be a surprise," Charlie told her, grinning.

"Look at this!" Elijah knelt down and pointed to something small and green hanging from the leaf of a plant.

"This is what I told you about, Charlie. This is a monarch caterpillar's chrysalis. When it opens, a butterfly will come out," Elijah explained. "Isn't it amazing?"

Charlie and Zoe stared in wonder at the green capsule, not much bigger than the tip of her finger, with tiny gold studs lining the top.

"A caterpillar went in there and it is being changed into a butterfly?" Zoe asked, astounded.

"Yes. It is called a metamorphosis," Elijah told her. He looked lovingly at Charlie. "You both have had a metamorphosis of your own."

"Yes," Charlie said in realization, nodding. She held his hand with one hand. "We have."

Free Bonus Novelette: Esther's Amish Secret

CHAPTER 1

Twenty-one Years Ago

Joanna Miller pulled the quilt up over her and her sister and whispered, "I have to tell you something that is both good and bad."

The sisters huddled together in a bed covered with an intricate, colorful Amish quilt. "What is it? Tell me," Esther insisted.

"You know I have seen Greg a few times, the man who works at Joe's old museum down the road—"

"I told you, you should not get too involved with an *Englischer.*"

"I've been a lot more involved than I've let on."

"What do you mean? Are you dating him? But he's not Amish. That's forbidden." Though Esther had to admit that the idea of her sister secretly meeting a nice young man at the museum—which was really an old antique store full of old stoves, toys, and player pianos—seemed wildly romantic and exciting.

"Yes, we have been secretly dating for several months now. Actually... We want to get married. We've been talking about it."

"What?" Esther cried out, throwing the quilt off them, not caring that her voice was above a whisper. She didn't want to wake their large family or their younger sister who slept soundly on the other side of the room. Their kerosene lantern cast a glow on the simple wooden nightstand and dresser made skillfully by their father.

Esther lowered her voice. "You're acting *ferhuddled*. Are you crazy? You can't marry him. You'll be shunned. You don't want that, do you?"

"Of course not. But I love Greg and he loves me. If our family and community have a problem with that, it's not my fault. I don't think it is wrong for me to marry Greg just because he is not Amish. He is still a Christian."

"No, no. This cannot be happening." Esther pressed her palms to her temples. "You can't get shunned." She turned and faced her sister. "Don't marry him, please. Please don't do it."

"I'm so sorry, Esther, but I love him. We truly love each other. I've already decided I'm going to marry him." Joanna shrugged and shook her head. "I'll never be happy if I don't marry him."

"Joanna, don't do it. Tell him no."

"I've already decided. I'm doing this, Esther."

"When would I ever see you?" It was clear that Joanna had made up her mind, and no one would be able to stop her.

"We are going to move to Portland after we get married. It's only an hour and a half away by car. You can come visit me there or I could secretly pick you up. I'll learn how to drive a car, you know. Can you imagine?"

Esther teared up at the thought of her favorite sister leaving forever, then they looked at each other and giggled again.

"I'll be sad to see you leave, but I am awfully happy for you," Esther said. "Will you have a fancy wedding with a white gown and flowers and everything? And a ring? And you'll even kiss at the ceremony?"

"Yes. I mean, it won't be too fancy. He's not rich, and we do need to save up the money for an apartment. But he did say he's going to get me a diamond ring."

"Oh, wow. Sometimes I wish we could wear jewelry and have wedding rings. Do you really think it is prideful?"

"No, unless you walk around like this." Joanna got out of bed and did her best impersonation of a prideful *Englischer*. "Look at my ring, isn't it lovely? It is so big that sometimes my hand gets tired from wearing it. Isn't it so beautiful and shiny?"

Esther fell on the bed laughing. "Promise me you won't be like that."

"I won't. I won't remain Amish and wear my dress and *kapp*, but I will always remember the values we have been taught and everything we have learned about God. The important things I will not change my mind about." Joanna settled back onto the bed.

Esther rolled over and turned off the kerosene lantern. "When will you be getting married?"

"He proposed today," came the excited whisper in the dark.

"What?" Esther grabbed Joanna's arm. "When will you tell *Daed* and *Maam*?"

"As soon as I get the courage. I wish that things were different. I wish there was no such thing as a shunning, and I wish *Maam* and *Daed* didn't follow the *Ordnung* so strictly. Why are the rules so strict? Will

312

our parents really be able to live with themselves if they shun their own daughter? How will they bear not ever speaking to me again?"

"They would see it as the right thing to do. We can't change their minds." Esther sighed.

"Will you come visit me in Portland?"

"Of course, I'll come visit you!"

"You'll have to lie. You never lie. If they find out you're speaking to me, you could be shunned, too, depending on when you get baptized," Joanna warned.

"I can do it without anyone finding out. I want to see you," Esther insisted.

"You could say you're going to Smyrna."

"Whatever it takes."

"You might have a proposal of your own soon. Irvin likes you," Joanna said.

"Really? You think so?"

Joanna swatted her sister in the arm and pushed the blanket off them again. "You're the one who's *ferhuddled*. Of course, he likes you. He trips over his own two feet and blubbers like a fool when he's around you. He might even love you."

"What?" Esther sat up and pulled back her dark hair that reached far past her waist. She thought it was her one beautiful feature when she could let it fall around her shoulders. Even though he'd never seen her hair, Esther wondered if Irvin found her pretty. She knew it was vain to wonder, but she couldn't help it.

Joanna nodded. "Remember that one time when he got his words so mixed up when you walked up to him that he blushed and ran outside, making up some excuse that made no sense about why he had to leave?"

Esther laughed a little too loudly, then clamped a hand over her mouth. Their younger sister stirred in her bed but did not wake up.

"That was so funny when he did that. He was so embarrassed. Poor guy."

When Joanna stopped laughing, Esther's smile faded. "*Was ist letz?* What is wrong?"

"You're my best friend. I don't know what I'd do without you." Esther's eyes welled up with tears, and a sob escaped her lips. She buried her face into a pillow, trying not to wake anyone.

"It's all right, Esther," Joanna murmured, rubbing Esther's back. She continued talking, but Joanna's words became muddled in Esther's brain as overwhelming sorrow covered her. Her vision blurred as she looked up at her sister, then Esther threw her arms around Joanna, crying into her shoulder.

Nothing would ever be the same. Once Joanna left, Esther would lose her best friend.

Eventually, Esther moved to her own twin bed. She closed her eyes, but thoughts about her sister leaving kept her awake.

She was going to have to lie after all. It was the only way she'd be able to visit her sister.

Nothing would stop her from seeing her sister.

***

Esther walked down the lane to the Unity Community Market, sent by her mother to get flour and rice for dinner. Irvin worked there, so anticipation of seeing him made her stomach swirl with excitement. Maybe *Maam* had sent her specifically, knowing Irvin would be there. Esther's parents were fond of Irvin, and Esther knew they hoped that Irvin and Esther would get married one day.

Lucky for them, it was something they all agreed on.

Esther opened the door to the market, and when the bell on it rang, Irvin looked up from stocking shelves. A wide grin lit up his handsome face.

"Hello, Esther. Glad to see you here," he said.

"Hi. I'm just picking up some flour and rice for my mother," she said, nervously skirting around him to get to the aisle with the dry goods.

"Are you alone?"

She pulled a large bag of rice off the shelf. "*Ja*. It's just me." That was when she realized just how quiet the store was at the moment. No music played like in regular stores, but still, it was quieter than usual.

"My father went home early. I'm here to close up," Irvin said, hurrying over to take the bag from her. "Here, let me carry that for you."

"Thank you." She let him take it, then moved on to the flour section. The silence hung in the air, thick like fog. She grabbed the bag of flour off the shelf, thankful for something to fill her hands.

"Want me to carry that too?"

"No, I've got it. Thanks. Well, that's all I need," she said, turning to walk to the checkout, and he followed her.

She put the bag on the counter and he totaled the amount, then she took the cash from her pocket and handed it to him.

"Esther, there's something I've been wanting to talk to you about," he said, and his hand trembled as he handed her change to her. He set his hands on the counter in an effort to still them.

Her heart leapt. "*Ja?* What is it?"

"How about if I walk you home and we talk on the way? It's almost closing time anyway. I'll lock the door and finish the rest later."

"Sure."

They stepped outside and walked back to her house. "Here, let me hold those."

"Thank you," she said, knowing perfectly well she could have carried the bags home with no problem, but she didn't want to hurt his feelings.

Several minutes passed in silence, as if he was searching for the right words. She made a few comments on birds and the weather to fill the silence, but it wasn't awkward with him, even when they didn't speak. Esther waited for him to find the words he wanted to say.

They approached her house and were running out of time. Soon other people would be around and they would no longer be alone, but they were still about five hundred feet away. "Well... Well... I was wondering if..." Irvin stammered, scratching his neck as if the air had suddenly got hotter.

"Irvin, you can talk to me about anything, you know," she said softly, reaching out and taking hold of his hand, and they both stopped walking to look at each other. She didn't care if it was bold or if someone saw her. She was rewarded with a crooked smile from him and a red blush that crept up his cheeks.

"Good. Well, I was hoping that... If you want to... I want to ask you if..." He shifted his weight and looked at the ground. "Um..."

"Irvin, just ask me," she said, almost certain he was trying to ask her if he could court her.

"Uh, I better go close up. I'm sorry, Esther." He shoved the bag of rice and flour into her arms and ran down the lane back to the store.

Esther stared at him, puzzled. What had just happened? Didn't he want to court her? Why had he run off like that?

***

"I have to do this." Esther watched in dismay as Joanna packed her few precious possessions in a backpack, her diamond ring flashing on her finger. Since they were raised to not put value in objects or possessions and Joanna would have no need for her Amish clothing, there was not much to pack. No photos, no diaries; only a few things from her childhood and things family and friends had given her.

"No! They will send you away!" Esther cried.

"That's why I'm packing now," Joanna said and picked up the bag with determination. "Greg is waiting outside. Let's get this over with."

"Joanna, wait. Are you sure you want to do this?" Esther grabbed her sister's arm.

"I've never been surer of anything. I choose the *Englisch* life. Amish life may be meant for you, but it's not for me. We can't wear what we want, or own vehicles, or be unique. We can't even play instruments, and you know how much I love playing the old pianos at the museum with Greg. That's how we fell in love in the first place. If I stay here any longer, I'll suffocate. I learned how to play the piano so quickly. I'm good at it, Esther. I want to be free to play the piano and marry who I love."

317

Esther frowned. Those things didn't matter to her, except marrying who she chose, and she loved Irvin. Esther didn't mind if she couldn't wear makeup or pants, or watch TV. Those things were not important. The simple life was what was important to her.

"You were always the good girl." Joanna sighed. "Always a good Amish girl. And I always got into trouble. I'm just not made for the Amish lifestyle. But I will always love you, Esther. No matter what happens. Don't ever forget that." She kissed Esther on the cheek and bolted down the stairs, skirt flying.

Esther stood there, frozen, but only for a moment before dashing down the steps after Joanna.

The front door opened and Joanna let Greg in. Their parents stood there, perplexed.

"Who is this, Joanna?" *Daed* asked.

"*Maam, Daed...* This is Greg Cooper. He works at the old piano museum down the street. We've been seeing each other for a while now."

"No... No..." *Maam* moaned.

Joanna took Greg's hand. "We've fallen in love. Greg and I are getting married," she said in a confident voice.

"He is an *Englischer*!" *Daed* roared, the purple vein in his neck protruding in fury.

"Don't do this, Joanna!" her mother cried, hand to her chest as though she was about to faint.

"We have already decided," came Joanna's steady answer. She stood up a bit taller.

"But you've been baptized. You chose the Amish way of life," *Daed* said.

"I've changed my mind."

"After everything we've taught you… You will be shunned. Our own daughter—shunned!" Tears flowed in tiny rivers down *Maam's* cheeks as she sobbed. "Joanna, you can't do this."

"I've already decided. Nothing will change my mind. I love Greg, and this is the path I choose." Joanna's eyes met Esther's. "If you shun me, so be it."

Esther felt the blood drain from her face, and her heart felt as though it might plummet to the floor. Was this really happening? Was Esther's own sister giving up their sacred way of life to marry this *Englisher* they didn't even know?

"Go, then," her father said firmly; he sounded as though he was going to cry. Her mother let out a wail as Joanna pulled Greg out the door. She heard her younger siblings cry out in confusion and sorrow.

Esther pulled her siblings into a hug, and *Maam* also came over to hold them. *Daed* paced back and forth, fists clenched. When he noticed how distressed his family was, he also began consoling the children.

Esther glanced out the window and saw Joanna and Greg get into Greg's car.

"Joanna!" Esther cried as she held her family. "How could you do this to us?"

Joanna got in the car and didn't look back before they disappeared down the dirt lane in a cloud of dust.

Esther felt as though a piece of her heart died that day, along with the sound of Joanna's name in the Miller house.

CHAPTER TWO

One year later...

They're leaving, Esther thought as she lay shaking on the cold ground in the dark Portland alley. She watched the two men walk away, laughing in their drunken wretchedness. She saw the flash of the knife going into one of their pockets as she sat up on the dirty concrete, hugging her knees, too shocked to cry.

How could they do this to me? How could they be so cruel and evil? I am ruined. No Amish man will want to marry me now, she thought. *What am I going to do? Will Irvin still love me after this?*

She had to get to Joanna's house. She was almost there, just a block away. Her sister would know how to help her. Esther gathered up the strewn pieces of her Amish dress and apron and pulled her white *kapp* back over her hair. She grabbed her small suitcase and stood. She wavered at first then told herself to get out of there before anything else horrible happened to her.

She hobbled down the street, feeling disgraced and empty. As she continued to walk down the block near the Maine waterfront, a hundred questions weighed her down. Her suitcase felt like it was filled with stones.

All she had wanted to do was surprise her sister with a visit. She had gotten off the bus and was close to her sister's apartment when she'd been...

Esther shuddered at the mere thought of the word.

Raped. She'd been raped.

Something dripped down her forehead. She raised a hand. Blood. They'd hit her. Her bloodstained fingers shook.

There had been people on the street and no one had even noticed what was going on in the alley. Or maybe they just hadn't cared. Didn't want to get involved.

What seemed like hours later, Esther reached the apartment. She rang the buzzer and heard her sister's questioning voice.

"Hello?"

"Joanna, it's Esther."

"Oh, Esther. What a surprise. Are you ok? You sound awful."

"Just let me in," Esther almost sobbed.

The door unlocked, and Esther trudged up the steps. Joanna opened the door and her smile fell as she looked at Esther from head to toe. She gasped.

"Esther! What in the world happened to you?"

"I got off the bus just down the street and was walking here when two men pulled me into an alley... They had a knife..."

Defeated, Esther broke down into sobs, shaking violently. Greg ran to the door and carried Esther to the couch. He got her a glass of water, first aid kit, and a blanket while Joanna comforted her sister, stroking her hair and murmuring comforting words in Pennsylvania Dutch.

"I understand what happened, Esther. You don't have to tell me if you don't want to," Joanna whispered. Greg politely gave them privacy, awkwardly looking unsure of how to make himself useful any longer.

"I had no idea people could be so vile," Esther cried, reaching for the box of tissues Greg had brought to her. "How could they do this to me? They've ruined my life. My life is over. How could this happen? What will I tell Irvin?"

"Some people are truly evil. Since I left Unity, I've been realizing that. I don't know how or why they did this, but I know your life is not over. I know Irvin loves you. It's so obvious. If he really loves you, he will still want to marry you." Joanna bandaged the cut on Esther's forehead.

"Really?"

"That's what love is, Esther. Loving someone despite all their dark and ugly secrets."

Unable to speak, Esther began weeping again. She felt as though her entire world was crashing down around her, that nothing would ever be the same again. How could she go on with her life after this trauma? How would she ever sleep again? Would she be haunted with nightmares and memories? And what about diseases or…pregnancy?

Her heart ached. *Oh, Lord, in your Word you say you are close to the brokenhearted. But I can't feel you right now. You feel so far away from me.*

Greg came back into the room cautiously. "Are you going to call the police?"

"No," Esther said firmly, once she could catch her breath. "That is not the Amish way."

"You can't let those men get away with this!" he said, outraged, his hands balled into fists. He looked as though he wanted to do more than just punch those men.

"I don't want anyone in the community to know that this happened to me, not even our parents. And especially not Irvin."

322

"This was not your fault. Don't feel ashamed," Joanna told her.

"I just want to forget this ever happened and move on with my life. I want to marry Irvin and have children and live the simple life. I don't want to go to the police and seek revenge."

"Justice isn't revenge," Greg muttered.

Joanna motioned for him to back off. He stalked into the other room.

Esther didn't expect her sister's husband to understand. He was not raised Amish like them. He'd never understand. Jesus had said to turn the other cheek, and that's what she would do. She would forget this ever happened.

"If the Amish community hadn't shunned you, this would have never happened," Esther mumbled angrily.

"Bad things happen, Esther. You can't blame innocent people for this. I chose to leave Unity and marry Greg, and if our family has a problem with that, I can't do anything about it. I made my choice. Don't be angry with the community for shunning me. They believe it is the right thing to do. Everything happens for a reason, even bad things."

"How will I recover from this?" Esther sobbed.

"I don't know. I can't even imagine what you're going through. I pray God will heal your heart over time somehow. I'll help you every step of the way."

"Thank you. Right now, I just want to go take a shower," Esther said, her skin crawling at the memories. A long, hot shower wouldn't erase those memories, but it might make her feel just a little bit cleaner.

"No, Esther, wait," Joanna said. "I mean, I know you don't want to report this, but I'm imploring you to reconsider. Those guys are out there, Esther, and they could be assaulting some other woman or girl right this minute. Don't you want to try to stop them from hurting anyone else?"

"Well, when you put it that way…"

"If you do decide you want to report this, you can't take a shower. I know you must want to desperately, but the hospital can run tests with a rape kit. It might help them track down the rapists. If you shower, it will wash away the evidence. At least, that's what I've heard on crime TV shows. I'm not really sure how it works, though. So, what do you think? Do you want to report this?"

Greg came back into the room. "I know you've always been taught to not report crimes, but you'd be helping the police so much. You saw what they looked like, and you heard their voices. Who knows? Maybe they'll be bale to arrest them with your help. Yes, vengeance is God's, but He doesn't want us to stand by and do nothing while innocent people get hurt."

"You're right." Yes, it was against what she'd always been taught, but in her heart she knew this was the right thing to do. "Okay. Let's call the police and go to the hospital."

***

"Hi, Esther. How was your trip to Smyrna?" Irvin asked her several days later when she returned, seeing her walking along the lane that lead to her home. It was a beautiful day, and the sun was shining brightly.

She felt so guilty for lying to everyone, telling them she was visiting friends in Smyrna, their sister community in northern Maine. The medical tests and endless questioning from the police that she'd endured had been more intense than she'd expected, but it would be worth it if those two criminals were arrested and convicted. "It was lovely," she lied.

"You know…" he said slowly. "If you are visiting your sister in Portland, I would understand. I'd do the same thing if my brother left."

"Really?"

"Of course. I don't always follow the rules." He gave her a goofy grin.

She couldn't help but smile. "Well, that's a relief. I did go visit her, but please don't tell anyone, okay?" Guilt niggled at her for not telling him the whole story, but she just wasn't ready.

"Of course. I won't. How are Joanna and Greg?"

"They're so perfect for each other. I miss her, but I'm glad she's happy. So how are you doing? How's work at the store?"

"Well, business has been good. My father told me when he retires, he would like me to take over, you know." He grinned, sticking his thumbs under his suspenders. "It is a good way to make a living that would support a family."

"I am so happy for you," Esther said, and she meant it.

"Actually, Esther, there is something I've been meaning to ask you," Irvin said, stepping closer to her.

By the look on his face, Esther instantly knew he was going to ask her if he could court her with the intention of marriage. Here they were, alone on the lane. It was the ideal time for him to ask. For the two of them, or any other unmarried Amish couple, spending time alone together was a rare thing.

She and her family had known for a while Irvin was interested in her, but he had been too shy to ask her to court him for so long until now.

And she was nowhere near ready for him to ask her. She had barely even admitted to herself that she had been raped, unable to even begin healing from the traumatic experience yet.

"I was wondering…" he began.

"Wait, I know what you're going to say. I want to, but I can't right now. I need some time, after everything that's happening with my sister. I'm going to go on *Rumspringa* and spend some time finding myself. Then I'll be ready. I hope you understand," she said. *Rumspringa* is a time when Amish youth are allowed to experience life outside the community.

"Oh…I see," he said, pausing to scratch his chin awkwardly. "I understand. I'll wait for you, Esther. No matter how long it takes."

Her heart warmed at his devotion but was also breaking at the same time. She loved him with all her heart, and she knew he loved her too. But if he knew the truth, would he still want her?

What if… What if she was pregnant? She had to find out.

"I'm sorry, Irvin," she stammered and hurried up the lane to the phone shanty. She opened the door to the small shed with a window and sat down at the desk inside. She called the local driver who drove the Amish to places that were too far for a horse and buggy.

The phone rang, and the driver answered.

"Hi, can you pick me up? I'd like to go to the grocery store in Pittsborough."

"Why not just go to the one closer to the community? Are they out of something you need?" she asked.

"No… I just want to go to the one in Pittsborough."

"Well, then, I'll be there soon."

After being driven to the store, Esther wandered the aisles, absentmindedly filling her cart with the things her mother had asked for. Today she did not notice the shoppers gawking at her clothing and whispering about her. Her whole life *Englischers* had looked at her strangely, wondering why she dressed the way she did or why she was at the store. Many *Englischers* did not realize that the Amish bought groceries in stores, too. Today, she didn't care about their stares.

She glanced over at the pharmacy section of the store as dread filled her belly. She knew she had to take the test to make sure she was not pregnant. Joanna had told her it needed to be done, and enough time had passed now for the test to be accurate.

"God, please. Please don't let me be…" she whispered. "I want children, yes, but not until after I marry the man I love." She did love Irvin very much, and she hoped one day that her wishes for children and a happy marriage with him would come true.

She meandered down the aisle and found the section that sold pregnancy tests. There were so many; she had no idea which one to get. So many boxes with different colors and different words on them—they blurred together before her eyes into a kaleidoscope of confusion.

Esther blinked, trying to clear her head. What if someone from her community saw her there and thought she had sinned? She had come to this store to be further away from the community, but there was still a chance someone she knew could be here. Esther glanced around and peered over the aisles.

What if they thought the father was Irvin? A sense of fear came over Esther. She snatched one of the boxes randomly and made a beeline for the cashier, tucking the small box under a box of cereal.

327

As she laid out her items on the conveyor belt, the cashier scanned each item. When she picked up the pregnancy test, she smiled at Esther.

"Good luck."

The sense of dread deepened. Esther did not believe in luck. But she hoped the Lord would spare her.

"Thanks," Esther muttered and paid for her items. She looked around, checking to see if anyone she knew was around. Once she gathered up her bags, she went straight to the bathroom.

A few minutes later, Esther stared at the small plastic stick that would reveal her fate. When she saw a plus sign appear, a horrid feeling of devastation sank and settled into her stomach. She leaned against the bathroom stall.

She was pregnant.

What was she going to do? What would her parents say? If she told them about the rape, then she would have to tell them she secretly visited Joanna, and they would be strongly against that. What would her community say? Would they think she was lying and that the truth was that she had sinned? What if Irvin wouldn't want her anymore?

"No!" she cried as her knees grew so weak that she couldn't stand. She sank down onto the tiled bathroom floor, even though her mother had always told her public bathrooms were so dirty. She didn't care about anything except figuring out what she would do.

Because, at that moment, she felt as though being an unmarried pregnant Amish woman was as good as being dead.

No, she decided. No one had to know. If no one knew, she wouldn't have to be embarrassed.

I will tell no one of this...except Joanna.

CHAPTER THREE

Esther marveled at the black and white images that the ultrasound technician showed her. She hadn't been planning on having one, but when the doctor had explained how it would help them monitor the baby's development, she changed her mind.

That was her child. Her baby. And yet it felt like an alien, a distant being she would never know.

"Well, well," the technician said, adjusting her glasses to get a closer look at the image. "Wait a minute. Looks like double trouble. You're one blessed woman."

"Double trouble? What does that mean?" Whatever it was, it didn't sound good.

The technician turned to her and grinned. "You're going to have twins, dear," she said.

"Twins?" Esther asked. The room spun a little as a wave of nausea assailed her.

"Do you need a drink of water, dear?"

"Oh, yes, please."

The woman hurried out.

Twins? Esther put a hand to her head. This really was double trouble. It was bad enough she'd gotten pregnant as a result of rape, but now God had chosen to give her two babies instead of one?

What kind of test was this? Esther had always been taught God doesn't give us more than we can handle.

But this was too much to handle.

The woman returned with a cup of water, and Esther sipped it slowly.

"You don't look too happy, darling. Usually women are thrilled when they hear news like this. Are you all right?" Esther noticed the woman eying Esther's *kapp* and dress. "Are you in some sort of trouble? Do you need help?"

Tears stung Esther's eyes as she looked at the floor, slowly shaking her head. "I was raped. I don't know what I'm going to do. I have to hide this pregnancy from my whole community..."

The woman was such a good listener, Esther told her the entire story.

"God has a plan," the woman, whose name was Sheila said. "I know right now it must be impossible to understand why on earth this would happen to you. But these two babies are human lives, precious human lives."

Esther shook her head. "I won't even know them. I probably won't even see them again after they're born. I don't know what I'm going to do, if I'm going to put them up for adoption or what. The doctor asked me if I wanted to abort, but like you said, these are human lives. I would never do that. They're not just cells or tissue. What right do I have to end a life, even though I was raped? It's not their fault. They have a right to live just as much as anyone else. Even if I never see them after they're born, I want them to live."

Sheila took Esther's hand and squeezed. "God has a plan for these babies, Esther. And you're the one who is going to bring them into this world. Maybe you won't ever see them again, but you chose to give these babies life, even after what happened to you. And that makes you the bravest woman I've ever met."

***

"We will miss you while you are away," *Maam* said, handing Esther a homemade bread wrapped in cloth. "Here, I made this bread this morning. Are you going to be all right?"

"Of course, *Maam*. I'll get a job and find someplace to stay," Esther said. "And if not, I will go to Smyrna. I'll be fine."

"I'd rather you go straight to Smyrna. We don't want you getting caught up in the ways of the world like someone else and being led astray…" *Daed* muttered.

"Edward," *Maam* chided. "Esther is a good girl. We don't need to worry about that."

Daed nodded. "Keep in touch."

"We love you," Maam said, swiping away a tear.

"I love you, too," Esther said, walking out the door with her bags toward the driver who was waiting in their driveway. The driver put her bags in the back. Esther got in the car and waved, and the car slowly rumbled down the lane.

As they drove, Esther looked out the window to see Irvin walking down the lane.

"Stop, please. Just for a moment," Esther said and got out of the car.

"Esther? I was just going to your house to say goodbye."

"I was going to stop by your house on my way."

"About the other day I'm sorry I ran off like I did. I just got nervous. I was going to ask you—" Irvin began.

331

Esther held up her hand. "No, wait. I know what you're going to ask me. And I think we should wait until I get back. I need some time on my own to do some soul searching before joining the church and getting baptized. I hope you understand."

"As you wish. I will wait for you, Esther. I'd wait for you forever." He gently took her hand and kissed it, sending Esther's heart fluttering. "I think you know how I feel about you."

"And I feel the same way, Irvin. Thank you for understanding."

"I'll be here when you return."

The way Irvin was looking in her eyes made Esther's insides melt, and she leaned into him. He wrapped his strong arms around her, softly kissing her forehead. "I love you, Esther Miller."

"I love you too, Irvin," Esther whispered, her eyes filling with tears. Would he still love her when she returned? Would he still want her when he found out the truth about what had happened to her?

"Nothing will ever change that," he added quietly.

Her heart filled with hope.

"I better go," she said, pulling away, even though she didn't want to. "Bye."

She got in the car again, and as they drove away, she turned around in her seat to see Irvin standing there, hat in his hand, waving.

Maybe he truly would love her no matter what. Or was that too much to hope for?

Esther went back to Portland to stay with Joanna for the remainder of her pregnancy so no one would know she was pregnant. She had told everyone that she was going on *Rumspringa*, and no one seemed to mind. She let them believe she was staying with her relatives in Smyrna, their sister Amish community in northern Maine. If they did suspect Esther was visiting Joanna, no one said anything, which she appreciated.

***

Esther, Joanna, and Greg were relieved and grateful when they received the news that the two rapists had been arrested. Several other young women had also come forward which had led to the police locating and arresting the two criminals. Esther slept a little better at night, knowing they were finally behind bars.

"I'm so glad you convinced me to report it," Esther said. "Thank you. I don't think I would otherwise."

"You did the right thing," Joanna said. "I know all the questioning was tough on you, having to relive it over and over. Not to mention the tests you had to have at the hospital. I'm sorry you had to go through all of that, especially after what happened."

"It was worth it. Have you heard anything new from the doctor?" Esther asked Joanna as they sat at the kitchen table drinking tea. Last time Esther had visited Joanna, Joanna had told Esther that her doctor was concerned with her fertility.

Joanna frowned. "I thought I'd be pregnant by now... They aren't sure what's wrong. They want me to have more tests done, but they said there's a possibility we won't be having children any time soon."

Esther reached out for Joanna's hand. "I'm so sorry. You always said you wanted a big family."

"Hopefully, one day things might change."

"It's ironic." Esther sighed. "And here I am wondering what I'm going to do with these two babies after they're born. I know adoption is an option, but I'd hate to never see them again. I don't want to give them

up, but I don't know how I can keep them. I just don't know what to do."
She rested her head in her hands, feeling defeated.

"Esther, what if I took care of them after they're born?" Joanna asked.

"What?" Esther looked up at her. "Are you serious?"

"Not permanently. Just temporarily. You're marrying Irvin soon, right? You could take them back after the wedding and tell everyone you adopted them. You could even tell people they were my babies. No one would ever have to know."

Esther paused, thinking. She twisted her prayer *kapp* ribbon in her fingers. "Do you think that could work?"

"I think it would."

"Actually, maybe that could work. I can stay here until I have the babies, like we planned, and then you take them. Then I can go home, marry Irvin, take them back, and no one will ever know the truth. I'd get my life back." A new hope filled Esther for the first time since she had been raped. Now she could fully trust the person who would take her children. When Esther saw the sorrowful look on her sister's face, she reached out for Joanna's hand. "But won't it be hard to give them up after I'm married? And what will Greg say?"

"Of course, it will be hard. And I'm sure Greg will agree. It will only be for a short time. I want to do this for you. I'd do anything for you, Esther."

"And I'd do anything for you."

CHAPTER FOUR

"It's a girl!" the doctor said, handing the second baby to Esther. Joanna was already holding the first baby, tears streaming down her face as she stood by Esther's side.

"You were amazing, Esther," Joanna said. "I don't know how you just did that. Wow, twin girls! They're beautiful."

"Yes, they are," Esther said, her own cheeks already wet with tears. "They're perfect." The twins were fraternal and did not look alike, even as newborns. One had light hair and a round face, and one had dark hair and an oval face. How could she ever part with them? Maybe she could just hold them both, just for a moment...

"May I hold her, too?" Esther asked Joanna.

"Of course." Joanna carefully gave the second baby to Esther, so she held one in each arm. They both squirmed and wailed, so loud for how tiny they were. Esther's heart almost burst with pride and...love. She loved them so much more than she ever knew she could love someone. So much more than she'd ever imagined.

To stop herself from breaking down, she knew she had to give them to Joanna to hold.

And she wouldn't hold them again until after she was married.

Esther had no idea how heartbroken she would be as she gave her babies to her sister. She felt as though she was giving away a part of her as she leaned back on the hospital bed, tears rolling down her cheeks.

They will be safe with Joanna and Greg, she told herself.

After the nurse took the babies for examinations, she and the doctor returned with solemn faces.

335

"What's wrong?" Esther said.

"One of the babies was born with a malformed ankle," the doctor said.

"What does that mean? Will she be able to walk?" Esther said, her heart racing with panic.

"Most likely, she will be able to walk normally, yes. However, she will need surgery to correct the problem. It may take only one surgery to correct it, or it may take several years for her ankle to be completely normal. It's hard to tell right now. We will need to run more tests to know more," the doctor explained. "It is possible she may need to have surgeries until she is about seven or eight years old, but after that she will most likely be able to walk and run normally. We will let you know more as soon as we know."

"Okay," Esther said, leaning against the pillow again. Would her poor baby be all right? Would she truly be able to walk normally?

"Don't worry, Esther. It's all in God's hands," Joanna said, reaching for Esther's hand.

"I know. But it's so hard not to worry."

***

"What are you going to name them?" Joanna asked as she held the newborn girls in the hospital room later that day.

Esther looked at the twins lovingly, wanting to hold them again, but she refused to, afraid she would grow attached. Then the leaving process would be so much harder.

"I decided on Leah and Charlotte. What do you think?" Esther asked.

Joanna smiled. "Those are lovely names."

336

Then the sorrow returned. She would miss them so much. Would they look like her? Would they be like her at all?

"Are you going to ever tell them the truth?" Joanna asked.

"That they're my biological children? I don't know. Maybe when they are older."

After running more tests, the doctor concluded that Charlotte would need a surgery on her ankle while she was still a baby. Hopefully it was correct the problem, but if not, she could need five or six more surgeries until she was six or even eight years old. It was still hard to know how well she would heal and how many surgeries she would need for her ankle to be normal. Hopefully, she wouldn't need more than one, but Esther still worried.

"We have the best specialists in the state here in this hospital," the doctor said. "Charlotte is in good hands."

As the doctor walked out of the hospital room, Esther turned to Joanna. "What are we going to do? We don't have medical insurance. How will we pay for the surgeries? And poor Charlotte. We live so far from the hospital. I just don't know what we're going to do."

"God has Charlotte in his hands, Esther. The Amish community has come together before to pay for people's medical expenses. Don't worry. We will figure it all out when the time comes. For now, let's take it one step at a time," Joanna said.

Still, worry niggled in the back of Esther's mind.

After they all went back to the apartment and spent several days together while Esther recuperated, it was time for Greg to drive Esther home.

Esther picked up her suitcase and turned to Joanna, who was holding both babies.

"Are you sure you don't want to hold them before you go?" Joanna asked.

"No. I know it will just make this harder than it already is." She stared longingly at the babies, remembering the past nine months which had turned out to be so incredible. Every time she had felt them kick inside her, every time she had felt sick to her stomach, how she had watched her belly grow more and more every day—then the miraculous delivery. She would never understand the miracle of life, how two precious babies had been the result of such a traumatic experience.

"I will just kiss them goodbye," she said, her voice cracking with emotion. A single tear fell from her eye and landed on Charlotte's soft head as she kissed her, and then Leah.

"Goodbye, beautiful girls. I will always love you, and I will see you soon," she whispered, then wrapped her arms around Joanna. "And I love you, my sister. I can never thank you enough for what you have done for me."

"It's our pleasure, Esther. Remember, I'd do anything for you." Joanna's eyes welled up with tears.

Esther smiled and walked out the door with Greg. Even though her heart was crumbling to pieces, she held her head high and never looked back.

As Greg drove her back to Unity, most of the ride was in silence. Esther stared out the window, quiet tears sliding down her cheek. She never realized how hard it would be to give the precious newborns away, even temporarily.

"Drop me off here, please," Esther said and Greg pulled over to the side in a concealed area near some trees. If anyone saw Greg driving her, they would know she had been visiting Joanna.

Esther grabbed her suitcase and set it on the ground. She looked Greg in the eye.

"I can't ever thank you enough. Both of you. Please keep me updated on Charlotte's condition."

"Of course, Esther."

"I'll call you after the wedding, after we settle in, so we can arrange sending them back here. I wish I knew when that would be. I'm sorry." When she had left the twins behind, she felt as though her heart was breaking in half. She couldn't wait to see them again.

"It's okay. Whenever you're ready."

Esther nodded, tears threatening. "Tell Joanna I love her."

She shut the car door. As Greg drove away, Esther walked through the dust of the dirt road back to her home, never looking back.

***

"The past few months seemed like an eternity while you were away," Irvin said the day after Esther came home. He leaned against the wall of the barn, twirling a piece of straw in his hands. "Everyone says you left to think about marrying me."

Esther smiled to herself. *Let them think that.*

"Everyone expects it, you know," Irvin said.

"Expects what?"

"That we will get married."

"Why, did you tell everyone how you feel about me?" Esther asked, blushing.

"No. But it is obvious, I guess. So, did you think about at least courting me while you were away?"

Esther stroked the nose of her father's black horse. "Yes, I did."

"You know what I was going to ask you when you turned me down to go on *Rumspringa* before I could even ask the question?"

"Yes." She smiled. "I knew what you were going to ask me. But I needed time first."

"And I am glad you had that time. Now that you're home again, may I ask you officially?" he asked, coming near her.

She turned to face him. "Wait. First, there is something you should know about me…"

"You can tell me anything, Esther. Nothing will change how I feel about you."

"Well, I hope that's true." She took a deep breath. It was time to get this over with. "After Joanna was shunned and moved to Portland, I went to visit her several times in secret."

"Oh, Esther. I understand. I told you before, I don't blame you for wanting to visit your sister. Did you think that would make me not want to court you?" Irvin held her hand, smiling at her.

He thought *that* was what she had to tell him? "Oh, Irvin. That's not even the half of it. I was raped in an alley while on my way to visit her." She'd said those words to the police countless times while they'd questioned her, but that felt so long ago. Saying those words again brought all the memories back, making it feel like it had happened only yesterday. She could still see their eyes, smell their alchohol-infused stench, see the glint of the knife.

Wasn't time supposed to heal all wounds? If only she could erase those memories forever.

She imagined Irvin pulling away from her, seeing her as unclean or damaged. Instead, she smiled with relief when he comfortingly rubbed her arms.

"Oh...Esther. I'm so sorry. That's truly horrible." A spark of anger flickered over his face, and he clenched his fist. "How can people be so evil? Do you know who did this to you? If I got my hands on them..."

"They were arrested. But the Lord tells us to forgive, Irvin. Revenge is not the Amish way." She gently touched his arm, and he relaxed a bit.

His eyes softened as he looked at her. "I'm sorry. You're right. They will have to face God's wrath. You know this doesn't change how I feel about you, right?"

"Well, there's more." What would he say when he found out about the babies? Would he still want her then?

"How can it get any worse?"

"I got pregnant." Her eyes pricked with tears at the thought of her two babies. Oh, how she missed them.

Confusion drew Irvin's eyebrows together. "But... What about the baby? What happened to the baby?"

She took a deep breath. Maybe after she told him this, he'd run. "There are two babies. Twin girls."

"Twins?!" Irvin all but shouted in shock.

"Shh." Esther waved her hands frantically and looked around.

"Sorry." He scrubbed a hand over his face. "Twins?" he whispered. "So, where are they?"

"Joanna has them temporarily. We agreed that after I'm married, I could take them back and let everyone think I adopted them. So, if you marry me, you'll have two daughters right after."

She pictured him rejecting her and storming out of the barn. This had to be too much for him. How could he possibly still want to marry her after all of this?

Esther clenched her eyes shut, bracing herself for the pain. This was it. The only man she had ever loved was about to tell her it was over.

Instead, she felt him pull her into a hug. She opened her eyes and looked up to see him smiling down at her sweetly. Love and warmth surrounded her.

"Do you still love me?" she asked, perplexed.

"Of course, I do. This does not change my intention of marrying you. I want many children, so having two daughters right away will be a wonderful blessing. I can't wait to meet them."

She let out a breath of relief. "Please don't tell anyone any of this. I would be so ashamed..."

He held her hands gently. "I understand, Esther. Still, you shouldn't be ashamed. This was not your fault. But if you want, this will be our secret. You did the right thing by giving the babies to your sister. I am so sorry that horrible thing happened to you. But I will never tell another soul. Thank you for telling me. And now that you have told me, there is something I must ask you." He took her hands. "While you were away, I realized I don't want to spend any more time away from you. I love you, and I've known for so long I want to spend the rest of my life with you. And I don't want to wait anymore. Esther, will you marry me?" His eyes lit up when they met hers. Because the Amish do not wear any jewelry, he didn't offer her a ring, but she didn't care. Irvin, Charlotte, and Leah were all Esther wanted, and soon they'd become a family.

She couldn't imagine anything more perfect.

"Yes!" she said. He stood and she threw her arms around him, even though any physical contact before marriage was frowned upon. She didn't care. And apparently, neither did he as he bent down and pressed his lips against hers for the first time. Her heart swelled with joy, and she held onto him even tighter.

She looked up at his face and sighed. She truly did love him. She had for a long, long time. For the first time since the attack, she felt truly happy.

"Let's go tell my parents," Esther said, taking Irvin's hand and hurrying out the barn doors. "They will be so happy." She pulled him along to her house and they burst through the door.

Her parents were in the kitchen. Her father was reading his Bible and her mother was chopping vegetables.

"*Maam, Daed,* we have wonderful news!" Esther blurted.

Maam looked up, eyes wide with hope. "You are courting, finally?"

"Even better. We are engaged!" Esther cried.

"Oh! Oh my! This is wonderful indeed," *Maam* said, fanning herself. She hurried over to them, giving Esther a hug and patting Irvin's hand.

Daed got up from his chair and hobbled over to them, shaking Irvin's hand. "We are so happy for you both. Esther, I am so glad you are taking such a fine Amish man for your husband. Irvin asked me for my permission to marry you a while ago, and of course, I said yes. We were hoping you two would end up together."

Esther smiled. "I figured."

"Well, how exciting it will be to announce it. Everyone will be so happy!" *Maam* said. "Have you told your parents yet, Irvin?"

"Not yet."

"Let's go now," *Daed* said. "We can all tell them together."

"Good idea," *Maam* said, already reaching for her shoes. They went out the door and walked down the lane to Irvin's family's house. On their way, they passed their neighbors, Mrs. Duncan and Mrs. Johnson, who were sitting on Mrs. Johnson's porch swing.

"Hello!" the two women called, waving.

"We have wonderful news," *Maam* said, already scurrying over to them, clearly unable to contain her elation. She looked as though she was about to burst with the announcement. "Irvin and Esther are engaged!" *Daed,* Irvin, and Esther followed her and approached the porch.

"Oh, we are so happy for you!" Mrs. Duncan said.

"That is wonderful," Mrs. Johnson said, then turned to Mrs. Duncan. "At least she found her way back into the fold, unlike her sister," she murmured, but Esther clearly heard her.

Irvin must have heard it too, because he gently touched Esther's hand. "Well, we should be going. We are on our way to tell my parents the news."

They said their goodbyes and turned to continue down the lane, going around the back of the house. *Maam* and *Daed* walked ahead, clearly excited to get to Irvin's house, while Esther and Irvin hung back.

"Irvin!" Mrs. Johnson called. "Would you come here a moment?"

He turned to Esther. "I'll catch up. I'll just be a moment. Go ahead."

"Sure." But knowing those two women, it wouldn't just be a moment. Irvin walked away and Esther turned to her parents, but they were already a good distance away. She shrugged and figured she might as well just wait for Irvin. She turned and walked toward the back of Mrs. Johnson's house.

"We are worried about you," Esther heard Mrs. Duncan say. She couldn't see them from this side of the house, but she could hear them. She edged closer to the side of the house to hear better.

"What if she is flighty, like her sister, and leaves the community? Some people have been saying Esther went to visit her in the city," Mrs. Johnson added.

"What if Joanna had a bad influence on her?" Mrs. Duncan asked.

"First of all, you don't know the whole story. Joanna's not a bad person, and she wouldn't have a bad influence on Esther. Joanna is one of the kindest young women I've ever met, and Esther is the woman I've chosen to spend the rest of my life with. I love her. And I won't tolerate you speaking ill of her and her sister. And I'd appreciate if you don't discuss the matter with anyone else. Am I clear?" Irvin asked firmly but politely.

Esther's heart swelled with pride at how he'd stood up for her and Joanna to these two gossips.

Apparently, he'd left the women speechless, something Esther had never experienced before with those two. Irvin came around the side of the house, and his eyes widened when he saw Esther standing there.

"You heard that?"

"Every word. Thank you."

Irvin pulled her close. "Those two gossip too much. It was time someone put them in their place."

Esther giggled. "I just wish I could have seen their faces."

"Come on. Let's go tell my parents the news." He took her hand, and they made their way down the lane together.

***

After Esther and Irvin were married, the community helped Irvin build a house, and the couple moved in. Their marriage started out wonderfully, just as Esther had always dreamed. But there was something missing.

She desperately wanted her children back. "Now that we are married, we can have them back. But Joanna's had them for almost six months now. They must have bonded so much. I feel bad asking for them back."

"But they are yours, biologically," Irvin said.

"You're right. And we did agree to it. I'll call her tomorrow."

***

The next day, Esther walked to the phone shanty down the lane. She picked up the phone on the desk and dialed Joanna's number.

"Hello?" came Joanna's voice.

"Joanna, it's Esther."

"Esther. How are you? How's married life? I'm so happy to hear your voice. The babies are getting so big. I wish I could have been at your wedding…"

"I know, I know. I wish you could have come, too. I'm doing well. Married life is perfect. Except…"

"Except you want the girls back," Joanna said. There was something in Joanna's voice, and Esther couldn't quite discern what it was.

But it wasn't good.

Esther took a deep breath. "I miss them so much. And yes, now that I'm married, I want to bring them home, just like we agreed."

Silence.

"Joanna?"

"This will be so hard, Esther. We're a family now. They love me, and I adore them. It'll be hard on all of us."

"I know. I know. Of course, you must have bonded so much by now. I feel terrible asking for them back even though they're my own children."

"Well, there's something I have to tell you. As you know, Charlotte had the surgery for her ankle, but that didn't cure the problem, as we suspected. She will need more surgeries until she's eight years old. It'll be many doctors' appointments and hospital stays until then. The doctor said she should be here where she can have direct access to the medical attention she needs and so they can see her regularly. And we have good medical insurance. If we adopted her—"

"Adopt her? What are you saying, Joanna?" Esther all but shouted, then lowered her voice. "She's *my* baby! She needs to come home. We agreed on this!" Esther could hardly believe what she was hearing.

"Esther, this is what's best for her, and you know it. You can take Leah home, but Charlotte needs to stay here with us. We both know you don't have medical insurance and never will, and it would be hard on you to take her to town for her doctors' appointments and surgeries with the buggy or by hiring a driver. And the hospital here in Portland is the best for her. The best specialists in the state are here. She needs to be here, Esther."

"But what about later on, when she's older? Can't she come home after she's better?" Esther asked, tears now freely flowing down her cheeks. She wiped her face and gripped the phone tighter, leaning on the desk in the phone shanty.

"That's just it. We don't know how long it will take for her ankle to be better or if it will ever be totally normal. She could be eight years old, but what if it takes even longer? Will you be willing to uproot her and thrust her into the Amish lifestyle after leaving her friends and family behind?"

"Irvin and I are her family!"

"She doesn't even know you. To her, we are her family. And when she's older, it would be so hard on her for you to turn her entire world upside down and have her come live with you." Joanna took a deep breath and softened her tone. "I don't know. We can worry about all that later. We don't even know how long this process will take. All we know is for now she needs to be here. And for her to have medical coverage, we need to adopt her."

"This is *ferhuddled*. They are *twins*. They are supposed to be together. One twin raised *Englischer* and one raised Amish… I've never even heard of such a thing."

There was only silence.

Esther closed her eyes. *Lord, what should I do?*

You know what is best for Charlotte, even though it is hard. She tried to ignore the voice in her heart, but she couldn't.

She knew what she had to do.

***

After deliberating and praying for a few days, Esther and Irvin both knew in their hearts that the right thing to do was to let Charlotte stay with Joanna and Greg until her ankle was healed, however long that may be, but they would take Leah home with them.

Esther and Irvin hired a driver to meet Joanna and Greg at the auto repair shop where Greg worked in Portland after he had closed the shop down for the day. They all sat down at a table and awkwardly looked at each other. The babies gurgled and cooed in the stroller.

Esther looked at the adorable twin girls. It was obvious that they were sisters, but their faces didn't look alike. "Which one is which?"

Greg looked at Esther. His eyes filled with tears. "This one is Leah."

Joanna held back a sob and buried her face in her husband's shoulder. Doubt and guilt assailed Esther, but when she looked at Leah, peace filled her. This would all be worth it to have Leah in her life.

Esther approached little Leah in her stroller and hesitated. She looked to Joanna as if to silently ask permission to pick her up.

Joanna nodded, her eyes red with tears.

Esther reached into the stroller and picked up her baby. She held her child tightly to her chest and tenderly kissed her sweet face, breathing in the scent of baby powder. Leah wiggled in her arms.

My baby, she thought. *Mine.*

Esther looked at the other twin, Charlotte. *You're my daughter, too. What will your life be like, raised as an Englischer? Maybe never knowing you have a twin?*

"We should get going," Greg said hoarsely and gathered up their things. Joanna stood and gazed at Leah longingly. Guilt stabbed at Esther's heart. She didn't regret her decision in taking back Leah, but she'd never forget the look of anguish on her sister's face.

Leah wailed, reaching her pudgy arms out for Joanna.

Tears stung Esther's eyes. It hurt that the child cried for Joanna and not Esther, the one who had given birth to her.

Joanna burst into sobs as Greg guided her out the door. Charlotte began to cry and Greg lifted her out of the stroller.

"Goodbye, Esther." Joanna looked at Esther with so much sorrow in her eyes.

Esther felt Joanna's pain. She and Joanna had been so close all their lives, but in that moment when Joanna turned away from her and walked out the door, Esther knew their relationship would never be the same.

***

"We are here," Esther cooed to the baby in her arms. "Your new home."

Irvin stopped the buggy and helped Esther down, then unhitched the horses. For the thousandth time, Esther wished she was holding both of her daughters in her arms.

At least I have Leah. Thank you, Lord, she prayed.

"Esther!" Mrs. Duncan called from down the lane, who was walking with Mrs. Johnson. Mrs. Duncan hurried over when she saw the baby, her feet shuffling surprisingly fast, faster than Esther had ever seen. "What do you have there, Esther?" Mrs. Duncan followed behind her.

"Oh, isn't she sweet? She's a cutie," Mrs. Johnson said.

Leah babbled and laughed, making the women giggle.

Esther's heart leapt, then fell to her stomach. She wanted to show off her daughter and tell them she was biologically hers, but she couldn't. She knew she'd have to lie, but it was so much harder than she'd imagined.

351

But she had to do it.

"This is Leah," Esther told the women who were now flocking around her and the baby. "My daughter."

"What?" the women asked, looking at her in shock.

Esther's heart wrenched, and she cleared her throat. "Our new adopted daughter is what I mean. We are taking her in because her mother was unable to keep her."

"But she looks like you." Mrs. Johnson's eyes lit up with realization. "Is this your niece? Is her biological mother Joanna?"

"Shh," Mrs. Duncan chided. "If Esther wants to tell who the mother is, she will."

They looked at her expectantly.

Esther nodded solemnly.

"So she is Joanna's," Mrs. Johnson said, patting Esther's arm. "It is good of you to take her in. And she is indeed precious."

Mrs. Duncan agreed, talking to Leah in a sing-song voice. Soon, Esther knew the news of Leah's arrival would be quickly spread all over the community if these women had anything to do with it. They would be the ones telling everyone she was Joanna's daughter.

Still, Esther had lied. But if it kept her past a secret, she could live with that.

For now.

"Well, we should let you get settled. I'm sure you have some bonding to do. Let us know if you need anything," Mrs. Johnson said.

"I'll make you a casserole," Mrs. Duncan added.

"Oh, thank you, but you don't need to," Esther said.

"Nonsense." Mrs. Duncan waved her hand as if swatting a fly. "You have a new baby in the house, so you get a casserole. I'll bring it by tomorrow."

Mrs. Johnson agreed to bring Esther food over the coming week as well. Soon, Esther knew the ice room under her house would be full of food. Whenever there was a new baby, a death, a fire, a wedding, or any big event, the community always came together to offer support.

As the women continued down the lane, Irvin came out of the barn after bringing in the horses and feeding them. "You know they're going to tell everyone."

Esther smiled. "I know."

"And you told them she's Joanna's?"

"Yes."

Irvin put his arm around her shoulder as they walked toward the house. "She's our daughter, Esther. Nothing will ever change that."

Esther's eyes pricked with new unshed tears. "I am so grateful for her. If only... I wish..."

"I know. Me too. I wish Charlotte was here too." Irvin's voice cracked with emotion. "Well, at least God has blessed us with this little angel. If He wants to give us Charlotte in the future after her ankle is healed, He will. We just need to trust Him."

Esther could only nod, knowing that if she spoke, she'd break down.

Irvin gripped the doorknob and looked down at the baby, who was babbling in Esther's arms. "We're home, Leah." He looked at Esther. "Are you ready?"

She smiled and nodded. "I've been waiting for this."

Esther's heart was full as they walked through the door of their home with their daughter, but still, a part of her heart ached.

Thank you for Leah, Lord. I am thankful I have her, but please, please bring Charlotte home to me one day.

And she believed one day He would. She would pray every day for Charlotte's return until then.

CHAPTER SIX

Twenty Years Later

Finally, God has answered my prayers! Thank you, God, Esther thought as she waited in the phone shanty for Charlotte to call her.

Charlotte, her daughter. Esther shook her head, still astounded.

Time seemed to tick by in slow motion as she waited for Charlotte to call. Earlier that day, Irvin had told her that Charlotte had left a message on the answering machine, explaining how Joanna had died of cancer and Greg had died in a car accident. Charlotte was wondering if she and her younger sister, Zoe, could stay with them. She said she'd call back soon.

At first Irvin was hesitant to let them come stay, but Esther had no hesitation.

Even though it risked her secret being exposed, she had to see her daughter. To have Charlotte and Zoe come live with her—it was what Esther had been praying for all these years. Though she wished it was under happier circumstances.

Oh, Joanna and Greg. Esther's heart wrenched at the thought of her sister and brother-in-law gone. How she wished she could have said goodbye, even for a moment, and told Joanna how much she loved her and how sorry she was. How very sorry she was for everything that had happened.

But she'd never get the chance now, not until they met again in heaven. Now all she could do was welcome Charlotte and Zoe into their home and hope they'd stay forever, if it was even possible.

"Oh, thank you, God, for this second chance. I can't apologize to Joanna, but I can do my best to love Charlotte and Zoe. Thank you, Lord, for answering my prayers and bringing Charlotte back into my life. I am so grateful," she cried out, letting her head drop on the desk.

The phone rang.

"Oh!" She jumped at the sound, her head snapping up, then she scrambled to answer the phone. "Hello?"

"Um, this is Charlotte Cooper. I'm—"

Oh, Charlotte, her darling daughter. She sounded so lovely, so grown up. What was she like? Was she kind and good-hearted? Esther's eyes welled with tears at the thought of all the years she'd missed with her. "Charlotte. I was hoping it might be you. This is Aunt Esther. I'm so glad you called back. Are you all right, dear?"

"Yes, we are, considering the circumstances. I am guessing you heard my message?" she asked.

"Yes. When your uncle told me, I decided to stay right here by the phone in the shanty. Your message was a shock. I had no idea about Greg and Jo—" Esther couldn't even finish the sentence as a sob rose in her throat. "I haven't spoken to my sister in over twenty years." Twenty years. Had it really been that long?

How could she have been so prideful? So *wrong?*

Charlotte said, "Oh, I am sorry to keep you waiting there by the phone. And I'm so sorry I had to break such sad news over an answering machine."

"Don't worry about that, dear." Tears coursed down Esther's cheeks, and it took all her willpower to not break down in sobs. She sniffed, swiping tears away. "Where are you now?"

356

"The Blue Moon Café."

"Do you need directions to get to our farm?"

"Yes, thanks."

Esther gave her some simple directions. "I'm really looking forward to meeting you both." *More than you can possibly know,* Esther thought. "I never knew Joanna had a second child." *Thank you, Lord, for blessing Joanna with a baby of her own,* Esther prayed. *Zoe is a miracle.* Esther sighed and continued, "Anyway, to answer your question, I do want you to come here. You are family, and you are always welcome in my home."

"Thank you so much. I can't wait to meet you. You have no idea what this means to us. My father's family lives in Canada, but we couldn't afford to travel there."

Esther was sure them coming to stay meant a lot more to her than anyone. "I have wanted to meet you for a very long time, Charlotte. It will be wonderful to have you."

Was this really happening? After all these years, Charlotte was finally coming home! Esther grinned, wanting to jump up and down and cheer with jubilation. So many nights she had prayed for this very thing, year after year, and now it was going to happen.

"I can pay room and board if you like…" Charlotte offered.

Pay? *Pay?* Esther waved her hand, even though her daughter couldn't see her. "No, no, that won't be necessary. You may stay as long as you like." Esther briefly went over some house rules, to which Charlotte agreed to. "We will see you soon."

Esther hung up the phone, still in shock. She was going to meet her daughter today. This very day! Would she be able to keep her secret

357

from her? Would she be so happy to see Charlotte that the words "I'm your mother" would fly out of her mouth?

She hoped she'd be able to contain herself.

All that mattered was that this very day Esther would get to hold her daughter in her arms.

***

"They're here!" Esther shouted from the window much too loudly. But she didn't care. Excitement bubbled up within her at the sight of the approaching taxi, and she ran a hand over the stray, squirrely gray hairs that she was sure were poking out from under her prayer *kapp*. No time to worry about that now.

Esther ran to the door and took a deep breath to compose herself. "Come, let's go welcome them," she said, and the entire family walked out to greet them.

The taxi came to a stop and the door opened. Esther waited impatiently as a young woman stepped out, carrying a pink bag. She had shoulder-length brown hair that was slightly shorter and layered in the back, which was probably considered a stylish haircut in the *Englisher* world. She wore jeans, a sweatshirt, sneakers, and a sorrowful look on her face. When she lifted her eyes to meet Esther's, everything else faded away. Esther's breath caught in her throat, and her eyes pricked with tears.

That was Charlotte. She was absolutely beautiful.

Zoe, Charlotte's little sister, got out on the other side of the car and stood beside Charlotte. Zoe had longer hair and was shorter, of course, but looked like she could be Charlotte's biological sister.

Her daughter and niece. They were wonderful.

"Charlotte," Esther said, approaching Charlotte with her arms

358

open. "You have no idea how glad I am to see you." A tear slid down Esther's cheek and she hugged Charlotte. Esther wrapped her arms tightly around her daughter. She savored every moment, drinking in the scent of Charlotte's shampoo and the softness of her hair that tickled Esther's face.

This moment was perfect. How many times had she imagined meeting Charlotte like this?

Thank you again, Lord, so much. I will always be grateful you brought Charlotte back into my life. Please, God, let her stay forever.

Esther smiled, overflowing with gratitude and elation.

"I'm so glad you're home, Charlotte."

She had a feeling their time together was only just beginning.

***

ABOUT THE AUTHOR

Ashley Emma knew she wanted to be a novelist for as long as she can remember, and her first love was writing in the fantasy genre. She began writing books for fun at a young age, completing her first novel at age 12 and publishing it at age 16. She was home schooled and was blessed with the opportunity to spend her time focusing on reading and writing.

Ashley went on to write eight more manuscripts before age 25 when she also became a multi-bestselling author.

She now makes a full-time income with her self-published books, which is a dream come true.

She owns Fearless Publishing House where she helps other aspiring authors achieve their dreams of publishing their own books. Ashley lives in Maine with her husband and children. She plans on releasing several more books in the near future.

Visit her at ashleyemmaauthor.com or email her at amisbookwriter@gmail.com. She loves to hear from her readers!

If you enjoyed this book, would you consider leaving a review on Amazon? It greatly helps both the author and readers alike. Just search for Amish Alias on Amazon.

Thank you!

GET 4 OF ASHLEY EMMA'S AMISH EBOOKS FOR FREE

www.AshleyEmmaAuthor.com

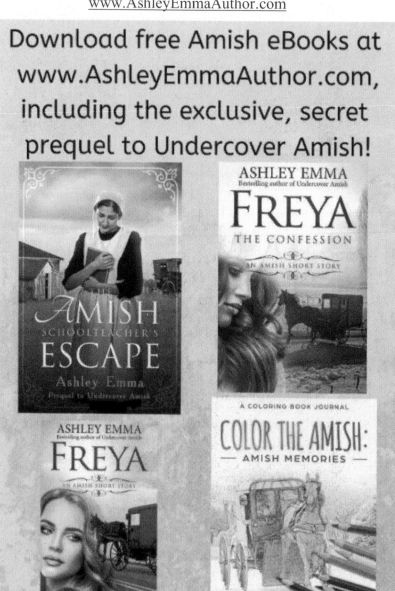

Other books by Ashley Emma on Amazon

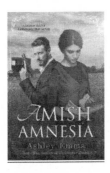

Coming soon:

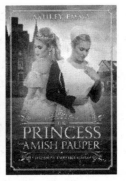

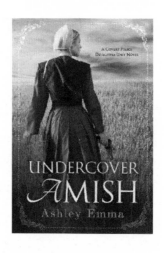

UNDERCOVER AMISH

(This series can be read out of order or as standalone novels.)

Detective Olivia Mast would rather run through gunfire than return to her former Amish community in Unity, Maine, where she killed her abusive husband in self-defense.

Olivia covertly investigates a murder there while protecting the man she dated as a teen: Isaac Troyer, a potential target.

When Olivia tells Isaac she is a detective, will he be willing to break Amish rules to help her arrest the killer?

Undercover Amish was a finalist in Maine Romance Writers Strut Your Stuff Competition 2015 where it received 26 out of 27 points and has 530+ Amazon reviews!

Buy here: https://www.amazon.com/Undercover-Amish-Covert-Police-Detectives-ebook/dp/B01L6JE49G

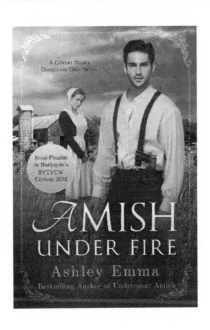

After Maria Mast's abusive ex-boyfriend is arrested for being involved in sex trafficking and modern-day slavery, she thinks that she and her son Carter can safely return to her Amish community.

But the danger has only just begun.

Someone begins stalking her, and they want blood and revenge.

Agent Derek Turner of Covert Police Detectives Unit is assigned as her bodyguard and goes with her to her Amish community in Unity, Maine.

Maria's secretive eyes, painful past, and cautious demeanor intrigue him.

As the human trafficking ring begins to target the Amish community, Derek wonders if the distraction of her will cost him his career…and Maria's life.

Click here to buy: http://a.co/fT6D7sM

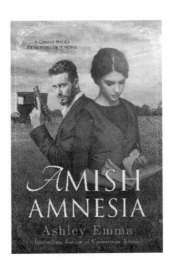

When Officer Jefferson Martin witnesses a young woman being hit by a car near his campsite, all thoughts of vacation vanish as the car speeds off.

When the malnourished, battered woman wakes up, she can't remember anything before the accident. They don't know her name, so they call her Jane.

When someone breaks into her hospital room and tries to kill her before getting away, Jefferson volunteers to protect Jane around the clock. He takes her back to their Kennebunkport beach house along with his upbeat sister Estella and his friend who served with him overseas in the Marine Corps, Ben Banks.

At first Jane's stalker leaves strange notes, but then his attacks become bolder and more dangerous.

Jane gradually remembers an Amish farm and wonders if that's where she's from...or if she was held captive there.

But the more Jefferson falls for her, the more persistent the stalker becomes in making Jane miserable...and in taking her life.

FREE EBOOK

After Freya Wilson accidentally hits an Amish man with her car in a storm, will she have the courage to tell his family the truth—especially after she meets his handsome brother?

Get it free: https://www.amazon.com/Freya-Amish-Short-Ashley-Emma-ebook/dp/B01MSP03UX

FREE EBOOK

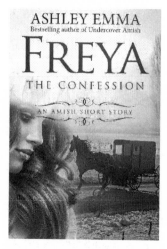

Adam Lapp expected the woman who killed his brother accidentally with her car to be heartless and cruel. He never expected her to a timid, kind, and beautiful woman who is running for her life from a controlling ex who wants her dead.

When Freya Wilson asks him to take her to his family so she can tell them the truth, he agrees.

Will she find hope in the ashes, or just more darkness and sorrow?

https://www.amazon.com/Freya-Confession-Amish-Short-Forgiveness-ebook/dp/B076PQF5FS

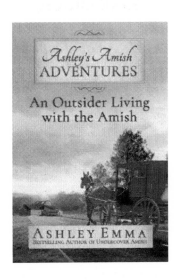

Ever wondered what it would be like to live in an Amish community? Now you can find out in this true story with photos.

https://www.amazon.com/Ashleys-Amish-Adventures-Outsider-community-ebook/dp/B01N5714WE

EXCERPT FROM AMISH AMNESIA

(This Series Can Be Read Out Of Order Or As Standalone Novels.)

Jefferson Martin reached his hands towards the campfire, inhaling the woodsy, smoky scent as he looked at the stars through the skeletal maze of tree branches above. After returning home from Afghanistan a few days ago, Jeff planned on spending his time off doing nothing but enjoying nature in Maine.

"Dad would have loved this," he told his sister, Estella.

"Oh yeah. He'd be making s'mores right now." Estella tossed her blonde hair over her shoulder, then smacked her forehead with a chuckle. "That's what we forgot! Stuff to make s'mores."

"Wow. I haven't had one of those since I was a kid." Jeff looked at her, grinning like the mischievous kid he used to be. "We should go to the store right now and get some, in honor of Dad."

"You mean you should go. I'll stay here and watch the fire." Estella smiled as she stoked the flames with the stick in her hand and pulled the blanket tighter around her shoulders. The night air was beginning to get chilly. "Get some coffee while you're at it, okay?"

"Okay." Jeff was already walking down the short path through the woods towards his car in the gravel parking lot near the restrooms. There was a small store a few miles down the road, and he figured it wouldn't take him more than a few minutes to drive down there and get back. He drove down the lane towards the main road, pausing at a stop sign.

He peered through the darkness at a car parked on the side of the road, curious when he heard shouting from inside the car. Suddenly a girl got out of the passenger side, and even from this far away she looked terrified and confused. She stumbled across the street, looking back at the car over her shoulder, the ragged clothing she wore hanging loosely on her thin body.

A man inside the car shouted profanities out the window at the girl. The first thing that came to Jeff's mind was domestic abuse, probably a fight between a couple. Sadly, he had seen it before. Still, his police and Marines training kicked in.

He was reaching for his door to go and offer his help anyway when the man driving veered his car out onto the street at about ten or fifteen miles an hour, as if the driver wanted to hurt her, not kill her. Jeff watched in horror as the car struck her knocked her over. She landed awkwardly on the ground with a sick thud, her body motionless on the street. The car stopped when it hit her instead of running her over, almost as if the driver was remorseful, then backed up.

Jeff slammed his foot down on the gas and sped towards the woman. The car quickly veered off in the opposite direction. It was dark and there were no street lights out here, so Jeff hadn't gotten a good look at the car or the driver. All he could tell was that the car was a dark-colored sedan.

Anger flared inside Jeff's chest and he shouted as the car tore off. He pounded the steering wheel in indignation, wanting nothing more than to chase the attacker down and force him to answer for his crimes. But it had been too dark to get a license plate, and this girl needed his help right now.

He slammed on the brakes, pulled his car across the road between the girl and potential oncoming cars, and jumped out, glancing again at his cell phone. No service. Of course, they were in the middle of nowhere.

Shoving the phone back in his pocket, he took another look at the girl, surprised when he saw she was more woman than girl. He checked her vital signs, relieved when he found a steady but very weak pulse. She was still breathing, barely. Her face, which would otherwise be pretty, had some old and fresh bruising and some small cuts. She was abnormally thin and pale. Her clothing was worn and too big, and she wasn't wearing shoes. Angry red lines from a rope or some other restraint wrapped around her wrists. She didn't seem to have any broken bones, but she was banged up pretty badly.

What had happened to this girl? Who had done this to her?

Rage coursed through Jeff's veins, and his protective instincts kicked into overdrive. He would find that guy, or whoever did this to her and make them pay. He wanted to hunt them down and do to them whatever they did to her, but he wouldn't be allowed to do that. Until they were arrested, all he could do for her now was protect her.

He gently scooped up the girl in his arms and brought her to his truck, laying her on the back seat and awkwardly buckling her in. Jeff slammed the truck door and flew down the street at record speed.

Luckily Estella had brought her own car to the campsite, so Jeff would call her once he got cell phone reception. First, he needed to call the local police. He held his phone again and groaned. Still no service.

Out in the woods near the campsite, a hospital wasn't exactly close by. Jeff didn't know how long he had been driving, but it seemed like hours later when he rolled into the hospital parking lot. He pulled in to the emergency room entrance and carried the girl inside.

"Help! She was hit by a car," Jeff called out. A few nurses rushed towards him with a gurney, and he laid her down on it gently, instinctively smoothing her dark hair back from her face before they wheeled her down the hall. Jeff began to follow, but a tired-looking nurse held up her hand to stop him. Jeff stumbled to a stop so he wouldn't slam into her.

"You can't come in while we treat her, sir. Are you family?" She adjusted her rectangle glasses.

"No. I found her at the scene."

"Okay. You can wait out here or leave your contact information at the front desk. Then we can let you know how she is doing later on." With that, she shuffled down the hall where the other nurses had taken the girl.

Jeff let out a deep breath. There wasn't much he could do at this point except park his car and wait. He would wait for the girl until he could speak to her.

Now that he finally had cell phone reception, he called the local police station to report the crime, which had been attempted murder and a possible kidnapping case.

Well, his vacation would have to wait. He'd been working at the Covert Police Detectives Unit in Portland, Maine, until he reenlisted in the Marines. After over a year of searching for terrorists in the desert, he'd been looking forward to time off at the Kennebunk beach house he and his sister had inherited. He needed to recover from a year's worth of dust, bullets, scorching sun, and the haunting memories that kept him awake at night. This time off was supposed to be for mourning the recent death of his father before he'd return to work at the Covert Police Detectives Unit,

375

but Jeff knew his father would have wanted him to take care of this girl to be priority. He would wait all night here if he had to until he found out how the girl was doing.

He dialed Estella's number and she picked up. "Estella, I'm not coming back to the campsite. I'm at the hospital."

"What? What happened?" Estella cried. "Are you okay?"

It looked like they weren't going to be having coffee and s'mores after all.

Chapter Two

The woman tried to open her eyes and found out that they felt like lead weights had been placed on top of them. When she finally got them open she was in a strange room with a very unpleasant smell. A strange staccato noise repeated rhythmically. A dull pain throbbed in her head, ribs, and legs. Every part of her body hurt, and it felt like she was being weighed down.

She wondered where she was and how she got here, looking at her hand and frowning as she saw the line that snaked from the I.V bag hanging over her bed. In the distance, she heard voices and tried to lift her head to see who it was. She couldn't and in the end, she gave up and rested her head on the pillow. She heard the sound of her door being opened and sighed in relief. She was finally going to get some answers and she needed a lot of those.

"Hey, how are you feeling?" a warm voice asked.

The woman looked up to see two other women standing beside her bed. She knew they were nurses from the clothes they wore. Which meant she was in the hospital. Of course, she was, something she should have figured out already from the smell and tubes sticking out of her arms.

"You've been through a lot, haven't you?" the other nurse said as she checked the IV bag.

The woman said nothing, still too disoriented to make sense of what they were saying. Her head hurt and her whole body felt stiff.

"Don't worry," one of the nurses attending to her said, "it's okay if you don't feel like talking yet. Rest and take it easy, okay?"

"Where am I and how did I get here?" the woman asked.

The two nurses exchanged a look before they turned to face the woman.

"Actually, we were hoping you'll help us with that. What do you remember about the incident?"

The woman frowned. "What incident?"

Again the nurses exchanged the same look before they turned around and looked at the woman again.

"What's your name?"

"My name...? My name is..." the woman paused, her mouth hanging open for a few seconds. No name formed in her mouth or brain. "I... I don't know," she whispered.

If you enjoyed this sample, check out the book here on Amazon or just search for Ashley Emma on Amazon:

https://www.amazon.com/gp/product/B07SDSFV3J

Thanks for reading!

Download free Amish eBooks at
www.AshleyEmmaAuthor.com,
including the exclusive, secret
prequel to Undercover Amish!

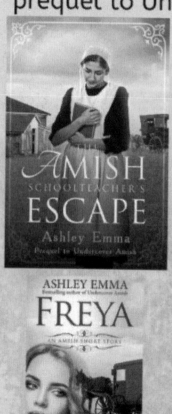

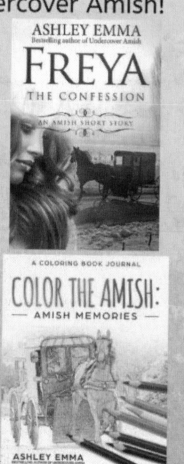

Other books by Ashley Emma on Amazon

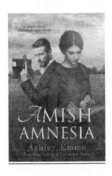

Coming soon:

 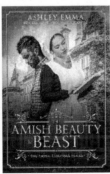 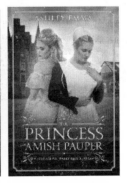

Made in the USA
Coppell, TX
04 March 2020